STORM
BREAKING

Altra and Florian

STORM BREAKING

BOOK THREE OF
THE MAGE STORMS

MERCEDES LACKEY

DAW BOOKS, INC.

DONALD A. WOLLHEIM, FOUNDER

375 Hudson Street, New York, NY 10014

ELIZABETH R. WOLLHEIM
SHEILA E. GILBERT
PUBLISHERS

First Printing, October 1996

1 2 3 4 5 6 7 8 9

DAW TRADEMARK REGISTERED
U.S. PAT. OFF. AND FOREIGN COUNTRIES
—MARCA REGISTRADA
HECHO IN U.S.A.

PRINTED IN THE U.S.A.

Dedicated to the memory of
Elsie B. Wollheim

OFFICIAL TIMELINE FOR THE

by *Mercedes Lackey*

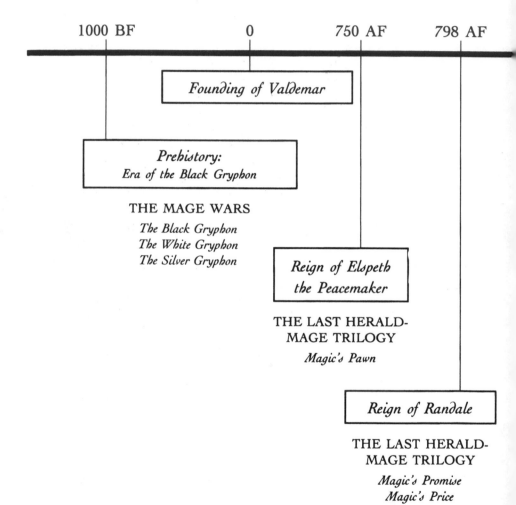

1000 BF   0   750 AF   798 AF

Founding of Valdemar

Prehistory:
Era of the Black Gryphon

THE MAGE WARS

The Black Gryphon
The White Gryphon
The Silver Gryphon

Reign of Elspeth
the Peacemaker

**THE LAST HERALD-
MAGE TRILOGY**

Magic's Pawn

Reign of Randale

**THE LAST HERALD-
MAGE TRILOGY**

Magic's Promise
Magic's Price

BF   *Before the Founding*
AF   *After the Founding*
°   *Upcoming from DAW Books in hardcover*

HERALDS OF VALDEMAR SERIES

Sequence of events by Valdemar reckoning

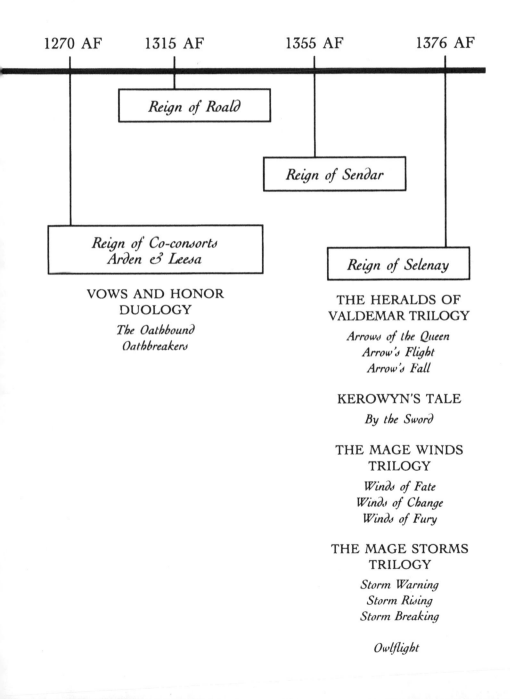

1270 AF   1315 AF   1355 AF   1376 AF

Reign of Roald

Reign of Sendar

Reign of Co-consorts
Arden & Leesa

Reign of Selenay

**VOWS AND HONOR
DUOLOGY**

*The Oathbound
Oathbreakers*

**THE HERALDS OF
VALDEMAR TRILOGY**

*Arrows of the Queen
Arrow's Flight
Arrow's Fall*

KEROWYN'S TALE

By the Sword

**THE MAGE WINDS
TRILOGY**

*Winds of Fate
Winds of Change
Winds of Fury*

**THE MAGE STORMS
TRILOGY**

*Storm Warning
Storm Rising
Storm Breaking*

Owlflight

Karal

One

Karal lay as quietly as he could, keeping his breathing even to avoid jarring his head. He kept his eyes closed against the light, hoping that the snow pack across his brow would eventually ease his throbbing headache. It was hard to think through the pain that stabbed from both temples and seemed to meet just above his nose. He was only vaguely aware of the rest of his body, muffled as it was in blankets, with hot stones packed all around to keep him from getting cold. The Shin'a'in who tended him seemed particularly concerned that he not take a chill from the clammy stone floor or the snow packs on his head. If this had been Valdemar, or even Karse, there would have been other recourses to ease the fiery lances stabbing through his temples—but unfortunately it wasn't. This half-melted ruin of an ancient tower held no such amenities as Healers or herbal pharmacopoeias, and he was going to have to make do with whatever their Shin'a'in allies could come up with, at least for the present. That meant willow tea and snow packs, and hope for the best.

I can always hope for the best. It could be worse. How much worse, though—that was something he was not prepared to contemplate at the moment.

It was a headache of monumental proportions, which was only to be expected, considering that he had personally been the nexus-point for all of the energies of a weapon so powerful and unpredictable that not even the Great Mage who had ended the Mage Wars had dared to use it. It had required a magic-channel, a *living* channel. Either no one in Urtho's contingent of mages happened to be a Channel, or else the Mage of Silence hadn't wanted to risk the life of such a person in the use of this weapon—in either case, it had remained un-used with a warning plaque advising against its use.

Or else he couldn't get any volunteers. Not that Karal could blame anyone for *not* volunteering. His first experience at being a Channel had been singularly unpleasant, but the sec-ond had been of a different order of magnitude altogether. He honestly didn't remember too much of what had happened to him, once the weapon had been activated. Both the Hawk-brother Adept Firesong and the half-Shin'a'in An'desha had assured him that was all for the best, and he believed them.

When both An'desha and Firesong agree on something. . . . He had the shivery feeling that he really didn't want to know exactly what had happened. If he knew, he'd have to think about it, and that gave him a very queasy feeling.

It was much easier to lie in his bedroll and deal with pain than to think.

Occasionally the sounds of the others, moving about in their daily chores, made their way past the pain, oddly muf-fled or magnified by the strange acoustics of the place. An'de-sha and the Shin'a'in shaman Lo'isha were talking softly, their voices blending together into a meaningless murmur, as oddly soothing as wind in leaves or the whisper of water over rocks. Someone, probably the Kaled'a'in *kestra'chern* Silverfox, was cleaning cooking utensils; soft metallic clinks punctuated the soft sounds of conversation. Nearer at hand, the Hawkbrother Firesong sang absently to himself; Firesong was probably mending something. Firesong always sang when he was men-ding something; he said it was to keep him from saying some-thing he would regret. He didn't much care for mending, or for any other chores—the Tayledras Adept had been used, all his life, to being waited on. Having to fend for himself was an experience that Firesong was not enjoying. On the whole, Karal was of the opinion that he was bearing up well under these pressures and added responsibilities.

So much for the human members of the group. And as for the ones who were not human—well, Karal knew where Altra the Firecat was. The furry, vibrating blanket covering him from neck to knee was Altra, not some arcane Shin'a'in cover-let. Somehow, unlike mortal cats which would inexplicably *increase* their weight when lying on a human, the Firecat had decreased his, making himself no heavier than a thick woolen blanket. Only the steady radiating warmth and the deep, soothing purr betrayed his presence.

Somewhere beyond the chamber where Karal was lying, one of the horselike creatures known to the Valdemarans as a Companion, the one called Florian, listened attentively to An'desha and the shaman. If Karal opened his mind a little, he would "hear" the voices that were only a vague music to his real ears, but he would hear them through the senses of the Companion. The bonds between himself and the Companion and Firecat were stronger now than only weeks ago. He had only to think of them to sense the whisper of their thoughts, and he was aware of their presence in his mind as a constant warmth. Something had happened during the time he could not remember that bound the three of them even more firmly together. Anything they saw, heard, or felt, he could experience himself if he chose. He didn't know if the reverse was true, but he rather thought it wasn't. *He* was the one who'd been changed, not them.

That was another thing he didn't want to think too closely about. The Firecat was not entircly a mortal creature, and the Companion, while mortal enough, like the Firecat was a human reborn into a body of magical nature. So if something had happened that bound *him* to *them*—and so very tightly that he no longer had to work to reach their minds—

He shivered, and the cold he felt had nothing to do with the snow pack on his head. *Oh, no. I can't have changed that much. This is probably just temporary, something that will go away when I'm stronger.*

He redirected his thoughts and noticed that at least now he *could* think coherently.

That's an improvement anyway.

Now where was everyone else? He kept his eyes closed and listened carefully, trying to locate them all by sound alone rather than take a chance that opening his eyes would wake the pain again.

The remaining nonhumans, the two gryphons, were busy packing up their few belongings. They muttered to each other with little hisses and beak clicks, and their talons scraped against the leather of the saddlebags they had borrowed from the Shin'a'in for their journey north. They had decided that they had been away from their twin offspring long enough, and no one in the group was heartless enough to insist that they stay. The thrill of walking where the fabled Black Gryphon had once walked was probably beginning to pall in the face of being away from their beloved little ones for far too long. And with the Gates down, it would be a long trip back, even for creatures that flew.

And it could very well be that coming as close as we all did to getting seriously hurt, Treyvan and Hydona have decided that they don't want to leave their little ones as orphans. Who could blame them for that?

Yes, he was definitely able to think more coherently now.

Coherently enough to notice my neck muscles are in knots. Hardly a surprise. Karal sighed a little, and relaxed tense shoulders into the embrace of his sheepskin-covered pack, which was now serving him as a pillow. *It's a good thing that I have clothing in there instead of books.* The snow pack *was* working after all; if he noticed that his shoulders hurt, that meant the headache wasn't overwhelming everything else.

Grand, so now I get to enjoy how much the rest of me hurts!

But as the pain behind his eyes eased, so, too, did the tension in his muscles, which were probably contributing to the pain of the headache in the first place. So annoying how all these things managed to feed back on each other!

Well, I'd be a poor Sun-priest if I couldn't make myself relax, now wouldn't I? Such relaxation techniques were part of every novice's training. You couldn't pray if you weren't relaxed; how could you keep your mind on the glory of Vkandis if you were being nagged by a cramp? He patiently persuaded his rebellious body to behave itself, getting muscles unknotted that he hadn't even known were tight. As he did so, the ache in his head ebbed further, thus proving his guess that part of the headache was due to muscle tension.

That's better. That's much better. If his head would just let him be, he might actually begin to enjoy this invalid state, at least a little. For once he felt completely justified in lying abed and letting others take care of him; the depleted state of his entire body had convinced him that he had actually *earned* a rest.

And after all, it wasn't every day he had a Tayledras Healing Adept waiting on his every wish. How many people could boast of that? He couldn't even sigh without having Firesong ask him if he needed anything, a rather odd turn of events given that Firesong was the one used to being waited on.

He wasn't at all certain what prompted Firesong's attentiveness—there were others who would certainly have played nursemaid if the Adept hadn't insisted on taking the duty—but the Hawkbrother did make a very good and considerate nurse.

I certainly wouldn't have expected that from him. It just doesn't seem like him at all.

Well, maybe it wasn't much like the Firesong *he* knew, but such a thought was as shallow as the flippant surface that was all the Hawkbrother would ever reveal to him, given a choice. He immediately chided himself for *that* thought.

That was unworthy as well as unkind. There is far more to Firesong than I will ever see. We are all trying to cope with extreme situations, and if that is the way he chooses to cope, he has a right to it.

Just at the moment, even when his head wasn't splitting, Karal was in no shape to do anything other than wonder and enjoy the attention. He could hardly move his hand without tiring himself, and simply getting to his feet to go to the privy area left him so exhausted, he could only lie in his bedroll and doze for marks afterward. That worried him; unless he regained his strength soon, he would not be able to travel. If he couldn't travel, he wouldn't be able to leave with the others when they returned to Valdemar. The impatient gryphon parents were not going to wait for the others, but the humans could not wait much longer either. If they didn't leave now, they might be caught and trapped here by winter storms.

On the other hand . . . it might already be too late. The Gate that brought us here is down, and if I were a mage, I wouldn't chance reopening it. We might be stuck here until spring. Even under the best of conditions it's going to take an awfully long time to walk back.

So long, in fact, that returning home might be the very worst thing that they could do at this point. The solution to the problem of the mage-storms he had depleted himself to provide was, once again, a temporary solution only. This might be the very best place for them to work on a permanent answer. They certainly had resources here at their disposal that they wouldn't find anywhere else.

For one thing, the ancient weapon that they had used to

cancel the Storm-waves had been only one of several available to them, and it hadn't been anyone's first choice, only the one they understood the best. Perhaps one of the others would provide a better chance. The Kaled'a'in had promised to provide a historian, a specialist in their own languages and the ancient writing they alone had preserved out of the Cataclysm. Perhaps when he arrived, he would be able to provide better translations than the gryphons.

We haven't even begun to explore this place, yet this was the heart of the Mage of Silence's stronghold. He is said to have been the greatest there has ever been, with vast resources. Can we really assume that we have seen all there is? There might be other rooms here, rooms they hadn't found yet, that might hold more answers to their problem. Maybe they would be much better off by staying here and looking, or studying the remaining weapons. It was an option no one had suggested yet, but he wondered if they all weren't thinking about it, much as they would prefer to return home.

The main problem as I see it is that we don't have anyone with us from the mathematicians and the Artificers. That alone worried him; the last two stopgap measures had been created, at least in part, by Master Levy's group of clever logicians. With the help of these scholars, all of them had been able to examine the problem from an original perspective. *We need them. Firesong might not like them, but we need them.*

He knew that with certainty; as if Vkandis Himself had placed that certainty in his heart, he was as positive of it as he was of anything in his life. This was not a problem that could be worked through unless all of the minds available contributed to the solution.

He sighed, and as he lifted a hand to move the snow pack off his eyes, he heard Firesong come to take it for him. The cold, damp weight lifted away. "Would you like a new one?" the apparently eternally-young mage asked.

He opened his eyes and shook his head—only a little, so as to avoid undoing the good that had been done. Firesong didn't look very much like a nurse; the incredibly handsome young mage had managed to pack a full wardrobe of his intricately styled, brilliantly decorated silk clothing into his single pack. Karal could not imagine how he had done it. At the moment, he was all in muted silver-blues which, at least, made it possible for Karal to look at him without pain. From his precisely-styled, silver-white hair to his immaculate leg wrappings, he was every inch the exotic mage and not at all servile. The amused smile he wore reassured Karal; if there had been anything really wrong with him, he was fairly certain Firesong would not be smiling.

"Not at the moment, thank you," he said, surprised at the rasp in his voice, as if he had been screaming until his vocal cords were raw. "You really don't—"

Firesong chuckled, surprising him. "Oh, there's a reason behind all of this," he replied with a smile. "You're ridiculously easy as a patient, and if I'm tending *you*, I don't have to do any of the more tedious chores." His voice took on the merest touch of arrogance. "I'd rather keep putting snow packs on your head than wash dishes, I assure you."

Karal had to laugh weakly. Now *that* sounded more like the Firesong he knew! "Oh, good," he said. "I was afraid that you'd suddenly been filled with the spirit of self-sacrifice, and I wasn't certain I could bear that for very long."

Now Firesong laughed, and tossed his long silver hair over his shoulder. "Keep your tender sentiments to yourself, Karsite," he said mockingly. "Out of my own self-interest I want you to stay an invalid as long as possible, and if you keep saying things like that, I might be tempted to do something to keep you that way."

"You promise, but you never follow through," Karal retorted, surprising himself with his enjoyment of the exchange. "I think my tender hide is safe from you."

"You doubt?" Firesong's brow rose, and he raised his gaze to a point somewhere past Karal; probably listening to Florian, the Companion. His next words confirmed Karal's guess. "Well, maybe you're right. A hoofprint in the middle of my face would not improve my looks—" He dropped his gaze to meet Altra's brilliant blue eyes. "—and I don't like the way that cat of yours is flexing his claws either."

:*I wouldn't hurt you where it showed*,: Altra said dryly, into both their minds. :*Silverfox might object to my alterations, however. But you would make a charming girl.*:

Firesong's silver eyes widened in mock fear, but there was a tinge of respect in his look as well. "Remind me never to anger you, Altra. That's a bit vicious even as a joke."

:*If I thought for a moment that you were serious, it wouldn't be a joke.*: The Firecat deliberately raised one paw and licked his flexed talons. Since Altra was the size of most large dogs, and his paws were correspondingly huge, those talons were wicked looking indeed.

That's not very subtle, cat, Karal thought warningly, knowing Altra would hear him.

:It wasn't meant to be subtle,: the Firecat replied in his mind only. *:There was a time when he contemplated injuring you. If he ever strays in that direction again, I want him to have something to think about.:*

Karal kept his face straight as Altra imparted that choice bit of information, so he did not reveal a reaction. That was certainly news to him.

And now everyone seems determined to protect me! But Firesong was waiting for him to say something, so before the mage could ask what it was that made him look so odd, he raised a shaking hand to rub his eyebrow. "Cats. You can't live with them, and the fur's too thin for a rug."

Altra gave an exaggerated snort of disgust as Firesong laughed aloud. "You *are* feeling better," he said, this time without the mockery. "Good. Maybe tonight you'll be able to stomach something besides that tasteless slop the shaman has been feeding you. Just try not to get well so quickly that I'm forced to wash my own plates again any time soon."

Before Karal could reply, Firesong rose to his feet to take away the dripping snow pack. He turned his head slowly to look in the direction of Florian and the others.

Sure enough, a little way past the chamber's entrance, Florian stood with his head just above An'desha's shoulder, looking at something the shaman was drawing on the floor.

He could, if he just relaxed a little, see everything from Florian's point of view. He didn't want to relax that much, honestly.

I just want my headache to stop. I want to be able to get up and do things like the others. I truly do want to stop being a burden. It isn't the place of a priest of Vkandis Sunlord to be the one given comfort, it is the priest's place to give comfort. . . .

He closed his eyes, and tried to find some meditation technique that would at least enable him to sleep despite the pain. If he fell asleep, at least he wouldn't be quite so aware of what a nuisance he'd become.

Without any warning footsteps, he felt a touch on his arm.

His eyes popped open, all he could manage in the way of a startled reaction.

He found himself looking up into a pair of extremely blue eyes, amused eyes, in a triangular face with golden skin. The eyes and the face topped a body wearing Shin'a'in garments of unornamented dark sable-brown; the color, he now recalled, that Swordsworn usually wore when they weren't engaged in one of their rare but vicious blood-feuds.

The Swordsworn had another name. *Kal'enedral. The ones Sworn to the service of Kal'enel, the Warrior.* He knew more about them now than any Karsite alive. The person sitting lightly on "his" heels would be one of the Swordsworn who had guided them here and guarded them on the way; who had, with the aid of k'Leshya, excavated a way into the Tower. He couldn't tell if this person was male or female; with the Swordsworn, it hardly mattered, since they were not only vowed to chastity and celibacy, but were by their bond to their Goddess, rendered incapable of a sexual impulse. That was a state that had no parallel in the Sunlord's hierarchy; although Sun-priests were not encouraged to wed, they were not denied that state either.

"Well, this was not what we intended when we opened our secret to you, young outClansman," the Shin'a'in said, in a clear, slightly roughened tenor voice that could have belonged to a man or a woman. The Sworn One spoke with very little accent, in remarkably good Valdemaran. Karal was relieved; his Shin'a'in was rudimentary at best. "We thought you would be here and gone again—"

The Shin'a'in paused then, as if suddenly aware that the "gone" very nearly had been "permanently gone."

Karal shrugged. "This wasn't our plan either, Sworn One," he said politely.

The Shin'a'in laughed. "True enough, and I think not even your God could have predicted this outcome. Certainly our Goddess did not! Or if She did, She saw fit not to grace us with the information. But now—well, given that the Gate that brought you here is gone, and our winter storms are closing in, we have determined that we will have to become true hosts."

At one point, Karal would have been shocked by the reference to a deity other than Vkandis Sunlord—more shocked that such a deity as the Shin'a'in Star-Eyed was spoken of in the same breath as He. Later, he would have been able to accept that, but would also have been driven speechless by such a *casual* reference to a deity, as if the person speaking had a personal relationship with Kal'enel.

Now he knew better; these Swordsworn *did* have such a relationship. She had been known to speak with Her special followers on a regular basis, and even occasionally intervene in their lives. Which was, after all, not entirely unlike the relationship Vkandis had with the Son of the Sun.

"I have been told that affairs were at such a turning point that any and all outcomes were equally likely," he said carefully, squinting around his headache. "Perhaps that is why She gave you no indication that we were to be unexpected tenants rather than guests."

"Well said!" the Shin'a'in replied warmly. "Well, then. Tenants you are, dwellers among our tents, and as such it becomes necessary that we provide you with something better than the hasty arrangements of aforetime. First, I am Chagren shena Liha'irden, and I am to be your Healer. Lo'isha is a good man and a fine shaman, but his Healing skills are rudimentary at best. I am better suited to helping you, trust me in that."

Karal could not help but show his surprise; a *Healer* among the Swordsworn? Chagren saw his expression and chuckled.

"Given our task of serving as the Guardians of the Plains, does it not seem logical that we must need a Healer now and again? I was a Healer before I was Sworn, and Swore myself in part because I was one of those who joined the battle with Ancar, and I vowed I would never again find myself unable to defend those who I had come to Heal. I petitioned. She accepted. Not *all* of us who come to serve Her so closely have tragic tales of great personal loss behind them." Then his expression changed, becoming serious for a moment. "Though there are many. Those who have seen too much to endure and remain sane often petition Her and are taken into Her ranks."

Those who have seen too much to endure— Karal glanced involuntarily at An'desha, and Chagren followed his glance. He looked back down at Karal. "Interesting. Your thoughts on that one?"

Karal blinked at the Shin'a'in's directness. "I sometimes wonder if there *is* any place for An'desha, after all he has endured."

Chagren lost that amused smile entirely, and his eyelids dropped momentarily to veil his eyes. "There is," he said after a pause, "if he chooses to take it. Among us there is no tale so strange that we cannot encompass it. Not among the Sword-sworn, I think, but among the Wise, those who wear the blue of the night sky and the day's ending. They are Sworn to Wisdom rather than the Sword, and I think it is among their numbers he would feel he has come home. But that is for him to decide."

The smile returned. "Meanwhile, it is for *me* to ease some of your discomfort, while my fellows bring the wherewithal to make this into a home for as long as may be. So. You have been Healed before?"

"Not really," Karal confessed. "The one Valdemaran Healer I saw decided that all I needed was herbs and potions, not real Healing."

"A wise Healer knows when to Heal and when to let time do the Healing," Chagren replied with approval. "Well then, *this* time you shall be the recipient of true Healing, such as, I believe, some of your Sun-priests are known to practice. I require of you only that you close your eyes and relax, and that when you sense my spirit, permit it to touch yours. That should be easy enough, yes?

"I think so," Karal replied as the headache returned with a vengeance. Any reluctance he might have felt vanished at the onslaught of further pain. He closed his eyes as instructed, and waited, slowly willing each muscle to release its built-up tension.

The moment he "sensed Chagren's spirit" he knew exactly what the Shin'a'in had meant; he felt something very akin to the sensation he had when he first communicated with Florian. And as he had when Florian had requested that Karal "let him into his mind," he let down those internal barriers he hadn't realized existed back when he had been plain Karal of Karse.

But this time, instead of thoughts and sensations flooding into his mind, a warm, soothing wave washed over him, and where it had passed, the pain was gone, leaving behind comfort and reassurance.

He opened his eyes; he thought it was only a moment later, but Chagren was gone. In his place stood a metal pitcher and cup, and in his chamber and the rooms beyond, new comforts and a few new figures had appeared as if conjured.

There was a small cast-metal stove at his feet, and he had

been heaped with more woven blankets. Several long, flat cushions arranged like a more comfortable bed than the one he currently occupied lay beside that. On top of the stove, there was a steaming pot.

Beyond his room, he saw at least one more stove and reckoned that there were probably more. Better bedding had appeared, and more amenities. Firesong appeared and glanced in the door to his chamber, and when the mage saw that he was awake, the Hawkbrother walked unhurriedly and gracefully to his side.

"You've been asleep through all the excitement," Firesong told him. "More of those Kal'enedral appeared with a veritable caravan of goods, and this place is now almost civilized." He smiled, and there was no mistaking the fact that he was pleased. "They even promised none of us will have to cook anymore, though we *will* still have to do the work of *hertasi*, I fear. That is just as well, since I do not believe I could have eaten another of my own meals, even if I died of starvation."

Karal croaked a chuckle, and discovered to his delight that it did not make his head hurt. "My headache is gone!" he exclaimed with glee.

Firesong nodded. "That fellow Chagren said it would be. I will probably be helping him the next time he Heals you. He told me what had caused your aching skull, and once he explained it to me, it was obvious—" He held up a hand, forestalling Karal's questions. "—and I will explain it all to you in detail, some time later, when we have the time for me to explain how and why a mage or a Healer is able to do what he does. Suffice it for now to say that you have misused that part of you that channels magic, as if you had bruised it by battering a rough stone around inside your skull, and that was why your head hurt. He was able to take care of the bruises, so to speak."

Karal tried to lever himself up, and found to his profound disappointment that he was still as weak as a newborn colt. "Too bad I'm not completely back to normal, but I suppose Chagren can't Heal everything at once," he answered with a sigh, as Firesong caught his elbow to help him.

"Obviously, he cannot," the mage replied reasonably. "There are some things, such as strength and endurance, that time will restore as much as he. Now, if you will move thus, and so, we will get you onto this more comfortable bed, and then you must drink what he left you, and eat, and then sleep again. For the next couple of days, making your way to the privy and back will be all the exercise you're fit for."

With Firesong's aid, Karal moved over to the pile of flat bed cushions, which turned out to be even more comfortable than they looked. The mage piled all of his blankets, rugs, and furs back on top of him, then handed him the metal cup. It proved to contain another herbal potion, but this one had a pleasantly fruity, faintly sweet taste, with a refreshingly astringent after-taste that quenched a deep-lying thirst no amount of water had been able to satisfy. At Firesong's urging, he drank a second cup, and while he finished that, An'desha appeared with a bowl and spoon.

"Chagren promised that you would at least be able to feed yourself, so that is *your* task for the day," An'desha said, handing him both. The bowl held real soup, not the tasteless gruel that Lo'isha had been feeding him. Although his hand shook a little, he managed not only to feed himself, but to finish every drop in the bowl. An'desha and Firesong sat watching him like a pair of anxious nursery attendants all during the meal, and An'desha took back the empty bowl with a grin of triumph.

"Soon enough you will be sweeping and washing with the rest of us," An'desha said as he rose. Karal leveled a sober gaze on Firesong as the young Shin'a'in left the chamber.

"I feel as if I should be sweeping and washing for both of you, you and Silverfox together," he said with guilt he could not conceal. "I am taking up so much of your time, and contributing nothing."

"*Now,*" Firesong replied sternly, "that says nothing of what you have done in the past, or will do in the future. And you are taking up very little of my time, since you sleep a great deal. Which is, by the by, what you should be doing now; sleeping, once you have another cup of this excellent beverage."

Obediently, Karal drank down a third cup and closed his eyes again, although he felt no real urge to sleep. But evidently there was something in the drink, or he needed sleep so badly that his body would take any opportunity to seize some, for no sooner had he closed his eyes and begun the first stages of his ritual of relaxation, than he was fast asleep.

* * *

Firesong waited until he was certain young Karal was deep in dreaming, then gathered up the now-empty pitcher, bowl, and cup and carried them off to be washed. The chamber through whose outer wall they had entered the Tower had been dedicated to cleaning—everything from pots to people. Judicious use of magic on Firesong's part had driven a pipe to the surface; at the surface was a black-enameled basin connected to the pipe that the Shin'a'in kept filled with snow. No magic melted the snow shoveled into the basin, just the sun supplemented by a simple horsedung fire. The pipe slanted down into the chamber where it was closed by a stopcock taken from a wine barrel, and simply turning the stopcock gave them water enough for about any purpose. Waste water went into a second pipe going down into the earth set just outside in the tunnel. So far, it had been sufficient.

Silverfox was at the washing basin, used both for dishes and clothing, and he felt a stab of guilt of his own that the *kestra'chern* should be wasting his time and talents on so menial a task as cleaning dirty dishes. This seemed as unreasonable a task as to ask a fine sculptor to shovel snow, yet there he was, serenely working away the soil of camp life with his slender fingers.

But the handsome Kaled'a'in looked up and smiled at his approach, and said lightly, "Would that all troubles are so easily washed away as these! All things considered, I have actually been enjoying myself on this little jaunt. I could almost feel that I am on holiday here!"

Firesong handed him the dishes with a groan. "Why do I suddenly have the sinking feeling that you are one of those benighted individuals who thinks that taking himself off to the utter wilderness for a fortnight or more constitutes a *holiday?*"

"What?" the *kestra'chern* replied innocently. "And you do not?" His blue eyes twinkled as he continued. "Think of the splendid isolation, the uncrowded vistas, the joy of doing everything for yourself, knowing you need rely on no one else! Self-sufficiency! Feeling yourself unconstrained by all the rules and customs that can come to smother you!"

"Think of the lack of civilized conversation, the dearth of entertainment, the deprivation of decent food, hot baths, and reasonable sleeping accommodations!" Firesong retorted. "*I* had rather endure a bored little provincial courtier babble for an hour than listen to a brook do the same, while my toes are cold and my nose even colder, and there isn't a cushion to relax upon. And I do not particularly take joy from washing dishes and mending clothing, I promise you. Those are tedious tasks at best, and wasteful of valuable time at worst!"

But Silverfox's clever, sharp features softened for a moment. "For you, perhaps, but unless he is in a circumstance like this one, a *kestra'chern* is never free of the needs of others. For you, this place is an exile, but for me, a holiday in the wild is an escape."

Now Firesong suffered another twinge of guilt, and he sat down beside the washtub. "And even here you are not free of demands," he said, reproaching himself. "For there are my demands on you—"

But Silverfox only laughed, and shook his long black hair back over his shoulders. "No, those are not demands, *ahela*, those are mutual desires. I could say that my demands on you are as improvident, but I won't. But there is this—for once, I can act on my own desires rather than concentrate on the needs of another to the exclusion of anything I feel."

Firesong felt the guilt for this, at least, lift away from him. "I . . . make you feel more free, simply by being as I am? In that case, perhaps I should be more demanding!"

The *kestra'chern* laughed, as the two gryphons, loaded with their travel packs, poked their beaks into the cleaning chamber with curiosity. "Why all the rrrevelrrry?" Treyvan demanded. "Arre potsss ssso amusssing?"

"That depends on who is cleaning them, old bird," Silverfox replied. "Are you ready to depart yet?"

The female gryphon, Hydona, nodded vigorously. "Now that morrre help hasss come, yesss. If I werrre young and unpairrred, I would ssstay, but—"

"But nothing," Firesong said firmly, reacting to the anxious tone of her voice, sensing she was afraid that he would demand that she stay. "Your little ones need you far more than we do. Not that we aren't grateful."

"When the keeper of hissstorry comesss, we will be sssuperfluousss anyway," Treyvan admitted. "He will be able to rrread the old wrritingsss here much morrre clearrrly than we."

It was obvious to Firesong that the gryphons were chagrined at their inability to decipher the ancient texts that had been found here, and they took their failure personally. They had all made an incorrect assumption about clan k'Leshya. They had assumed that the last clan that could truly have called itself *Kaled'a'in* rather than Shin'a'in or Tayledras had a purer form of the original tongue than either splinter group. Given that, the gryphons should have been able to decipher the ancient texts. And they had also assumed that since k'Leshya had come to dwell among the Haighlei, a people who shunned change, their language would obviously have remained as pure as it was the day that they all went through the Gates to escape into the West.

But while the Haighlei shunned change, the Kaled'a'in had not, and their language had drifted from the ancient tongue as inevitably as had Shin'a'in and Tayledras. Perhaps it had not drifted so far or so fast, but nevertheless, it had drifted, and in a direction that rendered the ancient writings as vague to the gryphons as to Firesong or Lo'isha.

However, providentially enough, there was among the pioneers of k'Leshya an individual who had not only come along to record what transpired in their new home, but one who had made a hobby of studying the most ancient scripts. While this historian was not the expert that a true scholar of the earliest days of White Gryphon would have been, he had volunteered to come and assist the party at the Tower, and he should prove more of an expert than the two gryphons.

That was the theory anyway. Very little in this strange situation had gone according to theory.

"I will be sorry to see you leave," Firesong said sincerely, "You both have been very patient about this, but even I can tell that gryphons aren't comfortable underground."

Hydona didn't say anything, but Treyvan shivered, all of his feathers quivering. "It hasss not been easssy," he admitted. "And all that hasss kept me here at timesss isss the knowledge that the grrreat Ssskandrranon walked thessse sssame chamberrsss."

Firesong nodded with understanding; not that long ago, he would have said the same thing in the same reverent tones about visiting the Heartstone Chamber in the Palace at Haven where his own ancestor Vanyel had once worked. That, however, had been before he had been kidnapped by that same ancestor and shoved, willy-nilly, into the affairs of the Kingdom of Valdemar. Being conscripted by a stubborn spirit to the aid of a place and people that were hardly more than misty history to him had given him a slightly more jaundiced view of "honored ancestors" than most folk had.

Oh, I'll leave them to their illusions. Skandranon is not likely to stick his beak into our affairs now, thank the gods; if he was going to show up the way Vanyel did, he'd be here already. If that was all it took to help them bear the feeling of being buried alive here, their illusions are valuable.

Besides, Skandranon had died peacefully, in extreme old age, surrounded by a vast flock of worshipful grandchildren and great-grandchildren. There were no stories of a haunted forest in which uncanny things happened connected with *his* legends, and his long line of descendants had legends of their own.

But Firesong couldn't help but wonder now and again just what his own ancestor Vanyel was planning. He'd given no indication that he planned to—as it were—move on, once the dual threats of Ancar and Falconsbane had been dealt with. By now he must have recovered from the effort of taking down the Web—and Vanyel at full strength had been powerful enough to wrest away control of a Gate *he* had not erected to transport five humans, four gryphons, a *dyheli*, two Companions, and two bondbirds all the way from a site at the edge of the Dhorisha Plains to the heart of the Forest of Sorrows beyond Valdemar's northern border. There was no telling what he might still be capable of.

I think I know why he didn't confront Falconsbane directly—but I would not have given odds in favor of Falconsbane if Vanyel—and Yfandes and Stefen—had been given leave to deal with him themselves.

"Do we take it that you arrre ssstaying, then?" Treyvan asked.

Both Firesong and Silverfox nodded, but it was Silverfox who answered. "That's why that caravan of Swordsworn showed up with all the new equipment. We just now told Karal, but that is only because he hasn't been awake long enough to listen to anything complicated. The Kal'enedral pointed out that we were lucky that we didn't encounter any winter storms coming in, but we can't count on our luck holding. If we're caught, we would have to do what the Shin'a'in do—dig in, hope we don't freeze to death, then settle in for the rest of the winter. Once the trail out is obliterated by a storm, there's no reestablishing it. If we're going to be stuck,

I'd rather be stuck here, where we can continue to research what Urtho left behind. I'm looking for secret doors, or concealed rooms, while the rest figure out what the effect of the cancellation wave we sent out will be, and how long it will last."

"I think you are wissse," Treyvan said gravely. "I do not think that Karrral would sssurrvive the trrrip, much lessss a grrreat sstorrrm."

"Nor do I, and that was why I voted to stay," Firesong said, then added with a sigh. "Even if it means living like a brigand until spring."

Treyvan gryph-grinned at that, and gave him a mock cuff with a tightly fisted claw. "Peacock!" he chuckled. "You arrre jusst dissscontented becaussse therrre isss no one herrre but Sssilverrrfox to admirrre yourrr handsssome face!"

"No, I am just discontented because I am not especially fond of sewing split seams and scrubbing pots, which is a perfectly reasonable attitude," Firesong retorted, and made shooing motions with his hands. "Be on your way; I'm sure you can't *wait* to get back to cries of 'But *Papa* said we can!', 'But Andra's mama lets her!', and 'Do I *have* to?' "

When he wished to exercise that talent, Firesong could be a wicked mimic, and he so accurately rendered a childish whine that both gryphons' eartufts went back in alarm.

"Perrrhapsss Hydona could go ahead of me," Treyvan ventured, then ducked as his mate leveled a killing gaze on him, "orr perrrhapsss not. Well, why not; we faced Ancarrr, we faced Falconsssbane, we faced the Imperrrial Arrrmy and the mage-ssstorrrmsss. What arrre two merrre childrrren againsssst that?"

"Worse than all of them put together, because they'll always get what they want?" Firesong suggested, and Hydona turned her deadly glare on him. "Of course, my opinion is hardly valid!" he amended hastily. "After all, *I* don't have children!"

Hydona snorted, but looked mollified, and Firesong wisely opted to keep the rest of his opinions to himself. "We'll all miss you," he said instead. "But you've done more than your duty, and children need their parents. Fly safely, friends."

"Thank you," Treyvan said simply.

Even though the Shin'a'in had labored to open the hole in the outer wall to give them all a wider door into the tunnel, it was still a squeeze for the gryphons to get through, burdened with their packs as they were. As a courtesy, Firesong sent a mage-light on ahead of them, though Treyvan was perfectly capable of making his own. Not that they were going to get lost in a straight tunnel, but the light might make the tunnel itself seem less confining.

Silverfox sat looking after them for a while after they were gone. "You know," he said finally, "they were the only creatures I ever envied when I was young."

"Gryphons in general?" Firesong asked. "Or those two in particular?"

"Gryphons in general," Silverfox replied, turning back to his dishtub. "The main thing was that they can fly, of course, but besides that, they are just marvelous creatures. They grow their own wonderful costumes of feathers, they are armed better than any fighter with those talons and that beak, and they can take on virtually any task except those that require unusually fine dexterity. They can even become *kestra'chern!* So I envied them."

"And now?" Firesong asked.

"Now I'm old enough and experienced enough to have seen the price they pay for all those gifts. You'd be amazed at how delicate their digestion is, they are devastated by certain diseases that are only an inconvenience to a human, and their joints tend to stiffen up and get quite painful as they age. I'm still of divided opinion about whether or not the drawbacks are worth being a gryphon," he added, "but I no longer envy them."

"I never did," Firesong said softly. "I only envied myself," and left it at that.

"... and the Mage of Silence brought all of the armies back to his stronghold here, in Ka'venusho," Chagren said, pointing with his charcoal stick to the appropriate place he had drawn on the floor. Karal nodded, and concentrated fiercely while Chagren related the rest of the history of the Mage Wars. He'd heard it all once from Lo'isha, of course, but Chagren had actually *experienced* a compressed version of this history. That had been during a special moment in his training, when he went to Kata'shin'a'in and entered a holy building that housed something he called the Webs of Time. Karal's grasp of language was not quite good enough to give him a clear idea of what *physical* forms these Webs were in, but Chagren said that they held the memories of those who had made them, and that under certain specific conditions, those memories could be awakened and experienced. Karal was disposed to believe him; after all that *he* had seen, what was one more supernatural marvel?

The gryphons had already given him their own version of the story, more heavily weighted with the heroism of the Black Gryphon, of course. Even Silverfox had a slightly different tale, as handed down among the Kaled'a'in *kestra'chern* from Amberdrake, Tadrith Wyrsabane, and the generations since them.

". . . so that is why this place was hallowed for us, even before we know there still were working weapons here," Chagren finished. "Mind, I said *hallowed,* not *holy*. We of the Plains do not count any human 'holy,' not even Her Avatars or the Kal'enedral. The Mage of Silence was a good man, a fine man, and flawed as all men are. What made him different from most other men was that he saw his weaknesses and spent all his life trying to keep them controlled, so as not to harm others with them; that he devoted a larger percentage of his life to the well-being of others than most ever even think of doing. What made him dangerous were the things he never troubled to control: his curiosity and his desire to meddle and change things for the sake of change itself."

Karal digested that; it was interesting to hear the various versions, not only of the story of the Cataclysm, but the way the three cultures viewed Adept Urtho. To the gryphons, at least, Urtho was the ultimate Great Father, which was hardly surprising, since they knew he had created them; to Silverfox he was both a familiar figure of history and a figure of semi-veneration, less than a god but far more than human. To the Tayledras, he was a figure of the misty past, and they recalled very little of him; most did not even know his name, and called him only "The Mage of Silence." To most Shin'a'in he was not even that—

Except to the Kal'enedral. To them, he was a man; powerful, good of heart and soul, but one who could not resist meddling in things he should never have touched. Without a doubt, that was because their version was flavored with their own form of prejudice against magic. Even Chagren was not immune from that prejudice, though he suffered from it less than some.

The Shin'a'in had been assigned the guardianship of the Plains by their Goddess Herself, although most of them were not aware that there really *was* something here that needed to be guarded from interlopers. Certainly, being a Goddess, She could simply have removed the weapons and dangers entirely had She chosen, but deities work in ways that are often not obvious even after centuries of scrutiny. It must have taken a direct edict from the Shin'a'in Goddess to get her chief servants, the Kal'enedral, to open the Plains and this Tower at its heart to strangers. He could hardly imagine what their reaction must have been to learn that they would be opening the Tower to *mages.*

Their faith must be very great, he thought, with wonder. *Look how long it took me to accept that Heralds and Companions were not demonic—they gave over their fears in a much shorter time.*

Or if they had not given up their fear, they had certainly worked past it. He had encountered no hostility from these people, only the wariness he himself felt, faced with strangers from a strange people.

Then again, perhaps the Kal'enedral had been very careful about which of their folk were permitted to aid the foreigners.

"I could do with a little less change myself," he said with a weak laugh. "But the mage-storms aren't giving us much of a choice in that."

Chagren grimaced, his aquiline features making the expression more pronounced. "Yet another mischance that some would lay at Urtho's door. Had he not made the choices he did, some would say that none of this would be happening now."

Interesting choice of words. Could it be that Chagren is taking a wider view of things? "But not you?" Karal asked delicately.

Chagren looked for a moment as if he was not going to answer, then shrugged. "But not me. I am not certain that Urtho's great enemy Ma'ar would not have unleashed worse upon the world; after all, look what havoc Falconsbane and Ancar wrought, who were lesser mages than Ma'ar. Then again, my *leshy'a* teachers had . . . experience with mages."

Now that was a new word; he thought he vaguely recognized the root. Something about a soul. "What kind of teachers?" he asked, to test his guess.

"I suppose you'd call them 'spirits' although they can be quite solidly real if She wishes," Chagren replied matter-of-factly, as if he spoke with ghosts every day. Well, perhaps he did.

"At some point in the lives of most Swordsworn they encounter one or more *leshy'a Kal'enedral*. There have even—" He broke off his words, and stared past Karal for a moment, and half-choked. His eyes widened, and he gave a slight bow of his head. "I believe, Outlander," he said in an entirely different and very respectful voice, "that you are about to find out for yourself."

Karal turned, to find that another of the Swordsworn was standing in the doorway; this one was very clearly a woman, but also very clearly a warrior in every fiber. She was dressed entirely in black from head to toe, and wore a veil or scarf across the bottom half of her face. A sword and long knife hung from her belt, and she bore the weight easily, negligently. In two paces she had crossed the chamber and stood at the side of Karal's pallet, looking down at him.

She could have seemed frightening, intimidating from her clothing alone, and yet there was nothing menacing whatsoever about her. Competent, yes; certainly imposing—but Karal would have had no hesitation in trusting her. Her blue eyes above the black veil were both amused and kind, and he sensed that she was smiling.

"Forgive me that I can't rise to greet you properly, Lady," he said with deepest respect.

"Oh, not at all," she replied, and her voice had a very odd, hollow quality to it, as if she were speaking from the bottom of a very deep well. "As I understand it, you're rather indisposed at the moment."

He narrowed his eyes, as he began to see, or sense, that there was something unexpected about her. She reminded him of something very familiar; in fact, there was some indefinable aura about her that was like—like—

Sunlord! She's—not—

"I must presume," he said carefully after a deep breath, "that Sworn Ones such as you who choose to instruct further generations do not bother to take a physical vehicle such as a Firecat or a Companion." *She's a spirit, that's what she is!*

Like An'desha's Avatars, only more here. *More real.* He felt positively giddy at his own daring, looking a spirit right in the eyes like this, and speaking to her as an equal!

"Say rather, *are chosen* rather than *choose,* and you have it rightly, young priest," the spirit replied, a hint of a chuckle in her hollow voice. "Though I have to admit that She has toyed a time or two with the notion of Black Companions. Or perhaps, Black Riders."

Since Karal could well imagine Florian's indignant response to *that* idea, he had to stifle a smile of his own. *Black Companions? Oh, the Heralds wouldn't like that at all!*

"I believe you've met a kinswoman of mine," the spirit continued. "She left her mark on you, which leads me to think that she regards you favorably. She's a hard one to please."

He tried wildly for a moment to think of who the Kal'enedral could mean. "Ah—you—Querna?" he hazarded, trying to imagine how that rather aloof lady could have left any kind of a mark on him.

The spirit laughed aloud at that. "No, young Clan-friend. *Kerowyn.* I see you've lined up anything that could serve as a weapon, hurled or otherwise, so that you can reach everything in the order you'd need it. That's the sort of 'mark' I mean. She's trained you so deep it's a habit."

Startled, he looked down involuntarily and saw he'd done just that, with the things he'd have to throw at the farthest point of his reach and his dagger right at his elbow. He flushed. What must Chagren be thinking now, that he distrusted them all? That they had let a potential assassin into their midst?

"Oh don't be embarrassed, boy," the spirit chided gruffly. "That's one of the best habits to be in. What if someone unfriendly got in here? What if one of our more fanatical brethren decided that She had been deceived by you lot, and you all had to die? Don't you know what we say? *Know where all the exits are. Never sit with your back to the door. Watch the reflections. Watch the shadows. Keep your hands free and your weapons loose.*"

Sunlord! he thought desperately, *I'm being bombarded with Shin'a'in proverbs! What a terrible way to die!*

He meant that lightly, but it seemed that the Kal'enedral intended to continue until she had recited every proverb on the subject of self-defense that the Shin'a'in ever invented. *"Never sit down to eat with your sword at your side—strap it to your back for a faster draw. Better an honest enemy than a feigned friend. When—"*

"*Who is wisest, says least,*" he interrupted, desperate to cut through what looked to be an unending stream of proverbs. Were Shin'a'in all like that? Even Kerowyn tended to spout Shin'a'in proverbs at the drop of a hint. And a spirit Kal'enedral probably knew every proverb ever composed!

The spirit laughed aloud again. "Well said!" she applauded. "Keep that sense of humor, and you might just survive this. Chagren, take special care of this one; he's deeper than he looks."

Chagren bowed low. "As you say, teacher," he replied.

Karal wasn't prepared for the spirit's departure; he barely blinked and she was gone. A chill ran up his backbone, but he was determined not to show it.

"If you see a Swordworn in black with a veil," Chagren said slowly, "it is *leshy'a*. There have been some few here among the rest of us. We think they come to ensure your safety . . . or ours. It's debated which."

"It's more likely both," Karal said, feeling a bit dizzy. "Kerowyn's kin to *her?*"

Chagren shrugged. "So she says. That is something new to me, but the *leshy'a* are not inclined to talk about their pasts. Often we do not even know their names. She is my first teacher of the sword, and came to me the night that I was Sworn—" He broke off what he was saying to shake his head. "I am babbling. And *you*, young outland priest, can consider yourself as having passed a kind of examination. None of the Sworn are likely to question *your* right to be here ever again."

With that rather surprising statement, he turned and left the chamber, leaving Karal alone with his thoughts, which were, to say the least, very complex.

Although there was one thought that was not at all complex.

So my right to be here will no longer be questioned. That's all very well for me, but what about the others?

Firesong sighed as he regarded his much abused shirt with a frown. His favorite sorts of garments were not meant for rough living and a camp existence.

"Glaring at it won't put the hem back up," Silverfox remarked around a mouthful of pins. "You might as well give up and do it the hard way."

Firesong growled under his breath, but took up needle and thread grudgingly. "All very well for you to say," he complained, "but you've been able to trade off sweeping and scrubbing the sleeping room to An'desha in return for cleaning his dishes. And you've traded Lo'isha massages for cleaning and airing the bedding. *I* haven't got anything anyone wants to trade for! Valdemar, barbaric as it was, is looking better all the time!"

Silverfox chuckled. "It could be worse; we could still be eating your cooking. I believe that our kin-cousins are being very generous in taking over the larger portion of the work."

Firesong growled again. "You only say that because you can do things even thc Kal'enedral are interested in. I'm a *mage*, that's all I know, and they don't want a thing I can do for them!"

Silverfox put down his needle to look up at him with sympathy. "You aren't just a mage. You are a lover, but you are so exotic to them that they could more easily entertain fantasies of bedding clouds. If there is *really* something you detest, would you please tell me and let me do it, or barter a massage or something to one of the Sworn and have him do it? You are a mage, *ashaka*, and I feel in my boncs that soon enough you will have more important things to worry about than hems and ripped seams."

Firesong started to reply, then shook his head and laughed at himself. "Why is it when you say things like that, you manage to deflate my self-importance rather than inflating it, and simply fill me with dread?"

Silverfox merely tilted his head to one side, and replied, "Do I?"

Let's change the subject, he thought. *I can do without too much introspection.* "Magic is working more reliably now that the counterforce is evening out the Storm-waves. It is still a horrid mess, but I think I can get a Gate up to the rim of the Plains soon; if I can do that, we can at least ask for a few more things to make life tolerable around here. How much would k'Leshya be willing to part with in the way of amenities, do you think? I haven't had a real bath in weeks and neither has anyone else. A big tub would be very welcome, even if its real intention was to water horses. A copper boiler to heat water would be even more welcome."

Silverfox looked thoughtful. "There might be a fair amount they could send us, both of leftover Tayledras gear and some of our own. And you know—if we could get a Gate open, we could get some *hertasi* volunteers to come through. They can't cross the Plains in winter without a great deal of hardship, and I wouldn't ask it of them. But they could come through a Gate, provided they were sure we could keep them warm enough over here."

Firesong closed his eyes for a moment in longing. Oh, how he missed his little army of *hertasi* helpers! If he had just one or two, he wouldn't have to do another tedious chore for himself again. They loved to do exactly the sorts of things he wanted to avoid here, and could probably show even the natives some lessons in organization.

"Before we try that, we ought to see if we can find out what Sejanes and the rest back in Haven have found out about Gating," he replied, after another moment of cautious thought. "Not that I wouldn't be willing to give up a lot for a couple of *hertasi*, but I wouldn't want to put them at any risk. It's one thing to toss a tub or a sack of meal through; it's quite another to risk a living being."

Silverfox nodded, and bit off his thread. "Should we send Karal back if we can get a Gate up that's safe for a living creature? He'd be better off with k'Leshya."

Once again, Firesong hesitated. *Now there's a question. He would be better off in a place where he could be properly cared for, but—how many more of the devices here need a Channel? What are we going to have to do in order to counter that final Storm, the one that's the reverse analog of the original Cataclysm?* "You can ask An'desha and Lo'isha if you like, but I have the sinking feeling we still need him. If he decides he's willing to stay here, we should let him." He took a few more stitches and knotted off his own thread. "I think he's going to insist on it. Sometimes that child makes me feel ashamed of myself. I sit here wailing and moaning because I have to pick up after myself, and he's fretting because he's too weak to help." He shook his head.

"Maybe that's *why* he's a priest and you're not," Silverfox said gently. "He seeks to give of himself even when there's nothing left to give. It hurts him, but it also makes him feel effective. We can't all turn out that self-sacrificing. Lady knows *I'm* not—"

He was interrupted by the sound of someone running. "Heyla, you two!" An'desha poked his head into their chamber. "Come to Karal's room. Altra made a Jump to Haven and he's back with word from Sejanes!"

Both of them dropped their mending and got to their feet, hurrying toward Karal's chamber—which once held the "weapon" that had discharged all of its formidable power through him. Firesong hadn't mentioned that to Karal yet; when they had elected not to move him, he had deduced that since all the chambers looked alike, Karal probably wouldn't notice which one he was in. *I'm not sure how he'd react. He might not care—or it might make him very nervous and unhappy, being in the same room where he nearly died.*

When they arrived at the chamber, they found Lo'isha, a few of the Kal'enedral, Florian, and An'desha already waiting there, with Altra on Karal's lap and an unopened message tube beside them.

Firesong blinked, and realized that after all the time of working with the mages and Artificers back in Haven, he'd been unconsciously expecting to see more people. *So it's just us now. I don't know if I like that. I hate to admit it, but those Artificers had some good ideas.*

"I hope this message is written in Valdemaran, but it probably isn't," Karal said. "I know enough of Imperial tongue to translate, though, if you want me to."

"Go ahead," Firesong said, motioning to him to pick up the tube. "I don't even read Valdemaran that well; you're the best reader we have except for Florian."

"And I can just picture Florian trying to unroll the paper!" Karal chuckled, though Firesong noted that Florian came to look over Karal's shoulder, probably to help with the translation.

If only Aya could read foreign tongues! he thought with envy. *We could each specialize in a language; it would be so convenient!*

Karal broke open the tube and extracted a roll of paper; he unrolled it with an accompanying crackling sound.

Evidently it *was* in Valdemaran; Karal's frown faded and he began reading immediately. Probably Florian was prompting him.

The letter began abruptly. *"Greetings, and* do not attempt to make or use a Gate. *We have already tried and the results were Unfortunate.* That's with a capital 'U' by the way."

Firesong winced. *I was afraid of that.*

"Things must be more unsettled than we thought," An'desha said with alarm. "My little magics have been working so well I thought certainly that the larger ones must surely be all right."

"That might simply be a function of where we are," Firesong reminded him. "For all we know, there are upper shields on the remains of the Tower, strong enough that we could do almost anything in here and not be affected by what's gone on outside."

Karal cleared his throat to get their attention again. Firesong turned back to him and nodded, and the young man continued. *"I fear this means you are exiled for the duration, colleagues. We built a small local Gate as soon as we could after you unloosed the power of your Device, and we attempted to transfer a few small nonliving items through it. I am glad now that we opted for caution and made those items of a nonliving nature, for the result on the other side was rather messy. Parts were recognizable, and that is the best I can say. Many suffered from desiccation, aging, or physical compression. Altra's Jumping seems to cause no such problems for the moment, even when he 'carries' someone with him, but he reports that it is becoming more and more difficult to Jump as time passes."*

At this, Altra himself raised his head and spoke up. :*I find that the distance I can Jump decreases as time passes. I am afraid that within a few weeks I will not be able to Jump across a given distance any faster than a Companion could run across it.*:

Firesong let out the breath he'd been holding in. *I wonder if I ought to go back to k'Leshya after all? I'm not sure I can continue to live like this and not begin to lose my temper, if not my sanity.* "Well, that's not welcome news," he said as casually as he could. "Is there anything else?"

Karal scanned the letter quickly. "Once the bad news is out, he gets a lot more formal and technical; the short version is that Altra can probably bring one or two people from Haven to here before he can't Jump anymore, but that we need to work on a way to communicate with Haven—maybe using scrying. Magic that doesn't transfer or move anything physical seems to work better than magic that does. I just hope that if there are shields protecting this place, they wouldn't interfere with scrying, too."

He handed the letter over to Firesong. "Here, you can get all the details yourself later; most of what he says only partially makes sense to me."

"I'll study it later," Firesong promised. "The question now is, what are we going to do? If we're going to have Altra bring someone over, we'd better do it soon."

"If we can get them," An'desha said slowly, "I'd like both Sejanes and Master Levy here."

Firesong rolled his eyes up at that, but had to grudgingly agree. "If they'll put up with the unpleasantness of Jumping, they *would* be the best choices," he sighed. "Sejanes has an entire magic discipline that is foreign to us, and Master Levy—" He paused for a moment, reminded himself to be charitable, and chose his words carefully. "Master Levy has a very unique way of looking at our problems. If not him, then we should have at least one of the Master Artificers here. Even I have to admit that we could not have accomplished anything here without their help."

An'desha and Karal both nodded vigorously in agreement, which made him feel a bit sour, but he had to admit that without the Artificers, they would be working without a resource as valuable as the presence of an Adept. *We need that utterly different viewpoint here. And Master Levy might even be as intelligent as he thinks he is.*

:*Master Levy and Sejanes have already volunteered,*: Altra put in unexpectedly. :*I was just waiting to see if you would welcome them here. I can go back for them now, if you'd like, although it will take a few days to get there and back with them.*:

Now Firesong was startled. A few days? Altra's Jumping distances *had* been severely curtailed! "If it's going to take you days, I think you had *better* start back now," he told the Firecat. "I don't want to think how much faster the situation could deteriorate if we wait."

The Firecat nodded, and vanished from Karal's lap. Only Lo'isha looked at all dubious when Altra was gone.

"What's wrong, shaman?" Firesong asked politely, seeing Lo'isha's troubled gaze.

The Shin'a'in shrugged. "I am only wondering if we should have asked permission of our hosts before we brought more folk in. Hopefully, they will not be offended by the addition of two more strangers."

Curiously, that slight objection had the effect of hardening Firesong's decision. "If we'd had them here in the first place, we *might* have a permanent solution instead of a temporary one," he said stubbornly. "I, for one, *want* them here. Wind and weather, Lo'isha, if you're worried that they might somehow overpower us and escape with secrets of Urtho's forbidden magic, Master Levy doesn't know the first thing about practical magic, and Sejanes is so old that if you spoke a harsh word to him all his bones might break under the force! They're hardly a threat, singly *or* together!"

"Oh, I agree, but it is not my opinion you must have," Lo'isha began, then shrugged again. "Or, well, perhaps it is. I suppose I have as much authority here as the Kal'enedral." He grimaced. "Much as I dislike taking on authority, I suppose it is time that I did so."

Since it was Firesong's opinion that it was more than time that he did so, he simply nodded and held his tongue.

Karal looked fatigued, and Firesong stood up abruptly. "I am going to search for another hidden room. I have the feeling that this place hasn't even begun to divulge its secrets to us. Anyone care to join me?"

Urtho may have been one of the most brilliant and compassionate minds in history, but his architects were no small geniuses themselves. Firesong already had found one small, hidden room by carefully probing the floor of the "washing" room when he noticed that water, dripped in a particular place, drained away through cracks invisible to the unaided eye. It hadn't held anything—in fact, it had probably performed the task of simple storage—but now he knew that there *might* be more such places under the floors here, and he had the feeling that if he just looked hard enough, he might find more than just storage areas.

"I'll help," An'desha said unexpectedly.

He smiled. "Come along, then," he replied. "I'm trying the skull chamber next."

The "skull chamber" was the one in which they had discovered a bizarre contraption that looked like the leavings of half a dozen Artificers and shamans all jumbled together with the

remains of a few feasts. The centerpiece was a highly ornamented cow skull, and none of them could even begin to guess
what the device was for. They would have been afraid to dismantle it, except that the delicate construction had already
fallen apart in several places already, and the shock of their
magical working had made it fall completely to pieces without any other ill effect.

Rather than use magic, since the chamber itself reeked of
mage-power, Firesong was using perfectly ordinary senses;
taking a cue from the water drainage, he had a skin of water
with a bit of ink in it to make it more visible, and he dribbled
it over the floor, watching to see if it moved or vanished.

With An'desha helping, the two of them were a lot more
effective than he was by himself. It was very boring work, and
he had expected An'desha to start a conversation, but he had
not anticipated the subject.

"You're thinking about going back, aren't you?" An'desha
said. "To k'Leshya, if not your home Vale."

He didn't reply at first; he pretended to be paying close attention to the water on the floor. "I'm not used to this sort of
living," he said, refusing to answer directly. "It's harder on me
than it is on you."

"I won't debate that," An'desha agreed. "And I hope you
don't think I'd put any blame on you for leaving. The gryphons did."

"But they have two children who need them," he snapped.
"I don't. I haven't any excuse for leaving except wanting to be
comfortable again!" He felt irrationally irritated at An'desha
for voicing all of *his* excuses, as if he were so transparent that
An'desha had no difficulty in anticipating what he wanted to
do and his rationalizations.

The trouble was that every time he looked at Karal, he felt
ashamed of himself.

"It's not as if you haven't done more than most people
would have already," An'desha said gently. "First you faced
down Falconsbane—"

"Mornelithe Falconsbane was a challenge, but no more
than that," he replied stiffly. "It's not as if I was alone in facing him."

"It's not as if you had any real reason to," An'desha pointed
out inexorably. "Valdemar wasn't your home. Falconsbane
didn't threaten the Vales. You'd done your duty in training

Heralds to be mages, and then some. You could have gone home once you'd done that much."

"Leaving whom to face Falconsbane?" Firesong demanded, his face flushing. "One of those half-trained Heralds? Elspeth? Darkwind, perhaps? None of them could have freed *you*. I'm not certain even Need could have freed you *and* dealt with Falconsbane."

An'desha simply nodded quietly. "But when it was over— you could have gone home then. You could even have taken me with you, and things might have turned out differently. You've long since gone past anything anyone could call your duty, Firesong. No one would fault you if you were too tired of all this to go on."

"And how am I going to compare to someone like Karal if I do that?" he demanded, flushing still further. "Too tired? How would I look, quitting now, next to someone who literally put his life in jeopardy over this?"

"You make him sound like a would-be martyr," An'desha chided. "Karal is quite a few things, including stubborn, occasionally bigoted, and now and then incredibly naive, but he's no martyr. And neither are you, nor any of us."

"So?" Aya must have felt his distress; the firebird sailed in the chamber door, adroitly avoided the snare of wires and junk, and landed on his shoulder. He petted the bondbird reflexively in a blind search for comfort. "If he's not a martyr, then—" He stopped, aware that his voice was getting high and strained.

He took two or three deep breaths. "An'desha, I don't know why you're baiting me this way."

Then, in a moment of blinding insight, he *did* know.

He's forcing me to think things through, so that I come to a real decision, instead of letting some unfinished business and an entire bundle of emotions sway me back and forth.

An'desha nodded, as if he saw all that written on Firesong's face.

I can't make a decision because I'm trying to demonstrate that I'm somehow better than Karal. And I can't make it out of guilt either.

So why am I staying?

"What Karal does is up to Karal, but—well, I'm not too old to take a youngster like him as a good example." He smiled weakly. "You all need me, just as you need Sejanes or Master

Levy, or Altra. I'm staying because even though I'm tired and I hate living here, it would be wrong of me to go off and leave you without my skills. I don't want to die in the cold and filth, but if I must, I will. It would be wrong to abandon all those people who are hoping we'll find a solution to the final Storm. It would be wrong to break my word to the people I promised I would help. Are those reasons good enough for you?"

An'desha laughed at that. "Don't think to bait me, Firesong; I was coached by an expert to steer you through your own thoughts and motives."

He scowled at that. "Are you happy with the result?" he growled.

"The question is not whether I'm satisfied, it's whether you are," An'desha countered. "And if you are, it is not for me to object. If your decision will interfere with other concerns, then that must be dealt with then."

He stood up and moved over to another section of floor. Firesong felt an imp of perversity rise inside him, and he knew he had to have the last word.

"And I didn't mention the best reason of all yet," he said silkily. Surprised, An'desha turned back to face him.

"What reason is that?" he asked, as if the words had been pulled from him unwillingly.

Firesong smiled. "Silverfox wants me to stay," he replied. "Can you think of a better reason?"

Darkwind, Elspeth and Vree

Two

Elspeth sighed, her breath streaming out in a fog of ice-crystals, and pulled the ends of the scarf wrapped around her neck a little tighter. Once again she sent a little thought of gratitude back over her shoulder toward Valdemar and the tireless k'Leshya *hertasi* who had fashioned her current costume. The little lizard-folk who had arrived with the bargeload of envoys from Clan k'Leshya had taken one look at her winter wardrobe and taken it upon themselves to refashion it, as if they didn't already have enough to do. The *hertasi* of k'Sheyna had already made her Herald's Whites in the style of the Tayledras, but those had all been of summer-weight fabrics. These new *hertasi* had remade her Whites in wool, fur, and leather, layered in silk according to patterns designed for her by Darkwind. These had been her Midwinter gift from him to her, and a welcome surprise they had been indeed, for they were certainly needed. Winter Field Whites *had* been designed for harsh weather, but not as harsh as the unprecedented weather currently holding Hardorn in its icy grip.

And Hardorn was where she, Darkwind, and a small group of mixed Valdemaran Guards and Kerowyn's mercenaries found themselves headed shortly after Midwinter Festival.

There hadn't been much choice; it was clear that Valdemar was going to have to send some form of envoy overland to Grand Duke Tremane, once it became impossible to put up any more Gates. Elspeth had been present when that last Gate had been attempted; the mangled crate that had come through had looked as if it had been turned inside out, and nothing in it was recognizable. It was just a good thing that the crate had only contained a few things for Sejanes and that they had been cautious enough to test the Gate with mere cargo before sending anyone living through.

But travel to and within Hardorn was not easy by any standard, even those of one who had journeyed from Valdemar to the Dhorisha Plains and patrolled the weirdling lands being cleansed and protected by a Hawkbrother Vale. In all of her life she had never seen snow this deep. The road they followed into Hardorn had been kept clear for traffic, but only enough to permit a cart pulled by two horses to pass. And even then, the wheels of the cart would scrape the walls of snow now and again. Every ten leagues a wider place had been cut, so that carts going in opposite directions could pass, but otherwise the snow was piled up on either side of the road until it reached shoulder-high on a horse. In places where the snow had drifted deeper than that, it could be taller than a rider's head. And the cold, the *wind*—In many ways, she was grateful that those tall snowbanks were there, because without that shelter they'd be facing a wind that bit as cruelly as any blade, and carried right down to the bone. *Hertasi*-designed tunics with fur linings and riding coats of sheepskin with the wool turned inside were the only things that made this journey bearable. She was quite grateful that the mysterious, industrious lizard-folk had been able to outfit the entire company with such coats before they all left.

"Why the sigh?" Darkwind asked, his breath puffing out in frosty clouds with each word. His bondbird Vree clung to the padded horn of his saddle, with no sign of discomfort whatsoever—except that his feathers were puffed out all over his body and his head was pulled down tight against his shoulders, so that he resembled a fat ball of wool with a beak. But then, Vree was a forestgyre, and Darkwind had once told her that they had come from stock adapted to harsher climes than this. Darkwind himself cut an odd figure, and not just because of his Hawkbrother costume or the bondbird on his saddlebow; Darkwind's mount was neither a horse nor a Companion, but a creature as intelligent and as foreign to Valdemaran eyes as a gryphon. It was a *dyheli*, a white *dyheli* at that, and the representative of his own race to Valdemar. His name was Brytha, and he had brought Firesong from k'Treva to k'Sheyna, then from k'Sheyna to Valdemar, and now consented to bear Darkwind on this current mission. Why? She didn't know; Darkwind didn't know either, and the *dyheli* seemed disinclined to explain. They were both grateful to him; although not the equal in endurance and speed of a Companion, the *dyheli* was better suited to this mission than a horse, more sure-footed and vastly more intelligent. The rest of their party rode tough Shin'a'in-bred horses, especially selected for endurance, shaggy as dogs with blunt, blocky heads.

"I'm sighing because I've decided that the one thing I will never say again is to say 'never again,' " she replied with a crooked smile. "Because as sure as I say it, I'm forced to repeat the act I swore never to repeat."

He chuckled ruefully, without needing any explanation. Neither of them had ever thought they would be riding back into Hardorn again. Their previous visit, although memorable, had not been particularly pleasant, either for them or for the Hardornens. When they had finished, mad King Ancar and his adviser Hulda were dead at their hands, mage-caused storms were lashing the countryside, the capital was in a state of total chaos, and the Imperial Army (taking advantage of the moment) was pouring over the Eastern border. And although very few Hardornens were aware of the fact, Elspeth and Darkwind were directly or indirectly responsible for most of the damage and chaos they left behind them.

Not that the Imperial Army was our fault, but that's just about the only thing we can say we didn't have a hand in.

And after the invasion came the real mage-storms, triggering incredibly vicious weather and unleashing real horrors on the unsuspecting countryside. *Those* were not the fault of anyone living, but they did make life in Hardorn even more miserable than anyone had ever dreamed possible. So riding into Hardorn didn't seem particularly likely *or* sane a few moons ago.

But that had been before Duke Tremane offered alliance; before it dawned on everyone in this part of the world that the mage-storms were a greater menace than anything mere humans could unleash on each other. Now things that wouldn't have occurred to anyone as possible scenarios were being hastily put into motion.

"Have you noticed something? The weather might be vile, but the *land* isn't suffering anymore," Darkwind observed.

"It's not exhausted and ill anymore, it's just sleeping, waiting for spring. I don't know about you, but that was one of the reasons why I didn't want to ever come back here again."

Elspeth nodded, and so did her Companion Gwena, the bells on her bridle chiming crisply in the sharp, icy air. *:Without Ancar draining the land of its power, things are returning to normal,:* Gwena replied. *:The land, and presumably the people, are no longer sickening. And much as I hate to say it—the blood and life-energy of all those poor folk killed in the invasion may have sped that recovery.:*

"That's a horrible thought," Darkwind observed with a shudder, for Gwena had made certain to include him in her Mindspeaking.

Elspeth shivered; intellectually she knew it was probably true, but it was horrible all the same. "That just sounds entirely too much like something Falconsbane would have come up with," she said reluctantly. "But then again, Falconsbane simply perverted things that were perfectly normal and good. And I suppose it would be even worse to think that all those people died and their life-energy went for nothing, or worse, was used by someone like Falconsbane."

:Mages and those with earth-sense have known for centuries that this is the reason why the countryside blooms after a war,: Gwena observed dispassionately. *:It isn't just that things seem better, and it isn't just that the people are ready to greet any positive signs with enthusiasm. It's because the lives lost go back to the land, and when the war is over, the land can use them to heal itself.:*

"We can at least be grateful that Grand Duke Tremane is *apparently* more interested in allowing the land to heal than in using that power for his own means," Darkwind replied, as he turned for a moment to stare off into the east. He said nothing more, and Elspeth thought she knew why.

They had only the word of three youngsters and Tremane's own people that he was to be trusted at all. Just at the moment, *apparently* was the only word any of them could use with regard to the leader of the Imperial forces. Those few facts that they had about Tremane were not much comfort.

Tremane had been sent by his master, Emperor Charliss, to conquer a weak and chaotic Hardorn for the Empire of the East. This assignment was to prove him worthy (or not) to be the Imperial Heir. The Imperial Army had taken roughly half of Hardorn before it stalled, held in place by Hardornen fighters, in mostly uncoordinated groups ranging in size from tiny bands to small armies, united only in their determination to oust the interloper. Since they were fighting on their own ground, they had the advantage once the front lines stretched out and the Imperial forces were thinned by distance. Nevertheless, if nothing had changed, Tremane would probably have been able to reorganize, regroup, and complete the conquest, possibly even carrying it into Valdemar.

But things *did* change, and in a way that no one could have foreseen; the change had come from a direction no one would have looked, for it had come out of the distant past.

We never do consider the past, do we? But we should have. Wasn't Falconsbane a revenant of that past? And shouldn't that have warned us to turn our eyes and thoughts in that direction? But then again, how can we truly plan for everything, every possibility? Even if we knew all of the threats at any one moment, the defenses for half of them would negate the preparations for the other half. We are better off being resourceful than omniscient, I think.

Once, before there had ever been a Valdemar, in a time so distant that there were no records and only the vaguest of hints about it in the great library of the Heralds, ancient wars had ended in an event known only as the Cataclysm. And until Elspeth had met with the Tayledras of legend, the Shin'a'in of the Dhorisha Plains, and the last, lost Clan of the true Kaled'a'in—progenitors of both the Hawkbrothers and the Shin'a'in—that was *all* those in Valdemar had known. Now, though, with the help of histories both arcane and mundane, the full story had been put together.

Elspeth considered that story, as she did every time she had the leisure to do so, intent on extracting the least bit of useful information from it. Despite the huge amounts of power involved, there were still human motives and actions behind what had happened so long ago. Even madmen would act according to their needs, so the more that one considered events of history, the more one could deduce what those needs had been—and once one understood the needs and motivations of the people involved, one could expound upon what else might have happened, or realize that an obscure detail was actually something significant in context.

There had been two Adepts back then, perhaps the most powerful that the world had ever known, called Urtho and Ma'ar. Ma'ar, the scion of barbarian nomads, had been infected with the mania for conquest, at first for noble reasons of uniting clans to keep them from annihilating each other. Urtho, the epitome of civilization and scholarship, had resisted him. But despite the best efforts of civilization, Ma'ar, Adept and Blood-Mage, had triumphed—

But only for a moment. In the very hour of Ma'ar's victory, a dying Urtho had brought defeat to his very door, with a pair of devices that released the bonds on all magic within their spheres of influence. One he triggered in his own Tower; one was sent to Ma'ar. The devices acted within moments of each other, and the results were both devastating and utterly unpredictable.

When it was over, there were two enormous craters where Urtho's Tower and Ma'ar's palace had stood. The first became the Dhorisha Plains; the second, Lake Evendim. And the interaction of the two series of shock waves created terrible mage-storms that had raged over the land for a decade or more, raising mountains and flattening them, disrupting magic, causing living creatures to change and warp out of all recognition, even transplanting entire sections of countryside from one part of the world to another.

Eventually the Storms faded, to be forgotten in the ensuing centuries, assumed by all to have been gone forever. But the forces released by the Cataclysm were stranger and stronger than anyone guessed, and now the mage-storms had returned, echoing back across time from the other side of the world, growing stronger with every new occurrence.

That was what had changed the situation Tremane had walked into, changed it out of all recognition. The situation in Valdemar had been bad, but not a complete disaster. Valdemar had only newly rediscovered true-magic, and did not depend on its power for anything. The other effects of the mage-storms, the vicious and unpredictable weather, the warping of living creatures, and so forth, could all be dealt with in one way or another. But for Tremane's forces, dependent on magic for everything from communication and supply lines to the means to scout the enemy and cook their food, it was a disaster as they found themselves completely cut off from the Empire, effectively blind and hungry as a fighting force. As for what was going on in the Empire itself, that was anyone's guess. Tremane had initially assumed that the Storms were a new weapon unleashed by the Alliance of Valdemar, Karse, Rethwellan, and the Shin'a'in/Tayledras clans. He had reacted accordingly—and in a direction entirely typical of the Empire, where treachery and assassination were so commonplace that children were given bonded bodyguards as cradle-gifts. He had sent an assassin to break up the Alliance.

That was the single act that Elspeth and any other Valdemaran found so difficult to think past. Valdemar had *not* attacked Imperial forces. Neither Valdemar nor any of her allies had shown any sign of aggression other than increasing the guard on the borders and covertly helping to supply the Hardornen loyalists. Tremane had no reason—except for the obvious fact that Valdemar was not suffering from the Storms as badly as the Imperials were—to think that this was an attack by Queen Selenay or her allies. Nevertheless, he had treated it as one, and had sent a covert operative armed with magic weapons to kill anyone of any importance at or in Selenay's Court.

The man had succeeded only insofar as murdering the envoy from Karse and the one from the Shin'a'in, and wounding several others. That was bad enough, but was sheerest good fortune that it wasn't worse, and no one made any mistake about that. If the assassin had waited until the predawn hours when people were sleeping in their beds, he would have succeeded in killing everyone from Selenay down to the gryphons.

Herein lay the heart of Elspeth and Darkwind's current problem. Now they were supposed to trust a man who used assassins against those he only *suspected* of aggressive action.

Elspeth found it difficult to think beyond that fact, even though Tremane had won over to his side the last person likely to ever forgive him—young Karal, the secretary and protégé of the envoy of Karse, Sun-priest and Mage, Master Ulrich. Tremane had even somehow convinced Solaris, Son of the Sun and High Priest and ruler of Karse, of his sincerity and his wish to make amends, though only the gods knew how he'd done that.

Well, he hasn't convinced me, and he hasn't convinced Darkwind, she thought stubbornly. *Whatever spell of words or personality he put them under, I hope it's going to be more difficult to work the same "magic" on us. I know mind-magic, and Darkwind is so foreign to Tremane's experience that he might as well be another species altogether. And what's more, I wouldn't be in the least surprised to discover that Kerowyn slipped half a dozen special operatives into our escort. Two sides can play the assassination game, if it comes to that.*

She hoped that it wouldn't, but she had enough experience now to make her plans around pessimism rather than hope. She didn't officially *know* that Kerowyn had planted her own agents, but she knew the Skybolts, and they were, one and all, "irregulars." Their skills were not those of straight-on fighters, although they could act and fight as a disciplined skirmishing unit and had in the past.

On the other hand . . . Solaris has Hansa, the other Firecat. If she *wanted to kill Tremane, there is no way he could stop her. So maybe that fact alone will make him behave himself from now on.*

That was certainly something else to consider. The Firecats possessed the ability to "Jump" themselves and anyone in physical contact with them from one location to another, and Elspeth was not entirely certain what their range was. Certainly it was good enough that Altra and Hansa served as messengers between Solaris and Selenay, and between the party in the remains of Urtho's Tower and the mages and Artificers in the Valdemaran capital of Haven. Solaris was perfectly capable of placing an assassin of her own right under Tremane's privy to poke a knife up into him if she so desired, and for that matter, there was no reason why Hansa himself could not kill a man if he chose. Although Firecats had the ability to *look* like common cats if they wished to, in their true form they were the size of enormous hounds, and their claws and teeth were correspondingly long and sharp.

Elspeth blinked at the images that thought conjured up. *My thoughts are certainly taking a grim turn today. Maybe I'm concentrating on spilling blood as an antidote to all this whiteness. Dear gods, it's cold—and we haven't seen another human soul since our guides left us.*

They'd been lucky when they'd reached the Valdemaran Border. A couple of Hardornen exiles—vouched for by Kerowyn's agents—had cautiously decided it was safe to return and acted as guides up until this morning in exchange for two pouches of currency and two packs of supplies. Now, though, they would have to go on without guides, because the husband and wife had gone as far as they intended.

Last night the party had reached the village from which the couple had originally fled. Even though it proved to be deserted, abandoned, like the other villages they had passed on this road, the two wanted to stay; even in thick white desolation they had a dream of a time in the future when there would be children running and playing in a verdant town square.

Their journey thus far had been an unnerving one, riding through a landscape devoid of humans. Elspeth could only wonder what had happened. *The land might be healing, but where are the people?* True, Ancar had decimated the population, but why hadn't they met with *anyone* on this road? Why were all the villages they passed through completely deserted?

The abandoned villages raised more questions than were answered, for everything had been taken except the heaviest of furniture, and there was no sign of violence. Was this the result of systematic desertion or systematic looting? Who was cleaning off the snow? Were the Hardornens hiding from an armed and possibly hostile group? Given the fact that this was a nation racked by war, that was possible. But *why*, when there was a Herald of Valdemar riding conspicuously in the front?

Perhaps because at a distance there's no reason to assume I really am a Herald. It's not that hard to get a white horse and a set of white clothing.

"What are our plans for stopping tonight, or do we have any?" she called back to the leader of the troop. They hadn't provisioned themselves for camping, though they had brought all their own food, assuming that rations might be short given the horrible mage-weather Hardorn had endured. It was a good thing they had, or they'd have had a choice between starving and (literally) eating crow.

"In theory there's a town ahead that used to have a weekly market and five big inns," the leader replied, his voice muffled by the scarf swathing his face. "Whether or not it's still tenanted—" he shrugged. "Someone's been keeping the road clean for traders, and I'm hoping it's them."

So was Elspeth, fervently. She was not looking forward to spending another night in an abandoned, derelict building. There was always one building that could be made to serve, and there was certainly no shortage of firewood, but she had always been glad of the presence of the others around her. She'd found it hard to sleep at night, with her shoulder blades prickling as if unseen eyes watched her. No one had actually seen or heard anything that could be taken as a ghost, but such places *felt* haunted.

She couldn't begin to imagine how Rusi and Severn could bear to stay back there in what was left of their village. Granted, there was plenty of material to make more than one of the houses sound and weather tight again. And granted, they were well-equipped to do just that. But the aching emptiness of the abandoned village would have sent her screaming for Valdemar within a week.

It was more than she could bear to think about right now. *I've done a great deal that people think is brave, but I'm not that brave.*

But that was also assuming that the land around the village was as deserted as it looked. When the mage-storms created killing weather and murderous monsters, would it have been safer and smarter to fortify the farmsteads and stay where the food was, or to come into the village and trust in numbers and weapons but chance the food running out? It wasn't a decision Elspeth had ever needed to make, and she hoped it was one nobody in Valdemar would be forced to face.

For that, all their hopes rested with that tiny group in the middle of the Dhorisha Plains, in the ruins of Urtho's Tower. If anyone could find an answer, it would be them. Although Elspeth and Darkwind were both Adept-class mages, Elspeth was relatively untutored and Darkwind had abandoned magic for so many years that despite his considerable prowess he still considered himself out of practice. As mages, they were of no help to the researchers who had gone to the Tower. They might be of some use with the Imperials, and they *would* be of great use as envoys.

She knew that Queen Selenay had debated long and hard before deciding to send Elspeth and Darkwind as envoys from the Alliance to Tremane. The Queen hadn't wanted to send Elspeth, but Elspeth was the only logical choice—she could make autonomous decisions, she had been trained both as a Herald and to wear the crown herself—she was the next best thing to Selenay when it came to being able to think *for* Valdemar. Elspeth had proven that she had good judgment, and because she was no longer the Heir since her abdication, she was of little value as a political hostage. Moreover, she had been trained by Kerowyn to defend herself against assassins; she could take care of herself in an ambush or an even fight, and she was as suspicious as even that redoubtable woman could have wished.

Then there was magic, in which she was an Adept; Tremane was no more than a Master, though of a far different magical discipline than the one she had been trained in. Very few of the Heralds of Valdemar were mages at all, much less Adepts, and although their Companions would be able to help them to some extent in matters of magic, it was no substitute for being mages themselves.

All that might not have been enough, except for Darkwind; he was an Adept as well, and of longer standing than she. He had been a Tayledras scout, which made him something of a fighter as well. He would have refused flatly to accompany anyone else; he was not a Herald, and his loyalties were to her, not Valdemar. Whereas she would hardly have gone anywhere without him, of course, and together they were a formidable pair.

Between her own qualifications and Darkwind's, there simply was no one as "right" to go on this mission as Elspeth, and if she had been anyone else's daughter, Selenay would not have hesitated for a moment to send her.

To give Mother credit, she didn't hesitate long. Elspeth was actually a bit pleased at that; Selenay had been treating her less as a daughter and more as—as an adult, and Elspeth had gotten the feeling, more than once, that when the Queen forgot to think of her as her daughter, she acted naturally. In a way, given the Queen's behavior of late, Elspeth had been a little surprised that her mother had given second thoughts to the mission. *I wonder if some of what has made her hesitate in the past was more guilt than anything else.*

Could it have been? Elspeth and her mother had never been comfortable with each other. *No matter how hard she tried, she always saw my father in me. In so many ways, I was more Talia's child than hers.* Now Selenay had the twins, children she could give her whole heart to; could she be feeling guilt that she *didn't* have that same maternal bond with Elspeth? Was that why she had always overreacted when Elspeth did something that might put her in jeopardy—because she felt as if she should have been *more* worried, more emotionally involved than she was?

An interesting theory, and one I'll never learn the truth of. I certainly couldn't ask her that, and the only other person who would know will never tell me. Talia would never betray anything she learned of Mother's heart, and rightly so. Elspeth gave herself a mental shake. Did it *matter?* Not really. Except that—if that was indeed the case, she wished she could convince her mother that it didn't matter. The last thing that the Queen of Valdemar needed was one more thing to feel guilty about. She already carried enough guilt for twenty people.

And I would rather be Queen Selenay's friend and fellow Herald than her daughter.

But the thought did present one explanation for some of Selenay's contradictory behavior, and it was certainly worth keeping in the back of her mind. She could watch for evidence of her own, and it would be interesting to act on that theory and see what happened.

Meanwhile, there was a long and difficult job ahead of her, and there was a danger they might all *freeze* to death before they even got to it if they didn't find some Hardornens soon.

"How much farther do you think this town is?" she called back over her shoulder. She glanced back to see—what was the Guard-Captain's name? Vallen, that was it—to see Vallen shrug, the movement barely visible beneath his multiple layers of fur, sheepskin, and wool.

"Soon, I think, but that is just a guess," he replied. Despite the scarf he wore about his face, his words came clearly over the muffled hoofbeats of their various mounts, over the creaking of the packed snow beneath those hooves. He gave his horse a nudge with his heels, and took the lead position as Elspeth and Darkwind moved aside to let him by.

Elspeth stood in her stirrups for a moment to peer up the road ahead, but if there were any signs of habitations such as plumes of smoke that could have been rising from chimneys, they were invisible against the uniformly gray-white sky. The sun was nothing more than a fuzzy, lighter spot about halfway down to the horizon.

She settled back down in her saddle; the way the road wound about, it wasn't possible to see very far ahead, and they only got a view of the countryside when the snowbanks allowed. *We could be right on top of this town and we'd never know it,* she thought.

Minutes later, the road gave another turn and dropped away in front of them. The snowbanks themselves inclined down to about waist-height. As if conjured up in a scrying crystal, the watched-for town appeared ahead of and below them, down in a shallow valley, the houses sticking up out of the snow like so many tree stumps in the snow-covered forest.

This was not the first time a town had appeared before them, but now, for the first time, there *were* signs that the place was inhabited. Some of the houses were nothing more than snow-covered lumps, but some had been cleaned of their burden of white. Thin smoke wreathed up out of about half the chimneys, to be snatched away by the wind before it climbed up to form a plume. There were a few figures moving about on the road near the town, and it was clear from the purposeful way that they moved that the party had been spotted, if not anticipated.

The place looked marginally better than the deserted villages they had already passed. Perhaps half the buildings were in disrepair; one or two had collapsed roofs, and it was hard to tell under the snow how badly some of the others had suffered. She had to guess that only the buildings with smoke rising from them were actually lived in, and she caught her breath at the thought that Ancar and all the other troubles visited upon Hardorn had literally cut the population in half. *Maybe more,* she reminded herself. *How many deserted villages did we pass through?*

Were conditions like this everywhere? If so—well, she did

not envy any leader the task of trying to bring this country back from such devastation. *If Tremane can get the Hardornens to accept him, he has more work ahead of him than I'd care to take on.*

A group of about a dozen people had formed up ahead of them on the road, barring them, at least for the moment, from entering the town. They were as bundled up in clothing as Elspeth's group was, making it difficult to tell anything about them, including their sexes; but in spite of that handicap, she thought that their stances showed a mix of fear and belligerence.

Fear? When had anyone ever *feared* her? They weren't so deep into Hardorn that the natives should be unaware of what a Herald was and what one stood for. How could they fear a Herald? Had Ancar created that fear in them so strongly?

She sensed the fighters behind her surreptitiously loosening their weapons, placing hands casually on hilts, and increasing their watchfulness. So it was not her imagination; they sensed hostility, too. Vallen reined in his horse and allowed her to take the lead; Darkwind signaled the *dyheli* to drop back with his head even with Gwena's flank. Elspeth brought them all to a halt about a length away from the "welcoming party" by gesturing with an upraised hand.

"We are peaceful travelers from Valdemar," she said in their own tongue, pulling her scarf down so that they could see her entire face—though she did wonder if they'd believe the "peaceful" part with so many weapons in evidence. "Who is in charge here?"

Two of the figures looked at each other, and one stepped forward, though he did not reveal his face as Elspeth had. Now that Elspeth was closer to them, the ragged state of their clothing was painfully evident. Their coats were carefully mended, but with patches that were not even a close match for the same material as the original.

"Me. I'm in charge, as I reckon," the foremost man said gruffly, and he folded his arms clumsily over his chest. He had no weapon in evidence, but Elspeth did not take that to mean that these people were helpless. If *she'd* been in charge, she'd have archers with drawn bows at every window.

She did not look up to see if her guess was correct.

"What're you here for?" the man continued. His arms tightened, and his posture straightened. His voice rose, angry and strained. "If you think you people in Valdemar are going to come in here and take us over, us and our land—"

"*No,*" Elspeth interrupted, cutting him off more sharply than she had intended. The man's nerves had infected her, and she took a deep breath to steady herself. "No," she repeated with less force. "We—Valdemar—has no intention of taking one ell of Hardorn land. Until Ancar attacked us, we were always the loyal friend and ally of Hardorn, and we intend to return to that status now that Ancar is gone."

He laughed, but it was not a sound of humor. "Ha!" he jeered. "You *say* that, but why should we believe you?"

"I swear it on my honor as a Herald!" she countered quickly. "You must know what that means, at least! Surely you have not lost faith even in that!"

This all had the feeling of a test, as if what she said here would make all the difference in how they would be treated from this moment on.

Do they have some way to communicate with other communities still? She couldn't imagine how anyone could cross this frozen wasteland faster than *they* were already doing, but the party of Valdemarans was confined to the road, and perhaps the natives had some way of cutting across country to spread news. Perhaps the old signal-towers were still working.

That could be the answer. And it could be how they knew we were coming.

"I swear it as a Herald," she repeated. "And as the envoy of the Queen. Valdemar has no designs on Hardorn, nor do any of the other parties to the Alliance."

—though Solaris had to restrain a few hotheads in Karse. Or rather, Vkandis did—

"We're only traveling," she continued smoothly. "We'd appreciate your hospitality for the night, though we did bring our own provisions. We know how difficult things have been for you, and we didn't want to strain anyone's resources."

There was a long silence, during which the man peered at her closely, and finally nodded, as if satisfied with what he saw. "That outfit's kind of outlandish, but you've got the horse, blue eyes and all, and *that* can't be faked." He shrugged, then, and made a gesture that she suspected told those hidden archers that all was well. "I guess we still believe in Heralds—

mostly since Ancar tried so hard to make us think you was some kind of witchy crew that had traffic with demons. I'll take your word as bond for you and the rest of this lot, but you better remember that *you* stand personal surety for them."

She nodded, trying not to show how unsettled his words made her feel. This was, literally, the first time she had ever encountered anyone this close to the border of Valdemar who *didn't* accept and welcome a Herald with trust. What had happened to these people to make them this way?

:Ancar is what happened to them, dear. They will be long in trusting anyone ever again,: Gwena said quietly. *:It may be that this generation never will.:*

"So where are you going, then?" the man asked, still wary.

"Tell him the truth, *ke'chara*," Darkwind said softly in Tayledras. "Don't dissemble. We might as well see now what kind of reception we're going to have while we still have the provisions to turn around and go home. We can't afford to fight our way across this country to get to Tremane."

She nodded slightly to show that she'd heard him; he was right, of course. If they couldn't get to Tremane's headquarters without fighting, there was no point in going on. "We're on our way to a town called Shonar," she said carefully, wondering how much or little he knew.

He knew enough; the man rocked back a pace. "You're going to Tremane?" he demanded. "The Impie Duke?"

She couldn't tell if he was angry or not, but she was already committed to the truth, so she nodded.

"We're the Valdemaran envoy to Tremane," she replied. "He—he wants to join the Alliance. Things that we have learned make us inclined to trust him to be honorable."

We hope.

There were murmurs from the group behind the man, and Elspeth took heart from the fact that they didn't sound angry, just thoughtful. The man himself considered them for a moment, then waved his followers aside. "We need to talk, Herald from Valdemar," he said with a touch of formality. "And there's no point in doing it in this cold. Come along; the inn's still in repair and heated, even if the innkeeper's gone, and if you've got bedrolls to sleep in, there's beds to put them on. If you can tend to yourselves and feed yourselves, we can give you fair shelter for the night."

That was the most welcome statement she'd heard yet on this journey, and she allowed Gwena to fall in obediently behind the man as he led the way to the inn.

The inn *was* in good repair, as promised, and so were the stables. The group dismounted in the inn-yard and led their mounts and the pack animals inside a stout building with a surprising number of animals in the stalls.

They must be keeping all of the horses and ponies in the town here, she realized after a look around. *That makes more sense than scattering them, one and two to a stable.*

The Hardornens quickly set to, throwing down straw from the hayloft to make up the remaining stalls for the visitors. As it turned out, they also had hay, though no grain to spare; that was fine, though. The Valdemarans had brought a string of *chirras* with them, loaded down with their supplies. The chirras did perfectly well on the hay alone, and there was plenty of grain in the supplies for the horses, Gwena, and the *dyheli*, Brytha.

Everyone in the party pitched in to help in the stables; Elspeth's cardinal rule, learned from Kerowyn, was that the welfare of their beasts came before the needs of the humans, and no one disagreed with her.

With the horses, chirras, Brytha, and Gwena warmly bedded down and fed and the sun setting behind the veil of gray cloud, they all trudged into the inn carrying their baggage.

Once inside, they stood in a tight group for a moment, looking carefully around. The common room, a large chamber with a huge fireplace at one end, stout wooden floor and walls, and smoke-blackened beams supporting the roof, had none of the air of neglect and decay that Elspeth had feared.

She guessed that the villagers had turned the place into their informal meeting house, for the place was too clean to have been swept out just for their benefit. The other door, the one that led into the street, kept opening as more and more people came in, and it looked to her as if most of the adults were gathering in the common room. They had all brought firewood with them as well, which relieved one question in Elspeth's mind—it would have been difficult for the Valdemarans to supply firewood for themselves.

The fellow in charge had not yet pulled off his coat, but he had removed the scarf from his face. He pushed to the front of the crowd, and waved a mittened hand at the staircase, and his weathered, careworn features were kinder than Elspeth had expected.

"Rooms are upstairs, take your pick," he said. "When you've settled yourselves, come down here where we can talk."

Several of those waiting came up the wooden staircase with their guests, bringing firewood to leave beside each hearth before returning downstairs. They didn't say anything, but Elspeth got the impression that was more because they were taciturn or shy than that they were hostile. With fires warming the chambers that had fireplaces, and bricks heating up to warm the cold bedding of those in chambers that didn't, the Valdemarans finally trickled downstairs to meet the eyes of their erstwhile hosts.

Elspeth took the lead, the rest following her. The natives watched Elspeth with covert curiosity, but the moment that Darkwind descended the staircase, they gave up any pretense of politeness and just stared, mouths agape with amazement. The corners of Elspeth's mouth twitched, but she managed not to laugh out loud at their expressions.

I doubt they've ever seen anything like my Darkwind. He must seem like something right out of a minstrel's ballad to them.

Darkwind really was quite a sight, with his long silver hair, his strange, exotic clothing, and the enormous bondbird on his shoulder. When he reached up a hand to Vree, casually lifted him off his shoulder, and cast the forestgyre into the air so he could fly across the room and take a perch on a beam, every Hardornen in the place ducked, and several looked as if they were afraid the bird was going to attack them.

For his part, Vree was on his best behavior, perching where there wasn't going to be anyone sitting directly beneath or behind him. That was extremely polite of him, for if he fell asleep, his instincts would overcome his training if he had to "slice." And a bird the size of Vree could produce an amazing amount of hawk-chalk.

She waited for Darkwind to reach her side, and took his hand in hers. "This is Darkwind k'Sheyna, a Hawkbrother from one of the Hawkbrother Clans in the Alliance," she said, as matter-of-factly as if she had said, "This is Thom, a farmer from the next valley." Their eyes bulged at that, and she didn't blame them. Even in Valdemar, up until recently the Hawkbrothers had been nothing more than a very spooky legend—what must these Hardornens think?

"He is my fellow envoy, my partner, and my mate," she continued. "Representing the Hawkbrothers, the Shin'a'in, and other interests. As I said, we are traveling to Shonar, to Grand Duke Tremane, as official envoys of Valdemar and other members of the Alliance."

The fellow who had taken charge of the meeting nodded. He had by now divested himself of his coat, and wore the clothing of a craftsman—a blacksmith, if Elspeth was any judge, by the scorch marks and mended places that might have been burn marks. He looked much shabbier than any blacksmith Elspeth had ever seen in Valdemar, where they tended to be the more prosperous citizens of a town.

Perhaps he is the most prosperous man here. What a thought! If he's as shabby as a beggar, how are the others faring?

The fact that he was the blacksmith would be the reason that Ancar had not "recruited" him for the army, given that he was able-bodied and neither too old nor too young to fight. A town this size depended on having a blacksmith, and the local smith would need to have more skill than an apprentice.

"I'm Hob," the man said, and gestured to one of the tables. If he'd been fed as well as he should have, his face would have been round, like an old, weathered ball. He was not starved-looking, but his bones were showing; just a hint that these people had seen bad times, as if she didn't already know that. "If some of your people want to go fix up your food, we'd like to talk with you and your—your mate, there."

"We'd be happy to share what we have," Elspeth began, flushing a little with guilt, but he shook his head.

"We've got enough to hold us, so long as spring don't wait to midsummer," he said. "And you'll need every bit you've got to get to Shonar. Thanks to, ah, some good advice, most folk between here and there have enough, but there's none to spare. I doubt you'll find anyone that can sell you so much as a sack of oats, and even if they would, it wouldn't be for money."

Elspeth looked back over her shoulder to Vallen; he nodded,

and with a gesture sent four of the guards off to the kitchen. The rest took seats with, and carefully *around*, Elspeth. Darkwind remained at her right hand, and she was not in the least deceived by his casual pose. If anyone so much as raised his voice in a way he considered threatening, the offending party might find himself facing the point of a knife or being held in the bonds of a most uncomfortable tangle-spell or racking paralysis.

And that's assuming I didn't act on a perception of threat first, for myself.

Hob sat across the table from Elspeth, and rubbed his nose, as if wondering how to begin. Finally he just set his shoulders and blundered in. "You say you're going to Shonar. How much do you know about this Tremane?"

Not long on tact, but I doubt he's used to being the leader of these people. He probably hasn't had much occasion for tact. Elspeth shrugged. "What we *know* is this; he's brought in his entire force to Shonar, and he's broken off all hostile actions with Hardornen loyalists. From what we've been told, he's going out of his way to avoid conflict with loyalist groups, which, you'll admit, in this weather isn't exactly difficult."

Hob snorted in agreement.

"Not only has he expressed an interest in joining the Alliance, he loaned us several of his mages to help us with—" she hesitated. How much would he understand if she told him about the mage-storms? "—with the magical problem that's at the heart of all the weird things that have been happening."

"The monsters? The weather? Them *circles?*" Hob's eyes widened and he grew quite excited. "Tremane helped you with fixing *them?*"

"He did, and he continues to," Elspeth replied. "It's a bigger problem than you may realize. It isn't just Hardorn that's been plagued by all these calamities. "It's Valdemar, the Pelagirs, Rethwellan, Karse, the Dhorisha Plains and, we're guessing, just about everywhere else, right out to the Empire. The Alliance, with Tremane's help, managed to fix things temporarily, in the area covered by the Alliance nations." She decided that it might be best not to mention Solaris' personal interview with the Grand Duke; after all, she only knew that it had occurred, not what had been said. "As for the rest that we know about Tremane, we have been told that the citizens of Shonar and the surrounding area have come to look upon him as their protector. We have heard that he has been doing good things for them."

"Aye," Hob said slowly. "We've heard the same. We've heard that them as was fighting against him have come over to his side, that he's been acting like—like we was his people. And now he's helping you in Valdemar?"

She nodded. He pursed his lips and exchanged glances with some of his fellow villagers. They weren't very good at hiding their expressions; what she was telling them agreed with some of what they had heard, and they were surprised to have an outsider confirm what they'd clearly thought were hopeful but unlikely rumors.

"We've heard as how things are pretty fat in Shonar, all things considered," he said finally. "We've heard that it's because of Tremane. We've heard he sct his men out helping with harvest, building walls around the town, doing other things like that 'sides taking down monsters."

She spread her hands in a gesture he could read as he chose. "We've heard the same things," she said. "I don't know yet how much truth is in what we've heard, but I'm certain that your sources arc completely different from ours. I can tell you this, not all of our sources are Tremane's people."

"And when two people say the same thing . . . aye." There was a great deal of murmuring behind him. He chewed on his lower lip. "All the same—"

"All the same, it's possible that he is putting on a good face for us, hoping to lure us into accepting him," she said, as bluntly as he would have. "We don't *know*, and we won't know until we get there."

Hob traced the grain of the wood of the table with his finger and avoided her eyes. "All the same, lady—we need a leader. There's nobody left of the old blood; damned Ancar saw to that."

"And people have been talking about accepting the *Duke?*" That was more than she had expected to hear, on *this* side of the former battle lines. "A foreigner? An Imperial?"

"The Duke, not his bloody Empire!" someone said in the back. "We heard his Emperor left him hanging out to dry when the troubles started; we heard he's not Charliss' dog no more."

"Hell, he couldn't be, could he, if he's comin' to you with his brass hat in his hand, looking to get into the Alliance," Hob said, looking hopeful. "He's proving himself for Shonar; if he proves himself for Shonar, why not for Hardorn?"

"But what if he doesn't just want to be your leader?" Elspeth asked softly. "What if he wants to be your King?"

Hob hesitated a moment, then shrugged. "That's all cake or calamity tomorrow, isn't it?" he said philosophically. "We got to get through the winter first." He favored Elspeth with a shy smile. "I can tell you this, there's one way we'd take him."

"Even as a King?" Darkwind asked quietly.

He nodded, slowly. "Even as a King. He'd have to swear on something we'd trust that he wasn't Charliss' man. Then he'd have to swear *to* Hardorn. And he'd have to do what Ancar, his father, even what his grandfather never did." He paused for effect. "He'd have to take the earth, in the old way."

Elspeth shook her head. "That's nothing I know of," she replied.

Hob smiled again. "The earth-taking—that's old, lady. Older than Valdemar, or so they say. What's old is sure, that's the saying anyway. They say them as takes the earth can't betray it. There's still a priest or two about that knows the way of earth-taking. If this Tremane'd take the earth and the earth takes him—well, there's no going back. He's bound harder and tighter than if we put chains on him."

Elspeth kept her feelings of skepticism to herself. After all she'd seen, there was no telling whether Hob was right about this "earth-taking" of his or not. "Well, you can believe that Valdemar has no interest in taking the rule of Hardorn away from the people; what *you* do about it is your business," Elspeth said carefully. "Our business is to see if what we've been told is true, and to advise the Alliance if it is not."

He nodded, and did not add the obvious question of how she expected to get herself and her party out in one piece if Tremane turned out to be playing his own game. That wasn't his problem, and she couldn't blame him for not volunteering to help if things got difficult. The people of Hardorn had all they could do to survive, and they had nothing to spare for foreigners out of Valdemar.

Comforting aromas of cooking food emerged from the kitchen, and Hob took that gratefully as his escape from the conversation. "Looks like your people have your food ready; we'll go leave you in peace with it. You can leave in the morning when you choose—and—ah—" he flushed a little "—you'll have better welcome farther along. Signal-towers are still up, and there's still a few as know the old signals. We'll be passing along that you're all right, that you're going on up to Tremane. Nobody'll hinder you; there're enough places with four sound walls and a roof that you'll get shelter at night."

As he stood up, Elspeth remained seated, but raised a hand toward Hob. "And does the Grand Duke know that the towers are still working?" she asked.

He laughed, which was all the answer she needed. So Tremane was *not* aware of this rapid means of passing news along. That could be useful, if it turned out he was playing a deeper game than they thought.

Hob and the rest of his people filed out, leaving the Valdemarans alone, and Elspeth turned first to Vallen as the kitchen crew put bowls of stewed dried meat and preserved fruit, and plates of travel biscuits onto the table. "Well?" she asked. "What do you think?"

He sat down across from her in Hob's place and picked up a biscuit and a bowl before answering. "This matches what we'd heard and didn't really believe," he said slowly, dipping his bread into his gravy, and eating the biscuit with small, neat bites. "Tremane sounds too good to be true. Altogether an admirable and unselfish leader." There was a faint echo of mockery in his voice.

"So does Selenay, if you look at things objectively," Darkwind reminded him. "And yes, I know, Tremane has no Companion to keep him honorable, but I'm not sure one would be needed in this case. At least for now, he's in a precarious situation. With the way things have fallen out, his position and his level of personal danger aren't that much different from the average craftsman in Shonar. He needs them as much as they need a leader; if they fall, it won't be long before he does, too. If they rebel, he has no population base to support his troops. This summer, they were fighting against him, and it wouldn't take much mistreatment to make them turn on him."

Elspeth nodded, agreeing with him, although Vallen appeared a bit more dubious. "He has armed troops, loyal only to him," Vallen pointed out.

"He'll have a hard time feeding those troops without farmers," Elspeth replied. "And he can have all the silver he needs to pay them, but if they haven't anywhere to spend it, their loyalty will start to erode. You can't keep an army under siege, starving, and far from home without losing it."

Vallen speared a bit of meat and blew on it to cool it. "All I can say is this," the Guard-Captain said, after he'd eaten the bite. "It's not all that difficult for a charismatic leader to sway the people immediately around him with words instead of deeds. It's a lot more difficult to do that with people out of the reach of his personality. They're inclined to look for something to corroborate what they've heard, and if there's nothing there, they forget him."

"But you're surprised at what you're hearing from Hob," Elspeth stated.

Vallen nodded. "Very. And not the least because a few months ago, these people would have fought with everything they had left to get rid of the man. *Now* they're considering accepting him as a leader. Doesn't it sound as if they've heard and learned something very compelling over the past few months? I just hope that what they've heard has more substance than twice-told tales."

Elspeth sighed and nodded, as she and everyone else applied themselves to their food. This was the first warm meal they'd had all day, and their supper last night had been hastily prepared over a smoky fire in the remains of a half-ruined house, not cooked in a proper kitchen. As the gnawing hunger in the pit of her stomach eased, and the warmth from their dinner filled her, she became aware just how tired she was. When she glanced around the table, there wasn't anyone except Darkwind who wasn't leaning his head on his hand as he ate. She felt the same way; worn down by the cold, and quite ready to go to bed as soon as she finished the last bite. Darkwind seemed in his element, and she would not have hesitated a moment in trusting the entire expedition to him.

Some of the others looked quite ready to fall asleep over

their plates. "It's the cold," Darkwind said quietly. "Don't worry, this is normal. It's being in the cold from dawn until dusk, without a chance to warm up, then going to bed in cold beds and unheated rooms. Tonight will make a difference, with a good hot meal and warm beds; tomorrow everyone will end the day without being quite so exhausted. If we can get shelter like this for the rest of the trip, our people will revive in no time at all."

He ought to know, and *she* should have remembered. Then again, perhaps she was not at fault for forgetting; when she'd worked beside him as a scout and border-guard at k'Sheyna Vale, they'd lived *in* the Vale. They'd return from their shifts on patrol to an *ekele* in the midst of a garden spot, as warm as a midsummer day. Before that, he'd refused to live inside the Vale, and there might well have been times when he'd returned home to a chilled *ekele*, or might even have remained overnight camping in the wilderness. Just because she had never personally experienced such hardship, that didn't mean he hadn't.

"Let's go to bed," Vallen said abruptly, after jerking his head up suddenly for the third time as he nodded off in spite of valiant efforts to stay awake. "I can't keep my eyes open anymore."

"I'll clean up; I'm good for that," Elspeth volunteered, and smiled at the look of surprise from Vallen. What, did he think she considered herself above such chores? Or had he forgotten that at the last several stops, she'd taken her turn at gathering fodder from the ruined barns, putting together makeshift stalls for the horses and chirras, and gathering clean snow for water? "I was a Herald-trainee once, or don't you recall? I've scrubbed my share of pots in my time, and I think I can manage without breaking anything."

Darkwind picked up empty bowls, knives, and spoons without comment other than a wink. Sometimes they both forgot the way other people saw them. She caught Vallen staring after Darkwind with an even greater look of surprise than he'd shown when she volunteered to clean up.

Does he think Hawkbrothers magic their plates clean? Oh, well, he probably does, and it doesn't occur to him that it would be harder work to clean a pot by magic than to do it by hand.

She gathered up what Darkwind couldn't carry, and both of them went into the kitchen.

This had been a particularly fine inn once, with a pump supplying water to the kitchen; the cooking crew had left water heating on the hearth. Both the regular Guards and Kerowyn's mercenaries were used to every aspect of this kind of mission; when it came to cooking, they were nothing if not efficient. It didn't take long to clean the bowls and cutlery and the two pots they had used for heating the food.

"I keep having second thoughts about this trip," Elspeth said quietly.

Darkwind nodded. "I can understand why you would feel that way, but I believe we are doing one of many things that could be the right path," he replied, carefully wiping out a pot and putting it away. It was a typically Tayledras response. "We must remain in contact with Tremane; that much I am certain of. *How* we do that—well, this is one way. There would have been others, but this is the way we chose, and I do not think we have chosen amiss."

"At least in this case, we'll have our own eyes and ears in Shonar," she sighed.

He smiled. "And tongues as well! We can also advise, if Tremane chooses to listen to us."

The pots, bowls, and utensils had all come with them, and she repacked them in the bags with the supplies. "Given the way things have been going so far," she observed, "it's only too likely, I suppose, for something entirely unexpected to happen out here. And in that case, the Alliance had better have people in place to observe and reassure. . . ."

Darkwind slipped his arm around her shoulders, turning his hug into a way to turn her toward the door to the common room. "And to fix, transform, leverage, and otherwise turn things for the better. Tremane, according to Kerowyn, comes from a culture in which treachery is a commonplace," he reminded her. "If anything unexpected *were* to occur, that would be the first explanation that would come to him."

She shook her head, and let him draw her toward the door. If she hadn't been too tired to think properly, she might have been able to make some kind of rational discussion out of this. As it was—

"You know, I almost feel sorry for Tremane," she admitted

reluctantly as they mounted the stairs to their room. Rank did have privileges, and she had laid claim to one of the rooms with a real bed and a fireplace; it had probably been one of the expensive chambers when this had still been an inn. She was looking forward to sleeping in a bed, warmed by a hot brick at its foot.

Well, maybe not sleeping, *at least not for a little while. I do have Darkwind here. . . .*

"I *do* feel sorry for him," Darkwind said unexpectedly, "And I believe I know why young Karal forgave him. Just because he has been forced to deal with daily treachery does not make him a treacherous individual. We do not know what he is really like, except that we may guess somewhat through his actions."

This speech had taken them up the stairs and to the space just outside the door to their room. Elspeth opened the door, drew him inside, and stopped the rest of the speech with her lips on his.

"I have had quite enough of Tremane to last me until morning," she said firmly, as he responded as she had hoped he would, by pulling her closer and simultaneously closing the door to their room. "I think we can afford not to think of him, for a little while, at least."

"Oh, at least," he agreed, and then said nothing more with words for quite some time.

Hob was as good as his word. From that time on, they began to see and interact with the people of Hardorn—those that remained, at least—and were given the limited hospitality that this sad land could afford. Elspeth continued to be surprised at the suspicion with which the Valdemarans were met. It didn't make any sense to her that the natives should persist in considering them the harbingers of another invasion. If they had been a real invading force, they would have had a small army at least. If they had been the advance scouts of an invasion, they wouldn't have come so openly.

She gradually decided that the reason had nothing to do with logic. Ancar had already poisoned his people's minds about the Valdemarans, and some of that poison still lingered. At the very beginning of his war with Valdemar, when his people had not yet been aware of the kind of man he really was, he had told them that his war was justified, that the Valdemarans were responsible for the murder of his father and most of the High Council, and that the Queen of Valdemar intended to annex Hardorn as a subject state of her own land. Later, of course, Ancar proved even to the most naive of his countrymen that he was never to be trusted, but some of his lies still remained in the back of peoples' memories. Perhaps they no longer even recalled it was Ancar who had spread those lies in the first place.

And to folk who themselves were never warlike to begin with, and who were now suffering privations worse in their way than even their life under Ancar, an armed force like hers—obviously well-trained, well-fed, well-armed, and in top condition—must look very much like an army. These folks hadn't yet seen the Imperial Army; they'd only heard rumors of it, how large it was, how incredibly *professional.* Away from the conflicts at the border, they had never seen anything larger than the garrisons Ancar bivouacked in their villages to insure their cooperation and to collect taxes. Perhaps their imaginations couldn't encompass the idea of an army, how large one had to be. Yet here was her force, quite large enough to take over every town in its path, and they didn't have to *imagine* what it was like, for it was real, and right in front of them.

The natives usually came around after a short meeting, such as she and her troop had had with Hob. At that point, the Valdemarans were treated like travelers instead of conquerors. Villagers would recall the old, hospitable customs, and would usually open the inn, the temple, or a Guildhall to them. Then there were warm beds, warm rooms, and once in a while, a bit of fresh meat to add to their own rations. There was no trouble with finding firewood this winter—not with half (or more) of the buildings in any given community standing empty and falling down. Sensibly, the survivors had moved into the best homes and kept them in repair, and were using the rest for materials and firewood. They might be on short rations, but they were going to spend the rest of the winter in warmth.

And that, Elspeth realized, (as she and her party continued to brave the cold that penetrated even the warmest of clothing and left them aching by day's end), was what would save these villagers. They could get by on less food, as long as they were warm enough. They might emerge when the snows melted as gaunt as spring bears, but they would be alive, for the cold would kill more quickly than short rations.

But the nearer they got to Shonar, the more people seemed cautiously impressed with Tremane, or at least with the stories they were hearing about him. Once the terrible, killing blizzards caused by the passing waves of mage-storms had subsided into more "normal" winter weather, he had begun making tentative overtures toward those who lived out past the area he had secured for himself and his army. He had sent his men out to clear the roads and keep them clear; he had encouraged such small trade as there might be in the dead of winter. If the rumors were true, he had also sent his men ranging in a limited fashion on monster-killing expeditions.

Supposedly, anyone within a three-day range of Shonar could come and request his help with killing a monster, provided that they knew either where it denned or what its range was. The Grand Duke evidently had no intention of sending parties of his soldiers off to wander about in the snow, trying to find a monster, and possibly making targets of themselves. Tremane would send out a team of twenty of his trained soldiers, all armed to the teeth and experienced in fighting mage-born aberrations, and all the natives had to do was lead them to the monster or to where it might be trapped or cornered. The soldiers did the rest; the natives got the privilege of deciding what happened to the carcass. Often, if it looked remotely edible, they would ask the Healer who traveled with the group to detemine if it was safe to eat, and the Healer invariably obliged.

In addition, once the monster or monsters were disposed of, the group would remain long enough to conduct a hunt of feral stock, which was generally not all that difficult to find. Half of what they killed they took back to Shonar; the remaining half they left to feed the natives. Since this was always more than the locals had before the hunt began, no one protested when Tremane's men claimed the "Imperial share." And in addition, while the hunts for monsters or feral cattle were going on, the Healer who always accompanied the expedition would tend to any illness or injuries among the natives.

In short, when the Imperial group returned to Shonar, they left behind a stockpile of much-needed meat, people who had received medical attention the like of which they had not seen since Ancar took the throne, and land that was now safer, if not as pastoral and tranquil as in generations before. If any new monsters appeared, the natives had only to request help again, and the entire scenario would be repeated.

Tremane would *not* give aid against wolves, bears, or bandits; the first two, it was said, he had decreed were perfectly well within the means of the natives to deal with. And as for the third—he claimed that he could not tell the difference between bandits and "patriots," and he was not going to try. This was a bit hard on the Hardornens who were suffering from the depredations of fellow humans, but perhaps it gave them incentive to track down those who had once been their neighbors and reintroduce them to a law that had been long absent from Hardorn.

All of this was very impressive in tale and rumor—more impressive in that the stories were remarkably consistent— but Elspeth waited to see what was being said nearer to Shonar.

Finally, they came within that three-day sphere of Tremane's influence, and they saw for themselves that the stories of Tremane's "philanthropy" were true.

Unexpectedly, they had stepped from a road cleared just enough to let a single cart pass, to one which had been completely shoveled free of snow right down to the earth or gravel of the roadbed—and one which obviously was kept free of snow. They saw for themselves the trophy heads (or other parts) from the monsters that Tremane's men had tracked down and killed. And they heard from the natives who had been fed and Healed out of Tremane's bounty just what a good and just leader he was.

No one was mentioning the word "King" yet, but Elspeth sensed that it was not far from anyone's thoughts. How could it be, when in the face of the worst times that Hardorn had ever experienced, this man was slowly imposing order and sanity on the face of the land? And it wasn't the arbitrary, selfish order of a tyrant, either; they'd seen enough of that under Ancar to recognize it if they saw it. This was law and order that they could live with and be at peace with.

Elspeth couldn't help but contrast their lot with that of their fellow countrymen who did not have the advantage of living within three days of Shonar. Reluctantly she had to admit that if she were in their boots, she'd have felt the same way.

More than that, she found herself agreeing with most of what he'd done and ordered here. A few things represented laws or customs from the Empire that *she* wouldn't have imposed, but the rest—it was just the hand and the mind of someone who was concerned about the welfare of the people and knew how to derive the greatest good from a limited amount of resources.

The day before they were to meet with Duke Tremane himself, Elspeth and Darkwind were approached by a solemn group of Hardornens as they ate their evening meal. This time the innkeeper still tenanted his inn, but it had been a long time since he had actually served guests. He had offered a chance for Elspeth and Darkwind to have a quiet dinner together, without the company of their escort, and the prospect was too enticing to turn down.

He put them in a small, private dining room, with the troop seated in the larger room outside. Elspeth had not realized how much she had missed being able to talk to him without worrying about the ears of others. There were things she had wanted to discuss that needed to wait until they were alone in their room—*if* they were alone, since they often shared their sleeping quarters with the others.

They lingered over their last drink, making the most of this private time—and that was when the innkeeper interrupted them.

"Town Council would like to talk, sir, lady," he said diffidently, poking his head into the room. "Alone here, if you please?"

Elspeth sighed. She did *not* please, but there was no point in saying so. "If they must," she replied, allowing some, but not all, of her annoyance to show.

The innkeeper vanished, and the delegation must have been waiting right outside, for they trooped through the door immediately.

"We won't take up much of your time, Envoy," said the best-dressed of the lot, a fellow who still boasted the velvets and furs of earlier prosperity. "It's just something we'd like you to—to say for us, to Duke Tremane."

"Not a complaint!" added a second, only slightly less elegant than his fellow. "No, not a complaint! Something he might want to hear, maybe—"

"There's been talk," the first interrupted, with a glare at the second. "We've heard the talk. Oh, I was Guildmaster for the Wool and Weavers Guild for this whole region—"

Which explains the finery, Elspeth thought.

"—and Keplan here was Master for the Leather and Furrier's Guild. So, as I say, there's been talk, and people have come to us with it. Duke Tremane's proven good for us, and there are some that want to make him our leader." The Guildmaster waved his hands expansively. "Some who are even saying— King."

The second interrupted his fellow Guildmaster. "Now, we've sent out word, *looking* for some of the old royal blood of Hardorn. We've got ways of sending word out farther and faster than you'd believe. And there's no one, not one person of the old Royal Family left alive."

"I can't say that amazes me," Elspeth told them dryly. "Ancar wasn't one to tolerate rivals. And he wouldn't let a little thing like the age or sex of a possible pretender stop him from removing someone he wanted out of the way."

The Woolmaster coughed. "Ah. Aye. And woe betide anyone that got in the way back then." He looked up hopefully to see if Elspeth agreed with this attempt to exonerate himself for not attempting to interfere. By that, she inferred that at least one opportunity *had* occurred, and he hadn't even tried.

But who am I to judge? I wasn't there, I don't know what happened. If he took the coward's path, his own guilty conscience may be punishing him enough by now.

"You were saying that there isn't anyone of the old royal blood left," she prompted. "So?"

"So—well—there's some consensus that we might offer Duke Tremane the Crown. With conditions." He held his breath and waited for her reaction.

"An interesting proposal," Darkwind said quietly. "I presume that the conditions would be unusual, since you mention them at all."

The Woolmaster switched his attention from Elspeth to Darkwind. "They could be," he said. "It's—well, it's something our old Kings hadn't done for generations. It's—"

"He'd have to take earth-binding," the furrier burst out. "We've got a priest of the old beliefs, one that knows the ceremony and can make it stick. He'd have to bind himself to the earth, to Hardorn, so that anything that hurt the land would hurt him!"

The Woolmaster stared at his fellow, appalled, but Elspeth only shrugged. "It sounds like a sensible precaution on your part," she told them. "And if the opportunity presents itself, we will convey your message to the Grand Duke. But we can't promise anything, and we certainly can't promise that he'll agree to any such thing."

"That's all we ask, Envoy!" the Woolmaster said, waving at his little group and backing up himself, with a great deal of haste. "That's all! Our thanks!"

As he spoke, he herded the others out in front of him, and with the last word, he shut the door to the dining room behind him.

Darkwind looked at Elspeth, and she grimaced. "Well," she said, into the heavy silence. "That was certainly interesting."

"And it leaves the question begging," he replied, with a rueful smile. "Just how *would* one present such a proposition to Tremane?"

"I think that we can wait until we ride into Shonar itself, and we get a chance to see what the Empire represents—as molded by the hand of Grand Duke Tremane," she replied. "That in itself will tell us whether or not there's any point."

Despite the icy wind cutting through her coat, Elspeth sat back in her saddle and stared until her eyes hurt from snow glare. "I can't believe they raised all this in a single season," she muttered.

:*And without magic,*: Gwena reminded her, shifting her weight in tiny increments to keep muscles warm. :*Granted, they did have a great deal of incentive—the possibility of hostile Hardornen troops attacking, and the certainty of monsters—what did that fine young man call them?*:

"Boggles," Elspeth replied absently, taking in the reality of a two-story-tall wall, and not a wooden palisade, mind, but a *brick* wall. This edifice circled not only the entire city of Shonar but the much larger camp and garrison of the Imperials, *and* an open sward that had once been the town's grazing commons as well. A monumental task? Without a doubt.

Then add to that the equally monumental task of constructing barracks buildings for the Imperial forces before the snow fell, and it became a job to stun the mind in its scope. How had he gotten all that built? Where had he found all the laborers?

"We're very proud of our work, *Siara*," said the "fine young man" in Imperial uniform who had met them half a day out of Shonar and escorted them in. *Siara* was evidently the generic title of respect applicable to either sex that the Imperial military used when the person doing the addressing did not know the true rank of the one being addressed. It was probably the equivalent to "sir;" mercenaries generally addressed their officers as "sir" regardless of gender, a perfectly sensible approach of which Elspeth approved.

"We all worked on the walls and the barracks, every man of us," the young soldier continued, his cheeks flushed in the cold. "Except when some of us went to work on the harvest, and then we traded work with townsfolk. However many it took to make up the work that one of us could do, that's what Duke Tremane traded, so the walls and the barracks could keep going up."

:*Sensible. Did you notice? The boy says that Tremane "traded" work for work, not that he conscripted workers.*: Gwena's head was up as she made her own survey of the walls. :*Granted, it wouldn't have been very smart to conscript workers for a wall you're building for your own protection, but that hasn't stopped rulers in the past from doing things equally stupid.*:

Elspeth nodded; no point in confusing the poor fellow by answering someone he couldn't hear. The Imperials were already confused enough by her insistence on special treatment and housing for Gwena and the *dyheli* Brytha, although they had agreed to such a condition before a single Valdemaran set foot on the road to Shonar.

Darkwind cleared his throat gently. "As impressive as these walls are, I suspect our fellow travelers are as cold as I am, and we are not growing any warmer for standing here."

The young soldier snapped to immediate attention and

stammered an apology. "Of course, *Siara*, forgive me! We'll be on our way at once!"

He nudged his own horse awkwardly with his heels, sending it ambling toward the gate ahead of them. He obviously (at least to Elspeth's eyes) was not used to riding, and the horse was certainly not a cavalry mount; thick-legged, jug-headed, and shaggy, it probably belonged to a farmer who didn't have any need for it in this season. He was probably grateful he hadn't had to ride out too great a distance to meet them; he handled the reins as if afraid the steady old gelding was going to rear and bolt at any second. The horse had no intention of doing so, he was just perfectly happy to be heading back to the city, a warm stall, and a good feed. She wouldn't hurt the poor boy's feelings by laughing at him, but she was very glad for the scarf wrapped around her face, concealing her mouth.

The guards patrolling the top of the wall looked down at them with interest as they approached, though with no sign of alarm. There was some nudging and pointing when those nearest caught sight of Darkwind's *dyheli*, but that was to be expected.

For her part, Elspeth saw absolutely nothing to make her instincts issue an alarm. Except for the uniforms, these men could have been any force in any of the Alliance nations watching the envoy of one of the other Allies ride in. There was no show of hostility from them, and no sense of entrapment on her part. They went through the gate without a challenge, and followed their guide through the main street of the city. It was strange, after all these weeks of not hearing their mounts' hooves do more than thud dully on the creaking snow, to ride once again to the peculiar music that Gwena's silver hooves made as they chimed against the cobblestones once they passed the wall, punctuated by the staccato clicking of Brytha's cloven toes. Townsfolk, evidently warned of their coming, gathered along the side of the street to cheer and wave welcomes and stare at Darkwind. She was reminded of the way they had last entered towns in Hardorn, as part of a traveling Faire. They hadn't stood out then in the midst of so much outlandish, gaudy, somewhat tarnished finery; probably onlookers had assumed that the *dyheli* had been an ordinary horse or pony in disguise. Now Darkwind had everyone's undivided attention, and to his credit, he seemed just as nonchalant as if there was no one gaping at all.

They passed several good-sized inns, and several more buildings that might have quartered them, and came out on the other side of the town. They were heading in the direction, not of the moundlike barracks buildings, but of a stone edifice rising at least four stories in height in the main, with towers of five or six stories above that. It seemed they were to be quartered in this fortified manor Tremane had appropriated as his headquarters; Elspeth wondered how many clerks, officers, and other underlings had to be reshuffled to make room for them. She was not going to be parted from her escort, and she doubted that Tremane was going to be foolish or naive enough to expect anything different, and that would mean displacing a fair number of people.

"The previous owner had a very small stable actually inside the manor," the young soldier said, as they approached a second set of walls about the manor. "The entrance is on the courtyard, and it is situated beside the kitchen. The Duke's Horsemaster said he thinks it was for very valuable mares in foal. There are four loose-boxes, and it's warm enough for people to sleep in at need. Will that do for your—ah—mounts?"

He looked questioningly at Brytha and Gwena, as if he still didn't understand what all the fuss was about.

For her part, Elspeth was just grateful that they'd not only found a decent place for the nonhuman members of the delegation, but that it was gong to be within the same building complex. "That should be perfect." Now it was her turn to hesitate. "We're going to want to see to them before we are taken to our own quarters, or even meet with Grand Duke Tremane for the first time. I hope he will understand."

The soldier's nod made it clear that he *didn't* think Tremane would understand, but that he was prepared to put up with the peculiarities of the Valdemarans.

Gwena chuckled in Elspeth's mind. :*Never mind, dear. The only person we have to persuade of my intellect is Tremane, and that won't take long. And it can wait until tomorrow; he's going to have enough shocks today as it is. Frankly, I'm more interested in a nice warm mash and a rest in a warm place than in meeting Tremane anway.*:

Gwena surely was easier to live with these days. *Or maybe*

I've finally grown up! Elspeth chuckled to herself, allowing herself to relax the tiniest amount. If there had been anything untoward, Gwena would probably have sensed it.

The walls about the manor were much, much darker than the walls around the city. These had been made of cut stone, like the manor itself, a dark gray that somehow stopped just short of being depressing. There were more guards on the top of these walls as well, but again, their manner was casual. While these men were professional, and ready to act on a moment's notice, their manner led Elspeth to think they did not consider themselves to be under any particular threat.

They entered a gate with an iron portcullis, but instead of passing under the walls into the yard between the walls and the manor, they went into an arched tunnel which actually passed under the walls of the manor. Torches dispelled part of the gloom, but not all of it. Elspeth did not miss noting the murder-holes in the ceiling above them, nor did anyone else in their party. The holes were spaced so closely that if the gates on either end of the tunnel were dropped, there would be no escaping boiling oil or other unpleasantness coming out of those apertures. This would have made her a great deal more nervous had the manor not predated Tremane's arrival.

Not that he wouldn't *use* them, he just had not put them there in the first place. The nasty mind that came up with them was a native Hardornen.

Possibly one of Ancar's ancestors. . . .

The delegation split exactly in half once they were in the courtyard. Half of Vallen's troop took the luggage to what was going to become their ambassadorial quarters, and the other half remained with Darkwind and Elspeth while they saw to the comfort of their mounts. Elspeth was just a little irritated at the too-obvious guardians, but she was experienced enough to realize they were a necessity. Until they really knew the situation here, it was better to be too cautious and formal, and reinforce the Imperials' perceptions of herself and Darkwind as people of diplomatic importance—which, of course, they were.

Her irritation was short-lived, for Vallen and his people made themselves useful instead of decorative, and things were soon settled in the stables to the comfort and satisfaction of everyone. One of the Imperials had remained to take them to their quarters, and with their own guards trailing behind, she and Darkwind followed him across the cobblestoned courtyard to one of the many entrances opening onto it.

"We've given you this tower," he said diffidently as he led them to a staircase, his Hardornen stilted, and painfully correct. "Duke Tremane hopes it will suffice your needs."

"I believe it ought to," she replied, as they climbed to the first residential floor. The half of their guards that had gone on ahead were already making themselves at home. This was quite a spacious room, furnished with beds and chests and not all that dissimilar from barracks in Valdemar. The second floor was identical to the first, but untenanted at the moment.

They continued to climb the staircase which wound around the outside wall. "These will be your quarters, sir and lady," said their escort, as they reached the third level.

They were standing in a public reception room set up on the third floor, with a table and chairs suitable for conferences, with writing tables and an arrangement of three comfortable chairs beside the fireplace.

"Your bedrooms and a study are on the fourth floor, and there is a storage room on the fifth," their escort said. "I am one of Duke Tremane's aides, and I will be at your disposal."

As Elspeth and Darkwind explored their personal quarters, he explained very seriously that they did not really want to use that top floor for anything except storage; it had no fireplace and was exposed to the winds in every direction. After poking her nose up there and seeing a thin layer of frost on the stones, Elspeth agreed.

Tremane gave them a decent period of time in which to get settled and into presentable clothing. Elspeth very much missed the comforts of the Palace at Haven; a hot bath here meant heating water over the fire in kettles, and pouring it into a tub the servants brought into the bedroom. The rest was just as primitive, and she wrinkled her nose at the sight of the chamber pot. But the alternative could be worse . . . and it wouldn't be the first time she and Darkwind had made do.

Finally, when they were presentable, Tremane sent another of his aides to invite them to dinner with him.

As good a time and place to open relations with him as any. When Darkwind gave her a little nod, she accepted for both of them, and they followed the young man down the stair and into the main body of the manor. They traveled down a dark and faintly chilled hallway for some time, with their only light coming from lanterns mounted in brackets at intervals along the wall. Finally they reached another stair, and the aide led them up into what was clearly another tower. In fact, if this tower held Tremane's quarters and was laid out in a similar manner to theirs, they could probably look right into his bedroom from their own.

An interesting thought, and one which showed a measure of trust from Tremane. If one could look, one could also shoot. . . .

They discovered, as the aide ushered them into a room that corresponded to their own reception room, that this was to be an informal meeting. The table was set only for three, with a single aide standing by a sideboard full of covered dishes. Tremane was already waiting for them, and Elspeth scrutinized him carefully, even as he was looking both of them over with the same care.

She would not have taken him for the brilliant military leader he was supposed to be. He didn't look anything like a professional soldier—but then, neither did half of Kerowyn's best fighters. He was losing his mouse-brown hair, and what remained was going gray. His intelligent face showed signs of age and strain both.

Tremane embodied contradiction. His shoulders were firmer and broader than any clerk's, but there were inkstains on his right hand. He wore a sword as one for whom it was a standard piece of attire, but there were lines at the corners of his gray-brown eyes that people got when they habitually squinted, trying to read in dim light. On the one hand— scholar. On the other—fighter.

He stood up after a moment, as if they had surprised him by arriving sooner than he had expected, and extended his hand. Elspeth found his expression impossible to read; closed, but somehow not secretive. A gambler's face, perhaps, the face of a man unwilling to give anything away.

But what his face might not reveal, other signs might. His clothing was a variation on the Imperial uniform, but with none of the fancy decorations she normally associated with someone of high rank. There was just a badge with a coronet and another with what might be his own device. Nowhere was there evidence of the Imperial Seal or Badge, although the badge of a crossed pen and sword looked as if it had been sewn in place of a larger badge.

Come to think of it, no one I've seen wears the Imperial Badge. That, more than anything else, told her he really *had* given over his allegiance to the Empire. Soldiers set a great deal of store by what device they fought under; if the Imperial Seal was gone, so was their loyalty to what it represented.

The lack of decoration, though—military men took pomp and decoration for granted. What did that lack of decoration say about Tremane? That he was modest? Or that he wanted to appear modest?

Tremane extended his hand to her, and she clasped it, returning his clasp strength for strength. He didn't test her, but his clasp was firm and so was hers. "I am pleased to meet you at last, Princess," he began. She shook her head, and he stopped in mid-sentence, tilting his head a little to the side in what was probably a habitual gesture of inquiry.

"Not *Princess*, if you please," she corrected. "I renounced that title some time ago in favor of other responsibilities. 'Envoy' will do, or 'Ambassador,' or even 'My Lady,' although I *do* still hold lands and title that are the equivalent to yours, Grand Duke. No one in Valdemar even considers me as being in line for the throne anymore."

Must not let him think he's being slighted by having someone sent to him who is of lesser rank.

"My partner and spouse, Darkwind k'Sheyna, is an Adept; his people do not have any equivalent titles specifying nobility," she continued, "But we judged his status as a mage to be significant in place of a title."

Tremane nodded, released her hand, and took Darkwind's. The two men gazed measuringly into one another's eyes before releasing their grips.

"I am very pleased to meet you both at last, and I would deem it an honor if you would dispense with titles and simply refer to me as 'Tremane,' as my people in my home lands did," the Grand Duke replied, softening his formal manner with a slight smile. "Would you take a seat? I fear you will find my fare somewhat plain, but these are not the times for overindulging."

It was Darkwind who replied, as he held out a chair for Elspeth. "I could not agree more, Tremane," he said. "But it does appear that the folk under your command are prospering better than most in Hardorn."

Tremane waited until both of them were seated before he took his own chair. "That is as much a matter of luck as anything else," he replied. "Luck, in that we have one resource that Hardorn lacks—manpower. There is enough to be scavenged if you have enough able-bodied men."

Tremane's aide offered Elspeth a simple dish of vegetables baked with cheese, and she nodded in acceptance. As he finished spooning a portion onto her plate and turned to Darkwind, she took up the conversation. "Nevertheless, you have impressed those natives here who live within your sphere of influence."

Tremane took a sip of his wine. "One of the virtues of the Empire is that its leaders are well-trained," he said, after a moment. "Its vices are many, but it *is* well-governed. At the best of times, its citizens had little to complain of."

"And at the worst?" Darkwind asked bluntly.

Tremane bowed his head for a moment. "So much power is easily abused," he said finally, and applied himself to his food, ending the conversation for the moment.

When it resumed, they spoke of inconsequential things. Tremane was a decent conversationalist, though not a brilliant one. He was *not* a courtier, or at least, not someone who devoted most of his time to such pursuits. But he was also too careful to be blunt, too practiced to say anything that might cause him or his people damage. He was a survivor of a very dangerous Court, and he had learned his lessons in that Court well.

When they bid their host a cordial, if guarded, good night, Elspeth knew only one thing for certain.

Grand Duke Tremane was a man who kept his own council, and it would be difficult to penetrate the walls he had built about himself. He would clearly protect his honor by maintaining silence at judicious times, and practicing deflection when possible. Anyone who attempted to divine this complex man's deeper motives would find themselves with a nearly impossible task, yet that was precisely the task Elspeth and Darkwind faced.

Melles

Three

Emperor Charliss sat enrobed in his heavy velvets of State, amid the grim splendor of the panoply surrounding his Iron Throne. He endured the burden of the Wolf Crown pressing down upon his brow, ignored the content of the peoples' chatter, and watched his courtiers vainly attempt to conceal their jittery nerves.

Outwardly, this Court was like any other, except in degree. Gossip, flirtations, negotiations, assignations, betrayals, confidences—the highborn, ranked and wealthy, all danced their dances just as they had for years, as their fathers had, and as their grandfathers had. Over the years their forms of jockeying and presentation had gone from custom to manners to mannerism, tempered by fashion and fear. Today, each attempted to hold their clothing and their overly-expensive accessories in their practiced ways, but their true state showed in their stilted movements, the nervous glances toward his dais, and in the faintly hysterical edge to their voices as they murmured to one another. His Court had always been noted for flamboyance of dress, but fewer and fewer of his courtiers were taking the time and care needed for truly opulent displays, which showed more clearly than any other outward signs that their minds and energies were directed elsewhere. They were afraid, and people who were afraid did not concern themselves with inventing a new fashion or impressing an enemy with their wealth.

Below the dais, people milled in the patterns dictated by rank and custom, but he was acutely aware of the holes in the patterns. The Court itself held little more than half the usual number of attendees. How could it be otherwise? Those who could leave for their estates already had, despite the fact that the Season was well underway.

This was wildly contrary to custom; *no one* who pretended to power or importance left the Court in winter. Summer was the time when the highborn of the Empire retired to their estates, not winter. Winter, that time of the year when snow and ice barricaded the isolated estates, one from the other, was the time to take one's place at Court and engage in revelry and endless intrigue, while one's underlings dealt with the tedium of estate caretaking, and become immersed in the round of social intercourse known as the Season. Those with youngsters to marry off brought them here to display them to the parents of other youngsters or potential older spouses. Those who wanted power jockeyed for position; those who had it campaigned to keep it. Those who pursued pleasure came here to pursue it. Only the impossibly dull, preoccupied, or solitary remained in their homes during the Season.

But not this winter.

When the first of the mage-storms had come sweeping out of nowhere across the Empire, disrupting or destroying all the magic in its path except that which was heavily shielded, the Emperor had been angry, but not seriously alarmed. Such a powerful work of magic could not have been easy to create, and he had not expected that the senders would be able to repeat it at any time soon. Granted, it had taken down every one of the Portals that were the fundamental means of long-range transportation across the Empire, but it had been possible to set them back up again in a relatively short period of time. The Storm had caused inconvenience, but no more. He had never had any doubt that the mages of the Empire would restore conditions to normal, and then he would deliver a punishment to the fools who sent such a thing. This punishment would send terror not only through their ranks, but into the hearts of anyone else even peripherally involved.

But then, without any warning, the *second* Storm had passed over the face of the Empire. That had been impossible, by the rules of all magic as he knew it. And then came a third. And after that Storm had passed, still *more*, and the intervals between them kept decreasing, even as the magnitude of the damage that each wrought increased.

The courtiers might not have been aware of the damage that was being done in the Empire as a whole, but they were certainly aware of the impact on their own lives. Mage-fires heating their rooms and baths no longer functioned. Mage-lights vanished, and had to be replaced by inferior candles and lanterns, normally only used by laborers to light their hovels. Meals, even in Crag Castle were often late, and frequently cold. One could no longer commandeer a Portal to bring something from one's home Estate. There were servants enough that discomforts were rectified to a certain extent—but not entirely. Those in the Court that had no truly *pressing* need to be here, and who had the intelligence to see what might happen if conditions continued to deteriorate, found reasons and the means to get home.

By now it was next to impossible to maintain anything of a magical nature without exhaustive work on shields, and every time another Storm-wave passed, those shields were so eroded that they required intensive repair. Transportation within the Empire was at a standstill, and communication sporadic at best. Physical constructions such as buildings and bridges that had incorporated static magics into their construction had crumbled. Every structural disaster created more disruption and fear, and sometimes involved great loss of life. Nor was that the only physical effect of the Storm-waves; great pieces of land had been changed out of all recognition, and bizarre monsters were appearing as if conjured out of the air itself. Migrating birds had altered their patterns, or flew entirely lost. Wide-leafed plants as tall as men, stinging to the touch, grew inexplicably from stonework and soil alike, and all over the capital and nearby provinces, vines strangled horses in the night. Carcasses of creatures that looked like nothing of this world were brought in as proof that these Storms were only making their world stranger and more horrifying with each passing day.

By this time anyone who stood the slightest chance of reaching his or her Estate by purely physical means had left the Court. At home, a courtier would at least have reasonable foodstocks at hand, and many had Estates that relied on old-fashioned, nonmagical, purely physical sources of heat, light, and sanitation. One irony was that the poorer and less pretentious of the courtiers, who had not had the spare means to spend on magical amenities in their estates, were now the least uncomfortable of their peers. As perilous as life on the Estates could become now, with monstrous creatures attacking without warning or provocation, the wise and forethinking knew it was not only possible, but probable, that life in the capital would become far more dangerous. How long before food riots set the disaffected against the wealthy?

Charliss gazed upon his courtiers through narrowed eyes, and his normally inscrutable face betrayed some of his annoyance. He wondered if these who were left realized just how perilous life here could become. There were a remarkable number of very foolish people here now; people he had heard saying some amazingly silly things. "I come here to the Season at Court to forget the world outside these walls," one woman had said testily in his hearing. "I don't care to hear anything about it while the Season is on; I have more important things to think about—I have balls to attend and five marriageable daughters to dispose of!"

But the world outside the walls of Crag Castle was vanishing, even as that woman danced and displayed her offspring, and no amount of willful ignorance was going to change that. Already those outlying provinces of the Empire that had but lately come under the rule of the Iron Throne had revolted, regaining their independence. Charliss did not know, in most cases, what had become of the Imperial forces that had been stationed there. Some few had made their way back to lands that were still within Imperial sway, but others had vanished into the silence. Perhaps they had revolted along with those they were supposed to rule; but more likely they had been slaughtered, or had merely surrendered and were now prisoners. *He* did not know, nor did anyone else. Reluctantly, he was forced to admit to himself in recent days that his Empire, powerful and vast, had one particular fatal flaw. It was entirely optimized toward controlling any and all threats from inside itself—from riots to political intrigue to civil war—but was pathetically unprepared for outside disrupting influences such as these Storms.

Within the Empire itself, with transportation reduced to the primitive level of horse and cart, matters were degenerating much faster than he could prop them up. Food was the most critical item; usually imported into the cities all winter long from the Estates that supplied it, foodstuffs were running short as even Imperial storehouses were emptied. Food *was* getting into the cities, brought by individual farmers or carters a sledgeload at a time, but there were not only distances to consider, but the dreadful winter storms as well. Prices for perishable items were trebling weekly, with the cost of staples following suit, though more slowly since he had ordered Imperial stockpiles to be put on the market to stabilize prices. In some cities food riots had already broken out, and he had ordered the Imperial troops to move in to quell the unrest by whatever means necessary.

At least on the Estates, which were used to supporting themselves, there was plenty of food in storage, and most nobles had their own personal forces to maintain order. There would be more cooperation than competition among their dependents and underlings, if a lord or lady was a wise governor of his or her property. If not, well, they would get what was coming to them.

There had already been extensive rioting in those cities where major public aqueducts, maintained by magic, had collapsed, leaving the entire city with no source of fresh water. He had been able to repress news of those riots, but he was not certain just how long he would be able to repress news of food riots if they became widespread. Somehow, when news was bad, it always managed to spread no matter how difficult the circumstances.

It was not the weight of the Wolf Crown pressing down on his brow that made his head ache, it was the weight of the misfortune.

Why am I the Emperor upon whom all this is visited? Why could it not have waited for my successor?

One bizarre effect of these disasters on the citizens of the Empire—as if there were not enough bizarre effects already—was that strange religious cults were springing up all over what was left of the Empire. It seemed as if every city had its own pet prophet, most of them predicting the end of the world—or at least of the world as the citizens of the Empire had known it. Every cult had its own peculiar rites and proposed every possible variation on human behavior as the "only" means of salvation. Some preached complete asceticism, some complete license. Some advocated a single deity, some attributed spirits to every object and natural phenomena, living or not.

Some sent the most devoted out to sacrifice themselves to marauding monsters in the hopes of appeasing whatever had sent those monsters—but of course nothing was ever appeased but the appetite of the particular monster, and that was only a temporary condition. Needless to say, *those* cults did not long survive, for either their followers grew quickly disillusioned and abandoned their leaders, or they grew quickly angry and fed their leaders to those same monsters.

The cults neither worried nor really concerned Charliss, even though many of them had recruited untaught or ill-taught mages, and were raising impressive, though short-lived, power. He left it to his own corps of mages to deal with that power or drain it. He left the day-to-day emergencies in the hands of his underlings, mostly from the military. He had more personal concerns; most of his attention these days was taken up with his own well-being, even his own survival, both of which were in great jeopardy. He had *depended* on reliable and consistent magic to maintain those spells keeping him alive and healthy after two centuries of life, and magic was neither reliable nor consistent anymore.

He *could* die before he was ready, and he had come chillingly close to it more than once. That, above all, was something he wanted no one to learn.

Many of his courtiers were mages, and he wondered how tempting it would be for one of them to take advantage of his precarious situation. He was under no illusions about the ultimate loyalty of his courtiers; he had once been one of them, and like them, his ultimate loyalty had been only to himself. There were two sorts of folk out there in the Great Hall now; those who were still here because they were fools, and those who were still here because they saw opportunities. The latter were drastically more dangerous than the former, and he never forgot that.

He had been able to keep his own existence from being

eroded by keeping the heaviest of shields upon himself, but he required an increasing number of lesser mages to do that, and he lost more ground every time another wave of Storms passed. Not even his corps of mages knew just how delicately his life was hanging in the balance.

At the moment, he had managed to keep the fact that there was even the slightest thing wrong with him a secret. His courtiers did not seem to notice any difference in his appearance, but it was only a matter of time before some sharp-eyed individual—or one with a good network of informants—learned that all was not well with the Emperor by assembling all of the small hints into one concise answer. The moment that happened, the panic in the cities would be replicated in miniature in the Court, unless Charliss could quickly exert total control over every courtier here. How could he do that, when every spare iota of time and energy was spent bolstering his failing reserves? He felt events slipping like sand between his fingers, and his very helplessness raised a rage in him that was as powerful as it was futile.

My Empire is disintegrating beneath me. Soon I may not have an Empire; I may consider myself fortunate to still retain a Kingdom—or a city—or my life.

But he did not despair. Despair was an emotion for weaklings and failures, with no place in the heart of the one who wore the Wolf Crown. Anger, a cold fire in his belly, rose in him until he felt he had to find a direction for it or burn away.

The realization of how his anger should be channeled rolled in and struck like a thunderbolt in his mind. He knew *precisely* where to place the blame for this situation, and his anger pointed like a poisoned arrow into the West and the home of his enemy.

Valdemar.

There could be only one source for his troubles, for the mage-storms and all they had wrought. Nothing like this had ever happened before he sent Tremane to finish taking Hardorn and consider taking the Kingdom of Valdemar which lay beyond Hardorn. Valdemar did not *have* magic as the Empire knew it, and yet they had defended themselves successfully against all of Ancar's magical attacks. The rulers of Valdemar had prevented his own agents from penetrating its borders for decades with great success; only a handful had obtained any intelligence, only three informants had ever gotten into the Court itself. Two of the three had not been mages, which had seriously hampered their effectiveness, and the third had been forced to forgo magic while she remained within the borders, which had the same effect. Valdemar had allied itself with foreigners as weird as any of the monsters currently springing up everywhere—with the grim Shin'a'in and the alien Hawk-brothers, with the monotheistic fanatics of Karse. Valdemar would be the only power to have come up with so completely unpredictable a weapon. The fact that—at least at last re-port—Valdemar and her Allies were not suffering the effects of the Storms only confirmed his "revelation." Surely only the people who had sent out such an encompassing weapon would know how to defend against it affecting them as well.

Besides, Valdemar had murdered his agents and envoys. That, he had personal proof of, for they had fallen through the Portal from Hardorn with daggers bearing the Royal Seal on the pommel-nuts. His advisers differed in their opinions on whether or not this had represented a deliberate provocation, an act of war, or simply a challenge, but there was no differ-ence of opinion on whose hand had done the deed. It had to be someone actually in the Royal Household, either the Heir or the personal agent of the Queen, not just any provocateur or Herald.

Tremane, parked on the very doorstep of Valdemar, had agreed with that assessment, but the measures that *he* had taken to disrupt the Alliance had gone seriously amiss.

Or had they?

It could be that he had never taken those measures at all, that he had concocted the story of his tame assassin out of whole cloth. Had he been planning to defect to the Valde-maran Alliance all along, in the hope that they would give him a Kingdom, when he saw that he could not win the war with the Hardornen rebels?

That would make very good sense, considering that Char-liss had made the promise of the position of Imperial Heir contingent on whether or not Tremane won Hardorn—the *whole* of Hardorn—for the Empire.

Given the choice between coming home in disgrace—

barely retaining his own Duchy—and winning himself a Kingdom, it could have been an easy decision.

All this was speculation, of course, but Charliss did have certain facts to guide him. Without question, Tremane had revolted, looting an Imperial supply depot, declaring to his men that the Empire had deserted them, and making common cause with the Hardornens he had been sent to subdue. Chances were that the Valdemarans had persuaded him, perhaps had even given him the idea to revolt in the first place. Tremane had been the best choice Charliss had from among those to whom he had offered the opportunity to earn the Heir's Coronet. Tremane was no fool, but nothing in his makeup had given Charliss the impression that he could be induced to revolt. He was intelligent, but not particularly imaginative. Yet one agent who had made his way across country against impossible odds had painted a very clear picture of Grand Duke Tremane's traitorous words and deeds.

That betrayal was as bitter as any experience in Charliss' long life and reign, and it would not go unpunished. It was a pity that Tremane had left no potential hostage in the form of a wife or child at Court, and that his Estate was so far away on the borders of the Empire that reaching it to despoil it was about as practical as going after Tremane himself. Of course, Charliss could and would assign it to someone else, but that was an empty gesture, and both he and the recipient would be well aware of that. No one would be able to get there until late spring at best, and if the Empire continued to fall apart, they might as well not try.

Still, a gesture would have to be made, hollow or not. These people below him, fools though they were, would have to be shown once again that he *was* the Emperor, and he was not to be trifled with.

He signaled to his majordomo, who rapped his staff three times on the marble of the floor to gain the Court's attention. Nothing disturbed the icy tranquillity of the majordomo's demeanor; men had been cut down by the Imperial Guards at his very feet and he had not turned a hair. Arrayed in a splendor of purple velvet and gold bullion embroidery, and bearing the wolf-headed Imperial Staff which stood taller than he was, no mage-made homunculus or clockwork manikin could have been more controlled than he.

So completely did his office subsume him that Charliss did not even know his name.

Silence fell immediately with the first rap, so that the next two echoed down the hall with the impact of Death himself rapping on a door. All eyes turned at once to the Iron Throne, and Charliss stood up to face them all, his heavy robes dragging at his shoulders. He braced his calves against the Throne, grateful for the invisible support.

He could have had the majordomo make the announcements, but that would lessen the impact, and it might give the impression that he was no longer vigorous. He could not have that, especially not now. He must appear to be as powerful now as the day he took the Throne.

His voice echoed portentously out over the crowd of courtiers, amplified and rendered more imposing by clever acoustical design around the dais. "Intelligence has reached Our ears that gravely grieves and angers Us," he said sternly into the silence. "We have received news from an unimpeachable source that Tremane, Grand Duke of Lynnai, has turned traitor to the Empire, to his vows, and to Us."

The gasps of surprise that rippled through the Court were not feigned, and only confirmed Charliss' impression that those courtiers still remaining were for the most part not among his brightest and best. He scanned for a few particular faces, men and a few women who were numbered among his advisers—and there was no surprise or shock registering there.

Good. It's agreeable to know that I haven't chosen any complete idiots.

"There can be no doubt of his intent or his thoughts," Charliss continued, as the gasps and murmurs died down again. "He has orchestrated the looting of an Imperial storage depot for his own profit, including the contents of the exchequer there, monies intended to pay the faithful soldiers of the Empire their just and well-earned stipends."

He cast a glance at the stiff figures lining the walls. *Ah, my own guards are looking black at that one. Good. Word will spread through the rest of the Army, and may the Hundred Little Gods help him if he shows his face where a single Impe-*

rial soldier can find him. Of all the truths in the Empire guaranteed to preserve life, limb, and prosperity, this was the truest: *Pay the Army, pay it well, and pay it on time.*

Charliss permitted a touch of his anger to show on his face and in his voice. "He has declared his allegiance to the Empire at an end, and has subverted his troops, entrusted to him, to renounce their oaths as well. He has broken off hostilities with the rebels of Hardorn, has entered into unlawful and traitorous alliance with them, and is acting in all ways to have set himself up as King of that benighted land."

Shaking heads and avid looks told him that every one of the power seekers still gathered here was hoping for profit from Tremane's downfall. Well, in the void left when a great tree fell, little trees could climb to reach the sun. Even in these strange days, that might still come to pass.

Now, however, was the time to alert these idiots to their danger. "Worst of all, he has entered into alliance with the vile and duplicitous monarch of Valdemar, which nation has sent unprovoked assaults by magic lately against this, Our peaceful Empire." He paused for a breath, steadying himself against the Throne under cover of his robes. That last was only supposition, but even those with intelligence networks the near-equal of his could not be certain of that, and really, would not care. Tremane had no friends here; those who had been nominally his allies would be scrambling for new men to attach themselves and their fortunes to. And proving that the current misfortunes had a recognizable origin might consolidate some of these idiots into a cohesive whole. There was nothing quite like a common enemy to make a force out of disparate and bickering parties.

Now to show them that the old lion had teeth. He put on his most dreadful look, the one that left even hardened guards with trembling hands and quaking knees, and made his next words thunder out like the pronouncement of some barbarian god. "We therefore declare Tremane of Lynnai a traitor, his title and lands forfeit, and his name anathema! We pronounce upon him the sentence of death, to be executed by any that have the means and opportunity! Let no loyal citizen of the Empire aid him, on pain of that same sentence; let his name be stricken from the rolls of his family, and let the House of Lynnai die with his father! Let his name be chiseled from monuments of battle, be erased from the records of the Empire, and let it be as if he never was born!"

That was the harshest sentence possible to pronounce within the Empire, and no few faces below him turned pale. For most of these people, this erasure was worse than a sentence of execution, for it extended Tremane's punishment into the Hereafter. If and when Tremane *did* die, he would have no immortality, for without some record on earth of who and what he had been, his soul would vanish at the moment of his death, or would wander aimlessly in the cheerless, empty limbo between earth and the afterlife, without any knowledge of who it had once been. . . .

Or so it was believed. When a citizen of the Empire believed anything, he believed in the immortality of records; when he worshiped anything, he always included his ancestors. To remove someone from his rightful place among his ancestors was to remove a piece of the very cosmos.

Charliss smiled grimly. *Now they know I haven't gone soft, just because I was prepared to name a possible Heir.*

He allowed his expression to soften. "We know that this has come as a great shock to all Our loyal subjects, the more especially as the Nameless One had been put forth as the potential Heir to the Imperial Crown. Such a betrayal harms you as well as Us, by threatening the security of the Empire. We would not see Our children distressed by the taint of betrayal mingled with uncertainty. Therefore, We now do name Our successor, and bestow on him all those lands, goods, and titles that were once the property of the Nameless One."

The looks of greed and avidity were back—though only briefly, and quickly controlled. At this moment, no one knew who Charliss was going to name, least of all the recipient. Once Tremane had been designated, Charliss had taken pains to show no partiality to anyone else; he had wanted to give Tremane as fair a playing field as possible in a Court as filled with intrigue as this one. And besides, by not showing favor to any one person, he had virtually opened up the field—if Tremane failed to conquer Hardorn—to *anyone*. The scrambling and jockeying had been most amusing when he'd had the leisure to take note of it. Every one of his advisers had the potential to be named Heir as far as anyone knew, and several of his mages as well. Those who thought themselves in the running were moving up through the crowd, almost without realizing that they were doing so, attempting to place themselves nearer the Throne, where he could see them better.

But his thoughts were wandering; the suspense was about to send one or two out there into a fit of apoplexy.

He had to end the suspense, although there would be several who were shocked or affronted at his choice. Nevertheless, Melles had been his second choice before he sent Tremane off to conquer Hardorn, and Melles had remained in that position all along. "We therefore do name as successor and Heir, the most worthy and knowledgeable adviser and most loyal servant of the Empire, Court Baron Melles."

He had just named Tremane's most fervent and implacable enemy. And if *anyone* was going to put in the astounding effort it would take merely to attempt to execute the Imperial death sentence on Tremane, it would be Melles. There was real hatred between the two of them, a hatred more powerful than Charliss had witnessed in a very long time. There was not much room for hatred in the Imperial Court; it was better to keep emotions superficial, for today's enemy might be tomorrow's ally.

Melles had been standing just to one side of the dais, visible, but unobtrusive, as was his normal habit. He was a slightly better-looking version of Tremane in some ways; thinner and not as muscular, with none of the physical attributes of a fighter. He was not balding; his hair was darker, and he was two or three years Tremane's junior. Otherwise, though, they could have been cut from the same cloth and sewn by the same tailor. Both of them had cultivated the art of being ignored and overlooked, though Charliss suspected that their motives for this differed greatly. He *knew* what Melles' motives were; now, in retrospect, he could guess at Tremane's.

Melles was not a hereditary noble like Tremane; he was a Court Baron, a man with a title but no lands, as his father had been before him. Melles' wealth came from trade, as did the wealth of most of the Court nobles, although the commodity that Melles bought and sold was quite unlike that of his live-stock-brokering father. It was no secret that an ambitious tradesman with enough ready cash could buy a Court title for himself, and with further applications of his wealth could arrange for the title to be inherited by his son. There was no shame in this—though many of the Court nobles were extraordinarily touchy about their titles, and many of the landed gentry made no secret of the fact that they considered the Court nobles to be purest upstarts. There was some friction between the two factions, although it was quite astonishing how quickly that friction vanished when a family with title but no fortune was presented with the heir or heiress to a fortune with no title as a matrimonial prospect.

Was that how the enmity had begun between Tremane and Melles? Had Tremane, or Tremane's father, snubbed Melles or Melles' father? It seemed unlikely that such hatred could spring from so trifling a cause. Oddly enough, Charliss could not imagine Tremane being rude to anyone, not even to someone he held in contempt. Tremane had always been too clever to make such enemies casually.

Well, it didn't really matter now. Whatever the cause, it served the Emperor's ends.

Barron—now Grand Duke—Melles moved forward out of the knot of courtiers at the very foot of the steps leading to the dais. He stood alone for a moment, then walked with solemn deliberation up the three steps permitted to one of his new title, bowing his head and going to his knee at the fourth. Charliss motioned to the guard at his right to bring up the coronet of the Heir from the niche at the side of the dais where it had resided since Charliss himself had resigned it to put on the Wolf Crown.

Although the acts of this ceremony appeared spontaneous, it was anything but. It was another dance, the steps dictated by the custom of ages past, every move choreographed centuries ago. Only the participants in the dance changed, never the steps themselves.

Even the guard who brought the coronet to Melles had rehearsed just this action a thousand times, even though there was no telling *which* guard would be directed to retrieve the circlet, nor who it would be given to. It was simply a part of an Imperial Guard's duty, rehearsed along with every other part.

The guard performed flawlessly, handing the circlet to Melles, who in accordance with tradition, solemnly crowned himself, just as he would crown himself with the Wolf Crown when Charliss died. Power and authority in the Empire came from within the man, and were not bestowed by the hands of priests, and in token of that, every Emperor and Heir bestowed the trappings of power upon himself.

Once crowned—not that the coronet was all that imposing, just an iron circlet in the shape of a sword, with a topaz matching those in the Wolf Crown set as the pommel-nut— Melles stood up, and bowed to his Emperor. Charliss surveyed him with satisfaction, thinking that he probably should have chosen Melles in the first place. Unlike Tremane, Melles was a powerful Adept who could, with a few decades of practice, be Charliss' equal in magic. Given that, and despite current conditions, it was just barely possible that Melles *would* contrive to bring back Tremane's head.

Charliss mentally resolved to resign on the spot if Melles managed to pull that one off. Not that he considered it *likely*, but such diligence would deserve a reward, and there wasn't much else Charliss would be able to give him.

And if he can do that, he'll be strong enough to take the Wolf Crown from me. It would be better to resign it with grace, and concentrate on keeping myself alive.

No matter how powerfully his enemies among the courtiers would gladly have plunged daggers into Melles' heart at that moment, not one of them would betray himself. "Go and take your well-deserved congratulations from Our Court," Charliss directed with cool approval. "We will discuss your new duties and privileges later."

Melles bowed, and backed down the steps. There was no throne for the Heir, nor any special place for him at Court ceremonies. Emperors of the past had not deemed it necessary or advisable to give their Heirs too much power or the appearance of it lest they acquire an addiction to it and crave more. As Melles turned at the foot of the steps to face those thronging to greet him, Charliss decided that the Emperors of the past had been very wise. Melles could certainly be one of those who would crave more than his just due.

Charliss decided to keep him on a short leash, as he watched the dance of power begin swirling about this new center.

One Tremane was enough, after all.

Melles had often thought, of late, that there had been so many upheavals that there was nothing that could evoke the feeling of surprise in him anymore. And although his intelligence network was extraordinary—in fact, it had been one of *his* spies who had brought word of Tremane's defection back to Crag Castle—he really had not expected to be named Charliss' Heir.

According to his own calculations, he wasn't the logical candidate, even though there were personal considerations involved. Since the onset of the mage-storms and the consequent disasters spread over the entire Empire, it had seemed to him that the Emperor would have to name someone who had absolutely no enemies at Court whatsoever. Whoever came after Charliss would have to cope with a much-reduced Empire, revolt everywhere, a possibly hostile Army; he would have to somehow convince the worst of enemies to act together and forge alliances until the Empire was stable again. Melles had far too many enemies who would rather die than work with him in any way; Tremane was not the only one, nor was he even the most deadly. Melles was a man who made enemies far more easily than allies. On the whole, he preferred enemies, for it was much easier to manipulate them than allies, and there was never the risk of disillusion when they realized they had been manipulated.

Friends were quite out of the question; a friend was a potential hole in one's armor, and he had not permitted himself such a weakness since he became a man. Then there was the matter of his position and duties under Charliss, which did not endear him to anyone. He could not think of a single person who *liked* him in the entire Court. Many feared him, some admired him grudgingly, others tolerated him as a necessary evil, but no one *liked* him.

But there they all were, flocking to fawn on him as if they couldn't wait to become his best friend. Some of them, in fact, might very well have plans in that direction, foolish as such plans might be. He was, after all, surrounded by fools; they wouldn't be here now if they weren't.

He smiled and accepted their congratulations with an expression that suggested that he would be eager to become their best friend. Why not? Even fools had their uses, and just like the Emperor who had bestowed his new title, he had never been the kind who threw away a potential tool.

The men thronged about him first, jostling one another in their eagerness to say something that he might remember later, reminding him of past favors they had done for him, offering favors for the future. It was quite astonishing, the sort of things they considered to be "favors;" he could not for a moment imagine why *anyone* could think that invitations to incredibly boring social gatherings featuring meaningless entertainments would ever be sought after.

And the *women!* They were worse than the men! If they were unmarried, they were pressing about him with looks and poses that were just short of open invitations to do as he pleased with them. If they were anything other than blissfully, happily married (and there were damned few of *those* at Court, especially now!) they were behaving the same. If they had daughters of anything resembling marriageable age—and plenty of these women had very liberal ideas about what constituted "marriageable age"—they were alluding to their daughters' admiration of him, and dangling invitations on their behalf.

As if any of them had the faintest notion who I am or what I look like—

No, that was unfair, Not all of these people were here because they were blind idiots who wouldn't have their Season spoiled by a few petty disasters. Some were here because they couldn't get back to their Estates, others because of their positions as Imperial Advisers, and some because they had no Estates. There were young girls—and not so young girls—who knew very well who he was and what he looked like, as they knew the identities, properties, and titles of every unwedded man expected to be at Court this Season. That was part of *their* duty, as they and their parents went about the serious business of husband hunting. He might not have been very high on their list of desirable matches until now, but they knew who he was.

And if he made an appearance at a private party, a musical evening, or other entertainment, each of them would proceed with grim determination to try to convince him that nothing would make him happier than to take *her* as his lawfully wedded soon-to-be-Empress.

That no less than an hour ago most if not all of these maidens would have cheerfully confessed that the idea of wedding him made them ill was of no consequence now.

Look how these same women throw themselves at Charliss, the old mummy! It isn't his handsome face that makes them act like shameless cows in season around him. Furthermore, Melles was well aware that if he had evidenced any preference for young *men* he would still be under siege from these women and their parents. After all, he would still be expected to *try* to produce an Heir of his body. The fact that only about half of the Emperors of the past had been the physical offspring of their predecessor didn't matter, he would still be expected to try.

And if some of what I've read in the private Archives is true, some of them went to some fascinating extremes in trying. . . .

Well, that didn't matter either. He wasn't a lover of men or boys, and not of little girls either. But he would wait until he wore the Iron Crown himself before he took a wife, and when he did, his first choice would be an orphan with no living family left whatsoever, just for spite!

"Yes, of course," he murmured to one of the women—after being certain that he was not agreeing to anything of importance. It would be a grand joke on all of them if he selected his bride from among the common citizens. It would certainly be easy to find an attractive orphan there!

He whispered an aside to one of the other advisers, a man who had been a disinterested ally in the past. *This is all going to my head. There will be time to think about women later; now is the time to concentrate on consolidating my base of power, and determining what can best be done to get the Empire through this crisis.*

Pleasures of all sorts would have to wait until the Empire was stable. Perhaps sometime in the future there might even be an opportunity to execute the Emperor's sentence of death on Tremane. But that time was not now, and he would wait for it to come to him. Hatred was an emotion that brought him a great deal of energy and entertainment, and he enjoyed it.

It was not for nothing that his enemies often compared him to a spider sitting in the middle of a web. If there was one virtue he possessed, it was patience, for patience was the only virtue that eventually brought rewards.

Now that the dance of courtiers and Court was over and the business of the Empire had been disposed of in Council, Melles got his private audience with the Emperor. Private? Well, not precisely; the Emperor was never alone. But no one of any pretense to wealth or rank in the Empire ever really noticed servants or bodyguards—

Unless, of course, that person was Melles, or someone like him. To the Emperor, without a doubt, they were invisible. To Melles they were possible spies.

The subject of conversation, as befitting the position and duties of the new Heir, was the state of the Empire. Melles was not particularly surprised to discover that Charliss had less information on this subject than he did. The Emperor had not been concerned with the day-to-day workings of his Empire for decades; he had been able to leave that to his underlings.

In Melles' opinion, he no longer had that luxury. "My Lord Emperor," Melles said patiently. "It seems to me that you have been insufficiently acquainted with the desires and needs of the common man."

They compare me to a spider in its web, Melles thought dispassionately, as he watched the old man glare at him over the expanse of a highly-polished black marble table. *They should see him when he is not playing his role. He looks like an ancient turtle deciding whether or not to stick his nose a fraction more outside his shell.*

Inside the sheltering back and arms of the Emperor's thronelike chair, that was precisely what Charliss resembled. And, like the turtle, Melles suspected that the Emperor really *did* want to pull himself back into his shell entirely.

He did not seem disposed to learn, or deal with, the basic changes in the Empire, and that fit with Melles' plans. *So what I need to do is to persuade him that not only is that a good idea for him, but also that he can trust power in my hands.* Melles already had a great deal of power; he had been in charge of dealing out whatever punishments the Emperor deemed necessary for many years now. Not quite an Executioner, and considerably higher in status than a mere law-keeper, when something unfortunate occurred to a member of the Court and the Emperor took special notice of it, everyone knew whose hand had been behind seeming accidents or twists of fate. Melles' value to the Emperor lay in making certain that it was impossible to prove anything when such accidents occurred.

The "accidents" weren't always supposed to be fatal, or at least not fatal to the physical body. Sometimes ruin suited the Emperor better than death, whether it be the ruin of a reputation or of a fortune. A ploy that Melles particularly favored was to contrive romantic liaisons that were entirely disastrous; it was amazing what people would do to prevent their follies from becoming widely known when that folly involved sexual favors, infatuation, or a combination of the two.

"Just what exactly do you mean by that?" the Emperor asked querulously.

Melles spread his hands wide. "I mean, Lord Emperor, that the common man is an extremely simple creature. You are thinking of him now in terms of the mob, which is a being with many arms and legs and no head, and as a consequence behaves in ways no rational man can predict. *I* am thinking of him as he is before he devolves to that mindless, intractable state." He tilted his head to one side; that had been a much longer speech than he usually gave to the Emperor, and he had learned to make certain that the Emperor always had openings in which to insert his own comments.

"So what is the so-called common man, when he isn't in a mob?" the Emperor mocked.

Melles was not about to let his own mask of serenity slip. Such mockery was as much a test as Tremane's assignment had been.

And I am not likely to be lulled by the illusion that I am the Emperor's only executioner. If he perceives me as a failure, I will not live long enough to rebel.

He inclined his head a little; not quite a bow, but enough to acknowledge his subservience even as he "corrected" the

Emperor's ignorance. "As I said, Serenity, he is simple. What he needs—desires—those things are just as simple. First of all, he wants the roof over his head to be sound and the food on his plate to be abundant. He wants that food to arrive every day. He wants to be left alone to pursue his work and the pleasures of his bed, home, and table. If you give him these things, he is not inclined to argue overmuch about the *means* required to deliver them. If he is deprived of them, he is likely to welcome whatever measures are taken to restore them." He raised a single finger to emphasize his next point. "Most, if not all, of your common citizens have been so deprived, and see only a steady decline in the quality of their lives, but if measures could be taken that will restore many of their comforts, those things they consider so important to their lives. . . ."

"I see your point," the Emperor replied, with no more mockery in his voice. He sat in silence, only the movement of his eyes betraying his alertness. He could have been a grotesque statue, if not for those glittering eyes. The Emperor did not fidget, did not visibly shift his weight in his chair, or perform any of the other tiny, unconscious movements of lesser beings. Partly it was a matter of training, for such utter stillness enhanced his image of supernatural power; partly, or so Melles suspected, it was simple good sense, to conserve his waning energy and resources.

Finally, the Emperor spoke, his voice low, deep, and grating. "You want me to give you the authority to order whatsoever you think is necessary to restore order at the level of the streets."

Melles nodded, very slowly, as those powerful eyes, blazing with the deadly life of a finely-honed blade, pinned him to his seat. He could not, dared not, return that glare. He was not here to challenge the Emperor, he was here to get the old man to share out some of his power. But he also wouldn't get anywhere if he didn't admit what he wanted. It was an interesting observation by one of his tutors that there were only three classes of people who could afford to speak the unvarnished truth—the very bottom, the very topmost, and children. The lowest classes could afford it because they had nothing to lose, the highest because there was no one who could call them to account for it, and children because they held no power and hence were no threat. Melles had never forgotten that observation, nor did he forget the implications of it. The Emperor could speak pure truth; Melles could not. When the Emperor asked a direct question, Melles had better be careful how much of the truth he told.

But there was another factor here. At the best of times, when the Emperor had been in his prime, he hadn't had time enough for everything. No great ruler did; that was why they had underlings and delegated their authority to those they thought could be trusted with it. Now, the Emperor was old, his powers waning, and he had the very personal and pressing matter of preserving what was left of his life to concentrate on.

The real question, the one Melles had no answer to as yet, was just how close to the end the Emperor was. That would tell him how reluctant Charliss would be to give up power to his Heir. Would he clutch his powers and possessions to him, or release them to clutch at life itself?

Those sharp, chill eyes measured him, and missed nothing in the process. "Very well." The voice was as cold as the eyes. "Have the orders written, and I will sign and seal them, granting you authority over city guards, militias, and authorizing you to make use of the Army in quelling local disturbances. That will be enough to see if you have the insight into the common man that you claim." A thin, humorless smile stretched the Emperor's lips. "If you succeed, I shall consider granting you more."

He waved a hand at the Emperor, in mute disavowal of wanting any other powers. "That will be sufficient, my Lord Emperor, I assure you. I wish only to restore order; without order, these seeds of chaos will spread to engulf us all."

Charliss only made a wheezing grunt full of cynical amusement. "I doubt that you intend to limit your grasp. But this is all you will get for the present. Go to the clerks and draw up the orders."

That was clear dismissal, and he took it as such. He stood, bowed with careful exactitude, and walked backward until he reached the door. The Emperor's eyes were on Melles every step of the way, and the slight smile on the Emperor's lips would have chilled the blood of a lesser man.

He reached behind him and opened the door without looking at it, backed through it, and closed it without taking his eyes off the Emperor. As the door closed, the Imperial eyes were still fixed on him, still measuring, still watching him for a hint of insubordination.

As the door shut with a decisive *click*, Melles let out his breath, slowly. *That went better than I had any reason to hope. He's still sane; if he stays that way, I can handle him.* He turned and stalked silently down the cold gray marble hallway with its high ceilings and austere decorations of captured weaponry from ages and wars long past. Like the room he had just left, the hallway was chilly enough to make him wish he had worn heavier clothing. Ostensibly, it was due to a failure in the enchantments of heating, but in fact it was deliberate, to discourage loitering. The hallway was meant to impress one who walked it with his own insignificance, and its acoustics underscored the message well.

Here, so near to the highest seats of Imperial government, the Audience Chamber, the Council Chamber, and the great Court Hall, one necessary adjunct to so much power was a highly-trained cadre of Imperial clerks to make decisions into orders. Nothing could function without written orders. Articles, commands, and doctrine, no matter how seemingly small, had no official life until they were quantified as documents. These pieces of paper were so vital to the working of the Empire, they were like water, food, or air to a soldier, and an official document would carry more power in its words than any courtier posturing and spouting similar verbiage.

And of course, there was such a group of vital clerks, a small army of them, ensconced in the one comfortable chamber on this floor, between the Court Hall and the Council Chamber.

An efficient Empire was one dependent on (though not run by) clerks, though they might not know it; their masters did, and always had, and took care to ensure the comfort of these all-important workers in the hive of Imperial rule. Large windows, screened against insects, let in cooling breezes during the heat of summer. And although the heating-spells had failed elsewhere in Crag Castle—legitimately—measures had always been in place in case of such a failure in the Clerks' Chamber. There were three great fireplaces on the wall shared with the Council Chamber, and two more on the one shared by the Court Hall, all of them burning merrily. Charcoal footwarmers sat under desks, and those all-important fingers kept warm and supple with metal handwarmers on each desk. Each clerk had his own oil lamp to read and write by, and there were pages assigned to this room only, to bring food and drink whenever called for.

Some—always among the "new" nobility who were not yet acquainted with the way things worked—grumbled at this treatment of "mere" clerks. What they were not aware of was that these clerks weren't "mere" anything, and most of them were higher in rank than the grumblers. Here the offspring of the noblest families in the Empire paid their service, even those intended eventually for the Army. They were accustomed to perferential and comfortable treatment, but that did not mean they did not earn it by their labors. There was never an hour when there were not at least six clerks on duty here, and there were twenty between dawn and dusk. Only the most skilled and most discreet served here, and their ability to remain closemouthed about what passed over their desks was legendary.

To open the heavily-guarded door and enter this haven of heat and light was a decided relief; Melles felt tight muscles relaxing under the influence of the gentle warmth. It was still early enough in the day that all twenty clerks were in attendance; Melles scanned the rows of desks, and went straight to the first unoccupied clerk he saw.

The young man he chose sat, like all the rest, at a large wooden desk with everything he required arranged neatly on top of it. A stack of rough draft paper, a smaller stack of Imperial Vellum, inkpots containing red and black ink, blotting paper, blotting sand, glass pens, and his handwarmer were all arranged in a pattern he found personally the most efficient. Off to one side was the book he had been reading, which he had immediately laid aside when Melles neared him. The only sign of individuality was a small egg-shaped carving of white jade in a motif of entwining fish.

The clerk himself was nondescript, unmemorable, as all of them were. They were taught how to be forgettable and self-effacing before they came to this duty. Here, they were a pair of hands and a brain full of specific skills, interchangeable with every other clerk in the room. Melles alone among his acquaintances had never taken a turn in this room, but that was because he had been serving Empire and Emperor by learning another set of skills entirely.

While the clerk made rapid notes, he dictated the orders; the clerk first made a rough copy, checking it word for word with him, then from the corrected rough, made a final copy on Imperial Vellum incorporating all the changes. Melles was being very careful in how he phrased these orders, giving himself precisely the amount of authority that the Emperor had specified and no more. Three more clerks were summoned to make copies at this point, for a total of five copies in all.

As yet, obviously, the orders were nothing more than paper. When he had finished, the clerk summoned a page from the group waiting and chattering on a bench beside the fire and sent him to the Emperor with the finished documents. The page would not walk down the corridor that Melles had just left; he would use a special passage between this room and the Emperor's chambers reserved only for the pages, so that he could not be stopped and questioned or detained.

Melles did not go with him; he was prohibited from doing so, nor would the Emperor's guards permit him to approach with documents to be signed in hand. This was to prevent him from somehow coercing the Emperor into signing and sealing them, or being tricked into doing so before he had read them. All these convoluted customs had their reasons.

At length, the page returned, and the glitter of the Imperial Seal on the uppermost document told Melles that all had gone well; the orders were approved with no changes. Had there been changes, the page would have returned with one copy, not five, which would have had the Emperor's revisions written on it. The rest, one of the Emperor's guards would have burned on the spot, so that the Seal could not have been counterfeited on them.

Melles accepted his copies with a bow of thanks, and left the room. The chill of the hallway struck him with a shock, despite being prepared for it, but he didn't hesitate for even a moment. Now his first priority was to get one copy of the orders into the hands of the Commander of the Imperial Army. The cooperation of the Army was needed before he attempted any of his ambitious plans.

He had been careful to phrase his orders in such a way that

the Commander's authority was not being subsumed by his own. The last thing he wanted was to make an antagonist out of General Thayer. The General made a very bad enemy, one who never forgot and never forgave. The orders as he had dictated them gave him the authority to coopt regimental groups or smaller, depending on need, but only if they were not currently deployed on some other duty. *If I can't quell a riot with less than a regiment, I won't quell it with anything larger. That's not a threat to Thayer, and it means I won't be countermanding any of his standing orders to the Army as a whole.*

With luck, he wouldn't need to use Imperial soldiers very often, but luck had not been with anyone of late. He already knew that he would have to disperse at least one riot in each city by giving the soldiers orders to kill. It would be the first time in centuries that Imperial soldiers had been used against civilians, and it would come as a tremendous shock. He hoped that the shock would be great enough that he would not need to repeat the lesson. The loss of civilians meant loss of taxpaying workers, and at this point the Empire could not afford to lose much in the way of taxes.

The Imperial Commander had quarters here in Crag Castle, as every Emperor since the Third had preferred to have the Commander of his Armies where he could keep a watchful eye on him. The Third Emperor had originally been the Imperial Commander, and he had not approved of the Second Emperor's choice of Heir. He had taken matters into his own hands the moment that the Second Emperor was dead, and had decided not to give his own Imperial Commander the kind of opportunity that he had taken advantage of. The rest had followed his wise example.

As Melles moved down various corridors and staircases, he passed through narrow zones of warm air alternating with much more extensive zones of chill to positively frigid air. Since the denizens of Crag Castle were now relying on fireplaces and other primitive providers of warmth, heating was unreliable and often unpredictable. There would be illness in the Castle before the year turned to spring; illnesses of the kind more often associated with poorer folk.

The times are . . . interesting. And likely to become more so before the end.

The corridors themselves never varied in decor, only in size and height; they continued to be built of the same gray marble, and continued to feature only captured weaponry as decoration. Once Melles left the area of the Emperor's Quarters and the official chambers of government, the hallways he traversed became much narrower, and the ceilings dropped to a normal level, but that was the only way to tell that he was not within the quarters of the Emperor himself.

The Imperial Commander was one of the highest-ranking officials in the Council, so his chambers were correspondingly nearer to the Imperial Chambers. Only those of the Heir—which Melles' servants were currently engaged in arranging to suit him—were nearer. The Commander's personal bodyguards stood at attention to either side of the door, showing that the great man himself was inside, as Melles had expected. Melles would shortly have a pair of those guards outside of his own chambers, now that he was the designated Heir. They were not just to protect the life of those they were assigned to, they were meant as protection for the Emperor. The Imperial Guards were an elite group, trained and spell-bound to the service of the Emperor. No force on earth could turn them against Charliss, and if either the Heir or the Imperial Commander proved troublesome, well . . . only the details of burial would prove troublesome once their guards were finished with them. It *was* possible to break the spells sealing them to the Emperor, and it was possible that the Storms themselves had already done so. The only way to be sure would be to approach them on the question of eliminating the Emperor, and if the spells were intact, that could be a fatal mistake.

Tremane had managed to leave his pair of Imperial Guards behind him when he went off to command the conquest of Hardorn, probably because the Emperor had not expected trouble from him away from Crag Castle. Perhaps, if Charliss had insisted that Tremane take along his watchdogs, things might have turned out differently.

Or perhaps not, except that the Guards would have solved our problem by dispatching Tremane for us, and I would still be Heir. There would still be mage-storms to contend with, the Empire would still be falling to pieces, and all else would be following much the same paths. The only change would be that they would have one less danger to worry about—Melles knew, as no one else in the Court did, that it was by no means certain that Tremane *had* allied himself with Valdemar. In point of fact, he hoped fervently that this was not the case. These mage-storms were bad enough, random and untargeted as they seemed to be; if the mages of Valdemar had at their disposal an expert, one who knew everything there was of any importance about the Empire, what would happen then? What if the Storms could be targeted accurately, to cause the most disruption and damage? If Tremane really *were* to ally himself with Valdemar, that might be what they would have to deal with.

As for what such a revelation would do to the Emperor—

When he was fit and not beset by so many problems, he would simply have been angry, gotten over it, and would dismiss his anger until someone brought him Tremane's head. Now, I cannot be sure, because it is possible that he, like the Empire, is disintegrating, and his sanity will crumble along with his physical body.

He nodded to the two guards, who saluted and stepped aside for him as he displayed the Imperial Seal on the documents he carried. He knocked once on the door, then opened it and stepped inside.

He entered an anteroom, lushly carpeted, with battle-banners on all of the walls, but holding only a monumental desk, three comfortable chairs, and a single servant dressed in a compromise between military uniform and private livery, who was obviously one of Thayer's secretaries.

"I have Imperial orders for the Commander," he told the bland individual behind the desk. "And if the Commander has time for me, I should like to discuss them with him."

Conciliate, be polite and humble. It costs nothing, and keeps the peace.

The secretary immediately rose to his feet, and held out his hand for the orders. "I will deliver the orders to him directly, High Lord Heir," he said smoothly. "Please take a seat. I believe I can assure you that the Commander will always have time to discuss matters of the Empire with you, for he left standing orders with me to admit you to his presence regardless of other circumstances."

As Melles suppressed his surprise, the secretary took the paper from his hand and exited quickly through the doorway behind his desk. Melles took a seat, examining the fingernails of his right hand minutely as a cover for his thoughts. He had been aware since he became a member of the Council that Thayer was an astute politician, but he had not known how astute. Most of the other advisers were still scrambling to decide how to handle Melles now that he was officially the Heir. That Thayer had left standing orders with his underlings to admit Melles at any and all times was an interesting development, and Melles wondered if it meant that the Commander was prepared to cooperate with the new Heir on all levels. If so, that would make Melles' tasks incalculably easier.

To have the Commander of the Imperial Army in my pocket . . . half the power of the Empire will be divided between us. And the rest, well, that can wait.

The secretary returned before Melles needed to find some other object to examine. "Please follow me, Great Lord," the young man said as he bowed deeply. "The Lord Commander is eager to speak with you without delay."

Melles rose to his feet and followed the secretary into the next room of the suite, this one very similar to the antechamber. The Commander had excellent taste; he had carpeted over most of the floor with one of the rich, plush rugs of the Biijal tribes of the Eastern Islands, some of the more attractive captured battle-banners hung on the walls, and there was a good fire going in the fireplace. Like the antechamber, this room held little in the way of furniture, just another monumental desk, several comfortable chairs, and two smaller tables. Oil lamps served for illumination in place of the mage-lights that would ordinarily have been here; with darkness falling, these had been lit and burned brightly.

General Thayer was waiting, the Imperial Orders in his hand, standing beside his desk rather than sitting behind it. In the silent protocols of the Empire, he was receiving Melles as an equal rather than Melles arriving as a supplicant. This was another good sign; Thayer was not going to challenge his authority at all.

The General could have taken his place in the ranks of his own forces; though his hair was as gray as granite, his body was as hard and tough as that stone. The very few fools who had challenged Thayer to single combat over one pretext or another had not survived the experience. Enemies and friends alike compared him to a wolf—enemies compared him to a ravening, insatiable hunter, friends to the powerful pack leader. Gray as a wolf he was, and his teeth and wits were just as keen.

That sharply-chiseled face wore a friendly, welcoming expression today, however, and although Melles knew the General to be an astute politician, he also knew that Thayer was no good at all at hiding his feelings. As surely as his mind was a great asset, his face was a great handicap in the game of politics. To counter that handicap, Thayer made every attempt to play the game in writing and appeared in person only when policy permitted truth.

The General extended his free hand toward Melles with a smile as the secretary bowed himself out, and Melles took his hand with an answering smile.

"By the Hundred Little Gods, I was hoping you'd come to me first before any of the rest!" Thayer grated. A hilt-thrust to his throat as a young man had left him with a permanently marred voice. "Congratulations, Melles. The Emperor finally made a good choice. Tremane was a little *too* popular with his own men to make me entirely easy in my mind about him."

"Whereas I am so equally unpopular with everyone that you find me more acceptable as Heir?" Melles raised one eyebrow delicately, and Thayer barked a laugh.

"Let's just say that when the Commander discovers that one of his generals is *popular*, it makes him wonder why that general is cultivating popularity." Thayer bared his teeth in a smile as Melles nodded his understanding. "Sometimes it happens that popularity is an accident, but more often than not it's been deliberately sought. You, however—"

"I, who am known as 'Charliss' Executioner' need not trouble himself about such trifles as popularity." Melles softened the comment with a wry smile. "I would rather have respect than popularity."

Thayer answered that sally with a lifted brow of his own. "In that, as in other things, we are like-minded. The Emperor, may he reign long, is not the only one who needs to worry about underlings with ambition, and I am glad enough to see Tremane eliminated. So, about these orders—your idea?"

Melles nodded, carefully gauging Thayer's reactions before saying anything. He need not have been concerned; it was clear that Thayer could not have been more pleased had he dictated the orders himself.

"Damned good idea! Come sit down so we can talk about this in detail." The General waved him to one of the chairs beside the fireplace, and took another, tossing the orders onto the desktop but making no move to place himself behind the desk. Melles took his seat, and the General moved his own chair nearer to that of the Heir before sitting in it. "Damned good idea!" he repeated. "Declare martial law, and you'll have the cits up in arms and starting a revolt in the streets, but bring in the Army without actually *calling* it martial law, and they'll fall in line without a whimper if you can restore order." He coughed. "Give them back their easy lives, and they'll call you a god and not care how you managed it."

"My idea is to use the smallest number of soldiers that I can to crush disturbances absolutely," Melles said cautiously. "I don't want people to begin muttering that we've called out the Army on them; I believe that is one thing the citizens of the Empire won't tolerate. If you'll look at those orders, you'll see I've been given direct command of city guards, constables, and militia. The way I see it, if I use those forces in the front ranks, and only use the Army regulars to back them up and add strength to their line, I'll get the effect that I want without it looking as if the Army is taking over."

"Good. Sound strategy," Thayer confirmed. "Out in the provinces they expect the Army to put down trouble, but the cits think they're above all that. Put down the first riots efficiently, kill a few of the worst troublemakers, and I don't think you'll have any trouble reestablishing order. I was hoping someone would figure out that we're in for a spot of domestic trouble and would plan on dealing with it."

And of course he didn't dare suggest it himself. Charliss would see that as a direct threat to his own authority, and I would have been asked to find General Thayer a— retirement. Thayer knows it, too. He nodded, and leaned back in his chair, feeling much more confident with Thayer as an open ally. "It's not common knowledge, but there have already been small disturbances, and I expect larger ones as food runs short and hardships build up," he said easily. "If we're ready—and ruthless in suppressing the troubles to come—I think the citizens will accept what we do as a necessary evil."

"Yes, as we've said, find a way to get them their meals and peace and the cits will accept anything short of burning down the city," Thayer retorted with contempt. "Now, how exactly do you want me to help? You want a special regiment detached to go wherever it's needed, or—" Thayer paused, looking eager, but a bit reluctant to put forth his own ideas. "Well, I'm a military man, I don't have any experience in riot control, but—

"You have an idea of your own," Melles said, leaning forward with interest. "Please. I'd like to hear it."

"We've still got limited communication mage-to-mage with all the military bases, and you know there's at least one near every large city," Thayer told him. "Now, if *I* were to move a certain number of men, a company, say, into each city—if *you* were to get the militias and city guards and so on organized in the way you want beforehand—well, as soon as a riot started, your city militia would naturally go take care of it, and just as naturally the captain of the company would offer his help. Your militia captain would accept it, and why not, they're both in military brotherhoods, as it were. With the backing of the Army, I don't see any reason why we couldn't squash any riot. And technically, since I doubt every hothead in every city would take it into his head to riot on the same day, you wouldn't be exceeding the number of men you asked for." He grinned slyly. "You see, they'd only be under *your* command for the duration of the riot; after that, they'd come back under my authority."

Melles allowed himself a dry chuckle. General Thayer was obviously a past master at the fine art of manipulating loopholes, and his strategy was an application of the very orders that he had written that he himself had not considered.

But then, I didn't have any reason to suspect that Thayer would make quite such an eager ally.

"That, General, is a brilliant plan; quite perfect for all our purposes," he replied, allowing approval to creep into his voice. The General smiled, a smile with just as much steel in it as warmth.

"Good. We're agreed on it, then." Thayer nodded decisively. "Now, in return, I'd appreciate it if you could do something about some domestic orders for me—not exactly requisitions, more like assignments. It all still comes under the heading of restoring domestic order."

"I'll do what I can." Melles had expected this; trading favor for favor was the accepted way of doing business in Imperial politics. He wouldn't commit himself until he'd heard precisely what Thayer had in mind, but Thayer knew that already.

"Put the Army in charge of all intercity transportation of supplies." Thayer looked him straight in the eyes. "As it is, stuff's being moved inefficiently, *what* gets moved is random, and carters are getting fat no matter what. The Army's suffering, because we're having to pay through the nose, just like the cits are. Conscript the carters, take over the Cartage Guild, make 'em subject to Army discipline, and we'll cure what's causing some of your riots in short order. Every dog in the Empire knows what's going on, and they'll be happy to see the Cartage Guild get what's coming to them. The cits are as tired of the profiteering as I am."

And you and your officers will get fat on the profits, instead of the Cartage Guild. Melles saw right through that one, but Thayer was right about several things. Transportation *was* a hit-or-miss matter right now, and the profits that the carters were making were obscene. Putting the Army in charge would reduce profiteering to an acceptable level, and get transportation organized. And there *had* been unrest over the profiteering; at least one of the riots had destroyed a Cartage Guildhall and the buildings near it.

No, there will be no weeping if I conscript the carters, their beasts, and their vehicles.

The question was, could he get away with that assignment, as an interpretation of the orders that Charliss had just signed?

He unrolled one of his own copies and scanned it quickly, then looked up into Thayer's flat brown eyes. "I think this particular set of commands gives me that authority," he said, knowing that the Emperor wouldn't care so long as he could keep anyone from lodging complaints against it. And since Thayer was going to have pressing reasons to prevent complaints. . . . "When I send out copies of the original orders, I'll see to it that this particular amendment is added."

Thayer smiled with satisfaction. "I'll have my mages get to

work," he promised. "By tomorrow night, there'll be companies picked; by the next day I'll have them moving into barracks in the cities. Don't worry; I'll send orders to select steady men, veterans, men who won't panic, won't shoot unless they're ordered, and won't exceed their orders. I'll send captains who have every reason to keep peace, steady men, not sadists who enjoy breaking heads."

Army efficiency, he thought enviously. *It's a beautiful thing to see working.* "My orders will have to travel by signal and sometimes courier, but they'll get to most of the Empire in a fortnight," he replied, and stood up. "It will be a pleasure working with you, Lord Commander," he finished, holding out his hand as the General stood up.

Thayer took it in another firm handclasp. "An equal pleasure here," he said. "And a damned sight better than working with one of the infernal groat-counters, let me tell you!" He followed at Melles' elbow, quite pleased to accompany his visitor to the door.

Melles knew what he meant; several of the possible candidates for Heir were men less of vision than of caution. Few of them would have the imagination to foresee the riots he knew were bound to come, much less to plan how to quell them. "Just remember—we want our actions to be as unobtrusive as possible—so that the citizens welcome the sight of soldiers in the streets rather than fearing it."

Thayer opened the door to the antechamber for him, nodding vigorously. "Exactly. I'll draw up a set of riot orders for you; you look them over and tell me what you want changed." He waved Melles through. "Grevas, see the Lord Heir out, would you? Lord Melles, I can't thank you enough for coming here yourself."

"Think nothing of it; I am glad that we could reach an understanding so quickly." Melles passed into the antechamber where the secretary received him with a deep bow of respect, then hurried to open the door for him. He waved his thanks at the underling, and entered the cold hallway feeling as if he had done a good day's work indeed.

Now, what else? Orders to requisition food if it's necessary, and it will be. And orders to requisition extra beasts and vehicles from the Estates, placing them in the hands of the Army. Have to specify rules about requisitions; taking a

farmer's only cart and horse is only going to be counterpro-
ductive. Put one of my secretaries on it. Mertun—he was a
farmer's son. That would be enough for now; too many orders
all at once, and it would cause more unease and unrest than
already existed.

And I need to consolidate my personal position. That, fortunately, was mostly a matter of reinforcing his own standing
orders to his special operatives. Those operatives would act as
needed, and bring him the information he required. And insofar as power in the Council of Advisers and the Court went—
well, most mouths would smile and utter compliments, and
he would accept them. Action would speak the real truths,
and his operatives would ferret out what those same mouths
said in private.

There was a single exception to all of that. If the Army
could manage to keep their lines of communication open, it
meant that they were able to get some magics to work. *Proba-*
bly those of short duration; and that may be the secret. That,
and a great deal of power forcing the magics through. I have
power, and I have more than one mage in my own pay. I sim-
ply hadn't thought to apply great power to small goals, but
maybe those goals are not so small after all, now.

He hurried down the corridor to his new quarters, only a
short distance from the General's, and found his own Imperial
bodyguards waiting at the door for him. They opened the door
for him with great ceremony, and he was greeted on the other
side by his own servants, who surrounded him and began fussing over him immediately with great ceremony and a little
fear.

Impatiently, he waved most of them away. His new quarters were fundamentally identical to his old, except that the
rooms were a bit larger, the furnishings (those that were not
his personal gear) more luxurious, and the suite itself was situated better with regard to conveniences. In the time he'd
spent conferring with the Emperor and General Thayer, his
servants had removed all signs of the former occupant, and
had made it seem as if *he* had always lived here. His own car-
pets were on the floor, his tapestries and maps on the walls,
his books in the cases and on the tables. He went straight to
his desk to draft the orders—or rather, elaborations—that
were to be appended to the Imperial Orders he had with him.

When he had finished, he handed the rough drafts to his own secretary, along with the four copies of the Imperial Orders he still retained.

"Take care of these—and have Mertun specify under what conditions a man's beast and vehicle are to be exempt from requisition," he ordered. His secretary bowed and took the papers out. Only then did he permit himself to relax, putting himself into the care of his valet. His secretary would see that three sets of the Orders got into the hands of the Imperial Clerks for distribution and dissemination. One set would remain here, for use as a reference.

He walked into his private chambers at the direction of his valet; with his own furniture here, in the same positions as in his old rooms, he could almost convince himself that nothing had changed.

Almost. *It's begun. I have started the avalanche; there will be no stopping it now.* He allowed his valet to extract him from his stiff coat of heavy, embroidered satin and help him into a much more comfortable robe. Within a short period of time he was settled in a chair beside a fireplace, with food and drink and a book on the table at his right hand.

He stared into the flames, amused and bemused by everything that had happened today. It had certainly been an *eventful* day, and one he would remember for a long time.

Nevertheless, his day was not yet over. He rang for his valet, and when the man appeared, murmured a certain phrase that meant his operatives were to be contacted and called in, one at a time. *My agents will have to watch for some new things now, as well as the old. My mages—well, if the Army can accomplish communicative magics, perhaps there are a few things that we can accomplish, too.*

It occurred to him that although vengeance on his old enemy Tremane was probably out of the question, at least he ought to be sure just exactly what Tremane was up to. Scrying was another magic of limited scope and duration, and it was just possible that enough could be learned by means of scrying to warn him if Tremane was actually a danger to the Empire.

He settled back, sipped hot spiced wine thoughtfully, and waited for the first of his spies to appear. No, much as he would like to, he could not dispose of that annoying Tremane—but he could not ignore the man either.

And in the kind of war *he* waged, the best and most reliable weapon was knowledge.

It was time to wield that particular weapon, and with more finesse and care than he had ever exercised before.

Lo'isha, Kal'enedril, and Silverfox

Four

The cavernous interior of Urtho's Tower was remarkably quiet with the gryphons gone. An'desha hadn't quite realized until now how much sound the gryphons produced—like the constant click of talons on stone, the windlike bellows-sound of their breathing and the rustle of feathers. He'd gotten used to those whispers of sound, and without them, his own voice seemed unnaturally loud despite the sussuration of other activity.

"Look here, it's really quite logical," An'desha said, with one finger under the line of characters—the same words, written in three different languages. Karal peered at them, his forehead creasing with concentration. "This is the Hawkbrother, this is the Shin'a'in, and you can see how similar—"

A muffled *thud* interrupted him, followed by the sound of alarmed and complaining voices. Startled, he looked up, past Karal and into the central room of the Tower.

He knew those voices, although he had not expected to hear them today. He got up and moved to the doorway, just to see if he was somehow mistaken.

He wasn't. The aged Imperial mage Sejanes, in his robes of oddly military cut, was a strange contrast to Master Artificer Levy in his practical, yet luxurious, black silk and leather. Both of them, however, looked pale and ill and much the worse for their travel. Walking ahead of them was Altra.

"By the Hundred Little Gods!" said Sejanes, every hair on his gray head standing straight out. "If I *never* have to travel this way again, it will be too soon!"

Master Levy swallowed, looking to An'desha as if he were

fighting to keep his stomach from revolting. His face had a greenish tint, and the knuckles of his clenched fists were white. "I . . . quite agree with you, Sejanes," he said in a strangled voice. "I believe that, given the option, I will walk home."

Altra looked at both of them with unconcealed contempt, stalking off into Karal's side room to bonelessly flop down onto the foot of Karal's pallet. An'desha followed him. An'desha didn't "hear" the Firecat say anything, but Karal pulled his mostly-untouched bowl of stew over to the cat, who gratefully inhaled it as if he hadn't eaten in weeks.

Meanwhile, Firesong, Lo'isha, Silverfox, and two of the Shin'a'in hurried over to greet the aged mage and younger Master Artificer. There wasn't much in the way of furniture here, but Silverfox brought both of them folding stools to sit on, and they sagged down onto that support with evident gratitude. An'desha didn't blame either of the newcomers for their reactions; he knew from personal experience that they were not exaggerating their exhaustion and illness.

An'desha had traveled once in the care of Altra the Firecat, in the creature's bizarre distance-devouring method of transportation called "Jumping," and he would not particularly care to experience it again. The Firecats were somehow able to cross great distances in the blink of an eye, and could take with them whatever or whoever was touching them. The experience was a gut-wrenching one, similar to a Gate-crossing, but repeated over and over with each Jump. The closer together the Jumps were, the worse the effect was. The amount of cumulative effect varied with each person, but from the look of these two, Altra hadn't paused much between Jumps and this latest journey had been quite a rough ride for them.

An'desha watched for a moment, but Firesong, Silverfox, and the rest seemed to have the situation well in hand. Sejanes clearly needed to go lie down, and Master Levy to sit down and have something to settle his stomach. After a brief rest, both of them were taken into the vacant side chamber that had earlier served as the gryphons' nest. Karal, meanwhile, was fussing over Altra, who, for the first time in An'desha's experience, was looking rather shopworn. Evidently the trip hadn't been easy on him either.

He remembered what Altra had said about the fact that even Jumping had become much more difficult. "Are you feeling all right?" he asked the cat, as Karal hovered over him anxiously.

:*I have felt better,*: the Firecat replied dryly. :*But I believe that with a short rest and food, I shall be fine. The currents in the energy-fields are vicious. It has become very dangerous to Jump even a tenth of my usual distances. I do think that from here on in I, too, would prefer to walk where I need to go, given the choice.*:

The clacking of hooves on the floor signaled the arrival of the Companion Florian. :*Oh, don't be ridiculous, Altra,*: the Companion said mockingly. :*Of course you won't have to walk. You'll convince one of us to carry you.*:

Altra ignored him, pretending to concentrate on the vital task of licking the bowl clean. That didn't take too long, and as soon as the last hint of gravy was gone, he curled up in such a way that he wouldn't be in the way of Karal's feet if the young Karsite needed to rest. :*I'm going to sleep now,*: the Firecat said with great dignity, and he closed his eyes firmly, still ignoring Florian's jibe.

Florian made a whickering sound that was so like a chuckle that there was no doubt in An'desha's mind what the Companion was thinking. "Oh, leave him alone, Florian," he told the Companion. "At least for now. You can't deny that he has done more than his share for some time to come. If Gating is dangerous, how could Jumping be less than hazardous?"

:*True enough,*: Florian replied equitably. :*You are correct, An'desha, and I am at fault here. Altra has served heroically, and I should not have teased him, especially not when he is as exhausted as his passengers. I beg your pardon, cat.*:

:*And I grant it, horse,*: came from the seemingly-sleeping Firecat.

Florian stepped over and touched his nose to the Firecat's fur in a conciliatory gesture, then backed off to the chamber entrance. He stood with one eye cast toward the main chamber, and the other watching over Altra and his friends, before finally quietly clopping off.

"Well. We have everyone we need," An'desha said to Karal, "Except perhaps that Kaled'a'in scholar we have been promised. We can certainly resume investigating the other devices we found."

"I keep thinking that there are more rooms and chambers

we haven't found yet," Karal replied, lying back down on his pallet, taking care to not to disturb Altra.

"There probably are," An'desha told him. "We've found signs of at least four more places where there might be storage chambers or even a passage to a lower level. The problem is that we haven't been able to get them open. Perhaps Sejanes or Master Levy will be able to help there." He smiled at his friend. "To tell you the truth, I suspect it will be Master Levy; I have the feeling that the tricks to getting these hatches open are purely mechanical."

Karal smiled back. "I think you may be right. That would fit well enough with what Treyvan was able to tell me about the Mage of Silence. It would be like him to put a mechanical catch in a place of magic, knowing that anyone who came here intending mischief would probably be expecting magic and not be prepared for mechanics."

An'desha chuckled. "And that would certainly put Firesong's nose out of joint. Poor Firesong! At every turn, it seems as if his great powers as an Adept are less and less important!"

Karal nodded and rubbed the back of his neck in thought. "It must be awfully difficult for him to face each day. Just look at what has happened. He went from being the brightest star in the skies to . . . finding his powers unreliable and lessened, with new methods to do what he used to do coming up every day. Some of them are even contradictory to what he has known as fact all his life."

An'desha frowned and nodded. "Sometimes I feel like I cheated him out of his glory by being who and what I am, but I know that none of us dictated or could have predicted the way things would unfold. I owe him my life, by the Star-Eyed's grace, and I am grateful to him, but I wish that he could feel the happiness now that he used to enjoy in the Vales. And as for things being contradictory—you've been experiencing much of that yourself, spiritually. So have we all, I think." He paused, fingers tented as he carefully considered his next words. "Still—Master Levy says that all things in our world, no matter how illogical they may seem, are still consistent under unseen laws. The spirits I have spoken with on the Moonpaths have implied much the same—that magic in all its forms works under those laws as surely as rain, wind, and beasts do. Perhaps Firesong, and all of us, are learning new aspects of the laws we have been subject to all our lives."

"With Master Levy here to confound us all with his teachings on universal laws, you'll need me for a secretary again," Karal said as he smoothed down his warm robes, brightening considerably. "I'll be glad to be useful again."

An'desha nodded with sympathy; he knew how idleness, even enforced, had fretted his friend, and he would also be glad to see Karal feeling as if he were contributing his share. Realistically, Karal was not able to help at all with brute-force physical tasks, but the role of secretary was perfect for him.

He would have said something, but he noticed that Karal seemed very tired, and it occurred to him that the two of them had been working quite steadily on comparing Shin'a'in, Tayledras, and Kaled'a'in writing ever since breakfast. Mental work could be just as exhausting as physical labor, even for those, like Karal, who had a knack for it.

"Why don't you look after Altra for a while," he said, cleverly using the Firecat as an excuse to get Karal to rest. "I'll go see if our hosts want to know anything about Sejanes and Master Levy."

Karal nodded, and caressed Altra with one hand while he closed his eyes. An'desha collected the empty stew bowl and made a mental note to get something more suited to Altra's tastes from the Shin'a'in.

He left Karal beginning to doze, Altra already asleep, and Florian watching over them both, and went out into the main chamber in the center of the Tower. Master Levy, already recovered, was examining the floor of that chamber on his hands and knees. He looked up as An'desha entered.

"Has anyone looked at the floor here?" he asked.

"We looked, but we didn't see anything," the Shin'a'in replied. "Why? Have you found something?"

"Perhaps." Master Levy got to his feet. "When I was still studying, I used to earn spending money by designing and helping to build hidden doors and chambers for wealthy or eccentric clients. I think there might be something here."

"Huh." An'desha looked closely at the floor, and had to shake his head. "I'll take your word for it. Do you think you can get it open—if there is anything there?"

"Perhaps," Master Levy repeated. "I'll have to examine it later, when I'm not exhausted. This is all sheer nervous energy, you see, plus a rather stupid wish to seem in better physical shape than old Sejanes, and it's all about to run out. I'm

going to get a bowl of that stew I smell, and then I am going
to sleep for a day."

An'desha laughed, as Master Levy shrugged ruefully and
with self-deprecation. As the Master Artificer drifted in the
direction of their little charcoal stove and the bubbling stew-
pot atop it, he started back toward Karal. But halfway there,
he turned, a little surprised, as a soft voice hailed him.

It was one of the few black-clad Kal'enedral, and with him
was another wearing dark blue. The one in black he knew;
Ter'hala, an old man whose blood-feud would technically
never be completed, because the one who murdered his oath-
brother had been Mornelithe Falconsbane. It was doubly
ironic that An'desha and Ter'hala had become friends over the
past few days. Ter'hala knew who and what he had been, of
course. An'desha, understandably nervous, had asked him
why he continued to wear black; Ter'hala had laughed and
said that he was used to the color and too old to change.

"Ter'hala!" An'desha greeted him. "Who is your friend?"

The Kal'enedral sketched a salute of greeting. "This is
Che'sera, young friend. He wished to meet you."

An'desha bowed slightly. "I am always honored to meet one
of the servants of the Wise One," he said politely, though he
could not for the life of him imagine what had brought so
many of the reclusive "Scrollsworn"—as he called them, to
distinguish them from the true Swordsworn—out of
Kata'shin'a'in and their stronghold there. "We are all truly
grateful for the hospitality and tolerance you have shown to
us."

*I wonder if the reason is that we've just added two more
meddlers to the group, and one of them is a mage from a
completely unknown land,* he thought, though he kept his
thoughts to himself. *Not that I blame them. We're the interlopers here; the Star-Eyed gave* them *the keeping of this
Tower and its secrets, not us.*

Che'sera returned his bow. "I am pleased to meet you,
An'desha," he replied, his voice so carefully neutral that
An'desha could not read any second meaning into the words.
"It is not often that one of the Plains who goes to become a
mage ever returns again."

"It is not often that the shamans permit him to return,"
An'desha replied, as calmly and carefully as he could, although he could in no way match the lack of inflection in

Che'sera's voice. "Until only recently, mages have been forbidden the Plains, even those of the People."

"Well, and you can certainly see why," Che'sera countered immediately, gesturing at the Tower remains about them. "This would all have been a great temptation. Can you say, had you become a mage of the Tale'edras, that you would not have been tempted to try to use one of these weapons against the one they called Falconsbane?"

An'desha shuddered. He still had far too many of Falconsbane's memories of the life he had led using An'desha's body for comfort—and behind those memories, marched others, a seemingly endless parade of atrocities stretching back into a dim past as ancient as this Tower.

"I would," he admitted slowly. "I would have been tempted by anything that might have brought the monster down. Anything that would have saved others from the horror he wrought."

Che'sera shrugged. "And yet it took *how* many of you, working together, to simply use the energy of one of these weapons rather than the weapon itself?"

"And yet you permit us here now." An'desha allowed one eyebrow to rise.

"We do, and that is in part why I wished to speak with you," Che'sera told him. "May we speak privately, you and I, for a little while, Shin'a'in to Shin'a'in?"

Now An'desha was considerably more surprised, and not at all certain what Che'sera had in mind. This was the first time in his reckoning that any of the Shin'a'in here had addressed him in such a fashion; most seemed uncomfortable with the concept of a Shin'a'in who was also a mage, and some seemed of the personal opinion that his half-foreign blood made him more alien than Shin'a'in. "Certainly, if that is what you wish." He nodded toward the sleeping chamber. "My friend Karal is asleep in there; he will not hear us, and if we speak quietly, we will not disturb him. I fear that is the most privacy I can offer, as it is in somewhat short supply here despite the vastness of the place."

Che'sera nodded. "That will do," he said, and gestured to An'desha to lead him onward.

An'desha did so, walking with great care past Karal and Altra, although neither stirred, nor in fact gave any indication that they were alive except for their steady breathing. At the moment he was suffering from mixed feelings; he was both curious and apprehensive to hear what Che'sera wanted to say that required privacy.

He gestured at his own pallet, waiting until Che'sera took a seat at the foot before seating himself.

"So," he said, wondering what he was letting himself in for. "What is it you wish of me, Sworn One?"

When Che'sera left him at last, he sat back against the gently-curving stone wall and simply thought of nothing for a while. He felt as if Che'sera had taken his mind, had turned it upside-down and shaken it, examined it, poked and prodded it, turned it inside out, and then, when he was finished, put it all neatly back in place with the ends tucked in.

He had probably been the most skillful interrogator that An'desha *or* any of Falconsbane's many incarnations had ever encountered. *You know, I suspect that at this point he could predict my reaction to virtually any situation, and do so with more accuracy than I could!*

Although his questions had covered virtually every subject, Che'sera seemed particularly interested in the Avatars. That was the one thing that hadn't surprised him, since virtually all of the Sworn had wanted to know about Dawnfire and Tre'valen sooner or later. Some of them here had actually been present when Dawnfire, trapped in the body of her bondbird, had been transformed into an Avatar in the first place. It had occurred to An'desha that as far as *he* was concerned, such a transformation was a poor substitute for returning Dawnfire to her proper human form. But then again, perhaps that had not been possible; granted, the Star-Eyed had been able to undo most of the changes Falconsbane had run on An'desha's own body, but that was in the nature of restoring something to its rightful state, not changing it into something else altogether.

Perhaps all that She would have been able to manage would have been transformation into a tervardi, *one of the bird-people, and that might have been a truly cruel "reward" for her, since the* tervardi *are frail and not very humanlike. At least this way, she is still fundamentally herself and she is anything but frail.*

He also sensed that there were other complications to the

story that no one had told him about. And there was, of course, the factor that Dawnfire had been mourned for dead, and her human body buried when the bond to it was snapped by Falconsbane. It didn't necessarily do for a deity to resurrect people; the question would inevitably arise: "Why this one and not *my* father, mother, sibling, lover." Better, on the whole, not to do any such thing. Look at all the effort that the Companions went to in order to preserve the secret of their own nature, and they weren't even returning as humans!

Just such philosophical questions had arisen in the course of Che'sera's questioning—though on his part, rather than Che'sera's—and the Sworn One had neatly deflected them. Perhaps it had been because Che'sera wanted him to think of possible answers for himself; there had been that kind of feeling as the conversation progressed.

And in all of that, I didn't learn a thing about Che'sera himself. Now that was truly unusual, since Falconsbane had been a rather skilled interrogator and some of that expertise was available to An'desha. Given the proper occasion, that was one of Falconsbane's abilities that An'desha did not mind coopting, but he had not been able to insert so much as a single personal question of his own the entire time the two of them spoke. Che'sera was most unusual, even for the Sworn.

An'desha rubbed his temples, feeling as if he should have a headache after all that Che'sera had put him through, even though he did not.

Activity, that was what was called for. There were dishes to wash, there was clothing to mend, and there were all manner of things to be done. Or perhaps he ought to go look at the food supplies the Shin'a'in had brought, and see if there was something more that could be done with them than the seemingly-endless round of soups and stews they had been presented with thus far. He wasn't precisely a grand cook, but he did have experience in dishes that no one else here did.

He rose and went in search of something useful to do.

The clothing and kitchen work had already been taken care of, but as it turned out, there was something new he could concoct in the way of dinner for them all. There was fresh meat, brought in by Shin'a'in hunters; there were beans and a few other winter vegetables such as onions, and there were spices and dried peppers. That particular combination reminded him of a recipe Karal had made up for him once, when they'd been too late to catch dinner with either the Court or the Heraldic students. He diced some of the meat and hot peppers and browned them together, added onions, beans and sweet spice, and set it all to cook slowly. While all of those ingredients had been used before, no one in the group had ever used them in that combination. It would definitely be different from anything the Shin'a'in had been cooking, and that was what he was looking for.

It had taken a long time to dice the meat as finely as the recipe called for, and having his hands busy allowed his mind to rest. His mind wasn't the only thing resting, however, and although Karal was still sleeping, others were awake again. At about the time he finished with his concoction, Master Levy was out in the main room on his hands and knees, looking intently at the floor, and prying at invisible cracks with some very tiny tools he took from a pouch at his belt.

An'desha washed up the utensils he'd used for his preparations, dried his hands, and went out to join him, though no one else seemed at all interested in what he was doing. "Is there anything I can do to help?" he asked, sitting on his heels just behind the Master Artificer.

"Well, there *is* something here, all right," Master Levy replied in an absent tone. "This is a movable stone, and I would guess that it drops down and fits into a slot carved into the rock. It may take me a while to figure out the release, though. Tell me something, do you have any idea if this mage thought in patterns, in *numbers* of things? As in—oh, the Karsites think in terms of one, seven, or eight—if they build a device with a catch, it will either have a single trigger-point or seven. That's because they have a single God, but in the usual representations of Vkandis as the sun rising, there are seven rays coming from it and in the ones of the sun-in-glory there are eight rays. The Rethwellans almost always use three, for the three faces of their Goddess. Most Valdemarans use three or two, three for the same reason as the Rethwellans, or two for the God and Goddess. It's not a conscious thing, it's just the kind of patterns that people establish as very small children."

"You might try four," An'desha said, after a moment of thought. "Urtho shared the Kaled'a'in faith, if he shared anything religious with anyone, and that's the same as the Shin'a'in. Except where it's free-flowing and curvy, there's a great deal of square and diamond symmetry in the decorations around here."

Master Levy grunted what sounded like thanks, and seemed to widen his scope of examination a bit.

Finally he sat back on his haunches, stretched all his fingers and shook his head. "Shall we see if we're supremely lucky and we're not dealing with a random placing?" he asked An'desha, his saturnine face showing rather more humor than An'desha was used to seeing from him. "If your guess is right, I think I've found all four trigger points; if *mine* is right, this far inside his Tower Urtho would not have bothered to be terribly clever about hiding his additional workrooms and the catches won't be difficult. I don't suppose you've got a clue about an order in which to push four trigger-points, do you?"

"If you're not supposed to push all of them at once, you mean?" An'desha thought again. "East, South, West, and North. That's the order in rituals, with the Maiden being in the East and the Crone in the North."

"That sounds as good a guess as any. Let's see what happens."

Master Levy reached out with one of his tools, but An'desha shot out a hand to stop him. "Wait a minute!" he stammered. "If you do this wrong, is anything likely to—well—go wrong? Will the ceiling fall in and crush us, or poison gas start seeping in here, or something?"

Master Levy paused. "There is that possibility," he began, and laughed at An'desha's expression. "Oh, for Haven's sake, it's not very likely he'd put someting like that *in the floor* now, is it? Where it might be triggered by accident just by people standing on it?"

An'desha flushed, embarrassed. "I suppose not," he replied, letting go of Master Levy's hand.

The Master Artificer continued his interrupted task, depressing a small spot in the stone of the floor. An'desha noted with fascination that it remained depressed so that if one had placed a coin on the spot, it would be flush with the rest of the floor. Master Levy then touched a second, and a third, both of which also remained depressed after he touched them, and although An'desha had not been able to spot the second place, once he had the distance between the first and second, he was able to deduce the locations of the third and fourth spot before

Master Levy touched them. An'desha held his breath in anticipation when the Master Artificer pushed on that last place.

Nothing happened for a long moment, and An'desha sighed
with disappointment. Master Levy, however, had his head
cocked to one side, and as An'desha sighed, he stood up,
looked fixedly at a place in the pattern of the floor shaped like
an octagon, then stamped sharply down on one corner of it
with his boot heel.

With a reluctant, grating sound, the stone moved a trifle,
dropping down by about the width of a thumb.

Master Levy stamped downward again, and the stone
moved a bit more. "It's stuck. Old, you know," he quipped.
He continued urging it with carefully-placed blows of his heel,
as it dropped down about the distance of a man's hand measured from the end of the middle finger to the wrist, then
began to slide sideways. Once there was a sliver of a gap between the octagonal stone and the rest of the floor, he got
down on hands and knees again, and peered at it.

By now, thanks to the sounds of stamping and the grating
of stone-on-stone, he had attracted the attention of everyone
in the Tower who was not asleep. "Will you look at that!"
Silverfox exclaimed, as the curious gathered around. "We
never guessed that was there!"

"I am looking at it. I think I'm going to need something to
pry with," Master Levy replied. "The mechanisms are rather
stuck, which shouldn't be too surprising considering their age.
I'm afraid once I get this open, it's not going to shut again."

"I don't see a problem with that," Firesong said, dropping
down on his heels to peer at the stone himself, beside Master
Levy, while Silverfox went off to get a pry bar from a Plains-
man. "If there's anything down there worth bothering with,
we wouldn't want to close it, and if there isn't, we'll clean out
the trash and use it for sleeping quarters or something."

Master Levy grunted and nodded his head as he felt along
the crack with great care, then put his nose to the crack to
sniff at it gingerly. "I don't smell anything that shouldn't be
down there," he said after a long moment while he concentrated on the scent with his eyes closed. "And I always did
have the best nose in my year-group. When the students were
experimenting, my Alchemy Master always used to count on
me to know when to evacuate the workroom if something
went wrong."

"Comforting, considering there might be a mechanism to release poisons into the room below, if not this one," said Sejanes, coming up to the rest with his hair all rumpled from sleeping. Silverfox arrived at that moment with the pry bar and shook his head at the Imperial mage.

"Not Urtho, and especially not in his own Tower," the *kestra'chern* said decisively. "He was a compassionate and considerate man, safe and resourceful but not vengeful. He would only create wards to protect things, not to punish. He wouldn't have taken the risk that a curious *hertasi* or some other innocent might set such a thing loose."

Sejanes looked skeptical, but didn't say anything. Silverfox, however, read the look correctly.

"You're not dealing with the Empire, Sejanes," he said. "You're not dealing with people looking to gain in rank by whatever means it takes. Urtho's personal servants and close friends were loyal enough to die for him—and many did, to his sorrow. Here in the heart of his personal stronghold, he would not have used safeguards that could harm his own people as well as intruders."

Master Levy inserted the tongue of the pry bar in the crack, and pulled.

The stone grated, and moved slightly, then kept on moving for a little after Master Levy stopped pulling. Now the gap was about as wide as a large man's palm.

"Do we want to investigate before we open this any further?" the Artificer asked Silverfox. "I defer to your judgment, since you seem to know more about the master of this place than anyone else here."

Silverfox looked pointedly at An'desha, who shook his head in answer to the silent question. "My knowledge is tainted, since it comes from his enemy," he said at once. "Ma'ar is far more likely to have underestimated a foe he considered sentimental and soft."

"It wouldn't hurt to drop a lantern down on a string," Silverfox said to Master Levy. "Then at least we'll be able to see what we're dealing with. For all we know, this is just a well, and not any kind of a storeroom or workroom."

"A source of water other than melted snow from the surface would be welcome," Lo'isha murmured quietly. Master Levy heard him, and nodded in answer to both statements.

This time it was An'desha's turn to go off and rummage for

a lantern and some appropriately strong string. They hadn't needed lanterns since they arrived here, although the Shin'a'in had brought some, just in case the magical lights failed. The magic lamps hanging from the center of the ceiling of each room had been quite enough to serve their needs and showed no signs of being harmed at all by the mage-storms that made magic problematic outside the Tower. An'desha dug one of the lanterns out of a pile of articles no one had found a use for, and got some string from the kitchen area. He filled the lamp with oil, trimmed the wick with thread clippers from a sewing kit, and lit it before bringing it out to the rest.

Master Levy made the handle fast to the string and lowered the lantern down into the cavity while the others crowded around. An'desha couldn't see anything from his vantage, and neither could most of the Shin'a'in.

"Well?" called Che'sera. "What's there?"

"Stairs, mostly," Master Levy replied. "So this isn't a well. I believe I see something like furniture at the bottom, but the light doesn't go very far down."

"It's not dimming in bad air, is it?" An'desha asked anxiously, vague memories of tomb openings intruding from one of Falconsbane's previous lives. "Even if there are no poisons, the air could have gone bad from what's been sealed inside."

"No, it's burning brightly enough. It's just a long way down to the next floor and the light is between me and what's down there," Master Levy replied. "It is an issue of contrast and visual acuity. Well, no help for it. Back to hard labor."

He inserted the tongue of the pry bar and continued to lever the stubborn stone out of the way, while at least a couple of the observers looked at each other, wondering why the Artificer used such flowery terms to say he couldn't see well. Suddenly, with no warning whatsoever, the frozen mechanism gave way. The stone slid beneath the floor into hiding, and Master Levy, taken completely off guard, fell over backward, the pry bar dropping out of his hands and clanging end-over-end down the staircase.

Only An'desha remained to assist the winded Artificer to his feet; the rest of the spectators made a rush for the stair with Firesong in the lead. In mere moments they had descended out of sight; then Firesong spoke a single word, light poured up from below, and muffled exclamations were drifting up through the hole in the floor.

"You might say 'thank you!' " Master Levy called after them, and sighed, rubbing his hip where he had landed. "We may as well go find out what they've discovered. I only hope it isn't Urtho's treasury; there isn't a great deal of good that gold and gems would do us in this situation."

"Urtho's treasury would have books, not baubles," An'desha assured him. "But we ought to go down, too, before they all get carried away in their enthusiasm."

Master Levy went with An'desha following him, taking the stone stairs carefully, for they were quite steep. They also went down farther than he expected, for the stone floor of the room above was at least as thick as his hand was long, perhaps a little thicker, which accounted for the fact that it hadn't rung hollow and had sounded like solid stone to their footsteps. It looked as if this room had actually been hollowed out of the bedrock after the Tower itself had been built.

Although the air was a bit stuffy and very dusty, with a hint of strange metallic scents, it was not at all damp. Nor was the room as gloomy and ill-lit as An'desha had anticipated. There were more of those magical lights everywhere, and as An'desha looked around, he had no doubt at all just what Urtho had used this room for. It was a workshop, with everything necessary for an inveterate tinkerer who was interested in literally everything.

Needless to say, the room was very crowded, despite the fact that it was just a little smaller than the main room above. This was not a mage's classical workroom, a place where *only* magic took place, and few if any physical components were needed. This was a place where anything and everything could be worked with, played with, investigated. Here was a bench with an array of glassware and rows of jars that had once held chemicals both liquid and solid—most of the former long since evaporated, leaving only dust or oily residue in the bottoms of their bottles. There stood another bench with a small lathe, clamps, a vise, and tools for working wood and ivory, and beside it a similar bench with the tools for shaping soft metals, and a third bench with the tools for cutting and polishing lenses, glass, and crystal. Looking incongruous beside that was a potter's wheel and glassblower's pipes, and along the back wall were a forge, a kiln, a glassmaker's furnace, and a smelter. They probably had once shared a chimney, long since blocked up by the destruction of the Tower above. There were more benches and work spaces set up, but from the staircase An'desha could not tell what they were, only that most of them had been in use up to the day of the Cataclysm.

An'desha simply stood and stared as the others wandered about, looking, but not touching. Master Levy, on the other hand, looked supremely satisfied by what he saw, as he surveyed it all from the staircase.

"Now this is much more in my way of doing things," he said, folding his arms across his chest and looking over the workshop with approval. "I believe I could have liked this Urtho."

On all of the benches—*all* of them—were projects in various states of completion. It was difficult to tell what some of them had been intended to do, if anything. There were pages of notes arrayed neatly beside each of these projects; it appeared that, in his workplace at least, Urtho was a tidy and methodical man. Firesong stood beside a particular bench laden with some very odd equipment indeed. He gazed on these pieces of paper with longing, although he forbore to touch them.

"This is maddening," he complained, hovering over a small sheaf of scrawled manuscript. "I'm afraid even to breathe on these things for fear that they'll fall to dust, but I think I may die if I can't read what's on the next page!"

But something about the way the "paper" looked stirred echoes in An'desha's deepest memories; he descended the last few stairs and made his way over to what appeared to be a small jeweler's workbench. There was a half-finished brooch there, nothing magical or mechanical, obviously *just* a piece of jewelry in the shape of a hummingbird to be inlaid with a mosaic of tiny agate-pieces formed into stylized feathers. "Wait," he muttered. The original design lay next to it, and after a close examination of the sheet, An'desha picked it up.

Silverfox stifled a gasp, and Firesong bit off a protest. He waved the intact and flexible drawing at them to prove it was not hurt by handling.

"Pick up what you want," he urged, "It's not paper. Or rather, it isn't like the paper we know and use now. It's a special rag-paper treated with resins so it wouldn't disintegrate.

You can write on it in silverpoint, crayon, or graphite-stick, but not ink; ink just beads up and won't penetrate."

"Really?" Master Levy walked to the bench nearest him and picked up another piece of the paper. "Very useful around chemicals, I would guess."

"Very useful around anything that might ruin your notes," Firesong observed, snatching up the papers he had stared at so covetously. "Oh—now *this*—oh, my—" He held the papers up so that Silverfox could peruse them, too, as between them they tried to decipher Urtho's notes in ancient Kaled'a'in, using the Hawkbrother tongue Firesong knew and Silverfox's modern Kaled'a'in as guides.

Che'sera looked at them curiously, but Lo'isha laughed at their immediate absorption. "Oh, we have lost them for a time," he said indulgently. "I know that look. The weaver is one with the loom!"

"Not entirely," Firesong responded absently. "But I will be very pleased when this scholar of Silverfox's shows up, so he can help us with this. If these notes are right, this *may* be the answer to our isolation here." He waved a hand at the bench and what looked to be a pair of mirrors serving as the lids to a matching pair of boxes. "These are completed, or all but some cosmetic frippery, and they're *supposed* to act like a pair of linked scrying spells, except they don't use true-magic, they use mind-magic. Apparently it can work over—unknown, incredible distances. Somehow they amplify it so that it only needs *one* person with mind-magic to make both boxes work, or so I think this says."

That made every head in the place turn toward the Adept, and he finally looked up from the notes he was sharing with Silverfox, shaking his hair out of his eyes. "Got your attention then, did I?" he asked, with a sly smile.

:*If these devices use mind-magic, they won't be disrupted by the mage-storms,*: commented a mental voice from above, and Altra flowed gracefully down the staircase, taking a seat on one of the steps at about head-height to the humans. :*That would be more than merely useful. If we learned how to use them, I could take one to Haven; if we learned how to make them, I could take another to Solaris. And I certainly have enough mind-magic to make them work, no matter who wishes to use them.*:

"I thought you said that you didn't want to Jump anymore," Firesong said sardonically. An'desha chuckled.

:I don't want to, but devices like these could replace that aspect of my duties as well as give us the resources of all of Master Levy's colleagues at Haven,: the Firecat replied with immense dignity. *:For that matter, if we could concoct a third device, I would not necessarily have to Jump it to Solaris; Hansa could come and get it instead.:*

An'desha hid a smile at the unspoken implication behind Altra's statement, an implication that Altra felt his colleague and fellow Firecat had been getting off a bit too easily in the transportation department.

:Our ability to Jump is partly true-magic, partly mind-magic,: the Firecat continued, for once without any hint of irony or mockery in his mind-voice. *:It is growing hazardous for passengers to Jump with us, as Master Levy and Sejanes discovered. It is no longer comfortable for us to Jump very long distances, and I was not exaggerating earlier about how I felt when we arrived. I was exhausted and drained, not a common occurrence until now. I can predict a time very soon when it could become actually inconceivably dangerous for us to Jump. But if we have a way to communicate with Haven and Karse—such a thing would be beyond price.:*

"I *had* deduced that for myself, thank you," Firesong replied with a touch of acid. "If you can just conjure up that Kaled'a'in scholar, we have a chance of learning how to use these things before the time comes when you can't take one back to Valdemar."

"The scholar will be here soon," Che'sera put in, looking up from the glassware bench. His dark-blue clothing reflected richly from the surface of the dusty glassware. "The main problem has been that since his assistant is a—what do you call the lizard-folk—?"

"*Hertasi*," Silverfox interjected. The handsome *kestra'-chern's* face lit up at Che'sera's words. "Ah, so it *is* Tarrn who is coming! Oh, that is very good, he may be frail, but he is the finest scholar in the ancient version of our tongue outside the lands of White Gryphon, and a good being as well." Silverfox seemed immensely relieved by what Che'sera had said, and that in itself made An'desha feel as if they were all beginning to make some progress at last.

"Yes. It seems the problem has been to find a way to bring

both of them in a gryphon four-harness carry-basket and still keep the *hertasi* warm without magic." Che'sera left the glassware-bench, and moved back toward the staircase. "When I left, a means had been devised, and they were planning on arriving within two or three days of when I expected to be here. They had only to manufacture this device, whatever it was, and then they could leave. I would have told you earlier, when I first arrived, but you all seemed quite busy, and I had business with An'desha that I wished to conclude before I dealt with anything else."

"That is even better news!" Now Firesong seemed much happier as well, so much so that he forbore to comment on that last statement. "I vote that if we can't, on superficial examination, find anything more important to investigate than these devices, we'll concentrate on those for our immediate goal. If we can communicate with all of the mages and Artificers on a regular basis, it will be as good as being at Haven with all the advantages of being here in the Tower to implement what we deduce."

He looked around at the rest of the party, most of whom shrugged with indifference or bafflement. "You and Sejanes should be the ones to decide. I'll be of very little use without a translator in any event," Master Levy said with great candor. "At the moment, I have nothing really to work on, as I believe we need to develop a new set of theories to match the changed conditions. Those, I feel, must come from things we can learn by studying the Cataclysm itself and Urtho's own methodologies. So until the translator arrives, what I can and will do, is attempt to find out if this place holds any more secrets in the floor."

"Very little use!" Firesong actually snorted. "After you were the one who *found* this place! No false modesty, thank you, Master Levy!"

"I may be of some slight assistance here below," Che'sera said, with great caution. "I shall examine those objects that seem to partake of the nature of the shaman, and see if I may make something of them. We Shin'a'in lost some things when the Cataclysm destroyed our land and sundered the Clans. I may be able to rediscover some of what was lost, and that may be of some help."

Hah! An'desha thought with triumph. *Now I know what you are, o mysterious one! Both Sworn to the Old One and a*

*shaman! Now, is it a need to keep an eye on all these mages
that brings you here, or was it the hope of keeping us from
finding things that the Clans would rather we didn't learn? Is
it an interest in what you might find within the walls of this
Tower, or is it something else altogether? Myself, perhaps?*

It could be, but he was not going to have the hubris to assume that the latter was the case. There were plenty of reasons for the Kal'enedral to want a shaman here; most of the
Sworn were not *leshy'a* with a direct link to the Star-Eyed,
though they could all walk the Moonpaths when they chose.
Although An'desha had seen more than one or two of the
Veiled Ones about, they had never stayed for very long, and he
had the feeling that they were not "permitted" to take a physical form for too long—perhaps just long enough to serve some
specific need, or be in themselves a kind of message.

*The Moonpaths . . . perhaps I ought to go walk them my-
self. I haven't seen or spoken to Tre'valen and Dawnfire since
we burned out that weapon of Urtho's.*

Firesong looked up, as if distracted for a moment, and cast
a speculative look at An'desha. "You know," he began, "it is
all too fortuitous, that we find these things."

An'desha smiled a little as he noticed Che'sera looking at
him in a similar way. He heard himself saying, "It is the way
of the Star-Eyed to provide such opportunities for those who
will help themselves. If I were you, I'd be careful with these
new finds, for She is unlikely to hand over easy answers. The
mind that controls the hand must use the tool wisely, and all
tools can harm their user."

Firesong grunted, and actually looked for a moment as if he
could be considering those words in the way a Shin'a'in would
acknowledge the cryptic advice of a shaman as being worthy
of meditation. Then the Adept shrugged a little and made off
with the sheaf of notes.

An'desha looked about the workshop to see what the others
were doing; Che'sera cracked a slight smile and rejoined
Lo'isha, huddling together over a workbench's treasures in the
far corner. Sejanes was examining the bench with some of the
equipment that An'desha could not immediately identify.
Firesong and Silverfox were halfway up the staircase in no
time, with their papers in their hands, chattering to one another and ignoring everything else about them. Master Levy
was already back up on what An'desha was now thinking of as

the "ground" floor, and Karal was probably still asleep. There might or might not be other Kal'enedral besides Che'sera about; they preferred to spend much of their time in the camp on the surface, and since he had arbitrarily taken care of dinner preparations, there was really no need for any of them to be inside the Tower at this point. This would be as good a time as any to walk the Moonpaths undisturbed.

He went up the stairs as quietly as he could, nodding to Altra on the way. The Firecat nodded back with immense dignity, then turned to follow Firesong and Silverfox, tail waving like a jaunty banner. Evidently *he* wanted to hear what they were up to, probably because they were the most interesting creatures in the Tower at this moment.

An'desha turned his steps in toward the sleeping chamber. Karal was, indeed, still asleep. He noticed as he paused in the doorway that Master Levy was in the side chamber where An'desha and Karal had found indications of another trapdoor. The Artificer was back down on his hands and knees and peering at the pattern in the floor. Florian was beside him, occasionally tapping a hoof on the stone at his direction.

An'desha tiptoed past Karal to his own sleeping place. *You know, if I look more as if I'm taking a nap, I'm less likely to be disturbed.* He pulled off his boots and curled up in his bedroll, arranging himself in what he thought was a very natural-looking position.

It occurred to him as he closed his eyes that he was being very secretive about this, when there really was no reason for him to do so. *On the other hand, I don't think I want Che'sera to know everything I'm doing until I know more about him.* If Che'sera turned out to be as rigid and inflexible as Jarim first was, or as hidebound as the shaman of An'desha's home Clan, it would be easier to keep away from him and his demands if he wasn't aware of everything An'desha knew or could do. *All I've told him is that the Avatars appear to me, not that I can go look for them. I think I'll keep it that way for now.*

He settled himself comfortably, then slowed his breathing and began the combination of relaxation and tension that marked a Moonpath trance. This, for those who were not trained in the technique, was more difficult than it sounded; too much tension and the trance state would never be reached, too much relaxation brought on a nap rather than a trance. Once he hovered on the edge of trance, with all of his attention focused, and nothing from the "real" world intruding, he sent his mind going *in*, and then *out*, in the pattern that Tre'valen had shown him, that felt like so very long ago.

He found himself, in his vision, standing on a path made of silvery sand that sparkled with a subdued glimmer, in the midst of an opalescent mist that swirled all around him. Or rather, he *seemed* to be standing there; this body was an illusory one, and he could change it to another form if he concentrated on it. This was a comfortable form, one he didn't have to think about to maintain, and it didn't seem reasonable to waste time and energy changing it to something else. He still was not certain if the Moonpaths themselves were an illusion; he had never bothered to test his surroundings to find out. The mist had no scent, and was neither cool nor warm; the sand beneath his feet neither so soft as to impede his steps, nor so hard as to be noteworthy.

"Tre'valen?" he called out into the mist, his voice echoing off into the distance in a way that had no counterpart in the real world. "Dawnfire?" The mist swirled about him, following his words with eddies of faint colors that faded within moments.

He had no answer immediately, but he didn't expect one. The Avatars were not in existence to serve and please *him*, after all, and he was well aware of that. Instead, he moved out along the path of soft sand, occasionally calling the names of his friends quietly into the mist. Eventually, if they were not occupied with something more important, they would come to him.

And so they did. They came winging through the mist in their bird shapes, forms the shape of a vorcel-hawk, but the size of a human, and with the sparkling, fiery, multicolored plumage of a firebird. He knew they were coming before they arrived, for they lit up the mist in the far distance like lightning within a thundercloud as they flew toward him, their flight paths spiraling around each other, leaving a double helix of light through the fog in their wakes.

Here they did not need to backwing to a landing as they would if they had taken "real" hawk-forms in the world. They simply slowed, then went into a hover above the path, then flowed into the vaguely avian-human shapes they normally wore to speak to him. Tre'valen was dressed as the Shin'a'in shaman he had been before he became the Star-Eyed's Avatar; but Dawnfire, though clearly Tayledras rather than Shin'a'in, wore a simple tunic that could not be readily identified as coming from any particular culture. Her long silver hair moved slightly, like the mist that swirled slowly about her. They both seemed to be completely ordinary humans—except for their eyes.

Not eyes, but eye-shaped windows on the night sky . . . the darkness of all of night spangled with the brightest of stars. So beautiful. . . .

It was said that Kal'enel Herself had eyes like that; in this way She marked these two as Her Avatars, a way that could not be mistaken for anything else.

"Younger Brother!" Tre'valen greeted him warmly. "It is far too long since we have seen you, but I pledge that we have not been idle in that interval!"

"Not all that long for a mere mortal," he corrected with a smile, "but a great deal has been happening to us as well. I was not certain if you knew about what we have uncovered and learned, and besides that, I wanted to make sure that you two were all right after the Working."

Not that I could have done *anything if they weren't.*

Dawnfire shrugged fluidly. "Poor young Karal bore the brunt of our Working, and we two were only a little drained," she said, and extended a cool hand to him, which he took in brief greeting. "It sounds as if you have not been idle either—you in the Tower."

That confirmed one of his guesses, that the Avatars, for all their power, were neither omniscient nor omnipotent. They were bound by some physical laws at least. Was that because they were not really physically "dead," as the spirit-Kal'enedral were? Or was it because they had been granted wider powers by the Star-Eyed?

"Would you like to tell me what you can, or hear what news I have first?" he asked.

"Your news; I suspect that much of what we have to tell you will be mere confirmation of what you already know," Tre'valen told him. "We have been ranging far in the world and in the Void, to see what changes the Working wrought on the energy-patterns of the Storms, and how far-reaching those changes were. I fear I bring no startlingly good news."

An'desha nodded, and detailed everything that had been

happening since the "Working" of which Karal had been the channel; from the effect that being the focus of so much energy had wrought on the young Karsite priest, to the departure of the gryphons and the arrival of Sejanes and Master Levy, to the comings and goings of so many Kal'enedral, to Che'sera's intense interest in *him*. Lastly, he described the events of the afternoon, the opening of the hidden trapdoor and the discovery of the workshops below.

They both listened with concentration and apparent interest—and surprise when he described the workshops. *So, the existence of the workshop is something that the Star-Eyed did not tell them, though Her agents have certainly been about. Interesting.*

"There may be answers there," Tre'valen said at last, and for a fleeting moment, his face took on that "listening" expression that Karal wore when either Florian or Altra Mindspoke him. An'desha wondered if the Star-Eyed *might* be speaking to Her Avatar at that instant, and his next words might have been a confirmation of that. "Certainly Firesong should pursue the investigation of the mind-mirrors; they should not be difficult to revive nor to duplicate, and they will serve you all in the days to come."

Oh, my; even more interesting. Perhaps my intuition about the Star-Eyed's providence was well-founded.

Dawnfire placed one long hand on Tre'valen's shoulder and, with a rueful expression, admitted, "This is the only concrete advice we can give at the moment. Would it were otherwise, but the future is still trackless and without a clear path. And even our Goddess is bound by constraints She cannot break, so that we may all work out our futures with a free will."

An'desha sighed, but saw no reason to doubt her. "So we are still muddling our way through a point when there are many futures possible? I had hoped after the Working that we would at least have gotten our feet on a clear path again!"

Tre'valen looked uneasy. "The danger has only been postponed, not negated, but luckily the forces involved have not worsened," he told An'desha. "You knew that the Working was not a solution to the mage-storms, only a reprieve, and that has not changed."

"We have been tracking the results of the Working since the initial release of the energy contained in Urtho's weapon." Dawnfire took up the thread of conversation. "The effect is all that one could have wished over Valdemar, the Pelagirs, Karse and Rethwellan and even Hardorn. The waves that you sent out *are* canceling the waves of the mage-storms, but— only to a point."

"What point?" he asked instantly, sensing that this was important, although he did not know why yet.

"Just beyond the border of Hardorn in the East," Tre'valen told him. "Also South, just at the borders of the Haighlei Empire, and around White Gryphon and its environs, but *they* know how to deal with the effects. And in any case, the Storms are weak there. North, well into the Ice-Wall Mountains. To the West, well, that is Pelagir-wilds and the Storms will hardly change *that*. It is East that concerns us, for the Empire is the recipient of the worst of the Storms, and they are causing great havoc there, among those who depend so much upon magic."

An'desha gave that some thought. "That could be good for us, or bad," he said finally. "Given what the Emperor did to us, I'm not at all sad to hear that they are having troubles. I'd rather that the Empire was so busy trying to hold itself together that they had no time to think of us, but Duke Tremane thought we were the source of the Storms, and what if the Emperor's people assume the same and retaliate?"

Tre'valen nodded. "Precisely. Warn your friends, An'desha, and when the mind-mirrors are working and in place, use them to warn Valdemar. Such things could be possible."

Could *be possible, he says. Yet if I understand the constraints the Avatars labor under, pointing out something specifically as* possible *may be the only warning they are allowed to give of a future they have seen. Or perhaps not. . . .*

Despite the unpleasant information, An'desha felt a warm glow of satisfaction. The Avatars avoided giving direct advice most of the time, but he was getting better at deducing what they wanted him to think about, and what information was the most critical to the current situation.

"What about the Storms themselves?" he asked. "Eventually, they're going to become strong enough to overcome the counter-Storm we sent out, aren't they? That's why we knew what we did was only going to be temporary—" He watched Tre'valen's face carefully and took his cues from the faint changes in expression, as he suspected he was supposed to do. "—so eventually, what happens? We're getting a—a reversal of the original Cataclysm, am I right? That was why we used this spot for the Working, because it's the place where the waves converge. Eventually the Storms are going to overcome the Working, and build up to something very bad?" He swallowed uncomfortably as Tre'valen's slight nod told him he was on the right track. "So then what? Obviously, the Storms that got set off aren't going to—go back into the weapons and things they came from. Do we get the Cataclysm all over again?"

Tre'valen shook his head, but not in negation, and Dawnfire spread her hands wide. "That is just what we do not know," she admitted. "And I confide in you—neither does She. There are too many possibilities, and some of them rest on very subtle factors. We do not yet know what the mages and Powers of the Empire will do, and that will have an effect. There are many things that you could do here, all of them effective, but in different ways and with differing results. *Probably* there will be another, lesser Cataclysm, unless you here manage to do one of the things that could avert or absorb it. There are many things you could do; you could do nothing whatsoever, as well, and from any action that is taken there are the possibilities of prosperity or ruin in varying degrees. Whatever happens, that is all we can tell you for certain."

He groaned. "That is not much comfort!" he complained. "But I suppose that it gives me enough to tell the others for now."

Tre'valen managed a ghost of a smile. "We never pledged to bring you comfort, younger brother," he chided gently. "Only enough help that you need not make your decisions blind, deaf, and ignorant."

"Let me ask about something closer to home, then," An'desha replied. "Che'sera. What is Che'sera to me, or I to Che'sera? Sooner or later he will deduce the source of my information, whether or not I actually say where it comes from in his presence."

Tre'valen's expression softened with affection. "What is Che'sera to you? Simply enough—a teacher, if you should decide, for yourself, that you wish to learn what he has to teach. And what are you to Che'sera? Largely, affirmation. He has been searching for someone to pass his knowledge on to, and he hopes that you will be that person. But it must be your decision, and he will not urge it upon you. He is—a good man, and much in the same way of thinking as Master Ulrich was; Karal will be like him, one day."

So. There it was, out in the open at last; his invitation to become a shaman. And not, perhaps, just any shaman, but one Sworn to the Goddess in her aspect as Wisdom Keeper. He sighed, wishing that he could be as certain of what he wanted as Karal was. But at least now he knew that Che'sera was neither a fanatic nor inflexible. That took a few worries from his shoulders, at least.

"You will be seeing more of us in days to come," Dawnfire told him, her sweet face full of seriousness. "I promise you, An'desha, we will tell you and help you all that we can; we see no good reason to leave you without aids and guides in this—"

Tre'valen looked out into the mists suddenly.

"—and right now, we must go," Tre'valen interrupted her. "There are more things we must investigate and watch for you. Fare well, younger brother! Time is running, and it is not on our side."

And with that, An'desha found himself alone again on the Moonpaths, as if the Avatars had never been there. With no further reason to remain, he sent his awareness dropping slowly back into his physical self, going *down*, then *out*—

As he slowly woke his senses, he heard Karal stirring at last, and smelled the distinctive scent of the meat and bean mixture he had prepared earlier. His stomach growled, and he opened his eyes.

"I brought you some dinner," Karal said, looking at him intently as he handed An'desha a bowl. "You were with *them*, weren't you?" Karal hooked his thumbs together and made flapping gestures with his fingers by way of definition.

He saw no reason to deny it, and nodded as he sat up slowly, and accepted the bowl and spoon from Karal. "They didn't tell me anything we didn't already know, or at least not much. I'll let Firesong and Sejanes know as soon as I've eaten."

Karal looked better than he had in days, and An'desha wondered if that was all due to the work of the Shin'a'in Healer, or if the Avatars had a hand in it. He suspected the latter, and not for the first time wondered what the link between Vkandis and the Shin'a'in Goddess was. The Avatars seemed quite drawn to Karal, and he to them.

On the other hand, they are very compassionate by nature, and he certainly deserves compassion and sympathy.

"Florian and I are going out for some fresh air. Do you want to go with us?" Karal invited nonchalantly. "I'm tired of being down underground like a hibernating bear; I want to see the sun before I go mad." He shook his head. "I can't imagine how that mage was able to stand being cooped up in here."

"You may see the sun, but you won't feel it," An'desha cautioned. "It's so cold that if you pour out a cup of water it'll be ice before it hits the ground."

"So I'll bundle up," Karal shrugged. "I've felt cold before. Karse isn't exactly a pleasure garden in winter, and up in the hills, there's snow on the ground for half the year. I'm beginning to sympathize with the gryphons; if I don't see some open sky, I'm going to start babbling."

"Then I'll go with you." It didn't take An'desha very long to pull on a heavy tunic, a second of the same weight, then his quilted Shin'a'in coat over it all, but Karal needed a little more help getting all that clothing on. He was quite steady on his feet, however, which An'desha took to be a good sign of his recovery.

By now, Master Levy was deep in his prodding and poking of the floor, and he jotted down measurements and diagrams in one of his notebooks. Silverfox and Firesong were sitting on their heels, the pages of notes neatly stacked in front of them, regarding another sheaf of their own notes with some dubiousness. "Where are you two going?" Silverfox called as the three of them passed by.

"We're going out for some fresh air," Karal replied. "Why don't you join us? We'll go frighten the Shin'a'in into thinking what you found in the workroom turned us all into monsters." He made a hideous face and Silverfox laughed.

"Fresh air? Not a bad idea." Firesong raised his head as Karal tendered his invitation. "We aren't making much more out of these notes. Maybe a little sun will wake up my mind. Go on out, we'll catch up with you."

An'desha noticed at once that their hosts had been at work on the tunnel to the surface—the opening they had made into the side of the Tower was large and quite regular, without any debris of broken masonry to trip over. The tunnel was also wider, though no higher, and there had been some extensive work done in shoring it up since the last time he'd come through it. It was *still* claustrophobic, but on this trip he no longer had the feeling that the tunnel was going to collapse and trap him at any moment.

He sent a small mage-light on ahead of Karal; he couldn't see past Florian's rump, so a mage-light was hardly of much use to *him*. Altra had declined to come, saying that he had seen quite enough of snow, and was planning another nap in Karal's bed.

He scented the outside before he saw any indication they were nearing the entrance. Although the air below remained remarkably clean, and the scents that lingered, thanks to some small magics on his part and Firesong's, were all pleasant in nature, there was a fresh quality to the outside air that nothing below could duplicate. Some of that was due to the cold, but not all.

The other thing they could not duplicate below was the light. As he stumbled out into the late afternoon sunlight, he squinted and put out a hand to steady himself against Florian's side. There wasn't a single cloud in the sky; the great bowl of the sky itself was an intense and blinding blue, and with all of the glare reflected off the snow, there was as much light coming from below as above.

Karal stood to one side, taking in huge gulps of air, his pale face taking on more color with every breath. Florian trotted off and kicked up his heels friskily.

Seen from the outside, the Tower itself was hardly more than a snow-frosted stub of melted-looking rock protruding from a snow-covered, rolling hill; the only projection above the otherwise flat Plains at all, not prepossessing except for its size. Because they had dug a long, slanting tunnel to reach the wall of the Tower below, the entrance came out quite some distance from the remains of the Tower itself, and it was at the foot of the Tower, precisely above the point where they had broken into the walls, that the Shin'a'in had pitched their tent-village. The round felt tents, white and brown and black, made a very orderly and neat array against the snow, so neat and orderly that it looked like a model rather than a place where people were actually living and working.

"Whoof!" Firesong exclaimed from behind An'desha, as Florian frisked and gamboled in the snow with Karal laughing and throwing snowballs for him to dodge. "Very bright out here! I shouldn't wonder if you could get a worse sunburn than in high summer!"

Silverfox ducked as Karal turned and lobbed a snowball at them. Karal laughed, and the *kestra'chern* pelted after him, swearing vengeance, while Firesong looked on indulgently.

"So," the Adept asked quietly, while Karal and Silverfox took shelter behind facing snowbanks, and hurled missiles at each other. "What did your Avatars have to say for themselves?"

An'desha flung him a startled glance, and Firesong chuckled at his expression. "You have a certain quiet glow after you've gone visiting them," the mage told him. "It's not terribly obvious, but it's there if you know what to look for. So? What did they have to say? Anything useful?"

"Mostly that nothing has changed that much. We've successfully bought some time for ourselves and our friends, things outside the areas we protected are deteriorating quickly, and eventually even our time will run out," An'desha said, wishing his news was better.

Firesong nodded, unsurprised. "And when our time runs out, we'll get—what? A replication of the Cataclysm? After all, everything is supposedly converging here."

"Maybe. Even They don't know for sure." An'desha sighed. "If She has any idea, She's not saying anything. If you want my guess, the gods are doing what They always do—unless and until *all* life is threatened with catastrophe, They'll see to it we have the tools and the information to find our own solutions, then leave us alone to find them. The Avatars think the things we're finding in the Tower will help us, but—"

"But there's no clear 'future' to see or even guess at." Firesong looked surprisingly philosophical. "I'm determined to see this as an opportunity; for *once* in my life there isn't a god or a spirit or the hand of fate or prophecy or anything else demanding that I trace a certain pattern on the pages of time. We're going to make our own future here, An'desha, and nothing is going to interfere with us to make it go some other god-ordained way. There's a certain satisfaction in that, you know."

"I suppose so," An'desha replied; he would have said more, but Silverfox suddenly broke off the snowball fight to peer into the north, and point.

"Look!" he exclaimed with glee, as Karal dropped his final

snowball without throwing it to squint in the direction he indicated. "Gryphons! Yes! They have a carry-basket, and I think they've brought Tarrn!"

An'desha shaded his eyes and narrowed them against the glare, and finally made out four sets of flapping wings with a half-round shape beneath them. He couldn't think what else would have that particular configuration except four gryphons and a large carry-basket.

"Come on!" Silverfox crowed. "Let's go meet them!"

He set off at a run; Florian loped up and half-knelt beside Karal, who pulled himself onto the Companion's back. The two of them quickly overtook Silverfox; Firesong cast an amused glance at An'desha and indicated the others with a finger.

"Shall we trundle along behind?" he asked.

"It would only be polite," An'desha pointed out. "And besides, the Shin'a'in have cleared a perfectly fine path between here and there. It would be a shame not to use it."

They followed in Silverfox's wake, though at a more leisurely pace. By the time they arrived at the Shin'a'in tent-village, the gryphons and their passengers had already landed and been taken into one of the tents. It was easy to tell which one; there was only one that was large enough to hold four gryphons at once, and only one whose pallet of snow had been churned by gryphon claws.

Dark-clad Kal'enedral nodded as Firesong waved to them, then went about their own business. An'desha pulled the entrance flap aside, and he and the mage entered the tent, being careful to let in as little cold air as possible. It took quite a bit of time for An'desha's eyes to adjust to the darkness inside the tent after all the snow glare outside; he stayed where he was while he waited, listening to the chatter of at least half a dozen creatures all speaking at once.

He looked around as soon as he could make anything at all out; he didn't recognize any of the gryphons, but he hadn't expected to. They were all arranged at one side of the tent, and it came as no surprise to see that they were eating—or rather, gorging. Not only would they have to recover from the stress of carrying their passengers all the way from K'Leshya Vale, but they would have to recover from the stress of dealing with the cold as well.

Karal was conversing with the gryphons, occasionally help-

ing them where the quarters were too cramped for them to
move themselves. Silverfox, however, was engaged in a high-
speed conversation with a gray-muzzled, but jaunty-looking
kyree.

This odd creature, vaguely wolflike as to the head and coat,
but also vaguely catlike in body shape and proportions, was
easily the size of a small calf. An'desha knew more about
kyrees from personal experience than from Falconsbane's
memories, as Mornelithe Falconsbane in all of his incarnations had very little to do with the creatures. An'desha, on the
other hand, was quite familiar with Rris, the *kyree* representative to the Kingdom of Valdemar and the Alliance. Rris might
look like this old fellow many years from now; his muzzle
was quite white, and his head was liberally salted with paler
hairs among the black. He was tired, but clearly in good spirits, and he chatted with Silverfox like the old friend he probably was.

Or to be more accurate, Silverfox chattered; the *kyree,* who
could only Mindspeak, nodded and made replies in his own
inaudible fashion. Until Tarrn chose to "speak" in the "public" mode, no one would hear him except those he chose.

With him, bundled in so many layers of quilted clothing he
resembled a roll of brightly colored Kaled'a'in bed coverings,
was a *hertasi.* He was practically sitting on a brazier, since the
lizard-folk were very susceptible to cold. It wasn't that they
were cold-blooded, precisely, it was that they were not able to
control their own body temperatures very efficiently. Opinions were divided on whether *hertasi* had been created by
Urtho or by an accident involving magic, but in either case
their physiology had some flaws, and this was the major one.
The poor thing could very easily lose limbs to the cold, or
would go involuntarily into a kind of hibernation. Layers of
clothing would not necessarily help this, especially not during
a long journey in bitter cold, hence the brazier now and whatever other measures the Kaled'a'in had taken. All that could
be seen of this *hertasi* was the end of the snout and a pair of
alert, bright, and apparently happy eyes peeking out of the
depths of the hood.

A great deal more of Tarrn was visible. An'desha knew
kyree from his acquaintance with Rris, but he had not had
much opportunity to get to know any *hertasi.* A few had come
with Silverfox and the Kaled'a'in delegation to Valdemar, but

he hadn't had much to do with them. And of course, Falconsbane was universally despised by both races, in all his lives,
so *he* would hardly have had any congress with them.

At just that moment, the *hertasi* spoke up; the *hertasi* associated with the Kaled'a'in tended to vocalize far more often
than they used Mindspeech, the exact reverse of the habits of
the ones associated with the Hawkbrothers.

"I believe I am thawed enough to make the dash for the
Tower," he said, in a high-pitched voice with hints of a whis-
tling sound underlying the tone.

:Excellent, Lyam,: the *kyree* replied. *:They tell me our baggage is already there, waiting for us. If we truly make a dash,
you won't get too much of a chill.:*

"Florian says he'll be happy to carry Lyam, if Lyam thinks
he can cling on," Karal spoke up. "Florian can get him to the
tunnel mouth faster than he can get there on foot." He turned
toward the *hertasi*, polite but a little uncertain in addressing
such an odd creature. "A Companion's gait is very smooth,
and I've never heard of one losing a rider, and you should see
one run!"

"I have never tried riding, but if I can get from White
Gryphon to here without the loss of limb or tail, I think I
should be able to survive an attempt on a Companion's back,"
the *hertasi* said with warm good humor. "And almost anything is worth not having to walk through snow myself!"

"We ssshall ssstay herrre overrrnight," one of the gryphons
said. "Thisss issss verrry comforrrtable, and we do *not* want
to go underrrgrrround even to sssee the Towerrr!" The others
nodded with agreement.

"It isss wonderrrful to be wherrre the grrreat Ssskandrrra-
non once wasss, but *he* did not have to crrrawl underrrgrrround," said another, flicking his wings nervously. "I do not
know how Trrreyvan and Hydona borrre it."

The *kyree* didn't shrug, but An'desha had the impression
that if he could have, he would have. *:Suit yourselves; you
will have to make do with my descriptions, then.:*

"Yourrr dessscrrriptionsss will be asss if we werrre therrre,"
the first gryphon said firmly. "I will fly the ssssky that Ssskandrranon flew, and that will be enough forrr me."

Tarrn stood up, and shook himself thoroughly. *:One more
dash, then, and we will be where no kyree or hertasi has set
foot in thousands of years!:* He seemed to relish the prospect

with scarcely-restrained glee, and the air of a creature a quarter of his apparent age. :*Well, friends, let us take these last few paces at the gallop!:*

Firesong, who had known many *kyree* and *hertasi* in his life, was comfortable with these two immediately. Tarrn had all of the warmth and wisdom of Irrl, one of Firesong's academic teachers, and Lyam had a great deal more assertiveness than most of the normally-timid Vales-bred *hertasi*. Although Firesong loved to be petted and made much of by his own *hertasi*, he had always found the shyness of the Vale *hertasi* something of an irritation. Someone once suggested that their manner was reflective of the deep trauma they had suffered during the Cataclysm, and that worried him deeply; if that was so, how would they react to another such event?

They'll cope, I suppose; it's the thing they do best. I don't know how they manage.

Both *kyree* and *hertasi* were at heart cave- and den-dwellers, and both of the new arrivals were obviously comfortable in the Tower. They settled into the same room shared by Karal and An'desha with every evidence of content. They had not yet moved in their luggage, but the Shin'a'in had brought appropriate bedding material for both of the new guests—and extra warming pans for both beds. As far as personal belongings went, the two had traveled much lighter than he had expected. Their main luggage consisted of boxes of very special writing materials; books of tough paper with waterproof metal covers that locked over the contents like protective boxes, and ink that would never run once it had dried, even if water was spilled directly on it. Tarrn was a historian; not a traditional *kyree* historian like Rris, who memorized and recited from memory, but the kind of historian like the Chronicler of Valdemar, who attempted to personally view as much as possible of epochal events, and to note the honest and bare facts in record-books called Chronicles. Only when those hard facts had been listed would Tarrn then make his own interpretations of the events, written separately in Commentaries. Tarrn was very serious about his calling; he would rather have the fur pulled out of his tail until it was as naked as a rat's than put a personal interpretation in the Chronicles.

Actually, that wasn't precisely true. Tarrn would dictate,

for, having no hands, he could not write. Lyam would do the actual writing. Lyam was Tarrn's third secretary in a long life as a historian, and his relationship with the *kyree* was obviously based on affection and mutual respect. Normally it was Lyam who cared for the *kyree's* needs, but with Lyam just now the one who was in need, Tarrn was seeing to it in a quiet and dignified manner that Lyam got first priority.

Lyam needed warmth more than anything else, and Karal volunteered to take care of him. Firesong had an idea that he knew why, too. At heart, Karal still considered himself to be the young secretary who had ridden to Valdemar from Karse, and he must be feeling a great deal of empathy for Lyam.

That's good; they are both strangers in strange places, and it will do them good to have a friend with the same— outlook? Status? They have a lot in common, anyway.

Tarrn, however, was quite ready for work, and looked it. He had been consulting with Silverfox all the way here from the tent-village. Firesong could not imagine where he was getting the energy.

He approached Firesong with Silverfox still in tow as soon as Karal took Lyam off to be wrapped up in warmed blankets and given something hot to drink.

"Firesong, Tarrn wants to speak with you privately, before we get to work," Silverfox told him, with a quizzical expression. "He says he has something for you, but he can't tell me what it is."

The *kyree* nodded his head as Firesong turned to look down on him with surprise. *:Indeed, Firesong k'Treva,:* Tarrn said with grave courtesy. *:I have. Would you come with me to where they have brought our belongings?:*

"Certainly," Firesong replied with equal courtesy. "Would you prefer that I Mindspoke with you?"

:That will not be necessary, but thank you,: Tarrn replied, turning and walking slowly toward the heap of bundles that the Shin'a'in had left just inside the main room of the Tower. *:It is not that this is a secret matter,:* the *kyree* continued. *:It is simply that I have not been given permission to say anything to anyone else before I discharged my obligation.:*

"Oh?" This was getting odder with every moment. Firesong couldn't think of anything or anyone among the Kaled'a'in of k'Leshya Vale who would have had anything to send to him.

Tarrn stopped beside the pile of belongings. *:If you will*

please remove the three bags of Lyam's clothing there—: he
indicated the drab bundles with his forepaw *:—you will find
what I brought you beneath them. It is wrapped in blue wool,
and it is very long and narrow.:*

Firesong easily moved the three packages, revealing a long,
narrow packet wrapped in blue wool cloth and tied with
string. Firesong picked it up.

And it Mindspoke to him.

:Hello, boy.:

The grating, decidedly *female* voice was all too familiar to
him, although it was not one he had expected to hear ever
again.

"*Need?*" he gasped, as he tore at the wrappings, trying to
free the blade within. Lyam must have wrapped it; the string
was tied in a complicated knot-pattern only a *hertasi* or a *kestra'chern* could admire. He finally pulled off the string, the
fabric fell away, and there was the ancient spell-bound sword.
She looked precisely as she had the last time he saw her,
strapped to Falconsbane's "daughter" Nyara's side as she and
Herald Skif rode out of Valdemar to become Selenay's envoys
to the Kaled'a'in and Tayledras, and possibly to the Shin'a'in
as well.

"Need, what are you *doing* here?" He hadn't been taken so
completely by surprise since—since he'd been kidnapped by
his ancestor Vanyel!

*:Nyara doesn't require me anymore; she's better off on her
own,:* the sword said to him. *:There's nothing at k'Leshya that
she, Skif, or the Kaled'a'in can't handle. You, on the other
hand, are dealing with very old magics. I* am *very old magic,
and I still recall quite a bit. I helped you once before, and I'm
hoping I can help you again.:*

Firesong held the sword in both hands, and stared at it. It
was very disconcerting to be Mindspeaking with what should
have been an inanimate object. A sword didn't have a face to
read, eyes to look into, and it was difficult to tell if *it* could
read his expressions.

*But there's something about all this that doesn't quite
make sense yet.*

"I find myself wondering if there is something more to this
than just an urge to help us here," he said finally. "You've
never put yourself in nonfemale hands before."

:Hmm—let's say I've never done it deliberately, but it has

happened, and it was usually with lads who had the same taste in men as my "daughters.": The sword chuckled, but he sensed there was still a lot more than she was telling, and he decided to press her for it.

:Try again,: he said sternly in Mindspeech. *:You're avoiding my question.:*

A sword could not sigh, but he got that sensation from her.

:All right. I could tell you to work it out yourself, but why waste time? You've got mage-storms disrupting magic; you've managed to get them canceled out for the moment, but we all know this is only a temporary respite, not a solution. I'm magic. I've managed to hold myself together this long, but each Storm gets stronger, and sooner or later I'm going to lose to one. I don't know what will happen when I lose, but it's going to happen.: She paused for a moment. *:Worst case is that I'll go up in fire and molten metal, the way the sword was made. Best case is that the magic will just unravel, and there won't be anything here but a perfectly ordinary sword.:*

He had never once thought that Need might be affected by the Storms; she had always struck him as being so capable, so impervious, that it never occurred to him that she might have been in trouble.

This bothered him. *:I can't promise anything,:* he said soberly. *:I don't even know if we're going to survive the end of this ourselves.:*

To his surprise, the sword laughed, though rather sardonically. *:You think I don't know that? If I go pfft, I don't want little Nyara to see it happen. She had enough troubles in her life and she shouldn't lose an old friend and teacher in that unexpected a fashion. Besides, if I'm going to go, I want to do it while I'm trying to accomplish something. How could I miss a chance at getting my hand in on what you're trying to do? It's complicated, it's dangerous, it's challenging, it's irresistible.:*

"If you say so," he said aloud, but strapped the sword on anyway, for she required *his* presence to be able to see and hear clearly. Without a bearer, it took incredible effort for her to perceive anything, and at that it was only dimly. He didn't often carry a blade, and she felt very odd, slung across his back in Tayledras fashion. "An'desha will probably be happy to see you, but you're going to have to explain yourself to the rest. They don't know anything about you."

And the gods only know what the Shin'a'in are going to make of her. Yes, Kethry had carried her, and Kerowyn after that, but still—she was yet another creature of magic inside the heart of the Plains. How much more were they going to be willing to allow?

:*I can't wait,*: Need replied, with a bit less irony than he expected. :*There's something rather amusing about the reactions people get the first time I talk to them.*:

Amusing? Oh, gods. Firesong buried his irritation at this particular complication in an already complicated situation; after all, Need was right about her abilities. She *did* know much older magics than anyone here, and that included An'desha. That might be crucial at this point, for there could be something ancient and long-forgotten that would give them all the clues they needed to solve this situation. She was a powerful mage in her own right—something near to an Adept, or she never could have made the magics that bound her human soul to an iron blade. He, An'desha, and Sejanes were the only true mages here; having Need with them gave them a fourth.

And if she is right, and the mage-storms overwhelm her along with the rest of us, she won't have to worry about how she unravels. If she dissolves into flame and melted steel, we here among all these dangerous machines of power will have far more to worry about than her.

On the other hand, dealing with Need's irascible personality was not going to be easy. He rubbed his temples, feeling another headache coming on.

She Mindspeaks; perhaps I can get Tarrn interested in her. When he is not translating for us, wouldn't she be fascinating for a historian?

He could only hope that was the case, because he had the feeling that Need was not going to give him a choice about becoming her bearer. In this all-male enclave, he was probably the closest she was going to come to an acceptable bearer, for by now, even the female Companions they had ridden here on had begun the long journey back to Valdemar.

"Well, we might as well get this over now," he said aloud, as Tarrn watched him with interest. "I assume, sir, that *you* have made the acquaintance of my metal friend, here?"

:*I have, and I hope she will continue to impart her tales of the past to me here, when our work permits,*: Tarrn replied gravely, which made Firesong feel a little more cheerful about the situation. At least he wouldn't be burdened with Need's presence and personality *all* the time.

"Well, most of my other colleagues here don't even know she exists, so we'd better introduce her to them before she startles one of them into dropping something critical by Mindspeaking to him without warning." Need remained silent after that little sally, which either meant that she agreed with him, or that she was insulted and was plotting revenge.

:*An excellent plan,*: Tarrn replied. :*Carry on.*:

He gathered them all together by the simple expedient of going into the central chamber, clearing his throat, and announcing, "Excuse me, friends, but something rather—unexpected—has come up that you really ought to know about."

That certainly brought everyone who understood Valdemaran boiling out, and the few Shin'a'in who didn't know the language followed the rest out of sheer curiosity.

Silverfox was the first to arrive, and stared at him as if he'd grown a tail. "Firesong," the *kestra'chern* began incredulously, "what are you doing with a sword?"

He removed Need from her sheath, just in case the leather and silk hampered her ability to Mindspeak at all, and held her out in front of him, balanced on his palms, as the others arrived. "Well, that's what I wanted to tell you all about," he said, flushing a little. "It seems we didn't get *two* additions to our little group here, we got three. I'd like you all to meet Need, those of you who haven't already encountered her."

"Need!" An'desha had only just emerged from the sleeping chamber, but there was no doubt that *he* was glad to see the mage-blade. "What is *she* doing here? This is wonderful!"

Firesong's expression must have been a bit sour, for An'desha took one look at his face and laughed. "Oh, it's that way, is it? You're the chosen bearer?" He looked down fondly at the blade. "Firesong is *much* too certain of his own expertise, dear lady; I trust you can teach him that there are other people here who are just as expert in their crafts as he. I warn you though, he looks much better this way than in a dress."

:*Don't be so hard on him, boy,*: the blade replied, amused. :*Leave that job to me. I've got more experience at it.*:

By now all the rest had gathered around, and were staring

with varying degrees of fascination and puzzlement at the sword. "What is this?" Sejanes asked, brows knitted.

"Is this by any chance *the* famous sword called 'Need' that the ancestress of Tale'sedrin Clan once wore?" asked Lo'isha, as the other Shin'a'in gathered in a knot behind him, murmuring. "The one carried by our Clan-sib, Herald Kerowyn?"

"The same," Firesong all but groaned. "To answer you, Sejanes, Need is a magically-made sword with the soul of its maker bound into it, and she is unbelievably ancient. Either she or Tarrn can probably tell you the story of *why* she did such a daft thing—"

:*Hardly daft. Reckless, yes, and probably less than wise, but at the time we didn't have many options, and all of those were worse than what I did. Of course, I could have just folded my hands and done nothing at all, but—let's just say that went against my conscience and my nature.*:

Those who didn't know what she was went wide-eyed with startlement at the sound of her projected mind-voice.

"The point is, she's from a time that actually predates the Mage Wars and the Cataclysm, at least so far as we can tell, and that makes her an expert in magics much older than the ones we know," Firesong said, noting as he spoke that An'desha's eyes were unfocused, which probably meant he was talking privately to her. "She has volunteered to come help us, since her last bearer no longer requires her tutelage."

Master Levy rubbed his chin with one hand as he looked down on the sword with speculation. "What happens if and when the mage-storms overwhelm us here?" he asked. "If she *is* magically made—"

:*Then unless I can manage to shield myself, which I'm not certain I can, I either go quietly or dramatically, and I don't know which it will be,*: Need replied bluntly. :*These Storms disrupt the patterns of magic so deeply they may as well be spells of Unmaking. But that would happen whether I was here or somewhere else, and I'd just as soon be trying to accomplish something. I told you, I'm not one to sit with folded hands, even if I still had hands to fold.*:

"Wait a minute," Sejanes objected, speaking directly to the sword, glimmering with reflected light from above. "If you predate the Mage Wars and the Cataclysm, how did you survive *them*?"

:*In a shielded casket in a shielded shrine in the heart of the triply-shielded Temple to Bestet, the Battle-Goddess,:* she replied promptly. *:And when the Cataclysm was over, the shields on the shrine and the casket were gone and I felt as if I'd been drained to the dregs. It took me years to recover, and by then I'd been moved to the armory since no one could figure out why I'd been put in with the Goddess' regalia in the first place. If I were inclined to such things, I'd have been indignant.:*

Sejanes nodded. "It would be difficult to find such a situation again," he observed, stroking his chin with one hand. "Indeed, it is quite surprising that you were in that situation during the first Cataclysm."

:The only reason they had shields like that was because of the war with Ma'ar. I don't know of any Temples now with that kind of protection,: Need went on. *:Or to be more honest, I don't know of any that would offer me shelter. I might as well be doing something useful, and I just might be able to save myself while doing it.:*

"Do you fear death so much?" Karal asked softly. Light rippled across the surface of the sword, as if Need reacted to that question.

Firesong expected a sarcastic reply, or none at all, but was surprised by both her answer and her sober tone.

:I don't fear death, youngling,: she said, with great honesty. *:What I'm afraid of is more complicated than that. I don't want to vanish without fighting, I don't intend to just lie down and accept "death" passively. There is the possibility that I could meet my end violently, and if that is the case—:*

"Then it would be better here," Sejanes said with finality, as a chill crept up Firesong's spine. "If there is a second Cataclysm and the effect penetrates this place, *your* demise will be insignificant compared to the violence that will be unleashed."

Light rippled along the surface of the blade again. *:Good. You'd already considered that.:* Need sounded relieved. *:I'd hoped I wouldn't be the bird of ill omen forced to point that out to you.:*

I would rather hope we can pull this off right to the very end, thank you. "No, just the one who forced us to think about it a little earlier than we wanted to," Firesong sighed.

Now she gave him one of her typical sardonic chuckles. *:Consider it incentive to find a solution,:* she told him.

Now, of course, those who had never met Need wanted to speak with her; Firesong handed her over to An'desha for that, although he was quite aware that she was not going to change her mind about her choice of a bearer. Somewhat to his surprise, Karal separated himself from the group for a moment and approached him.

"I'm not quite sure what to say, except that I know it isn't going to be easy or very entertaining to have Need literally on your back while we work our way through all this," Karal said quietly. "I've had teachers like her. They were very good, but not easy to live with, and you have my sympathy, for what it's worth."

"Thank you, Karal," he replied with some surprise. The last thing he had expected was sympathy or understanding from the Karsite!

"Just trying to—oh, I don't know." Karal smiled crookedly. "Believe it or not, I like and admire you, Firesong. We irritate each other sometimes, but who doesn't? And I never properly thanked you for what you did for me."

Firesong found himself blushing hotly, something he hadn't done since boyhood. "Oh, please," he replied, for once at a loss for words. "Don't thank me, we all—"

Karal shook his head. "I know very well what all of you did, and I won't mention this again since it obviously makes you uncomfortable. I just want you to know that it's appreciated and you are appreciated. And—well, I think I've said enough."

Considering that Firesong didn't think he'd be able to flush any hotter, Karal was probably right. When the Karsite rejoined the group talking to Need, it was a decided relief.

:Ahem.:

This time the mind-voice was Tarrn's, and Firesong was very glad to hear it.

"Can I help you, sir?" he asked, looking down at the *kyree*, who was in turn looking up at him with amused golden eyes. The white hairs of his muzzle contrasted strangely with the youth in those eyes.

:Since virtually everyone else is involved with speaking to our metallic friend, why don't we go have a look at those notes Silverfox says you are so concerned with? If this device is what I believe it to be, then the translation will be a simple one, and we may have some answers within a quarter-day.:

"Really?" Firesong's eyebrows rose.

:*Mind you, this is likely to be the* only *case where the translation will be so easy,*: Tarrn cautioned, :*And that is only because I am familiar with similar devices used by our gryphons. I think this is probably an improvement on those devices, allowing visions as well as thoughts and—*: He stopped, and shook his head until his ears flapped. :*—and we really ought to just see for ourselves before I make too big a liar of myself. Shall we?*:

Firesong got the notes and spread the pages out on the floor in one corner of the main chamber. He and the *kyree* bent over them in intense concentration, with Lyam taking notes beside them, and before very long, Tarrn *was* able to determine that the device was nothing more than an improvement on something he called a "teleson."

At that point, Silverfox joined them again, and by the time supper came and went, they had worked out not only the way to activate the devices, but also how to make more.

Provided, of course, that there were sufficient parts to do so. There were some esoteric components that needed to be prepared beforehand, and Firesong wasn't certain whether or not there had been any of those components among the parts in bins on the workbench. Both Tarrn and Silverfox were of the opinion that, although the Kaled'a'in could probably make more of these components eventually, it would take a great deal of trial-and-error to do so, given the vagaries of the way the language had changed over the centuries.

"Well, let's confine ourselves to activating the two we have," Firesong said at last, sitting back on his heels and stretching muscles that had cramped in his shoulders and back. "If they work, then we can see if we can make a third and get *it* to work. With communication open back to Haven, that will give us more than we'd hoped for; open it to Sunhame, and we're doubly advantaged. We can worry about being able to build more of these devices from scratch later, when we have the leisure."

"That seems a good plan to me," Silverfox concurred, rotating his head and neck to stretch out cramps of his own. "Let me go and get one of the devices and bring it up here, and that way we can actually test it over a little distance." He looked around. "We'll need someone with Mindspeech up here. That would be Tarrn, I suppose."

:That seems reasonable,: the *kyree* said agreeably. *:We will also need a mage—Sejanes, perhaps—to activate it.:*

"And I'll go down to the workshop and activate and man the other device down there," Firesong said, getting to his feet. He and Silverfox descended the stairs down into the workshop; Silverfox took one of the two devices from the bench and carried it carefully up the staircase again.

The instructions for activation had been quite unambiguous and equally simple, phrased in language that not even the passage of time had altered. Even a child, had he both true-magic and Mindspeech, would have been able to follow the instructions. It was obvious from the notes now that the reason these devices had not been put into use by Urtho was that *anyone* could "eavesdrop" on conversations held with their aid. That rather negated their value in a time of war. Urtho's notes had made it very clear that Ma'ar had many folks Gifted with Mindspeech in his ranks, and that he used it as he would any other tool.

Firesong only hoped that communications sent through these telesons would not be *forced* into the minds of those with Mindspeech; if that were to be the case, their use would be severely limited. Having to maintain ordinary shields was one thing; having to put up shields against something like coercion in order to block these communications out would be very uncomfortable. And for those who were untrained and unaware of their Gift, it would be impossible.

I don't want to drive people mad by having them suddenly forced to listen to strangers talking in their heads!

Well, there was only one way to find out for certain.

A very little magic was needed to help activate the device, and none to maintain it once it was active. There was nothing for mage-storms to disrupt; the device took Mindspeech and amplified it, using some resonance of an arrangement of crystals. The trick was, even those who normally would not be considered to have Mindspeech would be able to use it also; it only needed *one* so Gifted on one of the two telesons in order for the trick to work.

That would mean that Master Levy could talk with one of his fellow Artificers through the intermediary of a Herald, or a mage so Gifted could speak with Sejanes, who was not.

Hmm. And if the device isn't urgently needed, young Karal can talk with Natoli. The idea delighted him; now and again he had the urge to matchmake, and this was one of those times. It might be the strangest courtship ever on record, but if it worked—

Worry about that when you can get this ancient construction to operate! he scolded himself, and bent his concentration to doing just that.

A moment later—well, it *seemed* to be working. So far as he recalled the notes, it *looked* as if he had activated it. But—

:*FIRESONG?*: If it had been a real voice and not a mindvoice, the shout would have deafened him. As it was, it was excruciatingly painful!

"Aiii!" he shouted, clapping his hands over his ears, even though he knew that wasn't going to make a difference.

:*Sorry.*: That was a more normal "volume," although there was no sound involved. :*Is that better?*:

He didn't recognize the mind-voice; it certainly wasn't Tarrn. It also "sounded" rather odd, and he couldn't tell why. :*Who is this?*: he sent back cautiously, so as not to blast *their* minds.

:*Sejanes. I must say, this is an interesting way to speak.*: Firesong blinked for a moment, both to clear his thoughts and to try to pinpoint just why the mind-voice felt so strange. The mental images—

Wait, that's it. There are no mental images! There's no emotional flavor, no images, no leaking over of other thoughts! This is just like speaking, not like Mindspeech at all.:

And that, for those who were not Gifted and not used to sorting through the wealth of additional information that came along with Mindsent "words," would be a good thing. :*I believe we have a workable pair of prototypes,*: he sent back with glee.

His elation was matched by the others. After making certain that both devices were working according to the notes, and that all of the components were well-seated, the consensus was that they had earned a real respite.

But before they took that well-earned rest, everyone, Gifted and not, had a try at the teleson pair. The notes were correct; so long as one of the operators was Gifted, the result was the same, crisp, clear Mindspeech with no overtones of anything else. If both were Gifted, then the results were different; precisely like "normal" Mindspeech. To Firesong's relief, there was no "spillover" from the devices to those who were Gifted, although, as Urtho had indicated, the Gifted *could* "listen in" with perfect ease when the devices were in use.

Right now, that might be an advantage. It certainly wouldn't hurt to have more than two people at each Mindsent conference.

Altra had recovered enough from his last Jumps to take the device to Valdemar immediately, and insisted on doing just that, then and there. He saw no reason whatsoever to delay, and every reason to make all speed.

:With every mark that passes, it is more difficult to Jump,: he said firmly. *:Why wait? It will be easier to Jump with an inanimate object, but "easier" does not mean "easy." I want to get this over with!:*

There were no dissenting voices, so as soon as the mind-mirror teleson had been wrapped in a cushion of quilts to keep it from any possibility of damage, Altra left, saying that he thought he would return in four days.

"We'll know if the device still works or if it works at the distances that Urtho claimed in two days, of course," Sejanes observed as they all prepared for sleep. Not that any of them really thought he would get much sleep after all the excitement that day. "In two days he'll be in Haven, and then it will just be a matter of getting one of the Heralds to try calling us."

He crept into his own bed—the only one that *was* a bed, since it was not possible for him to get into and out of a pallet on the floor.

"Or one of us can call them," Karal pointed out, and yawned. He was already in his bedroll, with Florian curled up at his back, taking the place of Altra as a living bedwarmer. "You know, I was really excited a couple of marks ago and I thought I'd never be able to get to sleep, but now—" He yawned again, and looked puzzled. "—now it seems as if this is an anticlimax."

Firesong had the answer to his puzzlement. "Well, we're all worn out—it's been a very busy day—but there's more to it than that." He tied up his long hair to keep it from knotting up while he slept.

:Permit the old pessimist,: Need interjected. *:It's not an anticlimax, child, it's that this hasn't been the climax you think it should be. We have a new tool, and nothing more. If*

those devices hadn't worked, we would have gone on without them. We will find the answers here, if there are answers to be found, but the teleson is not one of those answers, and that is why it feels as if what we accomplished with them is only a minor addition to our work and not a major part of it.:

"Ah." Karal's face wore a sober expression of understanding. "I see what you are saying. We're not at the end of our work, just the beginning, and it's not even close to the point where we can celebrate. Well. That's a little disappointing, but at least we haven't fallen back."

"Exactly," said Firesong. "Which is all the more reason why you *should* get a good night's sleep. We'll need everyone in the morning." He leveled a sober look at Karal. "Especially you. I think we'll have work enough to make you and Lyam wish there were four of you."

"I'll be glad to get back to work," Karal said, with a weak smile, and on that note, Firesong extinguished the lights with a word, and it was not long before even he was fast asleep.

King Tremane

Five

What is the Shin'a'in saying? Darkwind asked himself, as he watched Duke Tremane trying to make out careful plans for the time when the mage-storms finally overcame the latest efforts to stave them off. *Ah, I remember.* *"The best plans never survive the first engagement with the enemy." How has the Empire done so well when they insist on having detailed plans for everything?*

The three of them sat around a small table in the Grand Duke's personal quarters, a table currently quite full, what with papers, glasses of water, and maps strewn across it.

"What do you two think?" Duke Tremane asked, setting aside the plans he and the Valdemarans had been discussing, and leaning over the table. As he looked up at them, his gray-brown eyes seemed anxious. "My scholars haven't been able to unearth any more information about the Cataclysm, and my mages have not been able to predict anything that these mage-storms have done."

Elspeth grimaced. "I don't know that much either, I'm afraid," she replied honestly. She glanced over at Darkwind, who shrugged slightly.

"I can only tell you of the effects the Cataclysm had, according to our records and traditions," he told the Grand Duke. "Those effects were widespread and all-encompassing. *All* magic was disrupted, from the Ice-Wall Mountains in the north to the borders of the Haighlei Empire in the south, and in an equal distance east and west of what are now Lake Evendim and the Dhorisha Plains. If any shields survived the Cataclysm, I am not aware of it, but I must add that the Kaled'a'in groups my people are descended from had none of the greater mages with them."

"So shields might survive?" Tremane persisted, fiddling nervously with a pen.

Oh, how he wants to have some way to get his sort of magic back! Now that this area of Hardorn was buffered from the worst effects of the mage-storms, Tremane had given orders for some judicious use of magic to take some pressure from scarce resources—mostly burnables. The barracks and headquarters were all heated and lit with mage-fires and mage-lights now, and about half the time food was cooked using mage-fires in the stoves. It did make things more comfortable, especially in the barracks, which had been heated with dried dung, and were hardly illuminated at all. But Darkwind and Elspeth could both tell how much the Grand Duke wanted to be able to use magic for all of the things he was used to; the only trouble with that idea was that it just wasn't possible to do so. For one thing, magical energy ran thin and low here; Ancar had depleted it sorely, and it would take a long time to recover. There was enough for lights and fires— but not for something more complicated, such as blind scrying, or creating mage-walls to keep the "boggles" out. For another, Hardorn was only *buffered*; there were still slight effects, and those were increasing, a little at a time, with every passing day.

Darkwind spread his hands wide, shaking his long, silver-streaked hair back over his shoulders as he did so. "That, I cannot tell you. The people to ask would be the k'Leshya, and they are somewhat difficult to reach at the moment."

He caught Elspeth's face taking on that slightly vacant look that meant she was Mindspeaking to Gwena, and he waited for her to say something. Tremane was always forgetting that Gwena was "present" in spirit, if not sitting at the same table, and the Companion would hardly forgo a chance to remind him.

"Gwena says that she can relay an inquiry to Skif's Cymry at k'Leshya Vale, and get the answer back in a couple of days," Elspeth said, her dark eyes crinkling at the corners, telling Darkwind that she was holding back laughter. Gwena had probably said far more than that, probably about Tremane and his faulty memory, but this *was* a diplomatic mission and such things would not be diplomatic to relate. "There are enough mages there that surely someone will know the answer. And she says if not, then she can relay on to Florian at the Tower and see if An'desha knows anything."

Not every Companion had that long-distance capability; in fact, there were only two in all of the world as far as Darkwind knew. One was Gwena, and the other was Rolan, the Companion of the Queen's Own. They were special; "Grove-born," the Heralds called it, and claimed that instead of being physically brought into being in the normal way, they simply appeared, full-grown, out of a grove in the middle of Companion's Field. They had unusually powerful abilities in mind-magic, and through most of the history of Valdemar there had never been more than one Grove-born Companion at once. But then again, this was, by all accounts both sacred and secular, a crucial point in the history, not only of Valdemar, but of this entire part of the world, and if ever there was the need for a second Grove-born Companion, this was the time.

Tremane chewed on his lip, and ran a hand over the top of his balding head. "You know," he said cautiously. "The fact that those weapons they are looking at in the Tower survived at all might indicate that some shields held, wouldn't it? Surely there were very powerful shields on that Tower at the time of the Cataclysm."

"And it might only indicate that things at the heart of the Cataclysm had some natural protection, like things in the eye of a whirlwind," Elspeth reminded him, twisting a silver-threaded chestnut curl around one finger. "I wouldn't count on that. I also wouldn't count on any of us, singly or together, being able to replicate shields created by the mages who lived back then. These were people capable of *creating* living beings—gryphons, basilisks, wyrsa—and I don't know of anyone living now who would even attempt such a thing."

Darkwind cleared his throat softly to regain their attention. "To get back to your question about the effects of the original Cataclysm—afterward, the natural flows of magic energy in those areas changed completely, and we can only assume that the same thing will happen again. And as for the physical world—well, we Hawkbrothers are still healing the damage that was created in the wake of the original Storms. If you think the monsters that you've seen so far are bad, wait until there are hundreds, thousands of them, when the number of warped and changed creatures equals or exceeds the number of normal creatures." He drummed his fingers on the table for a moment as he made some quick calculations. "To give you an idea, it has taken us something like two thousand years to clear an area approximately half the size of your Empire of dangerous creatures and even more dangerous magic."

Tremane brooded over his stack of paper for a moment. "So your suggestion would be. . . ?"

Elspeth and Darkwind exchanged another look, and it was Darkwind who replied. "If our group at the Tower can't do anything—warn everyone you can reach, create what shields and shelters you can, assume that they won't hold, and endure. Make your plans after you see what the effects are this time."

The Duke made a sour face, but did not respond. Elspeth tried some sympathy.

"Duke Tremane, I know this is difficult for you, but at least you are in command of an area in which much of the magical energy has been drained away, and which never relied on magic to get things done in the first place," she pointed out. "You can count on most buildings staying up, most bridges standing firm, count on fires heating your barracks as they always have, candles lighting the darkness, and food cooking properly in a well-made oven. Hardorn is prepared for everything except what the final Storm will do to the physical world—and in a way, you can even prepare for that, simply by knowing what the last Cataclysm did."

Tremane sighed, and rubbed one temple with his fingers. "Yes, I know this, and I also know that this is not going to be the case in the Empire. Things were falling to pieces so badly that when I mounted my raid on that Imperial warehouse complex, the men there hadn't heard from their superiors in weeks, and now—I can't even imagine the state of chaos the Empire must be in. It's just that things were difficult for us before, and the one comfort I had was that I couldn't envision them getting any worse. Now I have to, and plan for it, somehow."

Elspeth shook her head emphatically. "You can't *plan* for this, Tremane. All you can do is to warn people of what they *might* expect, and put things in place that will give you information once the worst happens. The signal-towers, for one thing. They work almost as well as Companions, and you ought to make it a priority to get them manned by people who know how to use them. You ought to make it a priority to get more of them in place if it is at all possible! If every little village had a tower, the way every village has access to a Herald, you'd be able to get help to people long before a messenger could have reached you."

Darkwind nodded. "Don't plan for specific events; doing that will inevitably prove to be an exercise in futility."

"Plan for flexibility, you mean?" The Duke considered that for a moment, and nodded. "All right, I can see that." Then he sighed. "And plan for communication, put ways of bringing in information in place while we still can. That's good, as long as the trouble spots are places where there are still people living. But if they aren't, there could be a nest of something brewing, some monstrous creatures, say, and we wouldn't know about it until the creatures had wiped out an entire town. Maybe not even then."

He rubbed his forehead, and Darkwind saw the shadow of physical pain in his eyes, in the tense muscles of his homely face. "I just wish there was a way to watch the *land*," he said fretfully. "I used to be able to get my mages to scry entire stretches of countryside, and that's what I'd give my arm to have working again."

Darkwind exchanged another look with Elspeth. :*What do you think? This is the best opening he's ever given us.*:

:*If we can make him believe in earth-sense,*: she replied, with some pessimism. :*Still, you're right. It isn't just the best opening, it's the only opening he's ever given us.*:

:*You, or me?*: he asked.

:*Me first, just to open the subject. I'm the local royalty, the local Herald, and the local expert in mind-magic. I could be expected to know about these things, and know if the Hardornens were just making something up. You pick up if you see an opening to insert something you know.*:

He folded his hands on the table in front of him as she cleared her throat. "Duke Tremane," she said, "I may have a solution to that particular problem, and oddly enough it is a part of a proposition that the Hardornens outside your domain wanted me to make to you on their behalf." She smiled apologetically. "I think you probably were anticipating that the loyalists might ask us to serve as their envoys as well as envoys for the Alliance. We promised we would put their proposal before you at an opportune time, but we promised nothing else; that seemed harmless enough."

He looked up sharply, and a little suspiciously. "A proposition? What sort of proposition?"

Elspeth bit her lip and looked down at her strong, well-muscled hands for a moment. They were hardly the hands of a pampered princess, and Darkwind had a suspicion that Tremane had noticed this. "Well . . . it's a rather interesting one. It seems that they've been watching how you manage things here, and you've frankly impressed them. There seems to be a general consensus that under certain very specific circumstances, they would not only be happy to arrange a truce with you, but they would be willing to offer you the crown of Hardorn itself."

He looked as if she had hit him in the back of the head with a board. It was the first time he had ever actually shown surprise. "The *crown?* They'd make me their *King?* What about their own claimants?"

"There aren't any," Darkwind said crisply. "Ancar was very thorough when it came to eliminating rivals. We were told that there weren't even any claimants on the distaff side; apparently he didn't in the least see any reason to exclude his female relatives from the purges, nor children, nor even infants. From all anyone can tell, he went back to the fourth and fifth remove of the cousins. By the time he was finished, well, *you* have as much right to the throne as any of the natives, that's how thin the royal connections are."

We learned most of that when we were here last, but I don't think it would be politic to mention that little trip.

Tremane didn't exactly pale, but he did look a little shocked. "And I thought that politics in the Empire were cutthroat," he murmured, as if to himself. Then he blinked, and collected himself. "So, just what *are* these specific circumstances you were talking about? And how will all this give me intelligence about what is happening to the land?"

Elspeth toyed with her glass of water. "This is where I am going to have to ask you to stretch your imagination a bit,

Tremane," she replied. "You know that mind-magic exists, now that you've seen the members of our party use it."

He nodded cautiously.

"You also have your own Healers who use Healing magic, which is similar to, but not identical with, mind-magic," she continued, "And you know that neither are affected by the mage-storms which are disrupting what we in Valdemar call *true*-magic."

"I'm following you so far," Tremane said with a nod.

"Well, as near as we can tell, there is another form of magic which is *like* mind-magic and *like* Healing-magic, but isn't exactly either of them," she told him, leaning forward earnestly. "It's called earth-magic, and it seems to have entirely to do with the land, the health of the land, and restoring that health. We think that's what hedge-wizards and earth-witches use, rather than true-magic; people who are trained in those disciplines—so they tell me—also refer to their power as earth-magic, and they call what you and Darkwind and I are accustomed to using by the name of *high*-magic."

:*Right. So you tell him about Hawkbrother Healing Adepts while I figure out how to segue this into the earth-binding ritual.*:

Darkwind nodded very slightly and caught up the conversational ball. "We Tayledras have specialized Adepts called Healing Adepts who have the ability to sense the poisoned places, the places where magic has made things go wrong, and fix them again," he told Tremane, who was sitting back in his chair with an odd expression that Darkwind could not read. "And if you need evidence of how well this works, it is in the fact that we *have* restored so much of the land to the pre-Cataclysm days. The special ability that makes this possible—Elspeth's people would call it a *Gift*—is something we all call the earth-sense."

"It's not just Tayledras Healing Adepts and earth-witches that use this. Both the King of Rethwellan and my stepfather Prince Daren have earth-sense, in fact," she said, taking the narrative back. "It seems that the Gift has always been in the Rethwellan royal line. They haven't needed it for generations, but it's obvious how useful it is when you know that even though Daren was not familiar with Hardorn and not ritually tied to the land here, he could *still* sense what Ancar had done to it when he came here to help Valdemar drive Ancar out. That actually proved to be of tactical value, since it gave us an idea of where Ancar was finding all the power he needed."

Tremane nodded, his brows knitted intently, and seized on the phrase that they had both hoped he would. "Ritually tied to the land?" he asked. "Just what does that mean?"

"The monarchs of Rethwellan—and I presume, of Hardorn—have always taken part in a very old ritual known as *earth-binding,*" she told him. "Because we in Valdemar do not have that particular ritual, I can't even begin to tell you how it works, or why, but when it is over, every major injury or change to the land is instantly sensed by the monarch. Ancar obviously never participated in that ritual, or he could not have done the things he did—I suspect that, as in Rethwellan, the earth-binding is part of the Hardornen private rites that take place just before the public coronation. Ancar crowned himself, without the usual rituals, so—" She shrugged. "My stepfather says that those who even have earth-sense latently can have it aroused by such a rite."

"The point here is that the people of Hardorn have found some of the priests of the old ways who know that ritual," Darkwind continued, as she glanced at him to cue him to take up the narrative. "*They* think that if you were to be tested for earth-sense and had it even latently, that would qualify you for the Hardornen crown. And if you were to undergo the earth-binding ritual, thus awakening the earth-sense and binding you to Hardorn, you would be a—a *safe* monarch for Hardorn, because you would be unable to harm, abuse, or misuse your land the way Ancar did."

"Because harming the land would hurt me." He lifted one eyebrow skeptically.

:Is he going to laugh?: Elspeth sounded dubious, and Darkwind didn't blame her. This was such a primitive, unsophisticated concept—for someone from the Eastern Empire, so sophisticated in the ways of magic that its power was used for practically everything, this must seem incredibly savage and crude.

But he didn't laugh, and in fact, he seemed to be thinking the concept over. "Can you tell me anything else about this earth-sense? Just what does it entail? How do you learn to use it?"

"Among my people, it isn't very complicated," Darkwind told him. "You don't so much learn to use it as you learn to keep it from using you. It's rather like Empathy in a way, or extremely strong Mindspeech. You actually learn how to shut it out so that it doesn't affect you all the time."

"Interesting. I can see how it would be inconvenient to be affected adversely by the very condition you are attempting to remedy." His brows creased in thought. "And does it go the other way? Does the physical condition of the King affect the land?"

"Havens, no!" Elspeth exclaimed. "For one thing, the King is not exactly as—as *monumental* as a country! It would be like a flea stepping on a horse. For another, it's only a sense, like the sense of smell, and. . . ." She trailed off in confusion as Darkwind shook his head.

"I hate to have to contradict Elspeth, but that's not entirely true, Duke Tremane," he said, feeling the need to be totally frank. "Under certain *very* specific circumstances, the health of the King who is bound to the land can affect the land. He can, in fact, sacrifice himself—give up his own life—to restore the land to its former health. This is something that my people know, and that the Shin'a'in not only know, but have even, very rarely, practiced. I must also say, however, that I personally do not believe that the Hardornens ever practiced that form of earth-binding. As with all crafts, there are scores, even hundreds or thousands of ways to do them, and nothing that they told us gave me any indication that they even know such a possibility exists. And I must also point out that to be valid, to have any chance of working, the sacrifice must be a *self*-sacrifice, entirely voluntary, and indeed eagerly sought by the sacrificial victim." He managed a thin smile. "Hauling one's King to the stone of sacrifice and spilling his blood upon the ground only serves as a sort of gruesome fertilizer to the local grass; it won't change anything else without that will to be sacrificed."

Tremane's brows crept halfway up his forehead as Darkwind imparted that choice bit of information, but he made no comment. After a moment, he stood up.

"I'd like to go think about this for a little," he said. "I assume you have a way of contacting someone if I make a decision?"

:I can find a contact,: Gwena said firmly in both their minds.

"We do," Elspeth told him.

"Then give me—about a mark," he replied. "I'll send for you, if you have no objections."

Since it had been a very long time since breakfast, and this would provide an excellent excuse to send their Imperial aide in search of food, Darkwind had no objections whatsoever, and neither did Elspeth. With a polite exchange of bows, they retired to their own quarters, leaving him sitting back in his chair, staring at the ducal ring on his finger, clearly deep in thought.

They were about halfway through a solid, if uninspired meal of bread and cold sliced meat and pickles, when Gwena announced that she had found the contact she had promised. *:Go to the Hanging Goose Tavern after dark,:* she told Darkwind. *:It will have to be you, since I don't think that Elspeth would be welcome in this particular tavern, and if there are two of you, he might suspect a trap.:*

Elspeth exchanged a wry glance with Darkwind and shrugged, applying herself to her food.

:You want to speak to the bartender who dispenses the beer, not the one who handles the harder drinks,: she continued. *:You tell him, "I drink my beer very cold." He is supposed to reply, "That's an odd habit," and you say, "I picked it up in the West." He'll nod and ask you what your message is. He has a perfect memory; he'll pass it on word for word. If Tremane decides to take the gamble, I suspect you'll have your delegation, priest included, within a few days. Maybe sooner. They might have moved someone into a village nearby, hoping you would be able to offer him the proposition soon after we arrived.:*

"I rather suspected that the loyalists had agents in the city," Elspeth said, as she ate the last bite. "I couldn't imagine how they knew so much about him just from 'hearing things.' But this sounds as if the network has been well in place for some time. It takes a long time to find someone with a perfect memory who is trustworthy enough to act as a message drop. It makes me wonder if this tavern wasn't a contact point for . . . other things." She smiled suggestively at Darkwind.

He chuckled. "I am just a poor Hawkbrother scout with no

knowledge of you city dwellers and your ways," he protested. "What other things?"

"Smuggling, maybe. Possibly intriguing against Ancar. And I'll *bet* the reason Gwena doesn't want me to go there is not because I wouldn't be welcome alone there either." She grinned at something Gwena said only to her. "I thought so." She reached out and patted Darkwind's hand. "The ladies working in this tavern will be selling more than just strong drink and food, my poor, uncivilized Hawkbrother. I suggest that you make it very clear to them that you aren't interested in their wares, or you might bring something inconvenient and uncomfortable home with you that would require a Healer's help to clear up."

He grinned back at her, and was trying to think of a clever retort when Tremane's aide came to fetch them.

The Grand Duke was waiting for them when they arrived, looking no different than when they had left him. They took their seats and waited for him to speak.

"Frankly, I am not entirely convinced that this earth-sense you told me about really exists," he said after a moment. "And I honestly do not think, if it exists, that *I* happen to have it. It just seems all too very pat and too coincidental that out of all the people who might have been sent here, *I* would happen to have this sense which is needed at this particular time." He frowned a little. "It's rather too much like something a tale-seller might make up."

"Possibly," Darkwind replied. "But you might consider it before you dismiss this proposition out-of-hand. If you take as your premise that earth-sense *does* exist, and that the extreme form of it could only be . . . induced, let us say . . . by this ritual, then the lesser, or latent forms would be very useful to anyone who was in a position to rule even a small area. Having such a thing could explain why some landowners are more successful at managing their property than others—why some landowners have an uncanny ability to gauge what is going on with their property and people, and why some have remarkable hunches that always prove correct."

"I can see that," Tremane acknowledged.

"So, given that, it is logical to assume that those landowners whose lines were so Gifted would be more prosperous than others, would accumulate more property, and would eventually rise to higher and higher positions of power over the many generations," Darkwind persisted. "And in short, it would actually be *logical* to assume that a man who had been a ruler of property or even a King would be so Gifted, because his predecessors could not have prospered so well without it."

Tremane laughed out loud; it was the first time that Darkwind had ever heard him laugh, and he liked the sound of it. He often judged aspects of peoples' character by their laughter; Tremane's laugh was open, generous, and not at all self-conscious.

"I think that if you had not been born among the Hawkbrothers, you would have become a diplomat, a courtier, or a priest, Master Darkwind," he said finally. "You certainly can turn a fine argument. Now, hear me out, if you please."

Darkwind and Elspeth both nodded, and Tremane set forth his own reasoning.

"You must know, and *they* must know, that with or without this *earth-sense,* if my men and I can recreate order here—as we already have done, you might note—people will come to my banner without the title attached to it. That is the great secret of Imperial success. We wait until a land is disorganized and demoralized, and then we move in, offering peace, order, and prosperity. Usually people welcome us. Then, when they see the high level that Imperial prosperity represents, word spreads, and the lands we move on generally are half-conquered before the Army itself ever reaches them."

"That makes rather too much sense," Elspeth put in dryly.

He nodded his acknowledgment and continued, tapping his index finger on the table to emphasize each point. "You must make it very clear to these people that no matter what happens, I intend to go on holding this particular piece of Hardorn from now on, for myself, my men, and those Hardornens who have accepted my rule and my order without any of this earth-binding business."

"I think they are already well aware of that, Tremane," she answered just as frankly. "But I will make sure that arrangement is openly acknowledged on both sides. To be honest with you, there is no way that you can be dislodged with the few resources these Hardornen loyalists have at their command. That would take an army. The only armies large enough are those commanded by the Allies, and we are here representing the Allies in a gesture of peace and goodwill, so I don't think you need concern yourself about losing your hold on this place."

"Good. Just so that we're all clear on that." He toyed with a corner of a piece of paper for a moment. "I can't say that I really care for the idea of subjecting myself to this ritual. It all sounds terribly primitive, somehow. But perhaps even if *I* don't believe I have this so-called earth-sense, the priest will be convinced that I do, and will let me go through with this ritual even if it is meaningless. Frankly, if that happens, it would be the easiest and quickest way to get all of Hardorn under my wing, and it would be done with absolutely no bloodshed." He smiled; an oddly shy smile, and Darkwind had the feeling that it was a rare smile, as if Tremane had even less to smile about than to laugh about. "How could I possibly turn away that kind of opportunity?"

"In your position, I certainly would not," Darkwind told him. "Well, is that the whole of your message?"

Tremane nodded. "And if you'll excuse me, I have matters regarding my men to see to. My aide can escort you back to your quarters, and if there is anywhere in the city you need to go, he can give you the proper directions."

:*That won't be necessary,*: Gwena said.

"Thank you," Darkwind replied, without giving any indication that he would take Tremane up on his offer.

Once again, after a polite exchange of bows, they departed for their own quarters. Elspeth had a thoughtful look on her face, but waited until they were alone again before saying anything.

She stood with her back to the cast-iron-and-brick stove holding the mage-fire, warming herself at it. A real fire also burned on the hearth, and between the two, their rooms were as comfortable as any in Valdemar. But the hallways of this fortified manor were still cold, despite the addition of such stoves, and they both tended to get chilled going from their quarters to Tremane's.

There was no doubt that this was one of the worst winters that Hardorn had ever experienced, even without the effect of the mage-storms. The main difference in the weather now that the mage-storms had abated, according to their aide, was that now there were only snowstorms, not killing blizzards, every two weeks or so. With the incredible blanket of snow covering the ground, the sun couldn't even begin to melt it before another layer fell.

The modified Heralds' Whites that the *hertasi* had designed for her seemed particularly well-suited to the icy landscape outside. He wondered what the Imperial soldiers thought when they saw her; did they believe that her costume was meant to reflect the season, as Tayledras scout gear did?

"You know," Elspeth said finally, in Tayledras. "This situation has some interesting parallels in the history of Valdemar—the Founding, specifically."

"Oh?" Darkwind joined her, hands outstretched to the warm stove, wishing that there was something like a Hawkbrother hot spring or soaking pool about. It never seemed possible to be entirely warm except in bed. He responded in the same language. "I wasn't aware of that."

"Well, Valdemar was fleeing the Empire rather than serving it when he and his followers trekked out in this direction, but when he got to the point where Haven is now and started building, he actually built beside an existing village," Elspeth replied, turning to face the stove and rubbing her hands together. "The locals there were not entirely thrilled with having a foreign power moving in, although they never actually *opposed* him. But once they saw the advantages of coming under his protection—and the way in which his own followers were treated—they began to act the way the Hardornens are with Tremane. And eventually, of course, they insisted that he call himself a King." She chuckled. "That was really rather funny; it seemed that every little petty ruler for leagues in every direction was calling himself a 'King,' and his own people were embarrassed to be led by a mere Baron. They had a crown made up, called in a priest to concoct a ceremony, and had him crowned before he had a chance to object. I gather that he was rather startled by it all."

Darkwind laughed. "That may be the first time I've ever heard of someone being tricked into becoming a King," he responded. "But you're right, I do see the parallels there."

She stared at the stove, frowning. "I think we can assume that Tremane is going to be offered the Crown, no matter what."

"I think that is a foregone conclusion, yes, lover," Darkwind admitted. "Even if he doesn't have earth-sense, the priest may perform the binding anyway, just to make him eligible. I think he was right about that."

She sighed and nodded. "The next question may be how we arrange for there to be the same checks on the King of Hardorn that there are on the Son of the Sun, the King of Rethwellan, and the Queen of Valdemar. Solaris has to answer to Vkandis, Faram has both the earth-binding and his family's sword to contend with, and Selenay has her Companion." She chewed her lip. "Then again—we may already have those checks partially in place. Solaris *did* curse him with speaking only the truth, after all."

"Yes, but not the whole truth," he reminded her. "There are ways of lying simply by not telling *all* of the truth."

She grimaced, and turned away from the warmth to pace the room as she often did when she was thinking. "You may think I'm going mad, but I'm beginning to agree with young Karal; I think this man has a basically good nature. That entire interview about the assassins when we first arrived. . . ."

Darkwind nodded, for he had come away with the same impression out of that interview; that Tremane was a man who would bear the dreadful burden of indirectly ordering the deaths of innocent people, and he would feel guilt about that for the rest of his life. *Real* guilt, not feigned. And it didn't matter that he had good reason at the time for his actions; what mattered was that he himself had changed over the course of these several months. What had been acceptable to him before no longer was.

But Darkwind also was aware that the man could be a very good actor. Most rulers were, to a greater or lesser extent.

"I still have some reservations," he said after a moment. "What occurred in the past is immutable. He *has* done terrible things to us, and without any provocation. Perhaps he has regrets now, but I find myself wondering if he might not revert to his old ways under pressure."

She sighed. :*I think we'd better continue this conversation in a way that can't be overheard,:* she cautioned.

:*Good idea. Sejanes had some magical way of learning Valdemaran and other tongues; there might be someone else here who can do the same thing.:* Granted, there might not be enough mage-energy for them to do so, but why take the chance? *:We Tayledras are more suspicious than any other race, I think, but I wish I knew if it was Tremane's better nature that had been subverted by the expediency of the Empire, or his expedient nature that has chosen to disguise itself as a good heart for—well—!:*

:He's in a position to do everyone more good than harm right now,: Gwena pointed out, joining the conversation.

:Gwena's right; and in fact, that's exactly what he has *done,:* Elspeth seconded. *:Look at his record:* granted, *he co-opted the best structure in the area for his headquarters, but other than that, he lives a relatively lean life for someone who is basically the uncrowned king of this area. He eats exactly the same food as his men, he isn't wasting precious resources on extravagant entertainments for his own benefit; in fact, he's pouring a lot of those resources back into the community here. He never asks his men to do anything he wouldn't, and he's usually out there leading them in person.:*

:He thinks first of his men, then of the local folk, then of their land and their beasts, and then *of himself,:* Gwena put in. *:That is the pattern that I'm seeing, and honestly, while some of that might be expediency, it can't all be explained by that.:*

Darkwind chuckled. *:I'm glad he's not handsome; I'd be jealous. He's managed to seduce both my ladies away from me.:*

Elspeth picked up an inkstand and pretended to throw it at him; he ducked.

:Consider yourself kicked,: Gwena retorted.

:Honestly, ke'chara, I would like to give him the chance to prove himself, and the way he handles the next crisis—which is going to be very, very bad, I think—will tell us what he's really made of,: Elspeth replied.

Darkwind chewed on that thought a while before replying, wondering if they were all making a terrible mistake. He *wanted* to believe in Tremane, and in the idea that the man was finally allowing himself to behave in a moral fashion rather than a calculated one. How must it have felt, to spend most of one's life having to plot each and every action without regard to whether or not it was ethically right? If he himself had been in that position, he'd have been driven mad.

:All right,: he said at last, *:but I have one proviso.:* His jaw

tensed as he hardened his mind. *:If he proves treacherous, and a danger to the Alliance—if he is going to cost more lives—we take care of the situation ourselves.:*

:You mean, kill him.: Elspeth nodded, very slowly. *:I don't like it—but I don't want another Ancar, much less another Falconsbane. He's used to using magic, and it would be very tempting to resort to the blood-path to get the power he's used to having.:* She shivered, and so did he; they had both seen far too much of the results of that path. *:We've done this before, and I'd rather the blood were on our hands, I suppose, than find that even more innocent blood had been spilled.:*

It was a nasty moral trap; when was murder acceptable? But that was the moral trap that the Tayledras had always been in. Darkwind himself had faced it many times—warning trespassers three times, and assuming that if they did not heed the warning, they were in Hawkbrother lands for evil purposes. How many would-be enslavers of *tervardi* and *hertasi*, mages hunting for yet more power for the wrong purposes, and would-be murderers of Hawkbrothers had he eliminated over the years? Enough that he had lost count.

Elspeth only had a handful of deaths on her conscience, but she was prepared to add another if the need was there.

:And with any luck, we'll all discover that our pessimism is unfounded,: Gwena said cheerfully. *:I'll tell you what; I will see if I can tell whether or not Tremane has earth-sense, while you make contact with the loyalists. Darkwind, my dear, we need to rummage through your wardrobe and find something in it that will not scream* foreigner *to every person in the town.:*

:What do you mean, we, *horse?:* he asked her.

Darkwind found his messenger—and Gwena's careful probe of Duke Tremane uncovered only a verdict of "maybe." Four days later, their aide knocked tentatively on the door to their quarters just after they'd finished breakfast. "Excuse me, Envoys?" he said, when Darkwind opened the door to him. "I don't want to interrupt, but there's a religious gentleman below who says that you called for him?"

Elspeth turned in surprise. Despite Gwena's assurance, she hadn't really expected an answer to their message this quickly. The man really *must* have been fairly close by; that argued for certainty on the part of the Hardornens that they had made Tremane an offer he would find irresistible.

"We have been expecting him, Jem," Darkwind told the young man. "We just didn't know when he would arrive. If you are reasonably sure that it is safe to do so, please show him the way up. Otherwise, if you are not happy with a potential breach of security, we can arrange to meet him in the town."

Jem flushed. "Oh, no. He's just an old man—it won't cause any problems. I just didn't know if you wanted to be bothered with him, if he might be a charlatan or—" He flushed even redder, realizing that he might have inadvertently insulted all of them.

"That's fine, Jem. Please show him here, and arrange for something hot for all of us to drink. And perhaps more food, he might not have broken his own fast yet," Elspeth said, in her kindest tones.

The aide bowed a little, still red with embarrassment, and left quickly. Tremane's aides were far more used to military situations than to the diplomatic ones they now found themselves hip-deep in. Elspeth found it rather charming, actually; military men were, in general, much easier to deal with and much more straightforward than civilians.

The old man and the second breakfast arrived at the same time; Elspeth privately thought that she wasn't too surprised Jem had taken him for a possible charlatan. There was nothing at all remarkable about him. His hair, gray and a touch on the shaggy side, looked as if he had not put a scissors to it lately. His build was that of a long-time clerk whose parents may have been merchants or tradesmen of modest means. His face, square, with a small beard, was lined with care, yet had smile-creases bracketing his mouth and eyes. His robes and cloak were clean and serviceable, but hardly impressive, he wore no liturgical jewels, and his manner was unassuming and cheerful. All of which, in her experience, meant that he was probably a very *good* priest; good priests, like good leaders, gave more to their followers than they kept for themselves, and were not particularly conscious of appearances.

They introduced themselves and offered the old man, who called himself Father Janas, their hospitality. As Elspeth had anticipated, he hadn't eaten, and he applied himself to the food with a hearty appetite. They kept conversation to a minimum until he had finished; once he had taken his cloak off, it was fairly obvious that, like most Hardornens, he had been sharing in the hard times. He wasn't emaciated, but he was thin enough that he had probably been on the same short rations as his followers.

"Oh, that was lovely," he said at last, when he had finished, and leaned back in his chair cradling a cup of hot tea laden with honey. "I'm afraid that my besetting sin is that I cannot resist good food." He laughed. "Since we are supposed to be concentrating on the spiritual world rather than the secular world, I suspect I shall be chided for my failing sooner or later by those to whom I must answer."

Darkwind smiled at that. "I would rather say that you were showing proper joy and respect for the bounty of the earth," Darkwind replied, and the old priest chuckled, a twinkle in his eyes.

"Well, shall we deal with the reason that I am here, rather than engage in rationalizing my shortcomings?" he asked, after taking a sip of his tea. "As I assume *you* suppose, I have come to test Duke Tremane for earth-sense, which will mean that I will awake it if it is there; and once I have done so, I will bind him to Hardorn. Now, nothing I have been vouchsafed has given me any indication that he does or does not have the Sense, and I am quite sure that *he* has no idea what is going to happen; do either of you?"

Elspeth shook her head. "We don't use that Gift in Valdemar, or, rather, if we do, it isn't used by Heralds, Bards, or Healers. And those are the only ones whose training I'm familiar with," she said. "My stepfather has it, but we've never discussed it much, and *he* was never formally bound to Valdemar. I've heard of other latent Gifts being awakened as a theoretical possibility, but no one in my lifetime has ever tried such a thing."

Darkwind shrugged, as the priest turned to him. "The Tayledras Healing Adepts all develop earth-sense along with their other abilities," he replied. "It doesn't come on them all at once, and if anyone has it latently, we've never bothered to awaken it. I haven't any idea how someone would react in such a circumstance."

Father Janas raised an eyebrow. "It can be rather dramatic," he said cautiously. "Assuming that one has it latently, rather than having a very weak version of the Sense, that is. We have always conducted this particular ceremony several days before the actual coronation of our kings, precisely because of that. It sometimes takes the recipient a good deal of time to get used to his new ability, if heretofore it has only been latent and when actuated proves to be very strong."

Elspeth nodded. "Rather like suddenly being able to see, I suppose," she offered. "Well, that is all very well in theory, but you are here to put theory into practice. How soon would you care to see Duke Tremane? Are there any preparations you would like to make, any vestments you need to change into before you are presented?"

Father Janas smoothed down the front of his robe self-consciously. "Much as I wish I could present a more impressive picture, I am afraid that I am wearing my best—indeed, my only vestments." He licked his lips and looked apologetic. "Ancar did not persecute priests and clerics directly, but he found many ways of doing so indirectly. I do not think you will find a single religious organization in all of Hardorn surviving at better than a subsistence level, and many simply vanished altogether as old members died and no new ones came to replace them." He shook his head sadly. "At any rate, it is all moot; I have no preparations to make, and I should prefer to see the Duke as soon as possible, as soon as he has the time free."

Darkwind rose to request their aide to take a message to the Duke. Elspeth had some other ideas, however.

She wrote a short note while Darkwind was talking with Jem, and asked the aide to take the message down to Tremane's chief of supply on his way back from delivering their request for an audience to the Duke. Jem looked baffled, but agreed; he was obviously not going to question why the envoy wanted to send a note to the supply sergeant.

"Just what are you up to?" Darkwind asked her, as they closed the door behind his retreating back and returned to their guest.

Elspeth seated herself before replying. "Tremane told me that he and his men had virtually gutted an entire Imperial warehouse complex," she told him, as well as their guest. "Now, given how the Empire likes to regiment things, even though there is no *official* Imperial religion, I am betting that somewhere among all the uniforms brought back are at least a few standard Imperial Army Chaplains' robes, or something of that nature. And I'm also betting that they look pretty much like every other priest's robes I've ever seen, precisely because an Imperial Army Chaplain would have to be able to conduct the rites of several religions, hence the uniform robe will be as bland and as *general* as possible."

"I follow your reasoning so far," Darkwind said, still puzzled. "But why should the supply sergeant let us have one of these uniforms, if they exist?"

She grinned. "I've been talking to the townsfolk. I know that it is Tremane's standard procedure to sell anything in stores that is not immediately useful to his soldiers if a civilian wants to buy it. You'll find a lot of townsfolk outfitted in surplused uniforms of some of the odder auxiliary disciplines, if you know what to look for. I asked specifically if I could purchase a set of chaplain's robes if there are any, and asked him to send them up as soon as he found them." She turned to the priest, who was a little flushed. "We'll have plenty of time to alter them into something approximating your own vestments before Tremane has time to see us."

Father Janas looked even more embarrassed. "Really, that's too good of you—"

She interrupted him with a cautionary hand. "You're being generous and forgiving; I know that this was a bit high-handed of me. But we may be more anxious to settle this than you are, and I'd prefer not to leave anything to chance. The Grand Duke isn't even certain that he believes earth-sense exists; I suspect his attitude is more that he is humoring us than anything else. We all want him to agree to go through with something he already considers to be mummery, and we want him to agree to do it *now*. The better the impression your appearance will make on him, the more likely he is to do that."

Darkwind nodded thoughtfully. "Actually," he put in, "using an Imperial uniform may serve us better than if you had come with your own vestments. He has lived with the chaplains. He is going to respect the uniform and what it represents without realizing he is primed to do so."

Father Janas uttered a faint laugh in self-deprecation. "Well, it is certainly true that most people rely on one's outward appearance for their first impressions, and I am afraid my appearance is hardly likely to inspire confidence."

His admission only deepened his obvious embarrassment, and Darkwind quickly changed the subject to that of the conditions over most of Hardorn. The priest was only too willing to talk about the hardships people all over the country had and were suffering, and the spirit with which they were enduring those hardships.

"Everything you saw as you journeyed here is representative of conditions everywhere in this land," he said, with real sadness. "People are not starving, but they are hungry. They are not freezing to death, but they are cold. There is not a single soul in this country that did not lose at least one member of his family to unnatural death in the last five years, and as you saw, entire towns and villages have been emptied. Temples and other places of worship are deserted, or tended by a few old men like myself. Worst of all, we have lost most of a generation of young men, and no matter how much better things become, how can we possibly replace them? Who will be the parents of our next generation of citizens?"

There are several thousand young men, none of whom will ever be able to return to the Empire, camped right here, Elspeth thought. *And most of* them *would be perfectly happy to become the parents of the next generation of Hardornens. I wonder if he's thought of that? I know Tremane has.*

At length Jem returned with the answer from Duke Tremane; he would be free immediately after lunch to receive the priest, and if necessary, could clear a good portion of the afternoon for the interview.

"That would be wise," Father Janas said, as Darkwind deferred to him. "Please return, tell him this would be very much to my liking, and ask him to do so."

Jem went back with the reply. Not long after he left, one of the many locals who had been hired to run errands within the Imperial complex arrived with a large, neat package and a handwritten bill. Elspeth accepted both, made a face at the mildly extortionate price the supply officer was charging, but rummaged in her belt-pouch for the correct number of silver coins anyway. They were Valdemaran rather than Hardornen or Imperial, but the price had been quoted in silver-weight and not a specific coinage. Given the circumstances, she doubted that anyone would care whose face was stamped on them so long as the weight was true. Those she sent back with the errand boy, as Darkwind handed the package over to Father Janas.

Just as she had suspected, the official uniform of an Imperial Chaplain was, once the rainbow of specific accoutrements for various religions and liturgical events were set aside, virtually identical in cut to the threadbare robe Father Janas already wore; it was even a very similar gray in color. He retired to the next room to change, and returned looking much trimmer.

Darkwind surveyed him with a critical eye. "Just what form does your deity—or deities—take?" he asked the priest. "Forgive me, but I think we need to make you look a little more impressive."

The priest looked confused but answered readily enough. "The Earth-father and Sky-mother are usually represented by the colors green and blue, and by a circle or sphere that is half white and half black, but—"

Darkwind had already turned to the pile of multicolored stoles and other accessories, sorting through the plethora of plain and appliqued fabrics, and came up with one stole that was green, and one blue. Quick work with his knife gave him four halves, two of which he handed to Elspeth. She had already divined what he was up to, and had gone into the other room for her sewing kit; a few moments later, she draped a stole about Father Janas' neck that was green on his right side and blue on his left.

But it was still too plain, and she took it back from him. While she cut half-circles of black and white fabric from two of the other stoles to applique to the ends of the new one, Darkwind left for their bedroom and returned with a bit of his personal jewelry. "This probably isn't much like something you would ordinarily wear," he said apologetically. "But it will probably do for now, and Tremane isn't going to know the difference between Hardornen and Shin'a'in work."

He handed a copper medallion on a tanned leather thong to Janas; Elspeth recognized it at once as the sort of token the Shin'a'in carried to identify themselves or their allies to Tayledras. She had once carried a similar token, meant to identify her to Kerowyn's kin, as well as to any Tayledras she might have encountered. This one was engraved with a swirling, abstract pattern on one side, and a deer on the other.

But a leather thong simply would not do. Now it was Elspeth's turn to go back to the bedroom and rummage through her jewelry.

Copper. What do I have that is copper?

When they had left, she had simply tossed everything she owned into a bag, including some of the pieces meant to go with the costumes that Darkwind himself had designed for her. A glint of copper at the bottom caught her eye, and she untangled an interesting belt made of a heavy copper chain entwined with a light one. She purloined the light chain to hang the medallion from, then as an afterthought, suggested to Father Janas that he use the heavy chain for the original purpose of a belt. That was the final touch that he needed, for the robe had been just a bit long on him; now with the new robe, stole, belt, and medallion, Janas presented quite a different picture from the man who had arrived.

He seemed to feel the change as well; he seemed less weary, stood a little straighter and with confidence matching his natural cheer. All in all, Elspeth reckoned that they had put in a good morning's work.

"It isn't precisely canonical," Janas told them, "But as you said, no one here is going to know that, and it *does* look— well—much more respectable, in the sense of *worthy of respect.* I can't begin to thank you enough."

"Thank us if all of this bears fruit," Elspeth replied firmly. "And speaking of which, here's our lunch."

As usual, it was rather plain fare, but there was plenty of it. Jem seemed startled by Father Janas' transformation, but treated him with more deference than he had shown initially, thus confirming Elspeth's feeling that the effort of reclothing the priest was more than justified. Jem lingered while they ate, which all of them read as an indication that Tremane was impatient to have the interview over with quickly. Spurred by that, they made quick work of their meal.

:I think we should let Janas take the lead in this now,: she told Darkwind.

:I agree; it will establish his authority from the beginning. After all, officially, we're only involved in this peripherally.

We were never more than the informal intermediaries,: Darkwind replied.

Elspeth signaled the priest with a slight nod as she set her
cup aside. He read the hint as adroitly as she had thought he
would.

"I think we are ready to see Duke Tremane if he is ready for
us," Father Janas said to the aide, standing up and settling his
new vestments with an air of brisk competence.

"He is ready for you, sir," Jem responded with all of the
respect that any of them could have asked. "If you would care
to follow me?"

He then looked for a moment with confusion at the two
envoys, as if he had, for that instant, forgotten that they were
involved. Clearly he was uncertain whether they should be
properly included in the invitation.

Father Janas solved his problem. "I have asked the Alliance
envoys to accompany me," he said smoothly. "If Duke Tremane has no objection."

Jem's face cleared as Janas took the question out of his
hands, and he bowed slightly to all of them. "Certainly, sir. If
you would all please come with me?"

All during the quick walk to the Grand Duke's private
quarters, Elspeth was conscious of an increasing feeling of ir-
rational excitement. *Something* was going to happen; she
wasn't quite certain what it was, but this visit was not going
to pass without an event of some sort.

*I wish there was something more of ForeSight in my family
than just an ability to get an occasional hunch,* she thought
fretfully. *It would be nice to have some warning when a
mountain is about to drop on us.*

At last they were finally closeted with Tremane, seated
across from him in three chairs arrayed before his desk. This
was not to be the less formal (Tremane was never *informal*)
sort of meeting that she and Darkwind had been having with
him of late; he had arrayed himself as the Grand Duke, the
Commander of the Army, and the local Power. He wore his
uniform, minus the Imperial devices, but with all of the other
decorations and medals to which he was entitled. He had both
a crackling fire in the hearth and a mage-fire in a stove, im-
parting a generous warmth to the room and a fragrant scent of
pine resin to the air. Sunlight streamed in through the win-

dows, whose heavy velvet curtains had been pulled back to let in as much light as possible. He had a choice of chairs to use here, and he had selected the heaviest and most thronelike for his use; the desk separated them from him like a fortress wall made of dark wood.

She was very glad now that she had gone out of her way to dress Father Janas appropriately. If he had entered this interview looking as shabby as he had when he had arrived, he would have begun on an unequal footing with Tremane. As Darkwind had speculated, she could see Tremane responding to the implied authority symbolized by a "uniform" he recognized, and Father Janas assumed his rightful position as an authority equal to his.

As for Elspeth, she was acutely aware of everything around her, her senses sharpened by her anticipation. Her feeling was so strong that it was amazing to her to see that Duke Tremane was concealing a certain amount of polite boredom under a smooth and diplomatic courtesy.

If Janas was put off by Tremane's attitude, he didn't show it. "Duke Tremane," Father Janas said, "you know why I am here. Those who have led the struggle against Imperial subjugation have heard of your defection from the Empire, seen how you have governed and protected the people here, and have come to the conclusion that *you*, at least, are not necessarily an enemy to Hardorn."

Tremane nodded at this recitation of the obvious, and waited for him to continue. Behind him, a knot in the wood on the fire *cracked* explosively; no one jumped.

Janas had clearly rehearsed his speech many times, until he was comfortable enough with it that he didn't have to think about it. "The consortium of loyal fighters believes that, since there is no one man who has been able to become their clear leader, and since no one in Hardorn commands the resources that you do, you may be the appropriate person to take up the defense of this land against outsiders and current adversity." He smiled thinly. "I will not mince words with you, Duke Tremane. These men are willing, given other conditions, to allow you to purchase the rule of Hardorn with the resources and men that you command."

He seemed a bit surprised by Father Janas' bluntness. "That

would seem reasonable," he replied with care. "And I am certainly willing to put those resources into Hardorn."

Father Janas nodded. "So I have been sent here by those men to discover if you are both fit and willing to lead this nation and help to defend it against those who would subject it to the rule of a foreign power—*including* the Empire." Janas tilted his head in inquiry. The fire popped again, scattering sparks, as he waited for an answer.

Tremane's reply was brief but polite. "I would welcome the opportunity to prove my worth, but I would like to point out that I am not, and never have been, a traitor to any cause. It was the Emperor and the Empire who abandoned us here; *we* broke none of the oaths that we had given. But now that those vows are broken, we see every need to hold fast to the oaths that we gave to each other. And if, in keeping those vows, we aid the people here, that is all to the good. Times are perilous, and whenever loyalty is found, it should be rewarded with loyalty." His face hardened. "But any new responsibilities that I assume must work *with* my vows to my men."

"There will be no conflict." Janas nodded, and there was a great deal of satisfaction on his face. "In keeping with our traditions, the ruler of Hardorn must be possessed of the quality we know as *earth-sense,* and be bound to the land if he has that quality. In order that your consent to be tested is informed, I shall explain precisely what that means."

He went into a much more detailed explanation than Elspeth or Darkwind had done, and in Elspeth's opinion, Tremane was a bit too cavalier about the entire thing. *She* had not been certain until this moment that the test for the earth-sense involved actually awakening it if it was latent. And Tremane was clearly preoccupied with some other thought as the priest explained that if he showed the symptoms of having the earth-sense, he would be expected to undergo the earth-binding ritual immediately.

Perhaps his own statements to Janas had reminded him of things he needed to deal with among his own people; perhaps it was only that he was not inclined to spend his time on something even peripherally connected with religion. She had the feeling that Tremane was a man who gave secular respect to religious authority, lip-service to the rituals, and otherwise gave no thought to the subject. And he considered the entire business of earth-sense and earth-binding to be essentially religious in nature, a matter of faith rather than fact.

:*He has already made up his mind that nothing is going to happen,:* Darkwind commented, as he watched Tremane's attention wandering. *:He is good enough at reading people to know that Janas thinks he can be a good leader for Hardorn, and I suspect he thinks that is the only "test" he needed to pass. I think he has decided that Janas will make a couple of mystic passes, then declare he has the earth-sense, mumble a few phrases, and say that he is bound to Hardorn, all without anything he can detect actually occuring.:*

:I think he's making a mistake, if that's the case,: Elspeth offered. *:I wish he'd listened a bit more closely because I don't think he really knows what he might be getting into.:*

Well, it was already too late to say anything, for Tremane nodded with relief when Janas finished, and said, "Please, I am quite ready if you can begin now."

And Janas was not going to give Tremane a chance to change his mind, for the priest stood immediately.

"If I may come to your side of the desk, sir?" Janas asked, and at Tremane's nod, moved around the desk until he stood behind Tremane's chair, and placed the tips of his fingers on Tremane's temples before Tremane had a chance to object.

The priest closed his eyes and opened his mouth before Tremane could pull away from the unexpected touch. Elspeth started, literally jumped, as what emerged from Janas's mouth was not a chant, but a single, pure, bell-like tone.

The sound resonated through her, filling her ears and her mind, driving every thought from her head and rooting her to her chair. She couldn't have moved if the room had suddenly caught on fire. She couldn't even be afraid; the tone drove out all emotion, including fear. It had exactly the same effect on Darkwind, who stared at Janas with round, vaguely surprised eyes.

But it did *not* have that effect on Duke Tremane.

Beneath Janas' hands, the Grand Duke stiffened, and his own hands came up to cover the priest's, but not as if he was trying to tear Janas's fingers away from his head. His eyes closed, and his hands were clearly holding Janas's hands in place. His own mouth opened, and a second tone, harmonizing with the first, emerged from *his* throat. The effect of the two tones together was indescribable, and even as Elspeth experienced it, she was unable to analyze it. She was suspended in time and place, and nothing existed for her but the two-note song that resonated with every fiber of her body and soul. In fact, every sense was involved; colors intensified and became richer, and there was a scent of growing things and spring flowers filling the air that could not possibly have been there.

How long that went on, Elspeth could really not have said. It took no time at all, and it took forever. The moment when it stopped was as dramatic as that when it had started, for suddenly Tremane's eyes opened wide, then rolled up into his head; his mouth snapped shut, cutting off the tone. He let go of Janas' hands, and he collapsed over his desk as if his heart had suddenly given out.

Elspeth was still frozen, unable to stir. Janas stopped his singing—if that was what it was—the moment Tremane fell forward. For a moment he stared at the Grand Duke in something like shock, shaking his hands as if he had touched a burning coal.

"Well," he said finally, "he *certainly* has earth-sense."

Before either Elspeth or Darkwind could move, the priest pulled Tremane back up into the support of his chair, and shook him gently until he awoke.

"Is—" Darkwind began, half standing. Janas waved him back.

"Duke Tremane is simply suffering from the confusion of having a very *powerful* new ability thrust upon him," the priest said in a preoccupied voice. "But there is nothing wrong with him, I promise you. In fact, he may well be more *right* than he has ever been before in his life."

Tremane was clearly still dazed, as Janas reached for a letter opener on the Duke's desk, seized one of his hands, and stabbed the tip of his index finger with it. He was so dazed, that he acted as if he hadn't even felt the point of the blade piercing his skin.

Janas held onto the Duke's hand so that Tremane couldn't pull it away, and reached into a pouch on his belt, pulling out a tiny pinch of earth. He inverted Tremane's maltreated finger over the bit of dirt, and squeezed until a single drop of blood fell and mingled with the soil.

"In the name of the powers above our heads and below our feet, I bind you to the soil of Hardorn, Tremane," he intoned, letting go of Tremane's hand and seizing his chin instead. "In the name of the Great Guardians of the people, I bind you to the heart of Hardorn," he continued, and took up the pinch of mingled blood and earth. "In the name of Life and Light, I bind you to the soul of Hardorn, and by this token, you and the land are one."

He held out the bit of blood-soaked earth to the Duke's mouth. Tremane opened his lips to receive it, and fortunately, he swallowed it rather than spitting it out, which would probably have been a very unfortunate gesture and a terrible omen.

Janas stepped back, watching the Duke narrowly, and Tremane blinked owlishly at him for a moment. Then, without any warning, he made an odd little mewling cry, and clapped both hands to his head, covering his eyes with his palms.

Now Elspeth started to rise, but the priest waved her back as well. "It's quite all right," he said, with immense satisfaction. "I can't begin to tell you how well this is going. He has the strongest earth-sense that I have ever seen in someone for whom it was latent until now—and just at the moment, he's a bit disoriented."

"Disoriented?" the Duke said from behind his hands. "By the Hundred Little Gods, that is *far* too mild a description!" He sounded breathless, as if he had been running a long and grueling race. "I feel—I feel as if I have been deaf and blind, and suddenly been given sight and hearing and I haven't the *least* notion what the things I am experiencing mean or what to do with them!"

He brought his hands down away from his head, but it was quite clear from the bewildered expression he wore and the dazed look in his eyes that he was undergoing sensations he had never experienced before. "I think I may be ill," he said faintly. "I feel terrible. I'm going to be very, very sick in a moment."

"No, you won't," Janas soothed. "That's not your own body you're feeling, it's Hardorn. The land is sick, not you; sick and weary. Separate yourself from it; remember how you felt when you woke up this morning? *That* is you, and the rest is the land's ills."

"That's easy for you to say, priest," Tremane replied feelingly. "*You* aren't in my head!" He was pale and sweating, and his pupils were so wide that there was scarcely any iris showing.

But Janas had already gone to the door and had called for Tremane's aides. "The Duke is not feeling well," he told them. "He needs to be taken to his bed and allowed to sleep. I think it would be wise to cancel any oppointments he has for the rest of the day."

Both aides looked alarmed at the state of their leader, and one put a hand on the hilt of his weapon and cast a doubtful glance at Janas, suspecting, perhaps, that the priest had somehow poisoned the Duke or inflicted a disease on him.

"It's all right," Tremane reassured them. "I think I've just been overworking. It's nothing serious."

As if that had been a coded phrase to tell the aides that nothing the visitors had done had caused his condition, both aides relaxed immediately and went to assist their leader to stand. "You know that the Healers have been warning you about overworking yourself," one of them scolded the Duke in a whisper that the foreigners were probably not supposed to hear. This was an older man, the Duke's age or even a few years senior to him, and the aide clearly considered it his responsibility to take Tremane to task. "Now look what's happened to you! You can't work yourself half to death and not expect to pay for it!"

"I'll be all right, I just need to sleep," the Duke said vaguely, and although he was not paying a great deal of attention to his surroundings or his visitors, he no longer seemed quite so disoriented, at least to Elspeth. It seemed more as if he had focused his attention inward, in a state of partial trance.

His two aides helped him into the other room, and Janas nodded at the door. Taking the hint, Elspeth and Darkwind rose and followed the priest out.

"Don't you need to be with him, to give him some kind of instruction?" Darkwind asked anxiously as they made their way along the cold corridors back to their own quarters.

The old man shook his head; he still had that air of great self-satisfaction. "No, he already has the instruction; that was what I was giving him at the beginning. It's all there for him to use, he just needs to sort things out while he sleeps. Don't worry, we've been doing things this way for centuries, not just with our monarchs, but with priests whose earth-sense is also latent. But I must say, this is probably the *most* successful ritual I have ever done!" He rubbed his hands together with unconcealed glee. "Now we'll have to get word across the country what has happened, plan for a coronation, find something like a crown—oh, there are a hundred arrangements we'll have to make."

He shook his head, interrupting himself, as they reached the door of their quarters. "I hope you won't think me rude, but I am going to *have* to leave immediately. There is just too much I have to do, and not a great deal of time to do it in. We'll be sending important people here soon, as liaisons with our new monarch. In the meantime, I think I can count on both of you to help him through the next day or two."

"I can certainly help *explain* what he is feeling," Elspeth replied, but with a little doubt, opening the door and waving him inside ahead of her. "I suspect it might be like the first time I was—ah—blessed with Mindspeech."

"Exactly, exactly!" Janas said, as he gathered up his old robe and made it into a neat bundle. Then he looked down in confusion at the clothing he was wearing, and for a moment, certainty was replaced with uncertainty. "Ah—I—"

"Consider the new vestments a gift from the Alliance," Darkwind said, divining his question before he could ask it. "And please feel free to approach us if any of your other liaisons might need similar outfitting."

Janas turned, taking his hand and shaking it with gratitude. "Thank you, thank you for all your help!" he said, brimming with so much effervescent pleasure that Elspeth could not help but smile back at him. "Now, I really must be off, there is absolutely not a moment to waste!"

He hurried to open the door to the hallway; fortunately, one of the sentries at the door intercepted him and offered to find an aide to ascort him out. He accepted absently as he pulled his shabby cloak on over his new finery, and the last that Elspeth saw of him, he was explaining to the aide some of the preparations that would need to be made to get ready for Tremane's coronation as the new King of Hardorn.

Elspeth closed the door behind them, and joined Darkwind who was sprawled bonelessly on the couch. She suddenly felt as if *she* had been running an endurance test, and collapsed beside him.

"Well," he said finally. "I confess I am at a loss for words."

"I have a few," she told him, putting her head on his shoulder. "But mostly, I can't begin to tell you how *relieved* I feel."

She turned her head so that she could see his face, and he smiled into her eyes. "You know how the Shin'a'in are always saying to be careful of what you ask for," he chided gently. "And you did *ask* for some sort of check on Tremane's behavior as a leader."

"I did." She took a deep breath, and let it out slowly. "I can't say that I'm at all *unhappy* about how this has fallen out. This means the probable end of conflict inside Hardorn. They're going to have a real, competent leader. He is going to be incapable of misusing the land or the people, and I have the oddest feeling that he won't even be able to *think* about going to war with anyone unless Hardorn is threatened first."

Darkwind kissed her forehead, then rested his head back against the back of the couch, staring up at the ceiling. "At the moment, I feel a great deal of sympathy for him. This may not be a punishment commensurate with what he did to our people, but he is going to be suffering real and sometimes serious discomfort for quite some time if I am any judge of these things."

"Because of the state of the country, you mean?" she asked.

He nodded. "Absolutely. You heard Janas; Hardorn is sick, injured, and only now beginning to recover. *He* gets to experience all that, until the land is healed again. What's more, when the mage-storms start up again, whatever they do to the land, he'll feel as if it's happening to him!"

She chuckled, a little heartlessly. "I wonder what having bits of the countryside plucked out and transplanted elsewhere will feel like?"

"Nothing *I* would care to share," Darkwind said emphatically.

She contemplated the prospect, and it didn't displease her. And she knew someone else who would find the new situation very much to her liking.

"I wonder how long it will take to get word of this to Solaris?" she mused aloud.

:Not long, trust me,: Gwena replied. *:And, oh, to be a fly on the wall when it does!:*

As the official-unofficial liaisons to Tremane on behalf of the rest of Hardorn, Elspeth and Darkwind found themselves dealing with a dozen requests the next morning that were the direct result of Father Janas' work the previous day. "You know, it is just a good thing that all this is happening in the dead of winter," Elspeth remarked to her mate, as she dealt with yet another request for "Royal Patronage" from a merchant in the town. "If we were in the midst of decent weather, we'd have half the country trying to get here for this coronation Janas wants to arrange."

Darkwind had handed most of the correspondence over to her, for the Hawkbrothers had no equivalent to royalty and the pomp and display that went with such personages. He shook his head. "I feel as lost as a tiny frog in the midst of Lake Evendim. Or a forest-hare in the middle of the Dhorisha Plains," he said ruefully. "Now I know what your people mean when they speak of feeling like a 'country cousin.' I haven't any idea what half these people *want* from Tremane."

"Frankly, neither have they," she replied dryly. "Royalty is rather like a touchstone to those who are accustomed to kings and queens and the like. One judges one's own worth by one's worth to the king, whether or not the king is himself a worthy person. All these people are attempting to gather about Tremane in the hope that some of the glitter will rub off."

She would have said more, but at that moment, there came a knock on their door. When Darkwind went to answer it, much to her surprise, Tremane himself stood in the doorway, guarded by his older aide, and looking a bit wan.

"Might I come in?" he asked. "Something in these memories of mine says that you might be able to help me. Sort things out, that is."

Darkwind waved him in; the aide remained behind, but with a look that said he would station himself at the door and not move until Tremane left again.

The Duke took a seat on their couch, and Elspeth made a quick assessment of him. For once he was hiding nothing; she suspected that at the moment he simply was unable to. He was still quite unsettled, disoriented, and distinctly wild-eyed. She handed him a fragrant cup of *kav*, a beverage the Imperials favored that she had also begun to enjoy, as much for the effect it had of waking one up as for the flavor.

"You know," he began plaintively, "when you came here, I told you that I accepted this mind-magic of yours, but to tell you the truth, I didn't entirely *believe* in it. You could have done everything you claimed simply by having two well-trained beasts and a clever set of subtle signals. Spirits, putting one's thoughts into someone else's head—that was all so much nonsense and only the really credulous would have given it much credence. . . ."

His voice trailed off, and Elspeth nodded. "Now, for the first time, you are in the grip of something you can't explain. Right?" she asked.

He nodded, looking oddly vulnerable and forlorn. "Magic is *supposed* to be a thing of logic!" he protested. "It has laws and rules, they are all perfectly understandable, and they bring predictable results! This is all so—so—*intuitive*. So unpredictable, so messy—"

Darkwind started to laugh, and the Duke looked at him suspiciously. "I don't see what is so amusing."

"Forgive me, sir," Darkwind choked. "But very recently a friend of ours, who truly and with all of his heart believed that *magic* was wholly a thing of intuition and art, having nothing to do with laws and logic, was confronted with the need to regard magic as you and your mages do. And he sounded *just* like you do now—the contrast is just—" He choked, trying to swallow his laughter, and Elspeth, who recalled quite well how Firesong had sounded, had to work very hard not to join him. That would not have done Tremane's spirit any good at the moment.

"When you have gotten used to this, I think that you'll find it has its own set of rules and logic, and you'll be able to deal with it in a predictable manner," she soothed. "This is simply as if—as if someone had dropped *all* of the rules of mathematics and geometry into your mind, and expected you to deal with them. You're overwhelmed with information, and I promise you that will change."

Darkwind managed to get himself under control, and took a seat next to the Duke. "I'll help you as much as I can," he pledged. "I am probably the nearest to an expert, until Janas or someone like him comes back here."

Tremane let out a sigh, and began slowly trying to ask questions for which the vocabulary was as new to him as the concepts. Elspeth listened carefully, adding what she could, and relaying when Gwena had any useful information to add.

:Poor man,: she said to Gwena, though not without a touch of faintly vindictive amusement. *:The only thing more unsettling to him right now would be for the ghosts of his ancestors to come back to haunt him, or for a Companion to Choose him.:*

:Oh, now there's a thought,: Gwena replied, and at Elspeth's reaction of alarm, sent a chuckle of amusement of her own. *:Don't worry. The only way that Tremane would ever be Chosen would be for most of the population of Hardorn and Valdemar to be swallowed up by the earth, and even then, I wouldn't put high odds on it.:*

:At least now he'll believe us when we say you've *said something.:* That was a satisfying realization.

Then something else occurred to Elspeth. *:Darkwind,:* she told her mate, *:I think this is best treated as something like Empathy. Janas may have put the rules for dealing with it in his mind, but if the Gift is so very strong, he may be so overwhelmed by the sensations that he can't actually relate them to what is happening. Try taking him through ground and centering, then shielding, just as you would someone with strong Empathy.:*

He nodded slightly, and changed his angle of attack on the problem. To Elspeth's way of thinking, this was actually going to be easier than dealing with someone with Empathy; there would be no changes in what he sensed as people around him underwent emotional changes. Since what he felt from the land was quite steady, with no sudden increases in intensity, once he learned to shield he would not have to learn to strengthen or weaken his shields.

In fact, he wouldn't want to; he *needed* to know when the land was harmed, and he couldn't do that if his shields were too strong.

She watched the two of them as Darkwind coaxed him through his first exercises. She came to the conclusion, watching his rapid progress, that there was more to what Janas had given him than mere instructions; once he had a grasp of the technique Darkwind was showing him, it didn't take him long to apply the technique correctly.

:Too bad we can't teach every young Herald the way Janas "taught" him,: she remarked wryly to Gwena.

:It would take an ability most Heralds haven't got,: Gwena replied frankly, and a bit enviously. *:For that matter, most Companions haven't got it either. I didn't realize until now just how remarkable old Janas is.:*

Oh, really! That made her reexamine the priest and his mission in an entirely new light, and wonder just what his real rank in the hierarchy of his religion was. Something equivalent to the Son of the Sun, perhaps? Probably only someone like Solaris would be able to tell for certain.

The only conclusion she could make was that the Hardornens had left nothing to chance in this venture, and had gambled a great deal.

But she kept all of this to herself; it wouldn't matter one way or another to the situation, and Tremane had enough on his hands right now with this new ability *and* the responsibility of becoming a King.

Becoming a King. What a strange idea that is. I can't think of any ruler in this part of the world who has been picked by his people since—since Valdemar. The parallels were coming closer all the time.

Tremane absorbed all that Darkwind showed him like dry ground absorbing rain; slowly the lines of anxiety and strain left his face, and the signs of disorientation and illness eased from his posture and expression. Finally, he sighed and closed his eyes with relief.

"I feel—normal," he said, as if he had never expected to feel that way again.

He opened his eyes, and Darkwind smiled with satisfaction. "That is precisely how you should feel," the Hawkbrother told him. "You shouldn't have to think about those shields for them to be there, since you are already acquainted with setting magical shields. They should remain in place until you take them down or weaken them yourself. *Now* the only things you will feel will be when something happens to Hardorn, for good or ill; you'll sense the change as soon as it happens."

Tremane colored a little, and coughed. "I seem to recall some injudicious words to the effect of *wanting* an ability that would give me that information."

Darkwind's smile turned ironic, but he didn't say anything. He didn't have to.

Surely every culture has a variation on the saying, "Be careful what you ask for, you may get it."

"Well, sometimes the Hundred Little Gods display an interesting sense of humor," Tremane sighed.

"They've displayed it more directly than I think you realize," Darkwind told him. "Are you aware that thanks to this 'gift' that Janas bestowed on you, that you are *literally* bound to Hardorn? You can't leave, at least not for long."

Tremane shot him a skeptical glance. "Surely you are exaggerating."

Darkwind shook his head. "I am not. You will not be able to go beyond the borders of this land for very long. Janas was not speaking figuratively as we both assumed when he made his explanations to you. I know enough of magical bindings to recognize one on you, and I doubt that anyone can break it. This is the magic of a very primitive religion, meant to ensure that a ruler could not get wandering feet and go off exploring when he should be governing."

Elspeth watched Tremane's face; though normally opaque, this experience had left him open—not as open as an ordinary person, but open enough for her to read his expressions. "What you're saying is, this *earth-binding* they put on me ensures that there is no possibility of going back to the Empire."

Darkwind held his hands palm up. "The most primitive magics tend to be the strongest, the hardest to break. Perhaps a better word would be *primal*. I suspect this one may date back to the tribes wandering this area before the Cataclysm. It was a fascinating piece of work to watch; no chants, no real ritual, just a tonal component as a guide for invocation, and of course the mental component. Simple but powerful, and that argues for a piece of work that is *very* old, and so proven by time that it is, in fact, a benchmark by which later magics could be judged." As Tremane sat there, with a dazed look in his eyes and a numb expression, Darkwind warmed to his subject. "It really does make sense. If you have a tribe that has recently settled, given up nomadic, hunting and herding ways and gone into agriculture, it stands to reason that your best leaders, the ones who are likely to be the most successful at defending your settlement from other nomads, are the people most likely to want to go back to the unsettled ways. If you want to keep them where they belong *and* give them a powerful incentive to hold the land in trust and not plunder and ruin it, you'd bind them to it."

"I get the point, all too clearly," Tremane interrupted dryly. "Seeing as I am the one blessed with this particular application of 'primitive' magic, and now am prisoner in an all too clear way." He rubbed his head with his hand, absently. "No disrespect to you, Darkwind k'Sheyna, but speculation about the origin of this bit of religious arcana is moot, and it can probably wait until the happy day when everything is settled again and you and Janas can argue about history to your hearts' content."

Darkwind was not at all embarrassed. In fact, he graced Tremane with the expression of a teacher whose student has missed the point of the lesson. But all he said aloud was, "Duke Tremane, if you wish to know how and why a magic works the way it does, you must learn or deduce its origin and purpose. In complex spell-work, the causes, triggers, paths, and effects are not always obvious, and are often fragile. In more primal spell-work, the variables may be fewer, but they are not necessarily any more obvious. You cannot unmake a thing—supposing you should choose to do so— without knowing how it is made."

"Supposing I should choose to do so. . . ." Tremane's voice trailed off, and he stood up to go look out the window. "I am not, by nature, a religious man," he said, with his back to them.

"We rather gathered that, sir," Elspeth put in, her tone so ironic it made Tremane turn for a moment to give her a searching look.

"There is not much in the Empire that would make one believe in gods, much less that they have any interest at all in the doings of mortals," he said, looking straight into her eyes.

"Tangible effect is the focus in the Empire. Results and tasks of the day take a distinct precedence over thoughts of divine influence or the spirit world. The closest thing to a religion of state is a form of ancestor veneration, which takes its higher form as the honoring of previous Emperors and their Consorts, who are collectively known as the Hundred Little Gods. Not that there are exactly a hundred, but it's a nice, round figure to swear by."

"I'd wondered about that," Darkwind murmured.

"Nor have I in the past been one to put credence in either predestined fate or omens. Nevertheless," he continued, "since arriving here, I have been confronted, time and time again, with situations that have literally forced me into the path I am now taking. I find myself beginning to doubt the wisdom of my previous position regarding destiny."

Elspeth could not resist the opportunity. "If you would care for some further proof that your previous position on the divine is faulty," she offered, "I am sure that High Priest Solaris would be happy to arrange for a manifestation of Vkandis Sunlord."

It was wrong of her, but after all that Tremane had been responsible for, she could not help but take a certain amount of vengeful pleasure in the way that his face turned pale at the mere mention of Solaris' name.

"That won't be necessary," he said hastily.

"As you wish," she murmured, with an amused glance at Darkwind.

:Well, talk about fire to the left and torrent to the right— not only does he have Solaris' curse of truthfulness on him, but the Hardornen earth-binding.: Gwena sounded unbelievably smug, but for once, Elspeth was in full agreement with her. :I do believe that Grand Duke Tremane is going to be very cooperative with the Alliance from now on—because if he isn't, he hasn't got the option to escape and he knows it.:

:And I just thought of another good reason for putting the earth-binding on your King,: Darkwind Sent silently, as Tremane turned back to the window. :If you bind him to a place so that he can't escape from it, he has to rule well, because he certainly can't ignore what he is immersed in.:

:Let's hope that's one of the things he's thinking about right now,: Elspeth replied. :He is a skilled leader and an in-

telligent man, and he is certainly a pragmatic one. It should dawn on him soon just how deep in he is right now, and then he will have to accept it and deal with the tasks at hand. For the sake of the Alliance as well as of Hardorn, I want him to know he has no other option but to rule wisely and honestly. We can't afford anything less.:

The Teleson Device

Six

Paper rustled quietly, the only sound in the cold, cavernous room. Baron Melles read the last page of Commander Sterm's report with a smile of satisfaction on his lips. Jacona, the throne city, was now effectively secured. Although the capital of the Empire was not precisely under martial law, his soldiers shared the streets and the patrols with the city constables, and both were happy to have the situation that way. He had tried his plan out here, where everything was directly under his careful supervision, and his ideas had all worked. They had not worked *perfectly*, but he had never expected perfection; they had worked well enough that he and Thayer were both pleased.

As he had predicted, the price of staple food supplies had increased as the availability had decreased, to the point where the average person either could not find or could not afford two out of three meals. That was enough to trigger food riots, his first shoot-to-kill order, and his second tier of plans. Jacona was already divided into precincts, with an elected official, the precinct captain, responsible for arranging local matters such as street repair with the city. That made organization much easier. The citizens of Jacona were now under strict rationing, with so many ration chits per commodity per week each, as arranged and administered by their precinct captains. Price controls went into effect with the rationing. No one was starving, and prices, while high, were no longer as extortionate as they were. Food supplies from the surrounding countryside had been assured, and those ration chits guaranteed that everyone would have access to a minimum diet. The chits did *not* cover luxury items, only staples, permitting those with higher incomes the ability to buy what they chose.

Naturally, there would be some citizens who would choose to barter away their own chits and even those of members of their families for cash or other commodities, such as alcohol. And, naturally, the Empire officially took no stand on this, so long as those who were involved were adults.

A child was different, and precinct captains were on orders to watch for children begging for food. If they found a child starving, and if its parent could not produce its ration chits or enough food to cover the household, the child (and its ration allocation) would be taken away and put in an Imperial orphanage.

That would be the end of that; once taken away, a parent could not retrieve a child, and it became the ward of the State. Once it turned fourteen, if male it would go into the Army; if female, underdeveloped, or sickly, an Army auxiliary corps or a workhouse—unless it showed extraordinary ability and qualified for higher training. But that was child welfare, and had nothing to do with rationing.

Naturally, there were luxuries and larger rations available for cash, and the Empire took no stand on this, either, so long as the commodities for sale on the gray market were not purloined from Imperial stores. Meals and services continued normally in the homes of the wealthy, although household expenses had doubled in the past few weeks. From what Melles had learned from his agents, prices on the gray market had stabilized, which meant that the wealthy would simply have to work a little harder to maintain their wealth. Many of them had already begun investment in coal, wood, and other fuels, or speculation in food items. There were a few with new-built fortunes in the city, because they had seen the trend of things and had moved accordingly. There were a few who were ruined, because their stock-in-trade consisted of small items that depended on magic, or because they were dealers in items like Festival costumes that no one wanted to buy under the current conditions. But so far as Melles could see, aside from these few unlucky or clever individuals, nothing much else had changed.

There were no more riots after the first serious one that gave Melles the excuse to issue his shoot-to-kill order, and which had resulted in the death of a dozen fools who happened to be leading it. There were occasional demonstrations, and a great many speeches on street corners, which were officially ignored. There were also no more collapsing buildings, or loss of service because magic had failed. This was because there were no more services left—or buildings still standing—that depended on magic.

There was plenty of work, though, and the one large change was that unemployment simply did not exist anymore. Those who demonstrated or made speeches did so when their working hours were over—unless, of course, they happened to be one of the few wealthy eccentrics who did not need to work to have an income. Where magical aqueducts no longer supplied water, and there were no communal wells, brigades of otherwise unemployed citizens with buckets brought fresh water from reliable sources to fill newly-constructed below- or above-ground cisterns. An entire newly-formed corps of citizens with handcarts now collected garbage, cinders, and ashes from fires, and animal waste from the streets and yards. Fortunately, the sewers were nonmagical in nature, and still functioned reliably.

Life in the city was not back to the way it had been, and never would be again until these mage-storms were over, but the ordinary citizen went to work, received his pay, ate regular meals, and slept securely at night. If he was colder this winter than last, or a little hungrier, well, that was the case for all of his neighbors, too. But not only were his streets kept clear of dangerous riots, they were also kept clear of vagrants and beggars—for vagrants and beggars swiftly found themselves in Imperial workhouses or work gangs, cleaning the streets and carrying water for the good of the ordinary citizen. This made the ordinary citizen happy. What made him even happier was the fact that Imperial workers were toiling day and night to find ways to restore more of the things that he had come to take for granted in the days of reliable magic. Already some things had been replaced—safe stoves that could burn a variety of fuels, from dried dung to coal, were now being made available at a moderate price from Imperial workhouses. Imperial bathhouses and laundries had been established, so that if a man could not afford to heat water for regular baths and laundry, he *could* still have those baths and get his clothing

clean for a few copper bits. The average citizen could look
forward to eventually regaining the kind of comfortable life
he had lost.

And if he had to give up some of his freedom to get that
life back, well, all but a few malcontents thought that was an
acceptable loss. Some folk even welcomed these new workhouses and work gangs, and were happy to see soldiers patrolling the streets and sweeping up those with nothing better to
do than to make trouble. It was true that crimes like assault,
robbery, rape, and burglary had dropped to almost nothing
after the deadly-force patrols had been deployed on the street
level.

*Well, assault, robbery, rape, and burglary by citizens
against citizens have dropped to almost nothing. No one in
his right mind is going to report a soldier or constable for
such a crime. And if there is no report, there is no crime, and
hence, officially no problem.*

So far, everything that he had set in motion in Jacona was
either working well or would be with a few slight adjustments. Now was the moment to plan the next steps. He put
both elbows on the desk, tented his fingers together and rested
them lightly over his lips, thinking.

He stared at the flame in the oil lamp on his desk that replaced the mage-light that had once burned there. The desk
itself had been placed near to the antiquated fireplace, which
held a better, more improved version of the official stove, a
contrivance of ceramic and steel that burned coal rather than
wood. More Imperial cleverness, that; coal fires burned hotter
and longer than wood, and although the smoke coming from
them was dirtier and might cause a problem one day, this new
"furnace" invention would get them through the winter. All
the fires in the Palace and in most of the homes of the noble
and wealthy had these furnaces, and the coal mines, which
once produced only fuel for the smelting furnaces for the
metal trade, now sent huge wagonloads into the city on daily
deliveries. A variation on this furnace heated the boilers that
once again delivered hot water into the bathing rooms of Crag
Castle and other edifices—and also supplied the hot water for
the Imperial bathhouses and laundries. Interestingly enough,
this entire situation was proving to be surprisingly profitable
for the Imperial coffers, for not only was the Empire collecting

more tax money, since taxes were based on profits, but the Empire was also something of a merchant, selling heating- and cook-stoves and the services of the bathhouses.

Theft of coal was punishable—like all theft—by being sent to a work gang. So were the crimes of inciting to riot, partici- pating in a riot, looting, chronic public drunkenness, vandal- ism, vagrancy, and delinquency. Any crime against property rather than against a citizen now bought the perpetrator a stint in hard labor rather than gaol or the Army. The new pol- icy made for quiet streets.

Tremane would never have ordered all of this; Tremane didn't have the vision or the audacity, and perhaps not even the intellectual capacity to mastermind such sweeping plans on such a broad scale at such short notice.

Melles continued to stare at his lamp flame, but nothing in the way of inspiration occurred to him. He reached for an- other, much shorter report, and leafed through it again. Per- haps before he thought more about the next stage of his plans, it was time to deal with his covert operations.

All in all, once the food riots were quashed, there had been fewer complaints than he had anticipated, and very little civil unrest. That came as something of a surprise, because he had assumed there would be a higher level of resistance to his new laws than there actually was.

So, all that meant was the good citizens of Jacona were being very good, going where he led like proper sheep.

There were, of course, a few wild goats out there still—the inevitable underground "freedom" movement, which he had also anticipated. How could there not have been? There were always those who would not be hoodwinked into accepting restrictions on their freedom, no matter how one disguised those restrictions.

The Citizens for Rights group correctly identifies you as the source of all of the new edicts and punishments, the report, written by the head of his network of low-level agents in the city, read. *They assume that the Emperor knows nothing, and that with enough work they will be able to draw his attention to your abuses and have you ousted. Failing that, and assum- ing that you somehow have the Emperor under your personal control, they plan on a general citizens' uprising to overthrow the entire government.*

That was also precisely what he had anticipated; not only did it not alarm him, he was actually rather pleased that he had predicted the development so accurately. His agent was not particularly worried, but he wanted more instructions about what to do now that he had identified the movement, its goals, and its members.

He picked up a pen and took a clean sheet of paper from the tray at the side of his desk. He wrote in code without having to think about the translation; he'd had enough experience at it that he could write directly to any of his agents in the correct code. This was a content-sensitive code, rather than an encoded letter; to all appearances, this missive was a perfectly ordinary letter about commonplaces, from a servant in the Palace to a relative in the city.

What it really said, however, was something else entirely.

Do nothing to openly disrupt the movement against me. As for the general citizens, continue to feed them misinformation; concoct tales of my helplessness in the face of the Emperor's growing tyranny. Make them think that I am trying to stem the Emperor's excesses and that Charliss himself is directly responsible for everything they object to. What I want is to hear that even the members of the Movement are starting to call me "The Peoples' Friend." Continue to identify all new members of the Movement, and if any really effective leaders emerge, identify their weaknesses and find ways to handicap them without actually removing them. Keep me informed at all times.

He started to seal up the envelope, then thought of something else and added a second page.

There are always bureaucratic mistakes; men taken up in a street-sweep who were actually on their way to work, outright victims of some soldier's personal feud. These people will know of each and every one—send me the particulars so I can arrange for investigations and turn a few loose with restitution. If any of them have young children suffering hardship without their father, mark them especially.

Now he sealed and addressed the letter and put it in the tray for his house agent to take to the appropriate drop. That last addition was nothing less than inspiration; all he would have to do would be to have one of the clerks deal with the paperwork to free the man, and send the family a little money, some luxury food items, and a basket of sweets for the children, and Melles would be a hero on the street. And he needn't trouble himself about petitioners plaguing him either. Now that he was officially the Emperor's Heir, the layers of bureaucracy between him and the citizen on the street were so many, so complex, and so labyrinthine that the average citizen would die of old age before he completed all of the paperwork required for an audience with him. This would only generate a little more work in the way of petitions, and there were plenty of low-level Imperial civil servants to take care of additional petitions.

Perhaps another man might have sent soldiers to arrest every member of the Movement—but another man did not have the depth of experience that Melles did. As long as he knew who belonged to these organizations, who were the real leaders and workers, and what their failings were, he was better off leaving them all in place. In times like these, insurrectionist movements were like cockroaches; squash one and a hundred more would hatch behind the wallboards. Rebels actually tended to thrive on a certain level of persecution, since persecution validated their cause in the eyes of others. In fact, many of them absolutely required feeling persecuted—and speaking loudly of it—in order to validate their own meager existence, since obviously only a Great Good would be opposed by a Great Evil. What made this even funnier, in a cripple-pitying sort of way, was that they would only proclaim their oppression to those peers least likely to disagree with them.

Melles, of course, played one facet of the same game on a much higher, more sophisticated level. People invariably polarized their views when they were given little information about a situation's complexities. If someone was not for your cause, then they must be against your cause; if not black, then white; if not day, then night. While the perennially-oppressed would use this tendency in human behavior to generate sympathy from others, Melles used it to steer public reaction. His actual plans and coups were more complex than could be briefly discussed by any layman, and he used fronts—like the labor groups and the police—to act as buffers and visible representations. He created simple concepts for laymen to absorb and react to, while giving little information about the greater, more complex goings-on. Thus, even the most clever leaders of rebel movements would be basing their actions upon incomplete information at best, low-end rumor at average, and utter fabrications at worst. Worst for them, anyway; for Melles it was simply human behavior according to schedule.

No, he would watch them, occasionally nurture them, frustrate and thwart them, and use them, but above all, he would let them have their little "committee meetings" and make speeches and inflame one another. That kept them quiet and mostly harmless. The more they ranted about being suppressed under improving conditions, the less anyone would listen to or believe in them.

It was better to remove the occasional competent and dangerous member than to go after the entire group. If he could not manage to do so in any other way, the really dangerous ones would tragically die while defending themselves against a street thug or a house robber. Then, before the person could be martyred, various carefully-contrived "secrets" about them would turn up during "investigation" of the death—evidence that they were child molesters, for instance—to spoil the probable public outrage there would otherwise have been, and that distaste would carry over to be associated with any of the person's movement. It would only take ten or twenty such instances for the general citizenry to feel relieved that these troublemakers were gone.

On the whole, he enjoyed the amateur "freedom fighters" as delightful entertainment, and if no group had sprung up, he would have had to start one just to have an organization to attract the real troublemakers. The most dangerous would be the very few individuals who realized that groups were obvious targets, and determined to undermine the authorities on their own. If he could catch someone like that, it would be by accident.

But the insurrectionist groups had their uses, not the least of which was that they gave the hotheads a place to vent their spleen. When they were making speeches, they were not setting fire to a storehouse of records, counterfeiting and giving away food chits, or breaking into a work camp and freeing prisoners.

Better a thousand fools' ineffectual speeches than a single food riot.

He moved that report from the "pending" tray to the "completed" tray, and turned his attention to the next in line. If conditions had not been so dire, he would have been positively gleeful; never had he possessed so much power over so many, and the sensation brought an intoxication he had not expected.

Report after report, from the heads of his specialized covert operations rings around the city, indicated that events were proceeding with as much smoothness as anyone could reasonably expect. The only things that could not be planned for were the effects of the mage-storms, and he hoped he had made enough allowance for the chaos those could cause. The precinct captains were political creatures, and although they were elected, he could replace them at his discretion. They could and would lie to save their jobs. The Imperial Commander was less likely to lie, yet still might shade the truth to conceal problems. His agents, however, were carefully picked and trained and they never reported anything but the facts, no matter how unpleasant. That was their job; he rewarded the truthful and got rid of those who were not—sometimes permanently, if they had been in a delicate or sensitive position. These reports confirmed his impression that the city was his: pacified, and lying quietly in the palm of his hand.

That was good, because he had no intention of leaving the capital, and he wanted it secured so that he could turn his attention to the Empire beyond without worrying about his personal safety and comfort. The power that gave him his authority was *here*, and although by now he could carry out his plans if the Emperor changed his mind and made someone else the Imperial Heir, it would be much more difficult to do so. He had the Army, but that might not be the case if the Emperor appointed a new man—and to subdue the rest of the Empire, he needed the Army.

Now that he knew what was working with Jacona, he knew what would work outside the capital. He returned to the longer report that he had set aside; this was the condensed version of what was going on in the Empire itself.

In the immediate vicinity, the countryside could reasonably be declared "pacified" as well. The sources of disturbance were those of chaos rather than man's intention—terrible weather and roving monsters rather than rioters. Within the small towns and villages, people were in no danger of going hungry, but they were terrified. Physical storms could sweep down at any moment, bringing snow that could bury a village to the eaves, winds that could rip a building apart, blizzards combining the two that lasted for days at a time. That was bad enough, but in the midst of the storms, terrible, malformed creatures came ravening into their very streets, monsters that no one recognized or knew how to kill. On the estates, things were sometimes even worse, for most nobles did not keep many retainers who were trained to fight; this close to the capital, keeping a small private army was generally frowned upon. So there had already been a case or two of a storm burying an estate, and before the servants could dig it out again, a bloodthirsty creature had appeared that kept them all penned inside—and in one case decimated the entire estate.

One less annoying minor noble to endure.

The Army was handling that situation with all the efficiency that anyone could ask for. Melles was both pleased and surprised to learn that General Thayer had deployed squads of monster hunters *before* ever implementing the requisition orders that Melles's secretary had drawn up. With scores of monstrous beasts hanging from hooks on display in village squares and estate courtyards, people had not only been happy to "donate" the items the Army requisitioned, they had even come forward with additional help. Some truly antique equipages had been made roadworthy—but also some very clever work had been put into the hands of the Army as well. Some genius of a village blacksmith had come up with a way to fasten runners on the wheels of carriages after locking those wheels in place, so that instead of having to wait until snow had been removed from the roads, carts could skim over the top of it. Practically speaking, what that meant was that the Army supply trains bringing food into the city could use roads with a single, narrow track cut for the horse or mule rather than needing to clear the entire road.

Pity that the wicker snowshoe for horses didn't really work, then we wouldn't have to clear the roads at all, or even use the roads. It is ironic that the poor are turning out to be the saviors of the wealthy, for only they had the knowledge of how to do things in completely nonmagical ways.

Other than that, life in the countryside was not at all bad; certainly better than in the city. Firewood was immediately available. So was food, in a greater variety than the cities were seeing now. Life on the estates was even better, and Melles was fairly sure that those nobles who had fled back to their possessions were by-and-large congratulating themselves for having had the wisdom to do so.

So much for life in the immediate vicinity of the capital. Now for the other large cities. . . .

With a few variations, it seemed that what had worked for Jacona would work for any large city in the Empire. He had to make allowances for local religion in a few places, and for one brand new cult in Deban that had virtually taken over the entire city, but for the most part, there were not too many changes he needed to make.

Finally, he finished the last of the replies he needed to make to Thayer and to his own agents in the field. His hands were cramped by the time he was done, and one of the servants had come in to check the fire and add coal twice. Despite the fire, the room was icy; for all its luxurious fittings, it was less comfortable than a warehouse.

Perhaps a sheepskin cover for his desk chair would help, and a charcoal brazier for under the desk. Better still, he ought to have his valet bring in the same kinds of amenities that the Imperial clerks used. He flexed his aching fingers and rose, feeling the cold in every stiffened joint. He knew with grim certainty that his battle with the encroachments of age was failing. Before all this nonsense with the mage-storms had begun, he had started on his own minor rejuvenation magics. He resented the fact that they had failed him now, at a time when he most needed his body to be in perfect health. He simply could not afford any distractions, yet what were all these aches and pains *but* irritating distractions?

Reminders of mortality?

He went to the heavy gilded and carved sideboard where the blown-glass decanters of liquor and special, cut crystal glasses were stored. His nose and feet were so cold they were numb; perhaps a drink would restore circulation and make him feel warmer. He was well aware that the warmth that came from liquor was a false, fugitive thing, but he wanted the comfort of it just now, and the pain-deadening effects that would ease his aching joints.

His valet entered, impeccable and correct in his livery of black and purple, just as Melles poured himself a small glass of potent, doubly-distilled brandy. The liquor gleamed in the glass with the deep glow of fine rubies, as Melles held it up to the light, admiring its color. The valet waited until Melles acknowledged his presence with a nod before speaking. "His Imperial Highness has called a Court, Lord Heir," the man said smoothly, one arm already draped with a suit of court robes in anticipation of the fact that Melles would need them. "Would you care to change your clothing here, or in your more private quarters?"

Melles sighed. This was the last thing he needed right now; he was tired and cold, and really wanted a moment or two to warm up and rest before he dealt with another crisis. But Bors Porthas would not have interrupted his working hours if this had been some bit of social nonsense; no, this must be something serious, and he had better steel himself to meet it.

"Here will do." No one was going to walk in on him unannounced, and Porthas, bland, self-effacing, incredibly competent Porthas, would have brought everything Melles would need with him. The balding little man with the thin, expressionless face was a miracle of efficiency, but that wasn't too surprising. He'd had plenty of practice in more demanding service before Melles retired him to this, his own retinue. In fact, there were a great many of the higher nobles of the Court who would have recognized Porthas' face as that of their own valued personal servant, forced by sudden illness to retire. . . . A fair percentage would have been shocked into speechlessness, and a few would have gone pale, recalling that they had sent floral tokens to the funeral of this particularly faithful servant.

Porthas looked remarkably healthy for a man who had been dead at least three times, and rendered forever incapable of leaving a bed on another five occasions. He looked ageless, in fact, and Melles was aware that not only could Bors Porthas perform every possible duty that would be asked of a valet, he could also still meet and beat many men younger than he in a bout of swordsmanship. As for his other talents—he was the only person Melles would entrust with certain jobs besides himself. That trim body was as efficient as the mind that was housed in it, and just as lithe.

Melles sometimes wondered if, after all the years of serving as Melles' agent, the life of a "mere" valet was stultifying. But then again, Porthas was no "mere" valet, any more than Melles was a "mere" courtier; he was the coordinator for all of Melles' agents, in the city, outside of the city, and most importantly of all, within Crag Castle. He and Melles alone knew the real names and identities of all of Melles' agents. And in the rare event that Melles would need to have a "removal" performed with precision and absolute secrecy, if he could not for some reason perform it himself, he would entrust it to Porthas. There was no one else besides he who was anywhere near Melles in level of expertise at their mutual profession. And he actually seemed to *enjoy* being a valet. Perhaps, after all his other activities, serving as a valet was restful and amusing.

He was certainly nimble enough at assisting Melles into the cumbersome court robes he despised. In sartorial matters, Porthas was not Melles' equal; he was Melles' acknowledged superior, and Melles was only too happy to give way to his expertise. When the last fold and crease had been arranged to Porthas' liking, Melles thanked him—without overdoing it, but making sure that the man knew that his service was noted and valued. With a smile of satisfaction, Porthas gathered up the discarded garments and retired to Melles' private chambers.

The long walk down the castle corridors, accompanied by the silent and ever-present Imperial Guards, allowed him to rid himself of some of his irritation. He knew that there was something in the air when he entered the Throne Room; nervous whispering did not cease at his entrance, as it often did, and the Iron Throne itself was vacant.

Melles made his way up to the foot of the Throne and his own proper place as First in the Court. General Thayer was already in attendance, with a frown on his face that told Melles he had no more idea than anyone else why the Emperor had called this particular Court into session. The General was also in full regalia, ceremonial breastplate gleaming over the somber livery of Imperial Army full-dress uniform, his ceremonial helm with its jaunty crest of purple horsehair tucked

under his left arm, from which position he could fling the useless piece of pot-metal at a would-be attacker while he pulled
his not-so-ceremonial sword with his right hand. On one occasion, the General had actually stopped his attacker with the
helmet before the man ever came within reach of his sword.

"Have you heard anything?" he asked Melles under his
breath. Melles shook his head, and the General swore several
pungent oaths, his face darkening. "I don't like this," he said.
"Charliss never used to call full Courts without notice. He's
been closeted with a messenger or an informant—and now he
calls a full Court. He's not acting rationally anymore, and the
Hundred Little Gods only know what he can inflate out of
tiny rumors. If he's heard something—"

"It won't be about us," Melles said smoothly. "We are proceeding splendidly, and the law-abiding citizens of the Empire
are very happy with us, and with the Emperor. Look at the
reports—look at the streets! And he signed every law, edict
and change to procedure we've instituted with his own hands.
Whatever he has heard, it will concern someone else's activities, and not ours."

At just that moment, Emperor Charliss appeared, draped
in his own ceremonial robes, moving slowly toward the Iron
Throne flanked by two of his guards, with four more following. Melles was shocked at his appearance, although he
doubted that anyone other than a highly trained Adept would
notice the level of deterioration in Charliss' protections and
rejuvenation magics. It only showed in small things—in the
careful way that Charliss moved, and in the signs of pain and
illness around his mouth and eyes—but it was very clear to
him that Charliss was losing his personal battle against age
and the mage-storms. And as Thayer had said, only the Hundred Little Gods knew what that deterioration was doing to
his mind.

In the past, the Emperor's mind had been the very last thing
to go; all of the Emperor-Adepts had died with their minds
clear even as their eyes closed for the last time. But that was
in the past, with magic working properly; what if the reverse
was happening, and Charliss' mind was decaying faster than
his body? What if the poisons of age were pouring into his
brain, acting like insidious drugs on his thinking processes?

The Emperor surveyed his Court with cold eyes, then

placed himself in the chill embrace of the Iron Throne, and regarded his assembled Court again, as if searching for signs of insurrection. Finally he gestured, and a single, weatherbeaten man in the garb of an Imperial soldier stepped out from behind the screen of guards, moving down the stairs to stand below the Iron Throne.

"One of Our agents has returned from the west," the Emperor rasped. "And meanwhile, there have been petitions and questions brought before this throne. Some among you doubt the wisdom of Our declaring a second heir, saying that the rumors concerning the Nameless One are only that, and that We should wait until We had real proof before We acted. We have brought you all here to witness this report, so that you may see that the Emperor rules over you because he is wiser than you."

The man stepped forward, went on one knee before the Throne, and began reciting a report in a dispassionate and unaccented voice. His report was virtually identical to everything that Melles already knew, and he didn't pay a great deal of attention to it. Granted, he had not realized that Tremane had looted the Imperial supply depot in Fortallan quite so *thoroughly*—the man had practically taken the very walls of the place, and Melles had to give him credit for the sheer audacity of the undertaking—but it was still hardly what he would call *news*. Charliss himself had known all of this; he'd made it public when he'd declared Melles as his new heir, and there should have been nothing in these words to cause the Emperor to feel the need to call a formal Court just so everyone could hear it.

In fact, there was something odd about the fact that Charliss felt the need to address the petitions and questions of Tremane's few friends in the Court. Charliss had always ignored such voices of dissent in the past. It wasn't at all like the Emperor to behave in such a fashion, anymore than it was normal for him to sit and listen to a report he'd already heard several times over. Nevertheless, Charliss was clearly agitated by what he heard, and grew more so with every word the agent recited.

Then the man reached the part of his report that was actually new information—a speech that Tremane had allegedly given to his troops, the contents of which were very clearly treasonable. Melles was fairly certain that the speech was accurately reported, in no small part because the agent kept referring back to notes he had taken, held in a small book that he took from his belt-pouch.

Melles paid very close attention to that speech, once he realized this was the reason that Charliss was so agitated. As the man spoke, the Emperor's hands clutched the arms of the throne, and he leaned forward with his eyes narrowed, cold rage in every nuance of his posture. This was a problem; the old Charliss would never have betrayed the fact that something angered him, but this was not the old Charliss. If the Emperor lost his temper violently in public, it was possible that his competence might be called into question. If that happened, his choice of Heir might also come under fire. The last thing that Melles needed right now was a Court on the verge of deposing the Emperor and finding a new and more tractable Heir.

Supposedly, Tremane accused the Emperor of violating his own sacred oaths to the Army. He accused Charliss of being the one who created the mage-storms, as a mad experiment in weaponry of mass destruction. He told his troops that Charliss deliberately sent them all out to be left in the area of effect of this new weapon, just to see what would happen to them. He claimed that Charliss had then deserted all of them, leaving them to face mage-storms and hostile enemy troops on their own, with no supplies, no pay, and no reinforcements. Lastly, he declared that they would have to make their own way, for the Empire no longer cared what became of them.

A strong speech, and one that Tremane might well have believed himself. Certainly, with no clear source for the mage-storms, one could make a case for them coming from the Empire rather than the insignificant little nation of Valdemar. Given that the Empire had centuries of tradition of magic use, and Valdemar, so far as anyone knew, had none, it would be far more logical to assume that combat-mages within the Empire had originated the mage-storms. In fact, if Charliss had actually possessed such a weapon, he might very well have used it in exactly the way he was accused. The Emperor was guilty of such callousness so often that a great part of his anger might stem from the fact that he had been accused when for once he was actually innocent.

Then the agent dropped real news, rather than just relating a speech. By working a team of mages together, his group had managed to get a clean scrying on Tremane until the last mage-storm had passed through. They had proof, besides the speech, of Tremane's perfidy. He had made common cause with Valdemar and her allies against the Empire. He had joined the Alliance, and would soon be crowned the new king of Hardorn, the land he was supposed to have taken for Charliss. And one of the stipulations that the Hardornens had insisted on was that he and his men, Imperial soldiers, would defend Hardorn against any further attempts by the Empire to invade and conquer their land.

It was at this point that Charliss exploded with fury, halting the recitation in mid-sentence.

Melles and Thayer exchanged a startled glance, for neither of them had ever seen the Emperor react in this uncontrolled a fashion. And the moment that the Emperor paused for breath—which was, thanks to his poor physical condition, after no more than a dozen rage-filled words—they both stepped up onto the dais and flanked him.

"*I* will handle Tremane, Lord Emperor," Melles said before Charliss could start again. "That is why you chose me, and believe me, he will live just long enough to regret his actions."

"And *I* will deal with the traitors who decided to cast their lot in with him," Thayer rumbled. "They are Imperial soldiers under my command, and as such, they will be executed by Imperial hands." Charliss looked up at them both, face still contorted with rage, and started to rise.

Melles again exchanged glances with Thayer, and nodded at the side door that led from the dais to the Imperial quarters. Melles moved his head in agreement, and each of them took one of Charliss' arms to help him to his feet.

"The Emperor wishes to confer with us as to the appropriate punishment for these traitors," Melles proclaimed, as they got Charliss up and standing between them. It wasn't a good answer, but it was better than saying nothing, and far better than letting the courtiers make something up for themselves. Before Charliss could say anything else, they had him moving, and once they had him started in the right direction, he continued until he was back in his austere, gray marble, high-ceilinged, private chambers. Wisely, the guards did not hinder them, perhaps because they knew that if Charliss went into a spitting, foaming rage in public, it would not do anyone any good except the rumor mongers.

Once Melles and Thayer got Charliss into a seat, however, the temper tantrum they had prevented from occurring in public broke out in private.

Charliss hissed, spat, pounded the arms of his white-leather chair, and probably would have thrown things if he'd had the strength to rise. Flecks of foam dotted his withered lips, and the pupils of his eyes were dilated. The guards stood at the door, eyes straight ahead, pretending to be deaf.

Most of what he babbled was incoherent, and it was painfully clear that Charliss had completely lost control of his formidable temper and of his ability to think. If it had not been for the fact that he was so angry he couldn't even control his voice, his shouts would have informed everyone in Crag Castle just how out-of-control he actually was.

But between his rage and his physical state, his voice didn't get much above a hoarse growl, and much to Melles' relief, he also could not get out of his chair to pace—or to destroy the contents of his chamber, as he had once or twice in the past decades. He could only beat impotently on the padded arms of the chair as he cursed Tremane's name and lineage back to the days of the First Emperor.

He and Thayer took turns trying to soothe the Emperor with promises of personal revenge and Imperial Justice, not that any of those promises had any likelihood of being fulfilled. The agent had made it quite clear that there were no more "loyal" Imperials with Tremane's troops; for one reason or another they had all defected over to him. The only way to get at Tremane now would be to send a magical assassin—and that would take the combined abilities of several mages. In light of all of the other pressing needs there were for the little magic that could be made to function, a magical assassin would be an extremely stupid thing to waste time and energy on.

While it was Thayer's turn to distract the Emperor, Melles sent one of the guards for his physicians, and looked around for something that might serve to blunt the Emperor's anger—or at least anesthetize him. This was a fairly public room, filled with gray or white-leather chairs arranged in small groups, with a white desk of bleached wood that was too clean to be used very often off in a corner, and rugs made of bleached sheepskin scattered about on the white-marble floor. There was a sideboard of gilded gray marble to Melles' right that was even more impressive than the one in Melles' rooms; it was loaded down with crystal decanters of liquors he recognized and those he did not. What, in the name of the Hundred Little Gods, would a drink as yellow as a buttercup or as blue as a berry taste like? Or one as green as new spring grass?

Or did he really want to know?

Probably not. If Charliss was used to entertaining the minor rulers of his possessions here, he would probably keep a stock of every vile concoction that every pelt-wearing barbarian ever invented in the name of "something to drink." Over the years, Melles had sampled a few of these, and he was not eager to renew his acquaintance with any of them. There were some things man was not meant to know—or imbibe.

By carefully sniffing the necks of each of the likely bottles, he found a decanter of the same potent brandy he himself had been drinking when the formal Court had been called. He poured a much larger portion than he would ever have drunk himself, and took it to the Emperor.

Charliss seized it in a clawlike hand and downed it without even blinking, then threw the glass across the room, where it hit the wall and shattered, leaving sparkling shards and a few ruby-red drops of bloodlike liquid on the white floor.

Melles raised an eyebrow at Thayer, who shook his head. Evidently the General figured he had the situation in hand and didn't need to turn the Emperor over to Melles just yet. Melles nodded, got another two glasses of the wine, kept one for himself and brought the other to Thayer. Then he stood back until Thayer needed him.

His enforced idleness gave him plenty of time to think about the Imperial agent's report. Tremane had shown more intelligence and initiative than Melles would ever have given him credit for, and on the whole, Melles was impressed. He would never have gotten the troops to stand by him, if he had not come up with a story to convince them that it was the *Emperor* who had deserted *them*. It was an adept use of polarity. And to somehow manage to make peace with the Alliance and convince the very people he had been fighting against to make him their new ruler—well, that was nothing short of a miracle. Melles would have given a great deal to know how Tremane had managed that particular feat.

Despite the fact that he hated Tremane with an unholy passion and would happily have seen him slowly drawn and quartered over the course of a lengthy dinner, Melles knew that in Tremane's position he would have done exactly the same things. For all the faults that Tremane had, stupidity wasn't one of them. He wasn't as brilliant as Melles, but he was not stupid either. He was lucky, though, and he had used all of the facts he had to make some reasonable conclusions. Melles had access to all the Imperial records, and he knew for a fact that Charliss had not given Tremane support or orders for months before the looting of the Imperial depot. Once Tremane's magics began to fail, he would have found himself fighting an unsupported war in unfamiliar territory, surrounded by enemies. He would have had no advantage over the enemy without magic to help. By the time the winter storms began, it would have been impossible to retreat across country to the Empire. So just what *did* Charliss expect Tremane to do at that point? Die in place, like a loyal fool out of the old Chronicles? Men like that had gone extinct in the days of the First Emperor, probably because they kept doing stupidly loyal things that bought them early graves. Charliss could not have concocted a better scheme to get rid of Grand Duke Tremane if he'd tried—except, of course, if he had appointed Melles to do away with him.

Not that Melles would have minded at all if Tremane *had* been such a loyal fool, but the fact was that he was loyal, like most men, only to a point. And after that point, he saw no reason to repay betrayal with more loyalty. And his luck must be phenomenal, for he had managed to pull an amazing victory out of a well that looked to hold only the bitter water of defeat.

But then, Tremane always had been unaccountably, inexplicably lucky. Fortune always smiled on the man and doubled the effects of his adequate competence. That was part of the reason why Melles hated him.

The liquor had enough effect on Charliss to get him to stop babbling; he still pounded the arms of his chair, but now he focused on Thayer, detailing the excruciating punishments he wanted Tremane and his men to endure before they died. Thayer did not bother to point out that Tremane and his men were quite out of reach of any Imperial punishments; he simply nodded gravely, pretending to pay attention, when in fact he was probably just hoping that Charliss' Healers would arrive before the Emperor erupted into incoherence again. Finally the physicians did arrive, and in a moment they had taken over from Thayer, swarming over the Emperor, pressing medicines on him, urging him to calm himself. Since Charliss' energy had been fading as the strong dose of liquor took effect, he was finally ready to listen to advice, to take those medicines, to allow his servants to take him to his bedroom and put him to bed. Thayer and Melles took the opportunity then to make their escape.

Thayer was in no mood to talk. "I was dragged away from writing out orders for troop movement in the provinces," he told Melles brusquely. "And I need to get those orders out, whether or not Emperor Charliss has other duties he needs me for."

Melles nodded, hearing and understanding the things that Thayer had not said. It would be best to get as many orders out as possible, quickly, while Charliss was otherwise occupied. It was all too clear that the Emperor was no longer entirely sane or stable. The problem was not that he was disintegrating; Melles and Thayer between them could very easily take over if he dropped dead this very night. The real problem was that he was not disintegrating fast enough.

Until he either abdicated or died, the Imperial Guards would make sure he *remained* the Emperor; that was their duty, and not only were they trained and sworn to it, they were *geased* to it. He would not be the only Emperor to have gone mad in the last few months of his life; the Empire had survived such rulers before, and truth to tell, with the difficulties facing the Empire now, being ruled by a madman was the smallest of its problems. At the moment, his obsessions were harmless enough. As long as he insisted on pursuing the twin goals of the destruction of Valdemar and the punishment of Tremane, Melles would be perfectly content. If all that happened was an occasional interruption of work, it would be a small price to pay to have the Emperor harmlessly occupied and out of the way of real business. Charliss was an Adept, and he did have an entire corps of mages who answered only to his demands—and it was entirely possible, if he decided to sacrifice all attempts to keep his anti-senescence magics working, that he *could* find some way to destroy Tremane, Valdemar, or both. Granted, such powerful magics would probably kill him and most of his mages, but that was to be expected, and it wouldn't bother Melles in the least. *He* did not intend to worry about anything as far beyond practical reach as Tremane, and Valdemar was even farther than that.

The real danger to Melles and all he needed to accomplish was that Charliss might recover his senses and his priorities enough to decide to meddle in what Melles had planned. That would mean nothing short of disaster, for the Emperor had his own nets of agents and spies that rivaled the ones Melles had in place, and he would know very soon just what Melles was doing, overtly and covertly. Most of it, of course, was simply good strategy, but there was that tiny fraction designed to make Charliss into a villain and Melles into a hero, and Charliss would probably not care too much for that.

Charliss would also have his own plans—which would not be a bad thing, if the Emperor was still sane. But he wasn't, and the situation was only going to get worse as time went on. If he began to meddle, he could easily undo everything that Melles and Thayer had worked so hard to establish.

Something would have to be done to keep that from happening.

All that flashed through Melles's mind as he stood in the frigid hallway with General Thayer. He nodded slowly. "We both have work to do," he replied. "We need to get our structure too solidly in place to dislodge by any force."

That was an innocuous enough statement, but a brief flicker of his glance toward the closed door of the Emperor's quarters brought an answering glimmer of understanding to Thayer's eyes. "Jacona's under control," Thayer replied. "It's the rest of the Empire that we need to think about now. And with your permission, I'll get to my part of it."

Melles clapped him on the shoulder. "And I to mine; after all, what *is* the Empire but soldiers and civil servants of various rank?"

The General nodded in agreement, and the two of them

went their separate ways; Melles hurried his steps to his own apartments with the determination to get enough in place that no matter *what* mad schemes Charliss came up with, it would make no difference.

He returned to his suite to find the ever-attentive Porthas waiting, ready to remove the uncomfortable court robes and replace them with loose, fur-lined lounging robes and sheepskin slippers. When he raised an eye at that, Porthas shrugged.

"I assumed that my lord would be working late into the night and would not wish to be disturbed. I had arranged for a meal to be brought here, and declined invitations on my lord's behalf for a card party and a musical evening." Even as Porthas spoke, he assisted Melles out of the heavy over-robe.

The moment that Porthas mentioned the card party and "musical evening"—the latter of which would probably be some idiot's wife, unmarried sisters, and unbetrothed daughters, all performing popular ballads with varying degrees of success—he shuddered. The card party wouldn't have been much better; when he played cards, he played seriously, and it would be a dead certainty that he would have been paired with an unattached female who either bet recklessly or was too timid to make a bid.

"You were correct, Porthas," he replied, as the valet eased him into the comfort of loose robes heated on a rack in front of the fire. "And I do have a great deal of work to do."

Charliss' actions today had given him the spur that he needed to make some fairly bold moves. That long report on the state of the rest of the Empire had left him with uncertainty earlier, but it was clear now that he had no time to waste.

First, the Empire; second, the Court. Thayer would have no part to play in that second act of consolidation.

He sat down behind his desk, and pulled paper and pen toward him. As he had already anticipated, local leaders throughout the Empire had already secured *their* immediate territories wherever possible. In places where the situation had not yet been secured, he had only to expand his existing arrangements, and he wrote out those orders first. The drafts would go to Thayer before they went to the clerks for copying, just to make certain that they weren't going to step on each others' feet, but the plans were simply extensions of what was already going on around Jacona.

Porthas placed a cup of hot mulled wine at his elbow; the fragrance of the spices in it drifted to his nostrils. He reached absently for it and sipped it, holding it with one hand while he wrote with the other.

The real challenges would come in dealing with those local leaders, people who had made themselves the top wolf in their own little territories, and would not care to hear from a bigger, tougher wolf than they were. Somehow he would have to persuade them that he had authority and power, perhaps in excess of what he *really* had, and that it was in their best interest to begin taking orders from him.

If he couldn't achieve that objective, he was going to have to eliminate them without direct confrontation, and put someone more amenable to authority in their places.

He put the cup down, out of the way, while he contemplated his options.

The real trick would be to get rid of them in ways that would not be traced back and connected with him. Getting rid of people was never difficult. It was doing so without leaving any tracks or signs pointing to who was responsible that was the hard part. Those clever, perceptive, and skilled enough to trace blame were few but devastating, and all plans had to be made with the assumption that such a sleuth would be investigating, though the odds were slim.

As with cards, duels, and death sports, look at the odds— but consider the stakes.

He picked up the report, leafed through it, and scanned the list of those local leaders and their brief dossiers again; his agents were good, and it was possible to get some idea of who would cooperate and who would not just from the thumbnail sketches of their personalities that had been provided to him. He had a short list of assassins to chose from, "special agents" who were adept at making deaths look like accidents or illness. It was going to be difficult to get them into place, given the current conditions, but it would not be impossible. With the help of the Army, he ought to be able to get any individual to the right location within a few weeks.

It would probably be a good idea to place his best agents on his most likely targets immediately, rather than waste time attempting to persuade some provincial idiot with an over-blown sense of his own competence. If the blow came before he even contacted a given fool, it definitely wouldn't be connected with him. That would leave the agent free to take on a second target if attempts at persuasion of someone worth saving failed.

He switched ink and paper, to the special colors of both that would tell these operatives that he had a job for them. The note he sent would be commonplace greetings, of course; no special agent would ever trust primary instructions that came written. This was a gamble on his part, for many of these people were free-lance workers. When they heard what he had to say, they might even turn *him* down; although they would be paid more for these targets than any of them had ever gotten for a job before, getting to their targets through the miserable conditions that existed now could be a real problem. And again, that was the privilege of an agent who was as good as these were; you couldn't persuade an artist to make a master-piece by standing him in front of an easel and threatening him with death. It might be possible to pick off one or two of these provincial leaders with ordinary assassins, and if he came up short on the number of agents he needed, that was what he would do.

But he really would prefer it if all of these operatives found the jobs enough of a challenge to take them on. They were very good. He, above all, should know; he used to be one of them, as did Porthas, and he had even trained some of them in technique.

There was nothing like being able to call on old school ties. . . .

As he wrote out his list of "invitations," it occurred to him that he actually did have a way to fulfill the Emperor's demands and "bring Tremane to justice," provided that the "justice" came in the form of a swift, sure blade or the sharp bite of poison. There were three of these assassins—four, if he counted Porthas, though he did not intend to do without that worthy's talents right here, who could and possibly *would* go to Hardorn and eliminate Tremane. Magical assassination being out of the question, physical assassination would take a year or more, but it could be done.

He paused to consider it, even though the idea did not appear to be a particularly good one. There was a certain amount of personal satisfaction to be had if he could somehow kill Tremane. *How* had the man managed to wheedle his way into the hearts and minds of the Hardornens? It did not seem fair that his old enemy should come through a situation that *should* have destroyed him, only to be made a King. Granted, he would never see his home again, and granted, Melles was going to be an Emperor, not a mere King. Nevertheless, the prospect was galling. It would have been satisfying to bring him down altogether.

Porthas took away the cup, and left a fresh one and a plate of sliced fruit, bread, and cheese in its place. This was a subtle hint that he should eat something. He took the hint, and ate without tasting any of it.

He weighed all the considerations. Given that the agent sent out would be brilliant, crafty, and given every resource, the likelihood of anyone from the Empire reaching the center of Hardorn was remote. Success would be remoter still, for an agent of the Empire, without the magical aids that would enable him to study the people and conditions surrounding his target, would be operating blind in a foreign land. He would stick out like a single red fish in a school of green fish.

In a way, it was possible to sympathize with the Emperor's obsession. Tremane *should* be dead at this point. Normally, he did not give in to his own emotions, but there was a sick anger in the bottom of his stomach that twisted and bit as if he had swallowed a viper, and it would probably never give him rest. He wanted Tremane dead, and he wanted to do whatever it would take to get him there.

But even when he had been an operative himself, he had known that there was a point past which it was inadvisable to pursue your target, no matter what your employer said or offered. This was one of those times.

He got up from his desk and poured himself another drink, ignoring for the moment the cup of mulled wine; not brandy this time, but a thick cordial with no alcohol in it, made entirely of syrup and stomach-soothing and gut-deadening herbs. He went back to his seat, let himself down into the embrace of the chair, and tried to convince his heart of what his head knew were facts.

When the enemy is "dead" to the world one inhabits, he might as well be dead in totality.

That was something his teacher had told him, and it was as true now as it was then. Tremane might as well be dead; his lands and possessions were confiscated, his name erased from the records, and he could never return here again. He would have to be content with a petty kingdom in a land of barbarians.

Pursuit of Tremane was a waste of resources, which were in very short supply, especially good operatives. There was no point in wasting a man who could serve Melles better elsewhere. It was time to bury the past vendettas with Tremane's name.

There was no point in following the Emperor into madness.

Every time a mage-storm washed over them, anyone with any pretensions at being a magician felt it; there had even been clever daylight robberies timed to coincide with the onset of a mage-storm, when the owner of a building would be incapacitated. The Storms were bad enough when they came during the daylight hours, but when they occurred at night, when everyone was asleep, they were worse, for they became part of one's dream and turned those dreams into nightmares.

Melles woke up in a sweat, clutching his blankets, out of a nightmare of tumbling through empty space. But the waking reality was no better, and he hung onto his bedding with grim recognition of what was behind the dream. Complete disorientation, nausea, the feeling that he was on the verge of blacking out and yet could not have the relief that unconsciousness would bring—this was a mage-storm to him, and he was profoundly grateful that Porthas and his guards were not mages and did not feel these effects.

At that, his own bouts with the Storms were not as bad as those of some of the other mages he knew, though he had not ventured to ask the Emperor how he weathered these things. He had a theory that the amount a mage suffered was directly proportional to the amount of magic he had tried to work in the interval between the Storms. If magic was tied to its caster, and the Storms disrupted magic, it stood to reason that when the Storms hit, they would give trouble to mage and magic together. As a consequence, he had tried to keep from working any magic at all, even giving up his own rejuvenation magics when they had not survived disruption.

When the Storm finally passed, and his dizziness and nausea vanished as they always did, he let go of the covers and tried to relax back into his goosedown mattress. With any luck, the Emperor would be "indisposed" today after *his* bout with the storm, and with further luck, the mage-storm would send his mental and physical state plummeting again. It was too much to hope that the Storm had killed him, but it was certainly possible that this time he might wind up bedridden.

That would be an excellent thing, for then Melles would have to stand proxy and speak *for* him. It might even be possible to frighten him into stepping down and making Melles the Emperor. He would not hope for it, and he would not urge it, for the Emperor might well take such suggestions very badly. It was a fine dream, though, and one he was loath to give up.

He closed his eyes and tried to relax in hope of resuming his slumbers, but it was of no use. He could not get back to sleep again. He opened his eyes and stared up at the canopy of his bed, or rather, at the darkness within the sheltering curtains of the bed. No light penetrated those thick velvet curtains, nor would it until morning, when the servants pulled back both window and bed curtains to wake him. Now that there was no magical way to heat Crag Castle, one needed those heavy curtains around the beds to keep the drafts out, just as one needed goosedown comforters and featherbeds, and many blankets. Even then, he often woke with a cold nose.

He was not a heavy sleeper, nor a long one, and never had been. Some would say that a guilty conscience kept him awake, or the memories of all of his victims, but the truth was simpler than that. Sleep, in his profession, was a dangerous necessity, the one time when he was completely vulnerable and had to entrust his safety to others. He had trained himself to wake completely at the slightest disturbance, and once he was awake, his mind leaped into activity whether or not there was any need for it. Once he was *that* wide awake, it was difficult to get back to sleep again.

He wondered what time it was. If it was near enough to dawn, it was hardly worth fighting to get back to sleep only to be awakened again.

He shifted his weight, and a scent of pungent herbs filled

the still air. Porthas had ordered the servants to add those herbs to the bedding, in anticipation of problems when the vermin-repelling spells failed. That was yet another example of Porthas' foresight; he'd seen some of the Councillors scratching surreptitiously at the last meeting of the Grand Council, and suspected fleas, since these were some of the same courtiers who kept dogs or other pets and insisted on having them here at Court. Vermin spread, with or without pets to spread them, unless one took precautions.

Fleas at Court! Well, they were not the only bloodsucking vermin here, only the most honest about it. In some ways, Melles would have preferred fleas to some of the other vermin he had to deal with on a daily basis.

That led his thoughts immediately to the current problem facing him: the Court. He had always known there would be some opposition to him as the Emperor's Heir, but he had not thought that all of his enemies would forget their own differences to unite against him.

His only solid ally was Thayer; in Thayer he had the Army—but *not* the Imperial Guards. Those were answerable only to the Emperor, and led by Commander Peleun, who was *not* a great admirer of Melles. How Peleun had managed to climb to the heights he had while still retaining a fair number of illusions about honor and fidelity was quite beyond Melles, but he had, and he was already causing some trouble. He didn't care for the idea of a former chief assassin as an Emperor—although Melles was following in a long and distinguished, if not openly acknowledged, tradition. He had preferred Tremane, who at least pretended to honesty, and had a fine career in both the civil service and the military behind him.

More important than Peleun, however, was Councillor Baron Dirak, who was in charge of the Imperial Civil Servants. *He* had been one of Tremane's staunchest allies, still defended him openly at Court, and was not at all pleased with Melles' rise to power. He'd had some hope of wedding a sister to Tremane, and was very bitter about losing that chance to power.

Either of these men alone could have caused him some small difficulty, but with both of them allied, things could become serious. And if his sources were correct, they were maneuvering to get Councillor Serais, head of the tax collectors, into their corner.

He had to consolidate his power in the Court. There were other candidates for the Iron Throne, many of them just as qualified as Melles. It was entirely possible that someone could send an assassin out after Melles. Peleun probably would be horrified at the thought, but Dirak would consider it, and there were others who knew how to contact the same list of "special agents" that Melles used. Melles hadn't been able to contact them all, and that meant there were at least a few top-level assassins unaccounted for. Peleun could use *his* power as the head of the Imperial Guard to allow anyone he wished in to see the Emperor at any time, and given the right set of circumstances, the end result of such an interview could be a brace of guards arriving to put Melles under arrest. With the Emperor's mind so unbalanced, it wouldn't be too difficult to persuade him that Melles was not enthusiastic enough in his pursuit of Tremane. That alone would be enough to get him arrested and replaced.

If he was arrested, his enemies would have the leisure to concoct as much evidence as they pleased to prove whatever they wished, and he would not be able to interfere. It was possible, of course, that Porthas would take up the reins and act in his absence, but Melles preferred not to count on such enlightened self-interest. It was far more likely that Porthas and all of his special employees would offer their services to what they perceived to be the winning side.

He was secure in the city; Jacona was quiet, and entirely his. He had issued his orders and sent out his assassins and negotiators along with Thayer's troops; within a few weeks he would know how successful he had been at taking the rest of the Empire under his rule. Now, while he was waiting for word from the countryside, would be a good time to consolidate the Court. That was one thing that his enemies never counted on; that he would continue to work on another aspect of his projects while waiting for results from the previous phase. They always started on a phase and waited to see what would happen before going on to the next, but that was a costly way to operate.

As for the Court—he would order no assassinations, at least not yet, and only use it as a last resort. If anyone died in the

next few weeks, even if it was completely an accident, he
would be the first to be suspected of initiating foul play. But
he had always used the knife as a tool, not an end, and the
skills that had made him the Emperor's most successful agent
included blackmail, information brokering, and—of course—
rumor creation. He didn't need to kill anyone to be effective.
It was more effective to keep a small but omnipresent *fear*
of death in peoples' minds than to actually deliver the blow
itself.

Peleun, Dirak, and Serais; he would concentrate on those
three, who were outwardly his enemies. The little fish were
probably waiting to see who came out the victor, and the bigger fish, the equals of those three, had not yet openly taken
sides.

Peleun's weakness was his fortune, or rather, his lack of
one; he didn't have a solid financial situation and he had been
speculating lately in commodities. He had been doing very
well, in no small part because he knew just what commodities
were going to be in short supply, thanks to his contacts with
the Army. The Army, of course, had taken over the Cartage
Guild, and although the Army did not own or profit directly
from the cargoes carried, there were Army records of what had
just come in that Peleun could easily get access to before the
goods ever came on the market. Everything had to go through
inspection, weighing, and taxation before so much as a grain
of wheat could be sold, and that took several days, enough
time for Peleun to purchase goods that were going to be scarce
before anyone else knew that supplies were going to temporarily dry up until the next cargoes came in. That was a great
weakness in the current market situation, for there was no
telling what might come in besides staples. There was no way
to effectively communicate back to the farms and estates, so
at some point, it might be impossible to find an apple, and at
another, there was nothing in the way of fruit in the market
but apples. All Melles had to do would be to see that Peleun
saw the wrong records, or completely falsified records, and
within a few weeks he would be a ruined man.

Dirak was a very nervous gentleman, timid and altogether
afraid of his shadow; perhaps that was why he had gone into
civil service in the first place. The current situation had him
gulping handfuls of calmatives on a daily basis; surely there

was something that Melles could do to further destroy his nerves.

And as for Serais—did he but know it, he was the most vulnerable of all. Some quick work among the Imperial tax records, and hundreds of thousands of gold pieces that had never existed in the first place would "vanish" from the treasury. Of course, the errors would eventually be uncovered, but it would take a great deal of work and require referring to all the original tax receipts, and Serais' reputation would be completely ruined by the time it was over. With any luck, he was probably skimming a little off the top anyway, and when Melles was through, that would have been uncovered as well.

That wouldn't be enough to keep the Court completely under his thumb, though. He had to give the malcontents within the Court another target than himself, just as he had done for the malcontents in the city. It could not be a target for *blame,* however, but a target of profit and reward. It would be very dangerous to *blame* the Emperor for anything, and there was no point in spreading rumors accusing anyone else of wrongdoing, when those rumors might well be turned on him. No, with all the uneasiness in the Court, offering people hope and profit would be far more effective.

What would happen when the mage-storms were over? What, exactly, would the Empire need? How could those courtiers who remained here profit from the end of the Storms? If he could give them a direction—even an entirely specious direction—that would get them too busy to concern themselves with him.

Last of all, he and Thayer should work together to at least make his position *look* unassailable. Perhaps by tempting one of his three targets to attempt to persuade the Emperor to do something—something that Melles could come out against— something that Melles would *know* the Emperor would never even consider. Reliable rumors that the Emperor was actually in favor of the given action would spur the target onward. By urging something the Emperor was against, the target would label himself as a troublemaker and potential traitor in the Emperor's eyes.

He smiled to himself. And what better action could there be than urging clemency for Tremane?

He felt his eyes growing heavier, and his body relaxing. He had a plan. In the morning, he would implement it.

Now he could sleep.

Melles smiled and nodded graciously as one of Viscount Aderin's six unmarried daughters blushed and dedicated her performance on the great-harp to him. He watched her attentively—which had the effect of making her fumble her fingerings—as she labored through a rendition of an old chestnut entitled "My Lady's Eyes."

Musical evenings were the best cure for insomnia that he knew, but attendance at this one was important. If one was going to plant information, this sort of gathering was the place to do so—a room full of very minor nobility, all of them hungry for advancement, all of them so eager for a crumb from the tables of the great that they would listen to and believe practically anything. They would never divulge where their information originated, in the hope that those they imparted their choice bits to would think that it originated with them and give them credit for enormous cleverness.

And none of them could be directly linked to him. He did not mix with them socially, except at extremely large gatherings like this one, which he had been urged to attend by the Emperor's Minister of Protocol. He was not related to any of them. No one had any reason to assume that he had any reason to *give* them information. For all intents and purposes, he was here to survey Aderin's daughters as possible marriage fodder, not to chat with Aderin's friends.

In fact, the girls weren't that bad. Three of the six were discreet and submissive, able to entertain without embarrassing him, unlikely to try to put themselves forward, attractive enough to satisfy him, and tractable enough to smile and ignore any little excess of his own. He could do worse, and very well knew it. This was probably why the Minister of Protocol had suggested the gathering, at least in part. There was some nervousness among the Ministers about the fact that he was not yet married and showed no signs of wanting that particular state. There *had* been a single Emperor in the past who had been uninterested in the opposite sex, and there had been trouble during his reign that he could have resolved with a marriage of state but had not done so. This had eventually led to a costly minor war, and at the moment, the Empire could not afford a *cheap* minor war.

Of course, he could always make the ministers happy by doing what the Sixth Emperor had done. With his reign starting on a shaky note, and unwilling to offend anyone by picking one girl over another, he had handpicked the daughter of a mere Squire, a very plain, very quiet child, and had educated her to be the perfect Empress. She had offended no one in his Court, because she had deferred to everyone; she had every skill needed in an Empress. Even the fact that she was plain had been valuable, because it was quite clear to everyone that she was the Emperor's place-holder and hostess, and nothing more. The Emperor had been able then to appoint dozens of royal mistresses over the course of his reign, all of them enjoying the same status, and he had threaded his way through many intrigues on the basis of which mistress he chose to favor at any one time.

That might be the best solution of all. And if he *had* to make a state marriage eventually, well, the Emperor could divorce his wife and remarry within a day and a night, and an insignificant place-holder would have no family to make trouble later. In fact, such a girl would probably be very happy to retire from Court with a generous settlement.

As he caught himself playing with the various possibilities of such an arrangement, he sternly brought his attention back to the real reason why he was here. He was going to plant rumors, and he had better get about it before people began indulging themselves a little too heavily in the mulled punch to properly remember what they heard.

Before the evening was over, he had started a whisper-campaign about Serais and the "missing" tax money, had suggested several lines of profit to be pursued when the Storms were over, and had hinted that when *he* was Emperor, those who confined their attention to conservative ideas and relied on "what always worked before" would take second place to those with innovation and creativity. Since these folk were among the lesser nobility, they had less access to rejuvenative magics, and hence the average age here was much lower than for the Court as a whole. Melles knew that the one thing he could do to attract the support of little fish like these was to suggest that he would be more receptive to fresh, new ideas than his predecessor. This indicated that there was room at the top—and that some old, tired titles might find their Council seats and Ministerial offices taken by those who had been languishing in their shadow.

It had been a profitable evening. And in addition, he had managed to deflect any accusation that he was actually pleased at Tremane's downfall by pretending to a low level of disappointment in "his old childhood friend," thus lending another layer of obscurity to his motives. Now there would be a substantial number of people with the impression that he and Tremane had been friends for most of their lives rather than rivals. So when he laid the trail to suggest that the Emperor might be willing to consider clemency for the Grand Duke, there would be people ready to believe the suggestion since it came from him.

This very evening, a bright young fellow who'd brought himself to Porthas' attention by his brilliance with both forgery and "fixing" account books had been smuggled into the tax office and was ensuring Serais' downfall. Peleun had invested everything he had to spare, and some that he did not have, in smoked ham, bacon, and fancy sausage, certain that the cargo that had just arrived from Tival was frozen fish, not meat. Tomorrow the double caravan of smoked ham, bacon, and fancy sausage that had arrived from Tival would go on the market, and Peleun would be very lucky if he could hold onto his house in the city.

And as for Dirak, well, Melles had something very special in mind for him. Besides being nervous, Dirak was devout—or perhaps it was better to say that he was superstitious. He was about to be the recipient of a great many omens of bad fortune, together with many minor mishaps that might lend further credence to those omens. If Dirak did not collapse with nervous exhaustion before the end of a fortnight, Melles would be very much surprised.

Melles was feeling pleased enough with the way that things were going that he dismissed Porthas early when he returned to his rooms. Porthas had been responsible for setting up most of what Melles had planned for his three enemies, and he was looking a bit worn, at least to Melles' critical eye. "I can take care of myself for once," he told the man. "I'm going to work for a few more hours, then go straight to bed."

"I would argue with you," Bors Porthas replied, rubbing his hand across his eyes, "but I'm too tired. I know my limits, and I've just reached them."

Melles uttered a short bark of laughter. "Good! I was beginning to think you had no limits, and I was wondering when you were going to set yourself up as my rival." He was only half joking about that; it was something anyone in his position had to consider.

Porthas snorted. "No fear of that, my lord. *You* are a target. *I* am not. To my mind, my position is the better one. Please sleep lightly and put an extra guard on your door, my lord. And *don't* try to dress yourself until I arrive to select your robes for the day. I do not want a repetition of the day you wore the sapphire tunic with the emerald trews. I would not be able to live down the shame."

Melles acknowledged the advice with a wave of his hand, and Porthas bowed himself out.

Since he would be doing without his valet's silent attendance, Melles set his desk up with everything he might need to work before he ever sat down. A servant would come in to mend the fire, but otherwise he would be left alone at his own orders until he chose to go to bed.

He had been working steadily on follow-up orders for his agents in Jacona involved with the freedom movement, and similar, but more general orders for similar agents in other cities of the Empire. He had noticed that the room seemed to be getting colder, and had been about to ring for the servant, when the servant finally came in, bearing a metal hod of coal.

He started to turn his attention back to his work, when something about the young man's posture sounded a mental alarm in his instincts.

He was already out of his chair and had slipped free of the cumbersome outer robe as he dove toward the floor, when the first knife hit the back of the chair and stuck there, quivering.

He rolled to his feet beside the fireplace and snatched up a fireplace poker as the youngster threw a second knife that he dropped down from a hidden sheath in his sleeve. Melles easily dodged that strike, too, and his lip curled with contempt. Arm sheaths—that was a trick for sophomores and sharpsters! And against *him*! What kind of fools were they sending after him anyway?

"You might as well hold still, old man," the young one whispered, pulling another knife from somewhere behind the back of his neck as he went into a lithe crouch. "You're going to die anyway, so you might as well make it easier on both of us."

Old man! Who did this young idiot think he was? But the stupid speech—*so* melodramatic and such a waste of breath—told him the kind of assassin he faced. He had to deal with nuisances like this one at least once a year; youngsters who thought they were better and faster than the old masters, and would use any excuse to take them on. He would have to kill this cretin; he had no choice in the matter. If he didn't make an example of the fool, others like him would think he'd gone soft and keep coming at him. Killing the boy would mean that the others would leave him alone for about another year.

But anger boiled up deep in his gut, and not just because some young freelancer, ill-trained and without even a nodding acquaintance with discipline, had decided to show that the master had lost his touch. No, this boy would never have come here if he had not been brought into the palace by someone who belonged here. That meant he'd been hired.

And *that* was an insult that was hardly to be borne. How *dared* someone send a rank amateur against *him?* Did they think his reputation was inflated? Did they think he could no longer hold his own against even a boy like this one?

Were they that contemptuous of him?

They were about to discover that it was not wise to tease the old basilisk; they would learn that it was only pretending to sleep.

He rushed the boy, startling him into skipping backward; he was used to the flickering shadows cast by flames instead of mage-lights, but the boy obviously was not. As he passed his desk, he feinted with the poker and picked up the tray of sand he used to dry the ink on his documents. The boy's attention was on the poker, not on Melles' other hand. Before he could get out of reach, Melles flung the contents of the tray into his eyes, then threw the tray itself at him. The boy deflected the tray clumsily with one arm; it hit him and clattered to the floor. He could not deflect the sand.

So far neither of them had made enough noise to attract the attention of the guards at the door, and Melles had no intention of calling for help. If the guards came, they'd kill the fool before Melles had a chance to find out who had sent him.

Blinded and in pain, the boy still had a few tricks left; with his eyes watering, he threw the dagger he held at the last place Melles had been standing, and rubbed at his face with one hand while groping behind his neck for another blade. Of course, Melles wasn't where the boy thought, but had dropped down below the level of a thrown blade. He lunged forward before the boy could register where he was, and swept the poker out in a savage backhanded blow at knee-height.

He shattered the boy's left kneecap, and the boy went down with a strangled cry.

"Who sent you?" he hissed angrily, as he stood up slowly, absently pleased that he was not at all winded. The daily workouts with Porthas had been more than worth the effort.

The boy responded with a curse about Melles's sexual preferences, rolled out of the way of another blow, and got his fourth knife into his hands at the same time.

"No matter what you've heard, I don't take any pleasure in that particular pastime," Melles said coldly. By now, his eyes had watered so much that the boy could see again, although his eyes were bloodshot and swollen. Melles was in no mood to take chances, even though he was facing a partially disabled foe, so he watched the young fool warily. The boy did not writhe or take his eyes off Melles, though the pain from his shattered knee must have been excruciating. "I suggest you tell me who hired you, and save yourself a great deal of pain."

The boy inched away, sliding over the slick floor, while Melles moved cautiously toward him. This time the curse was a bit more colorful and less accurate. Melles sighed, and shook his head, as the boy got into a standing position with the help of a chair. What did he expect to accomplish from there? He couldn't walk; his leg wouldn't hold him. And if he couldn't walk, his balance would be off. Didn't he know that? Was he so desperate he'd try anything, or did he really think he had a chance to escape?

Melles backed up, keeping his eyes on the boy at all times, until he reached his desk. Without needing to look to see where it was, he pulled the boy's first knife out of the back of the chair, weighed it in his hand for a moment to get the balance, and threw it.

It hit precisely as he had intended, in the boy's gut with a wet *thud;* the boy dropped to the ground again with a gurgle, unable to twist out of the way in time, as his own knife clattered to the floor. Perhaps the fool had thought he was going to try for the trickier hand shot. That was stupid of him, if he had. A gut wound hurt more and wouldn't kill immediately.

Melles walked over to the boy and stood looking down at him, with the poker held loosely in one hand. The boy had both hands on the hilt of the knife, trying to pull it out; his breath came in harsh pants, and his eyes were glazing with agony. "Who hired you?" he asked again.

The boy looked up, and spat at him.

He sighed. He was going to have to spend more time than he wanted on this, squandering time that could have been better spent on his orders, but there was no help for it. "You're going to tell me sooner or later," he said, without much hope for sense from this arrogant idiot, who *still* didn't think he was going to die. "You'll be better off with sooner."

This time the boy responded with a suggestion for an unpalatable dietary supplement. Melles brought the poker down on his other knee, and proceeded dispassionately to inflict enough pain to extract the information he wanted.

In the end, he managed to get what he wanted without too much of a mess, and the answer made him even more disgusted than he had been at the beginning of the futile exercise.

Duke Jehan. An idiot with just about as little sense as the cretin he'd hired.

And it was not for any great ideological reason, nor because Jehan was avenging Tremane, or trying to put one of the other candidates in the Heir's suite. No, it was because Jehan had somehow gotten the impression that if he managed to assassinate enough candidates, *he* would manage to be put on the throne because he was Charliss' second cousin!

Apparently he'd thought that if he used assassins to do his work for him, no one would connect him with the deaths! Melles had no idea who Jehan thought *would* get the blame if Melles himself was gone, but perhaps this would-be King of Assassins had gotten his order of targets reversed and had gone after the last on the list first.

He finished off the mewling thing on the floor with a single thrust of the boy's own knife, threw the knife down next to the body, and wiped his hands with a napkin, contemplating his next move. It wouldn't be enough to make an example of this boy, or Jehan would think he'd gotten off undiscovered and try some other way of ridding himself of his rivals. Melles had acquired immunity to most of the common poisons, but that didn't mean he wouldn't get sick if someone slipped a dose to him. That would cost still more valuable time, and might incapacitate him long enough for one of his *real* rivals to get in to the Emperor. No, he was going to have to give Jehan a real fright, and make him into an example for anyone else at Court idiotic enough to try something like this.

In the end, it took all of his skill to pull the job off—not to get into Jehan's quarters without arousing anyone, but to get past his own guards. The nurse who was supposed to be watching in Duke Jehan's nursery was easily incapacitated with a needle dipped in a poison that sent one into a deep sleep rather than death. Jehan's oldest son, slightly more than a year old, sat up in his crib and looked with wide eyes at the stranger who came to lift him out and place him on the floor. He didn't do anything more than babble, though, when the stranger gave him several pretty toys to play with.

Melles dropped the body, wrapped in a bloody sheet, into the crib in place of the child, and left the child himself sitting on the floor, happily absorbed in the bladeless daggers that had been intended to kill Melles.

That was a somewhat melodramatic gesture in and of itself, but Melles had the feeling that anything less wouldn't get Jehan's attention. He'd considered leaving the daggers whole rather than snapping the blades off, but if the baby was as stupid as its sire, it would probably have managed to kill itself with one of them. While that would have been no loss for the Court or the world, Jehan would have been so overwrought that the lesson would be completely lost on him. And killing babies, or allowing them to be killed, was bad for one's public image.

Melles slipped back across the palace and into his own rooms again, feeling drained and no less disgusted. He had lost most of the working hours of the night—and this late, although he had easily gotten the blood off the stone floor with the sheet, he'd used up all the hot water in his suite to do so.

He'd have to wash himself in cold water; one more mark against Jehan.

He put himself to bed, chilled and angry, but at least he was physically tired enough to sleep.

And hopefully, his little present would prevent Jehan and several others from sleeping for many nights to come. It wasn't much in the way of revenge, for him, but for now it would do.

Tarrn and Lyam

Seven

"Amazing!" Silverfox shook his head and stepped away from the teleson crystal, tossing his long, black hair to one side. "If I had not seen this, I would not believe it was possible."

"I couldn't agree more," Karal said. He had been watching over Silverfox's shoulder as the *kestra'chern* spoke with Treyvan. The round crystal lens mounted on top of the teleson had held a perfect image of the head and shoulders of the fascinated gryphon, and a thin but distinct echo of his voice emerged from the matte-gray metal box that held the crystal cradled in a quarter-moon-shaped depression on its surface. This was even more impressive than the time An'desha had done long-distance scrying on Grand Duke Tremane.

This was a distinct improvement over the original sets. A little fiddling and the addition of the crystals on each set as well as the mirrors—simple polished lenticular lenses that any glassworker could make—had made it possible to have images and the audible voices of the two users. All that had been in the notes that Lyam and Firesong had interpreted, but the crystals had never been installed. Perhaps that was why the sets had been on the workbench.

Karal gazed wistfully at the device, which was now being used by Sejanes and one of the new Mage-Gifted Heralds. "This is quite amazing. I wish you didn't have to have Mindspeech to use it."

"But you don't—" Silverfox began. "Or at least only one of you does."

Karal only sighed, very quietly. Silverfox looked at him

askance, with a question in his blue eyes, but it was Sejanes who guessed what lay behind Karal's comment.

"You'd like to use this to speak to that young lady of yours without any of us eavesdropping, wouldn't you, lad?" he said shrewdly. Karal blushed and didn't reply immediately, trying to think of an answer that was noncommittal enough without being an actual lie.

"Well, *you* need to use it to confer with the others back in Haven," he said, nodding in the direction of Sejanes, Firesong, and Master Levy. "That's important."

"And you aren't. Is that what you're saying?" Sejanes graced him with a skeptical look.

"What you are talking about is important," Karal replied, knowing that any declaration of how unimportant *he* was would only be met with a counterargument. "Idle chatter with Natoli isn't. It's not as if I really need to hear about what scrapes our friends are getting into, or who's passed to the back room at the Compass Rose."

Sejanes didn't counter that particular response. Instead, he provided a different answer. "We won't be using this device all the time. Personally, if there is a way, I don't see any difficulty with you using it to catch up on news with the young lady." He tilted his head at Firesong, An'desha, and Master Levy in unspoken inquiry. All three of them nodded their heads, completely in agreement with him.

"We all know that you would give it up to one of us if we even looked as if we *thought* we might want to use it, Karal," An'desha told him. "If you could think of a way that you can make it work without an eavesdropper, there's no reason why you can't use it, too. It's not as if you're going to wear the thing out, or use it up."

:Pish. I can Mindspeak. And so can Florian.: Altra wrapped himself gracefully around Karal's legs and looked up into his face. *:For that matter, so can Need. We certainly wouldn't embarrass you, would we?:*

"The Firecat says that he, Need, or the Companion could hold the connection for Karal," Firesong told all of them.

Karal started to protest, then shut his mouth, realizing that he was wrong on all counts and he might as well be quiet. The others wouldn't need to use the teleson all the time, Altra and Florian already shared most of his secret thoughts so why not these, and there could not be any harm in talking a little to Natoli now and then. His cheeks and the back of his neck grew hot. "As long as you don't mind," he said diffidently.

A snort from Firesong was the only reply to that statement, as a Herald in the teleson watched and listened with polite interest.

"*Shall I see if Natoli can be found later?*" the far-off Herald asked. "*If there's no one at the device, one of the Mindspeakers can project to you until Need, the Firecat or the Companion can come hold the connection.*"

:*I would think that would be quite satisfactory,*: Florian told Karal. :*And I think you ought to tell him that, so that he can arrange for Natoli to come as soon as the mages are finished.*:

"Ah, Florian thinks that would be a good idea," Karal said, trying to control his blushes. "Thank you."

He hurried away to find something to do before he got himself into any further embarrassing situations.

The most useful thing he could do was to serve in his proper place as a secretary, and right at this very moment the only person who needed the skills of a secretary was Tarrn. The *kyree* was down in the workroom, carefully describing everything before Firesong and An'desha took it all to pieces. Lyam had already made scale drawings of each workbench, and now he was making notes while Tarrn dictated. He gratefully gave up his place to Karal, even though the notes would now be in Valdemaran rather than Kaled'a'in. Tarrn didn't miss a beat, changing his Mindspeech from Lyam to Karal as soon as Karal held the notepad and graphite-stick. Karal rubbed his nose to keep from sneezing; they had stirred up quite a bit of dust just in walking about. It was amazing how much dust found its way down here once the hatchway was open.

"Why are you doing this, sir?" Karal asked, when they completed one bench and moved on to another. "I'm just curious."

:*A number of reasons,*: the *kyree* replied pleasantly. :*Later, if we are trying to put together another device, we will know what pieces were laid out on which bench in what order. We will have a historical record of how the workshop looked if we ever wish to reconstruct it. In this way, if for some reason the contents of the workbenches are ever jumbled together, we will know what tool goes with what project. It is not always intuitively obvious.:*

Karal nodded, and made another note on the identity of an object. All of that made perfect sense, but it would never have occurred to him to make such detailed drawings, or to measure the distance an object was from the edge of the bench.

:In a case like this, young scribe, records are always important,: Tarrn said. *:The more, the better. Once anything is moved, it is changed forever; perhaps that might not be important, but at the moment, we can't know that. The thing is to make drawings and notes on everything, and several exact copies of the documents we find:*

Karal laughed, which seemed to surprise the *kyree*. "It is a good thing that Urtho was a neat man, or you would be copying foodstains, I think, along with diagrams."

The *kyree* opened his mouth in a wide grin. *:It would not be the first time. I am a mere historian; how am I to know what is a diagram and what was a long-ago spill of wine? Perhaps a semicircle of dark brown may not in fact be a ring from the bottom of a mug, but rather a notation of where a teleson lens should go?:*

Lyam, now freed to go make more of those exact copies of the documents and notes they had discovered resting on the benches, trotted up the stairs. Karal had been amazed to discover just how much he had in common with the little lizard-creature over the past several days. Lyam was good-natured, patient, uncomplaining, and about the same age as Karal. Like Karal when he had first arrived in Valdemar, Lyam never expected to be anything more than a secretary. Lyam was probably right, but if anything was to happen to Tarrn, it would be Lyam who would apply the things he learned from the historian to complete a given task.

Tarrn, on the other hand, was a little easier to work for than Ulrich had been, largely because what Tarrn wanted and needed were simple things. It was quite possible for Karal to anticipate Tarrn's descriptions just by looking at the bench, although Tarrn often had a more succinct way of describing something than Karal would have come up with. And Tarrn, although he did have an air of quiet authority, was not as intimidating as Ulrich had been. Since he was physically much shorter than Karal, and since he looked like a friendly, shaggy sheep-herding dog, it simply wasn't possible to be intimidated by him, no matter how intelligent and knowledgeable he was. On the other hand, he seemed just a bit wary around Karal, which was not too surprising. The Karsites had a reputation for being extremely insular people, and it would be logical to assume that Karal harbored certain prejudices about four-legged "people." Tarrn could not have known about the Fire-cats, of course; very few people outside of Karse even knew such things existed.

The work went slowly but steadily. Tarrn had refused to allow anyone else to carry away anything after Firesong had taken the telesons and their notes. Since there wasn't any-thing down here that was needed immediately, the others had given in to his demands with good-natured humor. Since then, the meticulous description and drawing had been going on every day. Tarrn permitted people to remove articles from the benches only after he had finished with them, but since it wasn't always obvious when he was done with a bench, so far no one had moved much of anything.

Now they were down to the final bench, and Tarrn seemed very pleased with all that had gone before. This bench was virtually empty except for a few pots of dried-out paint and ink and some brushes and pens. :*A scribe's bench, I would guess,*: Tarrn speculated. :*Look at the height of the stool—how close the inkwell and the pots are to the front of the bench. Urtho never sat here, I'll wager.*:

"I doubt that any human did," Karal replied, noting the dis-tances down on the diagram. "This is a backless stool, where all the other seats are tall chairs, and to me, that says that whoever used this bench might have had a tail. The seat tilts slightly forward and has an angled, rounded cut-in toward the back, so, I'd say it was a *hertasi* that sat here. Probably Urtho's personal scribe or secretary."

:*Impressive deduction. I suspect you are correct,*: Tarrn re-plied. :*And this is good, since it means Lyam can use this bench for his copying work instead of taking an awkward position on the floor. Well, that is all we need from here. Do run up and tell the others that they can come loot to their hearts' content, would you please? Then if you would, tell Lyam about all of this, and could you help him move his supplies down here?*:

Tarrn gave the order carefully, phrased as a very polite request, as if trying to avoid giving insult. Karal would have obeyed him no matter what his attitude had been, but Tarrn probably wasn't taking any chances about hurting his feelings since they all had to live together in a very crowded environment. Lyam was very happy to transfer his work from the floor upstairs to the bench downstairs, and Karal helped him carry his effects. As Karal had thought, the backless stool was at the perfect height for the little lizard.

"This will be good," Lyam said, hissing his sibilants a trifle as he tested the seat. "The stool is perfect." The brushes proved to have failed to withstand the rigors of time; Lyam examined them, pronounced them useless for scribing, and added that nothing had changed much in the art of brushmaking over the centuries. It did give Karal a sense of awe to hold in his hand something that had last been held so long ago, but Lyam was right; the brush could have been made last week except for the fact that the bristles were crumbling.

"I admit to having a special regard for the tools of my trade," Lyam confided. The paint and ink in the pots were useless as well and were consigned to part of another bench to await their fate. Lyam and Karal cleared the top of the scribe's bench and set it up to Lyam's satisfaction. It did not escape Karal's notice that the graphite-sticks, silverpoint sticks, ink, pens, and brushes that Lyam arranged were in nearly the same places as those that had once served that long-dead scribe. Together they swept and cleaned out the corner, so that there would be no dust or dirt to smudge Lyam's new-made copies.

"Ah!" Lyam finally said with satisfaction, stretching his tail out and flexing his stubby hand-talons. "This is good, good light, and a good position! I can be very happy here, I think! Thank you, *gesten.*"

"You're very welcome. Really." Karal paused a moment as it struck him again, in a moment of astonishment, that he was chatting amiably with what could be loosely described as an intelligent dog and its lizard secretary, in the ruins of a magic-blasted tower once ruled by a legend. His musings were interrupted as the lizard secretary held up an ancient brush so that the tarnished ferrule shone dully in the workshop's light. "You know, simply by virtue of where this brush has been found, it could be worth enough in trade to feed my family for a season, but its highest value is in what it makes us think of when we see it.''

The *kyree* looked over at the *hertasi* with a look of pure pleasure, saying nothing. Lyam held the old brush reverently in both hands and continued. ''An artifact of Urtho's own workshop. This is history itself, Karal, as great as any carved monument or temple. History is in the small items as much as the huge ones. When we see an edifice, we see what the ancients *wanted* us to see, and that is important, but we find out so much more from what was so familiar to them that they thought little of it. And one day, perhaps historians will look back at our clothes, our brushes, and our everyday things, and learn who we were, too!''

:Now you know why I enjoy Lyam's company so much, Karal. He is truly a brother in spirit!: Tarrn's mind-laugh was joyous.

''Oh! I—well. It is easy to be overcome by all of this. It is wonder itself we are immersed in here,'' Lyam muttered, embarrassed, as he gingerly set aside the brush that had been the focus of his oratory. Karal and Tarrn exchanged knowing looks with each other. Even across time, species, and cultures, the enjoyment of history's ''wonder itself'' could be shared.

Karal left Lyam bent over yet another copy of the ancient notes; this batch seemed to be the jewelry designs. He would have offered to help, but although his drafting ability was up to making sketches of benchtops and their contents, it was not up to making copies of intricate jewelry patterns.

When he went back upstairs, Tarrn came with him, and immediately engaged himself in conference with Firesong and An'desha over another copied set of notes. Firesong and An'desha were chattering away, with odd breaks in the conversation as they listened to Tarrn's Mindspoken replies. Master Levy had replaced Sejanes at the teleson, and was talking to someone Karal did not recognize, but who wore Trainee Grays instead of Herald Whites. Sejanes, who was standing behind Master Levy, simply watching the conversation, turned at the sound of Karal's footsteps and waved him over.

''I understand from Firesong that you were the Channel for the last effort here,'' Sejanes said, when Karal was within earshot. The old mage looked at him expectantly, motioning him to follow as he moved away from the teleson and Master Levy's intensely technical conversation.

Karal nodded, wondering what Sejanes wanted. "Not that I have any idea of what a Channel is or does, sir," he added. "I'm afraid I put my faith in what I was told, that Channeling is instinctive." He felt very diffident, telling such an experienced mage that he had no idea of what he had been doing. He hoped that Sejanes wasn't going to be annoyed at him for mucking about with things he didn't understand.

Sejanes pulled on his lower lip thoughtfully. "That's true in a limited sense," he finally replied. "You could perfectly well go on that way; many Channels prefer not to know anything about what causes what they're doing. But there are things that can be learned that would make the experience easier for you, and perhaps less frightening. I could teach you, if you wanted to learn; that's why I asked about it. It could make an important difference in how you feel afterward."

Karal's mouth went dry, and he swallowed as a tremor of fear passed through him. How could he tell this old mage that the very last thing he wanted was to have anything to do with more magic? On the other hand, Sejanes seemed to understand how horrible it had been for him, and if there was a "next time," wouldn't it be better to undertake it fully prepared? "Well, sir, if I had a choice—I've done it twice, and I'd really rather not ever do it again. But if I have to, anything that would make things easier would probably be a good idea. So I guess I ought to take you up on your offer."

The old man chuckled at his lack of enthusiasm and patted his shoulder, as if to reassure him. "There's no shame in that reaction," he told Karal. "I've never Channeled, myself, but I've spoken to those who have and they would probably agree with you on both counts. I can't blame you a bit. Yet if we're going to start, I suspect we ought to do so before you lose your nerve about it. If you have some time to spare, we could begin now."

Karal shrugged with a nonchalance he in no way felt. "I'd rather not put it off and take a chance that I might need to channel power in the next few hours. The way my luck runs, I would need what you *might* have taught me if I hadn't delayed because—"

He stopped himself before he admitted how frightened he

was, but Sejanes saw it anyway. He left his hand on Karal's shoulder a moment longer. "I told you, it is no shame to be afraid, young one," he said in a low, reassuring voice. "Channels hold power as great as any Adept, and sometimes greater; the only difference between them is that Channels don't actually use what they carry. And perhaps that is what makes it harder for them. They are used by the power, rather than using it. What sane creature ever gives up control if he does not have to?"

Karal shuddered; he wouldn't ever *want* to use all that power. It would be more responsibility than he ever cared to handle under any circumstances, no matter how dire. "That's—that's quite a thought, sir. We—we of the Sunlord give up control to Him as a matter of faith. But we are still afraid sometimes, and He only helps those who try hard to deal with difficulties themselves. And I'm afraid I don't know much about magic at all, if it comes right down to it."

"Good. Then you have little or nothing to unlearn. And, yes, your faith will help you." Sejanes led the way to the chamber they were using for storage, purloined a couple of empty buckets and a pair of folded blankets for cushions to sit on, and took Karal over to a quiet corner. When they had made rough stools out of the upturned buckets and rested the cushions upon them, he began. Karal experienced a disconcerting sense of familiarity and an equally disconcerting sense of disconnection; Sejanes sounded like every good teacher he had ever studied under, but the surroundings were nothing like the classrooms of the Sun-priests where he had done all that study. And if he closed his eyes, Sejanes sounded so much like Ulrich except for the accent that it was uncanny.

"Mage-power, as we know and understand it, is an energy that is given off by living things in the same way that fire gives off heat and light in the act of consuming wood," he said, his manner easy and casual, his tone exactly the same as if he were describing the weather and not a power that could wreck kingdoms. "It tends to want to gather together, and tends to follow well-worn paths. In that, it is more like rainwater than fire."

"And mages can see this power?" Karal asked, though his mouth was dry with nervousness.

"That's what makes someone a mage," Sejanes replied. "I

can see that power any time I make the effort to—and someone like Firesong has to make an effort *not* to see it."

Karal glanced over at Firesong, who looked no different
from any other absurdly handsome Hawkbrother, and shook
his head. Seeing power all the time . . . was it like seeing
things with an extra color added? Was it like seeing particles
and waves swirling all around you like swimming underwa-
ter? And when the power got too strong, did it blind you, like
looking into the sun?

"Now, the power itself obeys rules," Sejanes continued.
"When the threadlike paths, or tiny streams, merge together
enough to make them of a different magnitude of strength, we
call them 'ley-lines.' These *tend* to be straight, at least in the
short term, and that, besides strength of power, is what makes
ley-lines different from the trickles that feed them."

"Is it the strength that makes them straight?" Karal hazarded.

Sejanes looked pleased. "We don't know for certain, but
that is the theory," he said. "It makes sense; a trickle of water
will meander more than a powerful river. We think that after
a certain point, the power can cut through the world taking
the shortest distance which, as Master Levy will tell you, is
always a straight line."

Karal nodded; no wonder Sejanes and Master Levy got on so
well!

"Now, sooner or later, since power is attracted by power,
these lines will meet. The places where two or more ley-lines
meet forms something called a 'node,' where power collects."
Sejanes looked at him expectantly.

Karal hazarded another question. "It can't collect indefi-
nitely, though, can it?"

Sejanes looked *very* pleased. "No, it can't, and it will either
be used up or drain away into the Void, and we honestly don't
know what happens to it after that."

Karal seemed to recall An'desha telling him something
about a third option, something that the Hawkbrothers used
called a Heartstone, but that was a complication he didn't
need right now. *First, learn the rules, and worry about the
exceptions later.*

"Now—about using power," Sejanes continued. "Mages
can use the power that they themselves produce. Mages can

use the power given off by things in their immediate vicinity. Mages can also store power for later use in reservoirs; those can be available only to a single mage, or can be a group effort, built by group contributions, for as long as the group lasts."

"Everybody?" Karal asked, more than a bit alarmed by the notion of a barely-trained Apprentice being able to use such power.

"Oh, no!" Sejanes chuckled. "No, fortunately, lack of training and practice provides some control. The common titles for levels of ability refer to what power they can tap, and not their absolute skill. As with any venture, some people are more skilled than others, but I digress. Apprentices can only use their own power or what is immediately available around them below the level of a ley-line. Journeymen can use ley-lines. Masters can use those reservoirs. If a mage is part of a particular school, he is given the key to the reservoir built by the mages of that school at the time he becomes a Master. At that point, part of his duty every day is to feed the reservoir as much power as he has time to gather. Eventually, over the years, with these reservoirs being filled more often than they are drained, they are ready for anything the Masters might need, but that power is tame, like water in a still pond."

"Because it isn't flowing anywhere?" Karal asked, and was rewarded by Sejanes's nod. "But what about nodes?"

"That," Sejanes said with a shading of pride, "is what only Adepts can do. Adepts don't need to bother with the reservoirs, though they sometimes do simply because they are so still—for very delicate work, for example, such as Healings. Adepts can tap into and use the raw power of the nodes. The stronger the Adept, the larger the node he can control. Ley-line power is harder to control than reservoir power or ambient power, because, as you guessed, it is 'moving,' so to speak. But node power fights the user, because it is moving swiftly, sometimes in more than one direction, and is wild and unconfined. Have you understood me so far?"

Karal nodded; so far this all seemed very straightforward. Perhaps Altra would also be able to help him with this, since the Firecat seemed something of a mage.

"Last of all of those who handle mage-power come the Channels." Sejanes nodded at Karal. "As I said when I began, the one thing that all life-path mages have in common is that they have what the Valdemarans call the Mage-Gift, and that ability enables them to actually see magic power. Channels, however, usually do not have Mage-Gift, or if they do, it isn't very strong."

"Why?" Karal asked.

Sejanes rubbed the side of his nose. "I don't know if there is a reason. There is some speculation that this is partly a protection for them, and partly a protection against them. The ability to sense magic power might be blinded the first time a Channel was used by very powerful magic. And if you can sense something, you can use it, so it might be better for all of us that anyone who can handle power stronger than any Adept would even *dream* of touching cannot actually use that power himself."

Again, Karal nodded. If you went on the basic assumption that any Karsite would—which was that it was Vkandis who granted such abilities—such a system of checks and balances made complete sense. Vkandis would not have placed extraordinary power within the capacity of mere mortals without some curbs on the system.

The explanation might also simply be that the act of attempting to actually *use* that much power rather than just direct it could be fatal. If mages who were also Channels died before they could wed and bring forth children with the Gift, such a combination wouldn't last for long. Look what happened to those with mind-magic in Karse. They'd been gathered up and given to the Fires for generations, and as a result, just before Solaris took power, there were so few such "witches" and "demons" that there hadn't been more than four or five Fires a year, with a single victim apiece.

Sejanes looked down at his hands for a moment, gathering his thoughts. "Think of a funnel; the wide end catches scattered drops of water or small pieces of matter, and focuses it down into a small, directed stream. That's what a Channel does, and roughly how a Channel does it. And because a Channel actually forces the power going through him to flow through a 'smaller space,' he increases the force of that flow and its 'speed,' if you will. So what a Channel needs to work perfectly is someone to guide the power in, however wild it may be, and someone to direct it as it goes out again. Remember that directing something—much like shunting a stream a few degrees—is much easier than using it."

Karal nodded numbly as Sejanes continued.

"Magic is much like water, Karal, but it is far more versatile. It can be manipulated by force of will, by natural aptitude, by specialized devices, and by other ways. Water, essentially, can only get things 'wet,' if I may use a crude analogy. Magic, however, can get things wet, turn things to dust, set them ablaze, make them into stone, give them life, put them somewhere else, and so on. But magic in its wild forms works in very gradual and subtle ways. It is not until magic is manipulated by someone that it has 'quick' effects. Without mages, magic takes its natural course."

"Like a river," Karal offered. "And mages make water wheels and dams and bridges."

Sejanes leaned back, apparently impressed. "That," he said slowly, "is essentially it. Yes. That is what we do."

Karal bit at his lower lip and offered, "And what happened here, is that long ago there was an explosion in the magic that—scooped a hole out. And the water—I mean, the magic—is rushing back to fill the hole."

"Close," Sejanes nodded. "Very close. You are a bright young man, Karal. Now, back to just what you are. A Channel. For whatever reason, a Channel collects power that is brought 'to' him, and directs it in a more purely directed, less stormy fashion."

"That's all there is to it?" Karal exclaimed. "I am a funnel?"

Sejanes smiled. "That's all the *theory*," he chided gently. "But now comes the practice that will help you keep parts of yourself from interfering with or even fighting that stream of power. And it will be all the harder because you will be dealing with something you yourself can only sense dimly, like playing blind-man's bluff with an unruly stallion. And to continue that analogy, I'm not going to show you how to catch and ride the beast, because it will kill you if you try. Instead, I'm going to try to teach you how to keep 'yourself' out of its way."

At the end of the lesson, Karal was quite certain that Sejanes' analogy of a game with an angry horse was the correct one. The inside of his head felt bruised, somehow, though certainly not as bad as he had felt after the first time he'd acted as a Channel. The lesson was over when Sejanes clapped him on the back and told him that he had done very well for his first attempt.

"You aren't the worst Channel I've ever seen, and we tend to use them more than you Westerners do," the old mage said cheerfully. "I don't know if the ability occurs more often in the Empire or if we Imperial mages are so lazy that we'd rather use Channels than focus power ourselves, and so we make an active effort to look for the ability. But you aren't the worst, that's for certain, and you've come to the lessons late in your life, so that's encouraging."

:*Faint praise, but better than none, I suppose*,: Altra observed, wrapping himself around Karal's legs. :*Natoli is waiting to talk to you.*:

"I'm going to assume that since my lord Altra is here, that your young lady is ready to speak to you," Sejanes observed. "Go on, off with you. By the by, you'll toughen up as you practice; this should be the worst training session you'll ever endure.

:*You'll notice he said* training *session,*: Altra observed, as Karal got up from his stool and followed the Firecat. :*That doesn't say anything about the real thing.*:

That hadn't escaped Karal's attention, but he really didn't want to dwell on it, not when he was finally going to get to see and talk to Natoli.

Karal took his place on the empty stool in front of the teleson; Altra draped himself over Karal's feet, and the Herald in the crystal winked, and stepped away. A moment later, Natoli moved into the place he had vacated.

She looked as if she had recovered from the boiler explosion. Her hair was a little longer than it had been when he left, and she looked at him as if she had forgotten why she was there. Suddenly he felt very shy.

"Hello, Natoli," he said awkwardly. "You look in good health."

He winced as he listened to himself; was that any way to speak to a girl he really wanted to be able to kiss?

"You don't," she said bluntly, peering at him. "You're too pale, and too thin. What have you been doing to yourself?"

That was so very typical of her that he had to laugh, and

relaxed immediately. "As to the first, we've been living under-ground, and we mostly don't get to see the sun. And as to the second—have *you* ever tasted Firesong's cooking?" He shud-dered melodramatically, and she laughed in return. "Seri-ously. We're mostly eating as the Shin'a'in do; it's not that bad, just a little odd."

"And you don't often see a fat Shin'a'in," she said shrewdly. "Things were quiet until Altra showed up with this contrap-tion. We Artificers all wanted to take it apart, of course, but when we were told that the first person to try would be skinned, we gave up on the idea." She grinned. "We'll have to make do with trying to duplicate it from those manuscripts. If we can, we'll send one by fast Herald-courier to Solaris, and then you'll get to talk to *her* on a regular basis."

"Must I?" he asked weakly. He was not ready to face Solaris just yet. He wasn't sure he would be for quite a while, actu-ally. Her Radiance was not a comfortable person to speak to, face-to-face. For that matter, she wasn't a comfortable person to communicate with, letter to letter; he always had the feel-ing that he was reading something intended for an audience rather than a personal letter.

"First we have to duplicate it," she pointed out, and smiled. "You know, I'm very glad to see you again. Sometimes, in the middle of the night, I'd wake up, and I'd wonder if you were—quite real."

Oddly enough, he knew exactly what she meant. "It's hard to imagine someone being real who's that far away," he agreed. "It's as if they never existed except in your mind."

She flushed a little, and looked away for a moment. "Any-way," she continued awkwardly, "we've been busy, though it doesn't have anything to do with the important things." She sounded wistful. "There's just nothing we *can* do right now to help with what you're doing, so we're back to the old proj-ects like bridges and steam boilers."

"There's nothing wrong with that," he countered. "Don't these things have to be done no matter what disaster might be looming?" He managed a crooked grin. "If everything else falls apart, your bridges will be there to get people across riv-ers that can't be ferried or forded. Surely that's worth some-thing."

She shrugged but looked pleased. "At least what we're

doing is useful," she admitted. "It's odd, though. The folk around and about Haven have the funniest attitude; you can tell them and tell them that the protection we've given them from the mage-storms is only temporary, but they act as if it's permanent. They aren't doing anything to prepare themselves for the worst, they aren't even thinking about it." Now she sounded and looked very frustrated. "When you ask them why, they just shrug and can't give you an answer, or they say something stupid, fatalistic, or both."

"I think," he said slowly, "that ordinary folk just can't imagine anything awful happening to *them*. It always happens to someone else."

"Well, you'd think after years of war and bandits and all they should know better," she replied acidly. "At any rate, now that things have settled down, they aren't at all interested in asking us about things they can do when the Storms come again, they just want to know how long it is going to take before a bridge will be up. Or if the steam boiler is likely to explode again."

"I hope *you're* on bridges," he said, trying not to show alarm. "And not steam boilers."

"Actually, I'm on metal stress," she replied, running her hand through her hair absently. "I get to make some very interesting and loud noises. We're trying to make tougher alloys, but I don't want to bore you with what we're doing. I spend some time in the forge, because at the moment, work on steam boilers is stalled until we can find a better way to make the boiler itself."

He sighed, resting his chin on his hands. "It wouldn't bore me, but I'd be lost," he admitted. "Sejanes is trying to teach me some specific kind of exercises for working with magic, and those would probably mean about as much to you."

"Probably." The conversation died for a moment. "Still, I hope you aren't—I mean, I don't want you to think that—" her face twisted with frustration. "Just, if you're doing something dangerous, don't take more on yourself than you can carry, all right?"

He smiled. "As long as you promise to do the same," he replied, and she laughed.

"Grain for the gander is good for the goose, hmm? Well, I'll promise to try, but my judgment is sometimes faulty."

"So is mine, so don't hold it against me." His smile took on an ironic edge. "We can't all be infallible Sons of the Sun."

"Oh, even Solaris admits to fallibility," she chuckled. "Believe it or not."

"Solaris?" he chuckled. "That would be an entry in the annals, especially if she admitted that she was fallible to you polytheistic barbarians."

"But she did!" Natoli protested, and as he continued to regard her askance, she looked surprised. "Oh! I'll bet no one told you, any of you! You will not believe what has happened with Grand Duke Tremane!"

As she outlined the astonishing developments in Hardorn since the arrival of Elspeth and Darkwind, Karal felt his eyes growing larger and larger. No one had seemed to think that any of this was significant enough to pass on to any of the other members of his party—

Which is probably because they all have their own preoccupations and not a one of them thinks anything is important outside those preoccupations! But you'd think someone would have said something to Sejanes!

"We have a Herald and a Companion stationed down in Karse in Solaris'—court, I suppose you call it—" she added.

"Conclave," he corrected.

"Conclave, then. We sent him down so that we could get information to her by way of his Companion and Talia's Rolan." She laughed. "Actually, it's not just 'a Herald,' it's my father, and he seems to be enjoying himself. Anyway, we sent her word about this, and the reply she sent back was: 'Since he has voluntarily placed himself in the hands of a higher judge of character than myself, I feel impelled to point out that Natoli, An'desha, and Karal were correct in their assessment of his basic character, and I was at least in part swayed by nothing more substantial than emotion.' What do you think of that?" She grinned, as if she had somehow won a great prize. Then again, winning a concession like that from Solaris would have been a great prize, particularly as it was her father who had sent the message on to Haven.

It's a small thing, but she just proved to her father that she doesn't have to be a Herald to accomplish something important, he realized. *And maybe she just proved it to herself as well.*

"I think she didn't use the ecclesiastic plural, which means that she was speaking for Solaris and not for the Son of the Sun," he told her, but he felt very pleased, nevertheless, for the sake of his own people. Historically, it was a tremendous temptation for the Son of the Sun to always think of himself as speaking for Vkandis, until even the most minor personal opinions were incorporated as doctrine. Solaris appeared to have overcome that particular temptation. "Which is not a bad thing."

"No, it's not." She appeared to have run out of things to say, and another awkward moment of silence descended. "I suppose you'll want to go tell all this to Sejanes. . . ."

He did, but he also didn't want to go, even though he didn't really have anything to say. The silence lengthened and became more strained. She glanced to the side, and her expression lightened a little with relief even while it darkened with disappointment. "Oh, here's someone for Master Levy. If Altra will hold the teleson open while you get him—"

"Of course!" he said, feeling both emotions himself. "Natoli, take care of yourself! And I—I miss all of you."

He didn't dare say that he missed only her, but he hoped she got that impression from his hesitation. "I—we miss you, too," she replied, with a smile more shy than usual, and vanished from the crystal. Karal ran to get Master Levy, who nodded and hurried to the device carrying a sheaf of notes as if he had been expecting to be summoned back.

Karal glanced around and couldn't find Sejanes in the upper rooms; he listened carefully and heard the old mage's voice coming thinly from the workshops below. He hurried down the stairs to find Sejanes chatting away comfortably with Lyam, though Tarrn was nowhere in sight.

"Sir!" he called, "I've got the most amazing news about Duke Tremane!"

"Well," Sejanes said, chuckling softly. "Well, well, well." He was inordinately pleased with Karal's news, and Karal could not help but wonder why.

That's an odd way to react, considering that Tremane has acted quite unlike a proper Imperial officer. "I thought you might be upset, sir," he ventured, tilting his head to one side. "Aren't you?"

"Upset? No, this is rather good news, all things considered," Sejanes replied, and chuckled again. "It seems that my former pupil has learned at long last that there are things that do not always answer to his logic. I am quite glad to hear this, truth be told. This is going to be a very good thing for everyone concerned."

Karal kept his inquisitive expression, hoping to prompt more information from the mage, and Sejanes enlarged on his statement.

"I am pleased for Hardorn, for that sad, maltreated land could not have found a better caretaker." He blinked, and his eyes fixed on some distant point beyond Karal. "I am pleased because Tremane could not have found a better trust than Hardorn. He was wasted on the Empire; he has the misfortune to be that rarest of Imperial creatures, a man of high rank who still maintains a shred or two of integrity and compassion. That is not to say, at all, that the military is composed of heartless men; far from that, in fact. He might have done well had he remained within the military, but as Emperor, he would have been a victim of one of three unpleasant fates—eaten alive by those conspiring to use him, murdered, or corrupted."

"That much I can see," Karal replied. "It's quite logical, but. . . ." He faltered, unsure how to ask what he wanted to know without being rude. Imperials were not—quite—irreligious, but they were hardly as devout as even the average Valdemaran. And when compared with the average Karsite, they were positively atheistic!

Sejanes seemed to understand what he wanted to know. "Not all citizens of the Empire are so immersed in practicality as you think." His gaze softened and turned inward for a moment. "Those most likely to become cynical, believers in nothing that they cannot see, are the career courtiers. Those least likely—probably the folk who live nearest the land, and those who live by magic. My young protégé was poised between the cynic and the believer, and he could have taken either path. He may be the rarest of all, one who can see the truth in both."

Karal wanted badly to ask just what Sejanes believed in, but he sensed that Sejanes would not tell him now. He might never. That was his right, of course. And it would be horribly impolite of Karal to ask him. If he ever wanted to tell Karal, he would.

"It is my own opinion, that whatever else has happened, Tremane has discovered that there are those other paths. Perhaps that will open his mind to those other possibilities." He rubbed his eyes for a moment, as if they were tired. "And I am pleased that he has an outside governor in this earth-binding, something to—shall we say—keep him from succumbing to other temptations."

"He is that weak, then?" asked Lyam, with the careless tone of one to whom Duke Tremane and his men were no more real than the folk in the Chronicles of a thousand years ago.

They might not be. The Kaled'a'in are so different from the Imperials that they must seem equally unreal to each other.

"Not weak," Sejanes amended, and his wrinkled brow knitted, as he searched for words.

He's trying to explain Tremane to a couple of youngsters for whom the Empire is only a name, who cannot even imagine the levels of intrigue that someone like Tremane must negotiate every day. Karal waited for the aged mage to find the right words. *And he can't know that the Temple of Vkandis is—or was, anyway—as much a hotbed of conspiracy as any court. I don't think Lyam could ever understand the stresses that Tremane must have been under, but I do. I wonder if Tremane ever got tired of it all, and wished for things to be simpler?* "No, he's not weak," Sejanes repeated. "The trouble is that certain habits, certain ways of reacting, become ingrained. It would be all too simple to revert to the ways in which business is conducted in the Empire, without thought for what was good for Hardorn. That, more than anything, would be the temptation; to take the way that is easiest, rather than the one that is best for the people and the land, and doubly so when resources are low."

Lyam looked baffled, but shrugged, accepting what Sejanes said for the moment.

Karal nodded. "Trying to do things the way he was used to would probably get him in great difficulties in Hardorn, wouldn't it?" he asked. "It might even break up the peace, and he might not know why that had happened. Now, he hasn't a choice, you see; he'll *know* what is best and he'll have to do it, or he knows how he'll suffer for it. And you know," he continued, feeling a certain amount of surprise at the insight, "the thing is, since people will know he *can't* do anything selfishly or maliciously, they're likely to be easier on his mistakes, if you take my meaning. They'll be more likely to forgive and explain."

Sejanes flashed a mildly surprised but appreciative look at him. "Exactly so. And I am very fond of Tremane; I should like to see him as happy as anyone burdened with power and the ability to wield it can be. He has a strong sense of responsibility, and this may be the one opportunity of his lifetime to exercise that responsibility with people who are likely to appreciate the care he will take." Once again, Sejanes' gaze turned inward. "He had his estate, of course, but those on it were used to being ruled gently. The folk of Hardorn were subjected to every ill imaginable. That will make them grateful to a gentler hand."

Lyam uttered the breathy equivalent of a laugh, showing very sharp, pointed teeth. "He will be finding himself burdened with more than power, I think. Earth-sense is as jealous a mistress as responsibility."

"But the earth-sense and his own responsibility will work in harness amicably, rather than pulling him to pieces between them," Sejanes countered. "Had he risen to power in the Empire, he would have spent every day being torn among fear, duty, responsibility, expediency, and the right. I think it might have driven him mad. I know it would have changed him into something I would no longer recognize."

The *hertasi* shrugged again. "Good, then. We take what small victories we can. I hope that all this gives him aid if we cannot stop the Storms. He shall need every help he can muster to protect these people who are now depending on him."

"It might." Karal knew something about earth-sense, though few Sun-priests had it. The ability was much valued among the farmers of the Karsite hills, where the soil was poor and the weather chancy. If you knew that it would be a bad notion to plant corn this year in a particular field, and a good one to plant clover, you might prosper when your neighbors failed. And if you shared your expertise with your neighbors, you might all be able to pay the tithe in goods instead of your own flesh-and-blood, come harvest time. It wasn't *exactly* a witch-power, and it wasn't *exactly* one of the things that would get you sent to the Fires, but it also wasn't the sort of thing that you spoke about to the Sun-priests. The Sun-priests in their turn were careful not to *ask* about it, and all was well.

"Another small victory, then." Lyam nodded decisively, and seemed to think that a change of subject was in order. "This Natoli, who gave you this word—is she kin to you? Or something else?"

That was not the subject the young Karsite would have chosen, and Karal felt himself blushing furiously, as Lyam's quick eyes and quicker wit filled in the truth. "Ah—" the little lizard said, not without sympathy, his head bobbing. "She is to you what Jylen is to me, I think." He sighed gustily. "I do miss her company, but I would not have her here. She could not have endured the journey, and I think she would have felt herself useless, which is a bad thing for anyone to feel."

"Natoli would have felt the same," Karal admitted. "Oh, *I* feel useless about half the time, and it makes me want to bite something. I'd rather not think how she would react."

"Nor I, Jylen." Lyam laughed. "A trimmer tail there never was, nor a more graceful snout, but neither belong to a maid with an overabundance of patience."

He shared a glance of fellow-feeling with Karal, and the young Karsite experienced a definite warming in the relationship between them.

"Well, Sejanes, I will take my leave of you," Lyam told the mage. "And of you, Karal. My stomach has an overly-intimate embrace with my spine, and I think I shall venture Firesong's cooking and see if it is as terrible as you claim. Surely he learned *something* from his *hertasi!*"

"It's not Firesong tonight, it's An'desha," Karal assured him, "And he and the Shin'a'in have agreed to share that particular chore from now on."

"Thanks to the Hundred Little Gods!" Sejanes exclaimed with clear relief. "Even enduring Shin'a'in butter-tea is preferable to eating what Firesong cooks!"

"In that case, I will haste my steps!" the *hertasi* cried. "In case the other starvelings aloft decide to leave me with naught but scrapings!"

He scrambled down from his stool and scampered up the

stairs with a staccato click of toenails on stone. Sejanes cocked an eyebrow at Karal.

"What about you?" he asked. "I was under the impression that young men were never quite fully fed."

It was Karal's turn to shrug uncomfortably. His stomach was still in something of a knot, and he wondered if Natoli was always going to affect him that way. If so, he was destined to grow much thinner.

"Lucky in love?" the old man asked, softly, and with a kindly and sympathetic manner. "Or unlucky? Either one can be hazardous to the appetite."

"I—I'm not sure," Karal replied, feeling his cheeks burning. "We don't know each other that well. . . ."

Sejanes reached out and patted his knee. "Uncertainty can be just as hazardous. But I take it that she *is* a trusted friend?"

"Oh, yes, absolutely," Karal said fervently. "There isn't anyone I would trust more."

:Humph.:

Karal glanced hastily down at his feet, where Altra lay coiled around the legs of his chair, hitherto unnoticed. How had the Firecat gotten there? The last Karal had seen, Altra had been sprawled on the floor near the teleson.

"There isn't a human I trust more. I trust her as much as I trust Altra and Florian," he amended hastily. "And for a great many of the same reasons."

:Better. Not perfect, but better.:

"That is an excellent beginning, then," Sejanes said, his tone just as serious and his demeanor as sober as if he was discussing the next solution to the mage-storm. "One should always begin with friendship, rather than a more ardent emotion. The former will last, if the latter does not. And one should also have enough in common with a young lady to *be* her friend. Unless, of course, it is a case of a prearranged attachment, and in that case, there is little that one can do besides hope that one's parents, guardians, or other adults involved have *some* notion of what might appeal to one in the way of a lifetime companion and attempt to find those things that one has in common with her."

Karal had to chuckle at Sejanes' careful way of putting things. He was delicately trying to learn if Karal and Natoli had been joined to one another by parental agreement, or if they might be violating other such agreements with their own acquaintance. "It's not prearranged, and I also don't think her father, Rubric, will mind that we're—ah, friends—since he's the one who introduced us in the first place. He's the Herald who's been sent into Karse as the liaison with Solaris. I think that Natoli doesn't make friends easily."

Sejanes brightened. "This sounds more promising with every word you add!" he said with real enthusiasm. "And your feelings at the moment? Attracted, but confused?"

"Very much so." Karal was as amused as he was embarrassed. Sejanes was certainly taking a very active interest in this situation! And if Karal had not known him, it would be very tempting to dismiss his interest as that of an interfering, old-maidish busybody.

But Sejanes had never interfered in anyone's private life, as far as Karal knew; he was hardly old-maidish, and gave no evidence of being a busybody, although he had intervened to offer to teach Karal something of magic. No, this concern seemed to arise out of some genuine interest in Karal, in the manner of a master with a protégé.

Just like Ulrich, his former master.

"You remind me in some ways of some former students of mine," Sejanes said quietly, echoing his own thoughts. "And you can tell me to go to the dogs if you think I'm prying where I have no right, but I hope perhaps I can give you useful advice about Natoli." He grinned conspiratorily. "I have had a number of lady friends over the years, and most of them were as highly intelligent as she seems to be. I believe I can remember what it was like to be young!"

Karal stared at him in mingled surprise and gratitude, for he'd had no one to ask for such advice. An'desha was mostly concerned with Lo'isha and the other Shin'a'in, when he wasn't working, as they all were, with the dangerous magics here. Florian and Altra weren't human, and although Lyam apparently had a lady friend, neither was he. Firesong—well, *his* advice would hardly apply to Karal's situation, even if he wasn't already wary of asking the Tayledras anything personal. He didn't know Silverfox well enough, he was *not* going to ask romantic advice of Natoli's teacher Master Levy, and the Shin'a'in were none of them approachable enough. The idea of coming to Sejanes would never have occurred to him.

But Ulrich would have helped me. . . .

Ulrich would have given him the same advice his father would have given him, or an older brother if he'd had one. Vkandis did not require that his priests be celibate, only chaste outside of marriage. Ulrich had told his pupil more than once that he had been romantically attached twice, and that only outside circumstances had prevented him from making either of those women his wife.

Karal knew a bit more than just that, though it was still bare bones. In the case of the second lady in his life, Ulrich and his intended had an extreme difference of opinion over the internal politics of the priesthood, and had not spoken again, not even after Solaris became Son of the Sun. The first time, early in his life, the lady had suffered a short but fatal illness, leaving him brokenhearted for many years.

Ulrich himself had never told Karal the stories; he'd learned of both from some of the Red-robe priests who were longtime friends and colleagues of his mentor. They had meant to compassionately keep him from inadvertently touching salt to Ulrich's open wounds, and warned him of the things he must not press unless Ulrich himself broached the subject.

But that had not prevented Ulrich from giving him some preliminary advice about girls, and the possible pursuit thereof, though at the time he had not been at all interested even in the idea. Perhaps Ulrich had a premonition that one day, he would need that advice.

But it was far more likely that Ulrich had simply been offering what he would give any lively young person who was his protégé; the suggestion that he himself had enough experience in matters of romance to offer advice. That set the scene for what was inevitable, and would have prevented him from going to his less-experienced peers for advice that had as much chance of being harmful as helpful.

Now Sejanes was offering the same thing, and Karal was only too happy to accept the offer.

"Thank you, sir," he said simply. "Do you have any ideas about what I should say to her?" He smiled sheepishly. "Don't think that I'm ungrateful, but talking with her is all I can do right now, given our current distance."

"That may be just as well," Sejanes replied mildly, but with a twinkle. "And yes, I have a few suggestions."

That was precisely what he wanted to hear.

Karal and Lyam scribbled on identical sheets of foolscap, seated side by side on a pallet bed, both of them taking full notes of this meeting. The entire group sat on pallets in a rough, three-sided square around the teleson, which was situated in front of Firesong. This was a new version of the old Council sessions that they had held in the Council Room of the Palace at Haven, and he wondered how many of the Councillors on the other side were gazing at the teleson with bafflement. Surely the device must seem to them as strange as any of the Storm-changed beasts that had been displayed for their edification. A tiny image of Queen Selenay gazed solemnly at them from the crystal lens. She had just asked him if he had any more information on when the mage-storms would begin again.

"I can't speak for magic, but I can for mathematical probability, and that has given us the ability to predict what is going to happen up to a point. The mathematics is relatively clear on this," Master Levy said gravely. "The cancellation effect of the power burst that was released from here is gradually eroding; we'll be seeing the resumption of stormlets in four days, but I don't think that even the most sensitive mage will detect them unless he is looking for them. That's all we know right now, and Treyvan will be in charge of the mages who will be looking for the stormlets and attempting to measure their relative strength. Once we have the resumption of stormlets that actually affect the physical world, we can measure how much they increase in strength and decrease in interval. We'll be able to calculate then how long it will take before the Storms have major physical effects again, and how long until they are dangerous. Once they are dangerous, however, they will build up to a repetition of the one released at the original Cataclysm. I have absolutely no doubt of that."

In the crystal of the teleson, Selenay nodded gravely. Although she alone was visible, the Haven teleson sat in the middle of the Council Chamber, surrounded by a full Council at their horseshoe-shaped table. All of them were able to hear what Master Levy said, although they only saw Firesong.

"Now we come to the question of the last Storm and the effect here, where all of the force will be concentrated. Here is where Need, An'desha, Sejanes, and I have performed our own calculations, and we're not optimistic," Firesong said with uncharacteristic restraint. "It is not good, Majesty. Although the shields of this place survived the initial, *outward* release, we do not believe they will survive the impact of the energies converging on this place. We think the shields will go down, and all the weapons that have not been rendered harmless will go then, and that will be bad."

"By 'go,' just what is it that you are saying?" asked one of the Councillors around the Haven teleson. "And just what precisely does 'bad' mean?"

Karal restrained a nervous titter. How would you explain "bad" to someone whose idea of a catastrophe was a major forest fire, a great flood, or a landslide? How do you get him to believe that it was possible to release forces that melted rock towers and dug craters the size of some countries?

"I wish I knew," Firesong admitted. "We don't know what most of them were intended to do, only that they were weapons deemed 'too dangerous' to use. It would be supremely ironic to discover that they cancel one another out, but I gravely doubt that we can count on that. Certainly the area of destruction will cover the Plains, and since we have enough warning this time, the Shin'a'in are evacuating."

The Shin'a'in are evacuating. The Shin'a'in, who never, ever left the Plains. Would that tell the inquisitive Councillor just how grave the situation was? Karal didn't know.

"Whether the effect will carry as far as Valdemar, I couldn't say, although if I were in your place, I'd count on it." Firesong held up a hand in warning. "And don't ask, 'What effect?' because I don't know that, either. We're trying to find out, but we're dealing with weapons created in secret by a secretive mage and the only notes are in a language that was current two millennia ago. We're doing the best that we can, and having more people here would only slow things down, but what we do may not be enough, or in time."

Karal noted the grumbling on the other side, but no one said anything out loud. *Probably because, as Natoli said, they just don't believe it can happen. Sheer stupidity on their part, but there it is.* In a way, he couldn't blame them; they were new to true-magic, relatively speaking. For most of them, the terrible things that Ancar's mages had done were only stories, and the first time they had seen anything like magic was when the mage-storms began. Nor could they imagine a force that could turn a flourishing country into a smoking, glass-floored crater. He noted that down, in a sidebar. Tarrn had told him that his observations could be important, so long as they weren't of a personal nature, and to note them down.

Most people don't believe that a disaster is coming, or that it can affect them, even when they're told repeatedly.

He was tremendously grateful that *he* no longer had to represent Karse at the Council; one of the Sun-priests who had fought with the Valdemarans against Ancar had come North at the same time that Natoli's father had gone South. He had never been comfortable in such a position, had never felt particularly capable of handling it, no matter what Solaris herself said. And certainly about half the other members of the Council had doubts now and again about his competence and even his integrity. But that Sun-priest had certainly seen magic and believed in it with his whole heart. Perhaps he could help convince the doubters.

"What about the weapons themselves?" someone else asked intelligently. "If we can get rid of them harmlessly, we'd be able to lessen the danger by that much. Is there any way of dismantling them?"

"When *Urrrtho* sssaid he could not?" That was Treyvan, his voice indignant. "When he left a warrrning to that effect? Arrre you mad?"

Ah, the things a gryphon can get away with saying, just because he's larger than anything or anyone else! Karal was glad that Treyvan and Hydona were there to say all the rude things that needed saying.

"We are proceeding very slowly in our understanding of these devices," Firesong said smoothly. "If there is a way to dismantle them, we will. We *may* be very lucky; at least one of them simply disintegrated with age, and time might have done what mortal hands could not."

It was interesting to Karal how Firesong had taken on the role of spokesman for the group. Not that anyone else had rushed to volunteer, but Firesong was by nature a bit lazy, and not apt to take on any more responsibility than he had to.

Then again, if Florian or Altra had held the teleson link open, the Councillors would have seen only Karal, the Companion, or the Firecat, none of which were good choices for inspiring respect. Sejanes had no mind-magic, nor did Master Levy. An'desha did, but he was no better choice than Karal, although thanks to his magic-whitened hair, he looked a bit older than Karal. Need could have gotten respect, but if Need had held the link, they'd all be seeing Firesong anyway. At least people respected Firesong; even feared him a little. One good thing; his acidic wit made a fine weapon to wield against intransigent or argumentative Councillors.

Then again, it is a chance for Firesong to be seen, appreciated, and admired, and who else has he had as an audience lately?

"First we have to discover *what*, exactly, they are supposed to do. Then *how* they do it. Then we might be able to judge if we have the ability to disarm them," Firesong explained patiently. "If you think of them as enormously complicated traps with a weapon in the middle, this will make more sense to you."

"But—" someone began, and stopped.

"Fortunately," Sejanes picked up smoothly, "this study does not at all interfere with our studies of the mage-storms, because that is taking place up there, among you. Here we are still operating on the assumption that we may have to trigger one of these weapons to counteract the final Storm. We already know which are the best choices, and together with the notes we found in the workshop below, we are studying them to see if the same solution we found the last time is viable this time."

"And what if you *can't* find an answer?" That voice sounded strained and somewhat panicked. So there was at least one person on the Council who was taking this threat seriously! Karal only hoped it was not someone who was inclined to take a panicked view of everything. Getting people to organize their own defense would be easier if they did not think of the person goading them to it as a chronic overreactor.

"You really ought to be operating on the assumption that we won't, and that all we have done is to buy you time to prepare," Master Levy replied truculently. *He* was very impatient with the Council, and had said as much before this meeting began. "We told you that in the beginning. When I left, the

Artificers were devising a formula to predict the pattern of the circles of damage."

"We're still working on it," said another voice. "The model isn't perfect, but we expect to have an answer before the stormlets start, and we'll check its accuracy with measurements as the stormlets increase in strength. By the time there's real damage, the formula will be tested and ready for use."

"So, there's your answer. If we can't come up with a simple solution, you simply keep people and livestock out of those dangerous areas, drain as much power as you can out of that stone under the Palace and shield it with everything you have, and wait for the final Storm to pass." Master Levy's tone said the rest; that any idiot should have been able to sit quietly and figure that much out for himself.

"While you all sit there safe and sound in the Tower?" someone else accused angrily.

That was a mistake. Karal braced himself for the riposte. Firesong was not in a good mood, and there was going to be blood on the Council table in a moment, even if it was metaphorical blood.

"Safe? Sound?" Firesong asked dangerously. "Where did you come by *that* incredible notion? Would someone please remove that man for incompetence and put him in the kitchen washing pans where he belongs? If *I* were the lot of you, I'd throw him off the Council. I do believe in encouraging those of lesser ability, but I think that appointing a congenital idiot to a Council seat is going too far."

There was an indignant spluttering on the other side, then a certain amount of commotion; Selenay continued to look serene, but her attention was not on the teleson. It was maddening not to be able to see what was going on.

"Well?" Firesong asked, when the noise had ended.

"We will take your recommendation under advisement," Selenay replied urbanely, and clearly as much for the benefit of her side of the gathering as for Firesong's. "You are correct in one thing, if a little less than tactful; this Council can no longer afford to seat members whose attention is so concentrated on minor details within their own sphere that they are paying no attention to the greater dangers that threaten us all."

"Here here," said another voice, one that Karal recognized after a moment as Kerowyn's.

Oh, my! That was unexpected! And Karal could think of three or four Council members who matched that particular statement, too! It seemed that after treachery and invasion and war and Alliance and more war and mage-storms, even Selenay's patience had begun to run short.

And about time, too. It was all very well to say that those three or four had been loyal during the worst troubles, and that loyalty deserved reward, but there was a limit. It was not wise to let the shortsighted continue to have authority in a situation like this one. Better to find them some position with rank and privileges and no authority, if Selenay still felt impelled to reward them. Right now, being too shortsighted could very well cost lives.

She might not see any reason to continue to reward these people; and that wouldn't be all that bad either. Sometimes the hand of censure needed to be used in order to make people believe it *would* be used, even against those who thought themselves above censure. In the words of the Shin'a'in, "Use the whip to get the horses out of the burning stable."

He was tempted to add that to the notes, but those were the kinds of purely personal observations that Tarrn had warned him against, and he kept them to himself.

:There are two Councillors that ought to be given the sack right here and now,: Altra observed with irritation. *:One of them is not entirely certain he believes in the intelligence of Companions. How can we expect him to plan for a magic-fed disaster? And the other is so wrapped up in why his district needs protection more than any other that he'll waste valuable time and probably try to divert resources he's not entitled to.:*

Altra didn't have to describe the offending members; Karal knew them well enough from that notation of their personalities. *:It's Selenay's Kingdom and Selenay's Council,:* he reminded the Firecat. *:If you'd like to make a recommendation as a Karsite representative, I'd do so privately to her. I'm sure that she would have no difficulty speaking with you after this is over.:*

:I'm not such a fool as to make one publicly!: Altra snapped, and shook his head until his ears flapped. *:Now I'm*

more than ever pleased that you're out of there. You don't need to have to deal with these idiots; they'd probably start blaming you for the Cataclysm! And I don't need to be there either; I'd be tempted to wind around their ankles as they started descending a staircase, and be certain of getting them replaced by someone with a bit more reasoning ability than a brick of cheese.:

He managed to send a mental image of himself coiling around the legs of the stupidest of the two Councillors, and of the man pitching down the staircase in a very comical fashion.

:Bloody-minded today, aren't we?: Karal observed.

:Vkandis help any rodent within a league of here,: Altra replied. *:When this session is over, and after I've spoken to Selenay, I'm going hunting.:*

:You won't have to go far,: Karal told him. *:The Shin'a'in were complaining about mice in the horse grain. Think you can lower your dignity for a bit of mousing?:*

Altra just snorted.

The Council session proceeded with admirable dispatch after that particular outburst. For his part, Karal admitted to himself that he was acting in some ways precisely like those unfortunate Councillors who could not or would not believe in the disaster threatening just below the horizon. *He* was conducting some parts of his life—as in, pursuing his interest with Natoli—as if nothing whatsoever was going to happen to change that life. And he was not going about in a state of barely-suppressed panic either. But the truth was that what he and Natoli did or did not do was not going to make a bit of difference to the Storms or the resolution of the problem, assuming there *could* be one. Neither was going about in a cloud of fear going to help resolve their difficulties. Fear wasn't an emotion you could sustain for weeks at a time either, so why try to keep himself in a continual state of near-panic?

But what he could do, he was doing, and at least one of his observations might turn out useful. It had occurred to him that the workshops had remained pristine and intact—more so, even, than the stored weapons—and that there might be even more shielding on them. Or perhaps there was a natural property of the stone, as there was of silk, that insulated everything inside from the effects of magic. Since they had always kept the hatchway open, there was no way to tell, and no one really wanted to volunteer to be shut inside just now.

Natural or not, it would have made sense to have the workshops protected from the possible effects of the weapons stored above—the more so as the workshops could serve as a shelter in case something up here went wrong. Or, alternatively, if something went wrong down *there*, the weapons stored up here would be unaffected.

But the workshops would make the safest place for those who were not involved to wait out the last Storm—and perhaps, for *all* of them to do so, if it turned out that there was nothing they could do. There was room enough for all of them, their supplies, and their attendant Shin'a'in friends to wait in a fair imitation of comfort. It would be difficult for Florian and the Shin'a'in horses to get down the staircase, but not impossible. The one drawback the place had was that it was at a level lower than the tunnel in—and if the stored weapons were affected—they might find themselves literally sealed inside, as the rock melted and ran or the remains of the building shook itself apart.

But if they waited in the tunnel or on the Plain outside, there would be no escape. He'd already discussed using the workshops in this way with the Shin'a'in, and they had agreed with him, going so far as to carry half of the supplies down there and store them, and making plans to evacuate the camp above into the workshops when the time came.

And as for the folk of the surrounding land, well, for the first time since the Sundering of the Clans, Shin'a'in and Tayledras were living together. More than three-quarters of the Clans were off the Plains and distributed among the nearest Vales. Some others had chosen to go to trade-cities and the like, where they had contacts or relatives.

Those remaining were heading South rather than North or West, taking with them all of the breeding horses and other herds, for only the baggage beasts and personal strings could be accommodated in the Vales. They were under the escort of the fighters of Kerowyn's old mercenary company, the Sky-bolts—those few who had retired or elected not to remain in Valdemar. They had returned to Bolthaven and formed a smaller company with the sole duty of guarding the Bolthaven mage-school run by Quenten, the town of Bolthaven, and the annual Shin'a'in Horse Faire. The herds would be safe in the wide and gentle Rethwellan valley below the fortified mage-school, as they would be safe in the hands of those who had benefited from the generosity of Kerowyn's Shin'a'in relatives in the matter of most excellent Shin'a'in-bred mounts.

Before too many more days had passed, the Plains would be empty of almost everyone but the little group here in the heart of the crater that was the Dhorisha Plains. A stranger would, for the very first time, be able to cross from one side to the other without hindrance.

Not that anyone would be stupid enough to try. The weather alone ought to prevent such an idiotic course. Only the Shin'a'in knew where game lurked in the winter; only the Shin'a'in had fuel sources and tents made to withstand the killing blizzards the Storms had brought. And in a landscape of endlessly rolling white hills with no landmarks, it would be suicide for most to try to navigate across the bowl of the Plains.

Besides, the Kal'enedral who were left were *not* your normal border-guards. It was not too bloody likely that anything would move into the Plains that they didn't know about the moment the breach-of-border occurred. And under the current circumstances, it would not be wise for anyone to assume that the Star-Eyed was not personally watching the borders. She would not even have to intervene directly in the event of an intruder; simply dumping a foot of ice on the cliffs ringing the Plains would prevent anyone but a skilled ice climber from getting down into the Plains proper. And dumping another foot or two of ice and snow on him while he was climbing, or arranging for an avalanche along the cliff, would see to it that not even an expert ice climber set a single living toe on the Plains below.

Good heavens, I'm as bloody-minded as Altra! Karal realized, as he serenely contemplated the notion of intruders turned into ice sculptures. But then again, they couldn't really afford to be anything less than ruthless now. The escort of Kal'enedral who remained to care for them had put their lives in the hands of their Goddess to do so, and knew it. Not only was there a good chance that the Tower would not survive the final Storm, but they were defending an indefensible position.

The Kal'enedral had defended the Tower in the past by keeping people far away from it; if there was a "lowest geographic point" to the crater that was the Dhorisha Plains, this Tower was probably cradled in the bottom of it.

Most of the Swordsworn had remained with the Clans, and rightly, to protect them during the evacuation. What if someone deliberately chose this moment to come looking for the Tower with a mind to stealing one or more of the weapons still in it? There would not be much that anyone could do to stop him if he came with sufficient force. It would have to be someone who was completely mad, but as the existence of Ancar and Falconsbane proved, there were people who were that mad, that power-crazed, to take such a chance.

But given all that this little group of seekers represented, the Star-Eyed would probably take care of such an expedition Herself—and if She didn't, it was just possible that Vkandis would.

Just as he thought that, a lull appeared in the discussion, and Karal decided to do more than add an observation to his notes. "It has occurred to me just now," he said slowly, "that there is a source of possible protection, at least for those of you outside the Tower."

"What's that?" someone asked warily.

His ears burned, for he might be stating the obvious, but it seemed stupid not to mention this. "Ah . . . prayer," he said diffidently. "Divine intervention. I mean, have you had people really *concentrating* on asking for help from other sources?"

"That is no bad answer," Lo'isha interjected, before anyone else could say anything. "If our Star-Eyed is like your gods, that could be a fat hare to pursue. You see, She only responds to peril quite impossible for mortals to deal with, and *only if asked*. Otherwise, She allows us to handle it ourselves. Your gods may only be waiting to be properly asked."

"Vkandis has traditionally been the same way," Karal confirmed. "I don't know what the gods do in Valdemar, but what is the harm in finding out?"

"None, of course," Selenay said gently. "And in our own pride and insistent self-reliance, we often forget that option. We would not be asking for aid for ourselves against other peoples, after all. We would be asking for aid for all peoples against an implacable force we don't completely understand.

Thank you, Karal, for not being afraid to state what should have been obvious. I will have the various notables draft up notices to their Temples to that effect."

Now Karal blushed, but with pleasure, and Altra's deep purr, vibrating his feet, was all he needed to gauge the depth of the Firecat's approval. He glanced sideways at Lo'isha to find the Shin'a'in gazing at him with a thoughtful smile that broadened when their eyes met.

Well, let's see if they're still pleased with me after this. . . .

"Please, Queen Selenay?" he added. "Don't exclude the Empire in those prayers. The *people* of the Empire haven't done anything to hurt us, and by now they must be in terrible straits. They've been suffering the mage-storms all this time, and from all Sejanes has told us, they need magic, they use it everywhere. For you, it would be as if fire suddenly stopped giving off heat."

She nodded very slowly, with just a touch of reluctance. "I will remember to phrase it that way," she promised. "And to remember that we have no quarrel with all of the people of the Empire, only with those who harmed us."

He stole a second glance at Lo'isha, then one at Sejanes. Lo'isha still seemed pleased with him, and the old mage positively beamed.

And what about Altra, Vkandis' own representative?

:What of me? I think you have done a very good thing.: Altra's purr did not let up at all. *:You manage to keep in mind that a nation is made up of people, most of whom have little or no control over what their leaders do. That is twice now, that you have urged mercy, and that is very good.:*

Even for Vkandis, notorious for being a vengeful god?

:Especially for Vkandis; please remember that religions are made up of people, most of whom have very little control over what their priests decree is doctrine. Keep in mind that given that the priests and the people have free will and the means to exercise it, gods may not always be able to control their priests either. So what the priests say, and the people believe, is not always the whole truth.:

Karal blinked at that. Altra evidently decided Karal was ready for a little more doctrine smashing.

:Time for a parable. Think of a very wealthy, very reclusive man with a dangerous reputation; say a former mercenary.

Assume he lives in a town but seldom leaves his home. Nevertheless—and not wanting people to think he is trying to buy good opinion—he sends his servants out secretly, day after day, to help the worthy poor, the sick, the helpless. Then one day while he is coming in his front gate, a woman with a baby is attacked by ruffians, and he reacts as he was trained, draws his sword, and cuts them all down in the blink of an eye. Say that later, in the inquiry, it was learned that those same ruffians were old enemies of his, looking for his new home. Now what are the townsfolk going to say about him?:

Karal knew very well what they would say. They would know nothing about the countless acts of mercy and charity that defined the man, they would know only the single moment of public bloodshed. At the least, they would call him vengeful, they would fear his temper, and might avoid his company. If there were those who envied him, it might even be whispered that he arranged for the attack on the woman in order to have an excuse for killing the gang. And although there would be a shred of truth in the stories of vengeance, it would by no means be the entire truth.

:Vkandis—any god—is far more than His people make Him,: Altra continued. *:It is the responsibility of the priest to lead them to that understanding, so that they do not attempt to limit Him to what they know.:*

That was what he had been groping for, these past several weeks! All the pieces for understanding had been there, but he just hadn't put them together in so elegant and simple a whole—

*:And just at the moment, the meeting is going on without your note-taking,:*Altra added, bending to clean a paw with fastidious attention to detail. *:Life is attention to both the large and the small, little brother. Pay heed to the sun, but watch your feet, or you'll fall ingloriously on your nose.:*

He bent hastily to his paper, with a soft chuckle inaudible to anyone else.

The meeting went on for far too long, but Firesong managed to annoy enough useless Councillors to guarantee that the next meeting would be much shorter.

It would have to be; Firesong had also cut short any attempt by the Councillors to turn the meeting into an accusation-

and-blame session (with most of both being aimed at the group in the Tower). That, Karal found difficult to believe the first time one of them started. They seemed to be cherishing a variety of bizarre ideas about what was going on here, not the least of which was that *they* would be safe when the final Storm hit, and those outside the Tower would be the ones in the most danger.

"What was wrong with those people?" he asked Lyam in amazement, as the members of their own group broke up and went off on their interrupted studies. "Where did they get those ideas?"

The young *hertasi* shrugged, his tail beating softly against the floor where they both sat, organizing their notes and putting up their writing supplies. "They think we wallow in luxury here, that we spend all our time in idle pursuits and speculations that have no bearing on work or reality. They half don't believe in the Storms; they think we've got a fabulous life here and we're prolonging our stay here to continue to enjoy this glorious place and our freedom from work and responsibility."

Karal glanced around at their "luxurious surroundings," taking in the elegant appointments. Well, the inlaid stone floors were certainly beautiful, and there wasn't a ceiling like this one in all of Karse and Valdemar combined. But in between—

True, the Shin'a'in pallets were colorful, and comfortable, but they weren't the equivalent of anything in the guest quarters at the Palace at Haven. And as for the rest, he didn't think that a single one of those Councillors had ever eaten, slept, or lived like this, and he didn't think any of them would ever *want* to. It wasn't as bad as the poorest Karsite inn workers endured, and in some ways it was a *little* more comfortable than the conditions of Vkandis' novices, but those highborn Councillors would probably think they'd been exiled to hard living at the end of the world.

And what they'd make of butter-tea, I don't know. They might consider it a form of penance.

"I don't know, Lyam," he said, finally. "Is this some sort of delusionary illness they're under?"

The lizard did not have many facial expressions, but he could and did cock up a brow ridge. "Actually, it's distance. A fair number of our people back in White Gryphon assumed that because we had been given k'Sheyna Vale that we must be living in the midst of incredible luxury. Anything that's far off must be better than anything at home, you see." He snorted. "Actually, if you want luxury, I'd recommend the courts of the Black Kings. I've been there, so I know. Silk sheets, private gardens, food worth dying for—now *that* is what I would call luxury!" He smacked his lips, or what passed for lips.

Karal sighed and shook his head, and Lyam patted his back. "Cheer up! The ones who think we're shirking are all idiots, and Firesong is going to get them to go away. If that Queen of theirs doesn't find them something harmless to do to keep them occupied, that is. I know his kind. He'll keep chipping at them until they quit."

Karal chuckled at Lyam's all too accurate assessment. "He can be diplomatic when he wants to be," he felt impelled to point out.

"Of course he can, but diplomacy is for when you've got time, and that's the one thing we're short of." Lyam shook his head as his expression turned grave. "Karal, I'm going to get serious for a moment; I want you to tell me something, and be honest. You've worked with these people—Firesong, An'desha, Sejanes, and all—for a long time. Can they do this? Can they really find an answer to the last Storm? Or should I look for a deep, dark den to hide in and hope it doesn't get melted shut behind me?"

Karal closed his eyes for a moment, taken by surprise by the sudden question. Perhaps that was why Lyam had asked it, so that he wouldn't have a chance to prevaricate.

"If anyone can, they can," he said at last. "An'desha holds the actual memories of Urtho's enemy Ma'ar, who was the second-most-powerful mage of the time of the Cataclysm. I just don't know if it's possible for mortal creatures to save this situation."

Lyam sighed. "I was afraid you were going to say that. "He slumped abruptly, and looked up at Karal with an unreadable expression. "Let's talk about our girls," he suggested. "You and I can't do a blazing thing to help *them*, so let's talk about our girls, eh?" In a mercurial change of mood, he grinned, showing a fine set of pointed teeth. "Nothing like girls to get your mind off your troubles."

"Or give you a different set of troubles to think about!" Karal laughed, only too happy to oblige.

Tarrn found them both commiserating over the way that females had to approach any difficulty sideways, like a crab, instead of meeting it head-on, a trait it seemed both *hertasi* and human females shared. He stood within earshot for some time, simply listening, with his pointed ears pricked sharply upward, evidently waiting for a natural break in the conversation before interrupting.

:*Lyam, have you any notion where the Shin'a'in stored the gray bag of books we brought with us?*: he asked. :*I find I need a reference.*:

"It's easier for me to find it than tell you where it is," the *hertasi* said, leaping to his feet. "Stay right here; I'll bring the whole bag."

He scampered down the stairs to the workroom, and Tarrn turned his attention to Karal. :*You and my apprentice seem to be getting on well,*: he observed mildly.

"We have a great deal in common, sir," Karal replied politely. "As you probably noticed."

Tarrn's mouth dropped open in a lupine grin. :*Young women, for one thing. Alas, I fear I could never give you reasonable advice on that subject; my kind are neuters, but by birth rather than by oath, as our Shin'a'in friends are.*:

That left Karal more confused than enlightened. "All *kyree* are neuters? And where do the Kal'enedral come into it?"

It took Tarrn a few moments to explain that, no, all *kyree* were not neuters, but that the neuters tended to be the scholars, tale-spinners, poets, and historians. Then it took him a bit longer to explain the oaths of the Sworn, and how the Goddess herself rendered them literally sexless, which was why it was so very difficult for anyone to be accepted by Her into Her service.

Karal was not precisely appalled, but he was certainly baffled. "I can't imagine why anyone *would* want to be Sworn!" he said to the *kyree*, "I mean, I beg your pardon, but—"

:*Don't apologize; I don't regret being neuter, and over the years I've often considered myself fortunate* not *to have to put up with what you do,:* Tarrn replied thoughtfully. *:As for the Sworn, whether Swordsworn or Goddess-sworn, I can well imagine any number of circumstances where a human would find the burden of sexuality intolerable. Such tales that brought them to that condition may be sad, even horrible, but at least among the Shin'a'in they have a refuge. And for some—well if their life has been spent entirely in the sphere of the intellectual, then there is no sacrifice.:*

Karal took a moment to look for An'desha, and finally found him, deep in conference with Lo'isha and another black-clad Shin'a'in. "I suppose I can think of at least one case where memories might be intolerable," he said slowly.

Tarrn followed his gaze. *:The thought had occurred to me as well. If we live. . . . :*

If. There was that word again, the one he thought about all the time, but did his best not to mention. "Are we likely not to?" he asked soberly.

As if called by his gaze, An'desha left the other Shin'a'in and walked over to them, just in time to catch Tarrn's reply.

:I don't know.: Tarrn was quite sober. *:I came here knowing that there was a good chance we would not, and so did Lyam. It is possible that what we record will serve to help others cope with the next Cataclysm in another millennia or two. Or it may help the survivors of this one. It seems that the only way we can be assured of survival is through the mechanism you yourself suggested.:*

"Divine intervention?" he said, dryly. "Ah, but there's a catch. We can't count on it; if we do, we *certainly* won't get it."

An'desha nodded as he sat down beside Karal. "That is the way of things with the Star-Eyed, at least, and this is the heart of *Her* land. If we were to call upon anyone, it should be Kal'enel. But Lo'isha says that She has been silent of late, as if She is no more certain of what is to come than we are."

:So what are we to do?: Tarrn asked. *:When the gods themselves are silent, what is a mortal to do?:*

"I don't know," An'desha admitted.

"You might try calling on old friends," suggested a helpful voice from above their heads, as brilliant golden light flooded down upon them.

Tarrn jumped straight up in the air and came down with his eyes wide and his hackles up. Lyam, whose head was just poking up out of the hatchway leading to the stair to the workroom, had to grab for the edge of the hatch to keep from falling. Even Karal, who had seen this phenomenon before, and An'desha, to whom it was familiar, gaped with astonishment as they rose to their feet.

Swooping down from the ceiling in a spiraling dance that involved Firesong's ecstatic firebird Aya, were a pair of man-sized hawks with feathers of flame. They landed with the grace of a dancer and the weightlessness of a puff of down, and the moment they touched the ground, they transformed into a man and a woman who still had a suggestion of bird about them. The man was dressed as a Shin'a'in shaman, but the woman was all Hawkbrother.

The Shin'a'in present all reacted the same way; they did not drop to their knees or grovel, but went rigid with the profoundest respect, and with naked worship in their eyes.

:What—is—this?: Tarrn managed, every hair on his body standing straight out.

"I am Dawnfire, and this is Tre'valen," the woman said, looking down at Tarrn with a smile. Her eyes were open wide, as were his, and they were perhaps the strangest thing of all about the two, for those eyes were the bright-spangled black of a star-filled night sky. "We're old friends of An'desha."

Altra and Florian appeared from one of the farther rooms, and made their way across the floor to the little gathering, and it seemed that they were the only creatures in the building capable of moving. They paused a few paces away from the bright creatures, and both made little bows of greeting in unison.

"Tre'valen and Dawnfire are Avatars of Kal'enel, Tarrn," An'desha said, very quietly. "And although I would not have claimed the privilege of saying they were my friends, they have been very good to me."

Tre'valen laughed. "Well, claim it or not, we are your friends, little brother. And more than that, we're here to help you as much as we can."

That astonishing statement broke the spell holding everyone frozen in silence, and everyone in the Tower converged on the pair except for Karal, who sat abruptly down.

We have Altra for Vkandis, Florian for the gods of Valde-mar—and now this. What is that Shin'a'in saying? Be careful what you ask for?

Well, he had asked for Divine aid; whether it would be enough remained to be seen.

Tashiketh

Eight

"All I know is this," King Tremane said, rubbing his temple in a gesture of nervous habit, "I haven't even tried to light a candle magically for weeks, but my mage-energy is going *somewhere*. If you can tell me where, I'll feel a great deal better."

Darkwind nodded, squinting a little against the brilliant sunlight streaming in through the windows of the King's Tower. That was what everyone called it now—"the King's Tower," as Shonar had become, by default, the new capital of Hardorn. It was a small and slightly shabby residence for a King, but Hardorn itself had seen better days. It would do Tremane no harm to be seen putting the welfare of his new country above his own comforts.

After a frenzy of make-do preparations, there had been a tiny coronation ceremony, wherein Duke Tremane had become King Tremane, and had been presented with a crown that (like the country) was rather the worse for wear. It even appeared to have been flattened before someone managed to wrestle it back into shape.

Still, it *was*—at least now—the authentic crown of Hardorn, and there was something to be said for that.

Tremane had accepted it graciously, worn it for the coronation, then immediately went to his private possessions and had a few things melted down and made into a very slim, gold band with minimal ornamentation that bore a remarkable resemblance to his ducal coronet.

That, in turn, had borne a remarkable resemblance to the slender coronet that Selenay wore, but Darkwind didn't see any reason to mention that. Frankly, the thin band looked dignified on Tremane's balding head, as opposed to the heavy crown. Even if it hadn't been battered, the original crown still looked rather silly, at least to Darkwind's eyes.

Crowns. This conference isn't about crowns. He turned his attention instead to Tremane's statement. "I think," he said slowly, "that your energy is going into the land—at least in making queries of where and what problems there are—and that *where* it goes tells you what places are most damaged. I suspect that those places producing monstrosities are the most heavily damaged, which is how you have been managing to pinpoint their lairs. You can probably stop the drainage if you choose."

Tremane considered that for a moment, then shrugged. "On the whole, I don't see why I should bother. It isn't a critical drain, and it isn't paining me or making me physically weaker. The only things I might want to do magically are things the earth-sense is giving me anyway. I just wanted to know *where* my energies were going; it could have been due to something more sinister."

That was astute of him, and a reflection on the changes in his thinking that he did not immediately assume it *was* something sinister and begin looking for an enemy. "Tayledras Healing Adepts can send their energies out to damaged land deliberately," Darkwind told him. "And they can redirect energy from elsewhere, using themselves as a conduit. You seem to have many of the same abilities, given to you by the earth-sense, rather than by accident of birth or because of training."

"Interesting." Tremane replied, his brows knitting slightly with thought. He leaned toward Darkwind as something occurred to him. "You know, there's another thing; I had assumed that I'd have earth-sense for all of Hardorn, from border to border, but every time one of those groups comes in to give me their—their pledge—it seems as if I can sense more than I could before. It's difficult to explain; it's as if I knew the place was there, but it was blank or shadowed to me. It's analogous to seeing into a room that was darkened and is now illuminated."

"That may be precisely what is happening," Darkwind admitted. "When someone has an affinity for a given area— usually a homeland, or at least the village they grew up in—a magical link naturally forms between them and the place. Location and divination spells work just a little easier when they involve that person's home area as a target, for example, over places the person may have been to only once. When these people open themselves up to your rule, they may also very well be opening up their home-affinity connection to you, too. Or, well, it could also be that the earth you take from them in the seisin ceremony links you to that place. It's fairly obvious to me that the seisin ceremony itself is a primitive piece of contamination-magic. As for details of how you can use that to advantage, I don't know; you'd have to ask someone who already has the sense."

He hadn't missed the hesitation before Tremane picked the word "pledge." Poor Tremane was enduring a great deal of personal embarrassment for the sake of these people, if only they knew it. Little groups were trickling in all the time to swear fealty to their new king, and they were using an ancient ritual they referred to as "seisin," a ritual probably as old as the earth-taking ritual. There was no doubt in Darkwind's mind that it was just as potent as the earth-taking, and just as primitive.

And it profoundly embarrassed the urbane and efficient Tremane, as most "primitive" rituals would embarrass him.

Nevertheless, it was effective, and he didn't think he needed to point out to Tremane that the reason he could sense another new area every time his new liegemen swore to him was that he literally was adding to the area he had "taken." It was entirely possible that the pinch of earth he had ingested at the ceremony that gave him this new power had been carefully made of a bit of every soil the priests could get their hands on, for that very reason, thus adding in the extra power gain from contagion.

"Speaking of your new subjects, Tremane, there's another group coming in at the gate now," said Elspeth, who happened to be standing by the window. "They're pretty heavily armed and I see someone with a pennon at the front." She frowned and shaded her eyes with one hand, looking down into the courtyard. "Is that—yes, it is, four sets of strawberry-leaves. It's a baronial coronet on the pennon-head. Congratulations! You've hooked one of the few big fish remaining in Hardorn."

Darkwind barely suppressed a smirk. *:For the first time*

since I've been with you, ke'chara, *I've just seen a Herald . . .
act as a Herald.:*

Elspeth just made a short choking sound, while Gwena tittered in their heads.

Tremane sighed, but it was with visible relief. "I'd better go right down and greet them properly, then," he said. "Can we resume our meeting later?"

"No reason why not," Elspeth said for both of them. "We'll meet you down there with Gwena and the full panoply. If you've gotten a baron, we'd better confirm your treaty and association with the Alliance."

Darkwind smiled; this was not, by any means, the first time that Gwena, he, and Elspeth had dressed up and assembled to impress the new liegemen. It had rather startled some of them to see a "horse" indoors, until they saw Elspeth's white uniform and realized that it wasn't a horse at all, but a Companion.

Tremane laughed unexpectedly; it seemed to Darkwind that the new King laughed quite a bit more than he would have expected, perhaps because he had a strong sense of humor about himself. "You should hear the things my housekeeping staff has to say about hoofprints in the wood floors. Do you have the same problem in Valdemar?"

"Sadly, all the time," Elspeth told him. "We've never found a way to prevent them, and we've tried everything." She moved away from the window with her arms crossed over her chest and a twinkle of amusement in her eye. "A silver piece says this one will be more impressed by Darkwind and Vree than by Gwena and me."

"I'll take that bet," Tremane responded easily. Darkwind stood up, smiling mostly to himself. Tremane had become much more relaxed around them since the earth-taking ceremony, treating them more often as colleagues and equals than as foreign ambassadors. Darkwind thought he knew why, although he doubted if Tremane himself was aware of the reason.

The land "knows" Elspeth and Gwena; the Valdemarans have always been good stewards of the land and good friends to Hardorn since Vanyel's time. It also "knows" me, since serving and healing the land are what the Tayledras were born and bred for. Because the land knows and trusts us, it is making Tremane feel comfortable around us and inclining him to trust us as well.

Tremane's new link with Hardorn was going to affect him in any number of ways that he was not always going to be conscious of, but Darkwind didn't see anything but good in that prospect. Very occasionally Tremane grew momentarily disoriented by some new information the earth-sense threw at him, but for the most part he was coping well. Eventually, as Hardorn recovered from the damage that had been done to it, Tremane would find that the land sustained *him* in moments of stress, rather than the reverse.

There was a knock on the door, and Elspeth joined Darkwind as Tremane's aide—now styled his "seneschal," though he still acted and probably thought of himself as a military aide-de-camp—entered diffidently.

"Sir—I mean, Your Majesty—there is a party below who—"

"I know, I'll be there directly," Tremane interrupted. "You know the drill by now; go see to the arrangements, and as soon as I look appropriate I'll be down. Blasted crown," he muttered, as the aide saluted, recollected again that Tremane was a King now and not a military commander, and bowed himself out. "Where did I put it this time?"

"Where you always put it, Tremane," Elspeth laughed. "Locked up in the chest."

"Right, with the robes that are too damned heavy to wear and not warm enough to make any difference in the Great Hall." Tremane swore with annoyance under his breath, and Darkwind wondered how he would ever have survived being made Emperor if he disliked the panoply of rank so much. "I won't miss winter one tiny bit. Thank you; I'll see you in the Hall and we can get this nonsense over with. Again."

"Oh, this time it looks as if it will be more than worth the effort," Elspeth assured him, as she preceded Darkwind into the hallway.

"Will it?" he asked her, as they descended the staircase to their own quarters.

"I think he'll be pleasantly surprised," she said. "I don't know much about Hardorn heraldry, but I think this new fellow may be the highest-ranking native to survive Ancar, and that means he'll be bringing a fair piece of the country with him. Not to mention his escort, and they looked as if they probably represent some major armed forces."

"So how old is this baron?" Darkwind asked. He had a good reason for asking; the surviving nobles of Hardorn tended to be mostly very old, or very young. The former had survived by being no threat to Ancar, and the latter by being hidden by their relatives, usually with reliable farmers or other family retainers.

"I'd say early teens; fourteen, fifteen at the most," Elspeth replied.

"Hence the reason he'll be more impressed by a Hawk-brother than a Herald. He may not even know what a Herald *is*, until someone tells him." Darkwind shook a finger at her. "You're stealing Tremane's silver, you little cheat."

"Then he shouldn't bet with me. He ought to know by now that I never propose a bet unless I'm certain of the outcome." She nodded at the guards on either side of their door and opened it herself. Their own guards from Valdemar stationed inside the door brought their weapons up until they saw who was entering; then they grinned sheepishly and returned to a deceptively relaxed posture.

"Is that any way to treat a monarch?" Darkwind asked her, and sighed as he began climbing the stair to their private quarters. "Never mind; forget I asked. I suppose it won't hurt him."

"I never treat Tremane casually in front of anyone else," Elspeth reminded him, taking the narrow staircase a little behind him. "This is calculated behavior; it shows him that I consider him my equal and will treat him as such. And as Mother often reminds me, the fact that I abdicated in favor of the twins does not make me any less a princess. It's not a bad thing in this case to have one of the Blood Royal acting as ambassador."

"True, all of it." The next floor was the purview of their guards and staff, who were currently lounging about, engaged in various off-duty occupations in the main room of their circular suite. Elspeth and Darkwind both waved at the rest of their entourage as they passed through, but did not stop on that floor. He continued the conversation. "Well, I take it you think this latest delegation is worth bringing out the full formal gear."

"Every feather, bead, bell and bauble," Elspeth said firmly. "Full Whites for me, and the circlet, with badges *and* medals. And don't pretend you don't like to dress up, my love."

"I wouldn't dream of it." The scent of the balsam incense he used both to perfume the air of their private quarters and to discourage pests met them as they reached their own floor. "Unlike you so-called 'civilized' peoples, we Tayledras know how to create clothing that is impressive, functional, *and* comfortable."

"Don't put *me* in that 'civilized' category!" she protested. "We Valdemarans feel precisely the same way! Well, we Heralds do, anyway, and that category includes the ruling family."

"Impressive?" He raised an eyebrow even as he went to the chest containing his clothing and raised the lid. "I'll grant you the functional and comfortable, but you Valdemarans have no sense of style, or at least, you Heralds don't. You horrified my poor *hertasi* with your uniform, you know. They thought you were wearing the sacks your clothes were supposed to be carried in."

They "argued" about clothing, style, and decoration happily all the time they were changing into their formal clothing, she into the Whites that he had redesigned, with the additions of rank, and he into the most elaborate outfit he owned, although by the standards set by Firesong, he was rather drab. His draped clothing of scarlet, gold, and warm brown was augmented by a sculpted leather tunic with a padded shoulder, and when he was dressed, Vree left his perch by the window and lofted straight to him, to land on the shoulder with a fraction of the impact he would have used in making a landing on a perch. Having Vree on his shoulder instead of his wrist served a double function. First, no falconer would ever have let one of his birds sit on his shoulder; that was a tacit invitation to facial scarring or losing an eye if something startled the bird or if it suddenly decided that this was a good time to strike out for freedom. This marked him to the knowledgeable as a Hawkbrother with no doubt. Only a bondbird could be trusted to sit this way, with no jesses, no hood, and no means of "control" over him. And second, if the exotic clothing would not set him apart from the rest, then Vree, who was much larger than any forestgyre or other gyrfalcon these people had ever seen, certainly would.

Elspeth, who had a lifetime of rapid changes-of-outfit to fall back on, waited with an exaggerated expression of boredom for him to finish his belt adjustments. "Bring your head over here," Elspeth commanded, the feathered and beaded ornaments meant to be braided into his hair dangling from one hand. She already wore the beaded feather he had given her as a token of love, one of Vree's own primaries, braided into her own.

"Should I leave the rest of me here?" he suggested. She made an exasperated *tsk*ing sound, and pushed him down into a chair. Vree flared his wings to stay balanced. She wove the feathered cords deftly into his long hair, as cleverly as if she had been born in an *ekele* rather than a palace.

"There," she said, bending to kiss him, then rapping him lightly on the top of his head with her knuckles. "Now you're presentable."

"So I am. And so are you." He rose and headed for the door, this time taking the lead down the stairs. The entire procedure, from the time they entered the room to this moment, had taken a fraction of the time it would take Tremane to get ready. But then again, they were not going to have to be laced into ceremonial armor either.

Their own entourage was so used to this by now that there had been no need for Elspeth to ask anyone to go get Gwena, drape her with her ceremonial barding and bells, and bring her to the Great Hall. The Companion was already waiting for them when they arrived at the side entrance they would use to get in place before either Tremane arrived or the delegation was allowed to enter. The members of Tremane's staff were quite used to seeing a "horse" wandering about the halls now, and let her go her own way when they saw her. Waiting with her were all of the dignitaries that could be hurried into formal clothing or uniforms on short notice, though there was always a chance that not all of them were what they were dressed up to be. Once, after most of Tremane's staff had gone to a meeting with the town council, Darkwind recalled, someone had actually borrowed an Imperial officer's tunic and a handful of medals and coerced the cook into it for one of these ceremonies! Since the folk coming to pledge their loyalty were likely never to set eyes on Shonar again, it did no harm to anyone to have impersonators fill in the ranks of Tremane's Court if it was necessary, to give the impression that every petty lordling with a handful of men was being given the highest of honors.

This time the reverse was true, for not only were all the real officials present, but the mayor of Shonar, Sandar Giles, had been on his way for a meeting with one of Tremane's under-lings when he saw the procession of armed men heading for Tremane's manor. He'd sent a now-exhausted runner hastily back to the town for his mayoral finery, and now stood wait-ing with the rest while the servants did what they could to make the Great Hall bearable.

"One of Tremane's mages is in there, warming the place up," Sandar was saying to Tremane's aide, who was look-ing distinctly uncomfortable in his nonregulation, heavily embroidered tabard. It looked like—and probably was—something that had been found in an attic and been pressed into service as the "official" clothing of His Majesty's Sene-schal. A great deal of the Court garments had been made out of salvaged material or dredged out of attics. For that matter, Sandar Giles' outfit showed a touch of the moth's tooth around the squirrel-fur trim and the woolen hood, as if he had gone to storage for his grandfather's mayoral outfit.

Small wonder Tremane has difficulty taking all this seri-ously. His "court" is hardly up to the standards of even his old ducal household, I should imagine. Elspeth and I are the only ones who are not threadbare and much-mended.

But none of the various delegations that had come riding or walking in to Shonar had looked any better, and most had looked much worse. By the current standards of the country, Tremane's Court probably looked remarkably prosperous.

Before this is all over, we may look back on these times fondly, as the days when we were all doing well. It was a grim thought, but one which he and Elspeth often shared. If the mage-storms could not be held back—

Well, there was nothing to be gained by dwelling on that now. Under Tremane's direction, people were readying them-selves for worse to come, and Hardornens, unlike Valdemar-ans, were perfectly willing to believe in "worse to come." Once the ceremony was over, but just before the delegation left for home, Tremane would give this new lot their direc-tions on surviving the final Storm, as he had every other dele-gation so far. That those directions were mainly guesses hardly mattered; they would have direction and confidence that he had the situation on the way to being under control.

The door opened, and a thin, gawky man came through it, a fellow with thinning hair, who squinted at them from be-hind a pair of glass lenses set in a lead frame that rested on his nose. "It's warm in there now, and it should last through your ceremony," the mage said, and made shooing motions as if they were a bunch of hens he wanted to drive before him. "In with you now! The sooner you get the ceremony over with, the less likely that the spell will wear off before it's over!"

None of them needed a second invitation; the hallway was freezing, and the promise of warmth was all the encouragement they required to move quickly.

Elspeth and Gwena hung back until the others were inside, and Darkwind remained with them. Gwena was quite careful whenever she came inside the manor, and despite the complaints from Tremane's household staff, she left very little sign of her presence after these ceremonies. Some of the Hardornen warriors, who forgot to remove spurs or came striding in wearing heavy, hobnailed boots, did worse damage than Gwena, who picked up each hoof neatly and set it down again with the greatest of care.

Gwena was arrayed in the "riderless" version of Companion full dress; no saddle, but with a blue and silver blanket cut like her barding, decorated at all the points with silver bells, a blue-dyed leather hackamore with silver tassels at the cheekpieces, and reins bedecked with more silver bells. Had there been more time to ready her, the decorations included even bells and blue ribbons to braid into her mane and tail, but she had to be content with her mane and tail flowing freely.

"You look lovely, as always," Darkwind told her.

:Thank you,: she replied coyly, and gave her head a tiny toss so that the bells chimed. :I'm afraid we four are making a more impressive show than Tremane's own Court, but that can't be helped.:

"At least we are making our support unmistakable," he pointed out, as they took their appointed places among the rest.

There was some shuffling as the dignitaries of Tremane's Court sorted themselves out, then the young Seneschal nodded his head and the main doors were flung open to admit the latest delegation.

At the head of the procession was a youngster—no boy, but young, too young to need a razor—of about fourteen. Under his scarlet cloak and tabard, he wore full armor that had seen hard use, and his eyes were far too old to belong to that young face. The dented and slightly tarnished baronial circlet about

his brow did not detract from the painful dignity with which
he carried himself, and by his build and the muscles beneath
the armor, he was clearly no stranger to real fighting. Behind
him, more men in full armor followed in pairs, ranging in age
from powerful graybeards to men only a little older than the
boy-baron. One of the two immediately behind the boy carried
a small wooden box. They paraded in slowly, surveying every
person there with suspicion, and Darkwind smothered a smile
as the boy's eyes lit on the Alliance envoys, widened, and flit-
ted from Elspeth to Darkwind and back, finally remaining on
Darkwind.

:*I won,*: she Mindspoke unnecessarily.

The entire delegation came to a halt at the foot of the low
dais. By now, several of the Shonar artisans were at work on a
real throne for Tremane, since the original throne of Hardorn
had been lost in looting and fires, but it would not be finished
for another week or two. In place of a real throne was a prop
throne, made for an Imperial theatrical production, and modified by those same artisans. They had sanded off the gilt paint,
which had probably looked fine at a distance but only looked
cheap and shoddy up close, and had removed all of the glass-
paste jewels set into the back. What had been carved wolves
adorning the back were now hounds, the Hardornen symbol
of fidelity. The swords making up the legs and arms, and inter-
laced on the back below the hounds, had become tree
branches, and the wood had been rubbed with oils and polished until it shone. The shabby cushions had been replaced
with brown velvet purloined from drapes taken from storage.
However, in the course of all the recarving, the wood had been
pared down in some places to a precarious extent, and Tremane had been warned to be very careful when sitting on it.
Everyone was going to breathe a sigh of relief when the new
throne took the place of the old. It could be taken for a terrible
omen if Tremane's throne collapsed beneath him in the middle of one of these ceremonies. Tremane had good-naturedly
commented that having a fake Imperial throne recarved into
a fragile Hardornen throne was entirely appropriate.

Tremane kept the delegation waiting just long enough for
them to get a good look at the rest of his Court, and to take in
the banners on the wall behind his throne, which represented
those who had already come in and brought him their pledges.
Most of those who had sworn their oaths had taken their ban-

ners from the arms of the former nobles of the region, although more often than not there had been no one who actually qualified to take those arms. Tremane had solved that quickly enough by confirming the delegates in their places as the new lords, and bestowing the old titles upon them as soon as their pledges were confirmed.

Sadly, besides a number of ancient titles going begging, there was plenty of empty land lying fallow and abandoned, but Tremane had plans for that, too. Once summer arrived, it would be settled, and former Imperial officers who were ready to retire would be ennobled and put in place as overlords. They would be allowed to take with them as many Imperial soldiers as wished to retire to farming and had found brides among the Hardornens; these would be given freehold-grants on reclaimed farms. Thus, the newly ennobled would have garrison and work force in one, and the newly wed couples would have more of a base for their start than most. After that particular announcement, the number of engagements and handfastings had skyrocketed, and if some of the good farmers and fathers of Shonar had been a bit reluctant to welcome Imperial sons-in-law at first, their reluctance had evaporated when they learned of the royal bride-price the foreign sons-in-law would bring, thanks to the foresight of their new King.

Darkwind hid a smile as the young Baron kept taking covert glances at him, as if the youngster had never seen anything so outlandish in his life. Darkwind had been told that rumors of his presence and powers were circulating out beyond Shonar's walls, rumors which got more and more fantastic with every league distant from the city. He wondered what the boy had heard, to make him look so wide-eyed.

There was a bit of a stir at the door just off the dais, and Tremane's major-domo stepped inside.

The major-domo rapped three times on the floor with the butt of his staff. "His Majesty, King Tremane of Hardorn!" the man announced in ringing tones, his clear, commanding voice showing precisely why he had been plucked out of the ranks to fill this position. "And his Majesty's Chief Advisers!"

Tremane and his four Chief Advisers filed in with ponderous dignity. Of course, his Chief Advisers were also members of his bodyguard, but their weapons were not carried in an obvious fashion, and there was nothing about them to advertise that fact. Tremane wore his ceremonial armor, the

Hardornen Crown, a tapestry tabard with his own arms (requisitioned from his former squire), and was draped in a fine cloak of silk edged in heavily embroidered silk trim purloined from the same curtains that had provided him with material for the seat cushions of his throne. The cloak was also part of the props for some unknown play; it was ridiculously long and required the services of two small boys recruited as pages to carry the trailing end.

Both pages were from the group of five children that Tremane and his men had rescued from the grip of the first killing blizzard; Tobe and Racky were their names, and they took their duty as Tremane's pages very seriously. They had been nicely outfitted in page costumes cut down from Imperial officers' uniforms by their mothers, who nearly burst with pride at the notion that their boys were serving the new King.

Tremane took his seat gingerly, which translated into a ponderous sort of dignity to outside eyes. The pages arranged his royal mantle out before his feet, like a peacock's tail, just on sanity's side of preposterous, and retired to their positions behind the throne. The young baron tensed as Tremane nodded to him.

"Baron Peregryn, I understand that you are from Adair," he said quietly. "You are a very welcome addition to the Court."

Darkwind watched the boy and his entourage to see if they noticed the relative informality of Tremane's address. After much consideration, he had decided to completely do away with the royal plural, because Ancar had been so rabid in its use. Darkwind saw two of the older men exchange brief nods, and it seemed to him that they wore expressions of satisfaction.

The young Baron took two steps to the foot of the throne and went immediately to one knee, and the rest of his entourage followed his example in dropping to theirs. "I have come to offer you my pledge, King Tremane," the youngster said, in a high tenor that trembled only a little. "And in token of this pledge, I bring you seisin of my lands, and those of the men pledged in their turn to my service."

Young Baron Peregryn reached behind him without looking, and the man carrying the small wooden casket placed it in his outstretched hand. Darkwind watched their movements carefully, analyzing everything they did, and making some guesses about the relationship the Baron had with his men.

He is *the acknowledged leader, no matter how young he appears to be, and he and the older men have worked and fought together a great deal. They trust him—and he trusts them. He has youth, enthusiasm, and charisma, and they have experience, and they all work to weave these things together. This one will be worth watching for stories and songs of noble deeds.*

The boy opened the casket and held it out to Tremane, who took a double handful of soil from within and held it for a moment.

"Thus do I, Tremane, King of Hardorn, take seisin of the lands of Peregryn, Baron of Adair, and of those who are pledged to him," he proclaimed in a voice suitable for a battlefield oration. He dropped the soil back into the casket, and held out his hand to Tobe, the older of his two pages. Tobe handed him a small dagger, and with his face completely unflinching, he slashed his palm shallowly, held his hand over the casket, and allowed his blood to run into it and mix with the earth inside.

"Thus do I, Tremane, King of Hardorn by acknowledgment of the soil of Hardorn itself, give the pledge of my body to the lands of Peregryn, Baron of Adair, and of those who are vowed to his service." The other page, Racky, took the dagger and handed him a linen cloth, which he used to bind the wound across his palm. Meanwhile Tobe took the casket from Peregryn, mixed the soil and blood thoroughly with a miniature spade, and then used the spade to divide the moistened soil between the original casket and a small box. Tobe handed the casket back to Peregryn, who received it with the same reverence as he would a holy relic. Tobe gave the box to the Seneschal, who would take it to the cellars of the manor and add it to the urn of soil already there.

All of this mixing and dividing gave Tremane a chance to recover from the shock of adding yet another stretch of land to his "senses." Darkwind knew that by the time he reached his own quarters again, the slash would be completely healed—and now was the moment when he would confirm his right to be King by telling Peregryn what, if anything, was wrong with his lands.

"If anything!" No, there will be a great deal wrong, there. *Adair is supposed to be in the north, and there would have been reflections off the Iftel Border before Firesong and the rest instigated the Counter-Storm.*

Tremane's eyes had the glazed look that meant he "felt" something very strong, which probably meant very bad. "Your lands, Baron Peregryn, include a small river valley, bounded by a lake, a hill shaped like a sleeping cat, and a forest of pines," he said slowly, as if he were talking in his sleep. Peregryn's eyes widened, and several of the men behind him began whispering urgently together. "Beneath that hill there is a cave, and within that cave there is a place where magic is pooling and stagnating. Living there is a beast, changed by magic into a monster. You cannot kill it directly; it will cost too many lives. You cannot poison it. To kill it you must feed it a cow which has been fed on datura-flower for three days. It will gorge itself, and the action of the flower will make it sleepy and it will go to the cave to hide. You must then collapse the cave or brick it up, sealing it inside."

Tremane went on, reciting the locations of several more pockets of trouble, together with suggested solutions for eliminating the problems. Peregryn wouldn't be able to implement all or even most of those solutions until summer, but at least now he and his men knew where all the trouble spots were, and would be able to deal with them one at a time. As Tremane spoke, more and more of Peregryn's men began whispering together, their expressions taking on the slightly stunned look of men who were hearing something they could not believe, and yet *could* verify. Evidently several of Tremane's revelations matched problems they already knew about—and knew that Tremane could not have learned by any normal means. Finally, Tremane fell silent, then blinked, shook his head a little, and his eyes cleared of their daze.

"I trust that will help?" he said dryly. He would remember everything he had said, of course; this was not a true trance, more of a state of intense concentration. And behind him one of his clerks had been taking down every word and would give Peregryn a copy before he left. If Peregryn was unable to deal with any of the problems Tremane had identified for him, there would be a record of what the problem was and where, and eventually Tremane's own men would move in to take care of it.

"More than simply 'help,' Your Majesty," Peregryn replied shakily.

He would have said more, but one of the men of his group,

overcome with fervor and enthusiasm, leaped to his feet, brandishing his sword over his head.

"Long life to King Tremane!" he shouted, his voice actually cracking with excitement. "All gods bless King Tremane!"

That goaded everyone else in the entourage, and eventually Peregryn as well, to get to their feet in an eruption of cheers. Tremane remained sitting on his throne—in part, Darkwind knew, because he couldn't stand just yet—and bent his head to them in gracious acknowledgment of their accolade. Some of the oldest men were openly weeping; these were the ones who eventually thrust themselves forward, flung themselves at Tremane's feet, and kissed his hand with tears streaming down their faces. It was a moment of extreme and powerful emotion, and Tremane himself was not unmoved by it. The King took great care to clasp every man's hand, using both hands, listening to him babble, until he was ready to rise again and let another take his place. It was quite obvious to Darkwind that Tremane recognized these old warriors for what they were, and knew how difficult it was to get any sort of accolade from them, much less this kind of emotional outburst.

These older men always proved to be those who had survived the purges and who had expected to die without ever seeing Hardorn return to peace and prosperity. Darkwind knew very well why they wept, and so did Tremane. "I have given them back their dreams and their hope," he had said, a little in awe himself, after the first time this had happened. "They see a future now, where their grandchildren can expect to grow up without fear of being murdered on a royal whim."

And he was right; that was precisely what those old men saw: a future, where before had been only darkness and doubt.

It took some time before the young Baron and his men managed to calm themselves down, and more before all of the appropriate ceremonies had been fulfilled. Tremane apologized for having to house them in a barracks; they hastened to assure him that they would have been perfectly willing to camp in the snow. Tremane directed his supply sergeant—who now bore the impressive title of "Procurement Adviser"—to bestow upon his new liegemen the "usual gifts" and they made a token protest. The "usual gifts" were all surplus items, so much in surplus that their value in the town would be seriously depreciated if any more came on the market. Surplus

Imperial clothing, surplus hand tools, surplus weapons. Some of Tremane's people had argued against that last, pointing out that he would be arming those who had lately been his enemies. But Tremane felt, and Darkwind agreed with him, that giving them weapons demonstrated his trust in them. It was a gesture worthy of a King.

Besides, these new liegemen *needed* the weaponry that Tremane gave them. Their own supplies had been depleted in their war against the Imperial forces. If they were going to rid themselves of their land's boggles, they needed weapons.

This wasn't at all altruistic. Practically speaking, Tremane would rather that *they* went after their boggles instead of turning to Imperial soldiers for help. They knew the lay of their own land, where a boggle might lair, where it could run. His men wouldn't, couldn't. Better to let the local experts handle it, if there was any chance they could.

By the time the presentation was over, Baron Peregryn and his men were, however, so happy they were beside themselves. They never even noticed that Tremane had gone pale, and was sweating, his hands clenching the arms of his throne so hard that the knuckles were white.

:*He isn't getting up, because he can't,*: Elspeth said, her Mindvoice sharp with alarm. :*It's more than simple disorientation this time. It's really striking him hard.*:

:*What's wrong?*: he asked, hoping she'd know.

:*I can't tell, and neither can Gwena.*: There was frustration there as well as alarm. :*All I can tell for certain is that he's in nearly the same state as he was when his earth-sense was first awakened. This has something to do with the earth-sense itself, and something to do with this new area he's taken seisin of.*:

Neither of them dared move to help him, not while the Baron and his people were still present; Tremane was clearly attempting to conceal his weakness and it was their responsibility to follow his wishes. He reached for her hand as she reached for his; their hands closed on each other and they stood waiting, tensely, while the last of the amenities were played out.

Finally the Baron and all of his men trooped out, to be accommodated overnight in one of the barracks. In the morning, Tremane would meet with them again and give them warning and instructions concerning what everyone here was now calling the "Final Storm," and what to do to weather it. Then, when everything had been organized for their return, they would go back home with a small caravan of supply sledges. Only after the doors closed behind them, could Tremane fold his body over his knees and his own people rush to help him.

But he waved them away before they could do more than ask him what was wrong.

"I'll be all right," he said, and Darkwind let out the breath he had been holding, for he *sounded* normal, just a bit shaken. "It's nothing physical, and I don't believe it's anything to worry about. Just—something unexpected just happened; let me sit here for a moment or two more while I get over it." He looked over at Darkwind and smiled ruefully. "Quite frankly, it feels as if someone just dropped me off a very high cliff, and I stopped just short of the ground."

Elspeth knelt at his side, and Darkwind joined her. "It's the new Barony, isn't it?" she asked. "It's something there. Is it the Storms starting again?"

As if her questions gave him a focus for his own sensations, he seized on them. "Yes. No. Yes, it's Adair, and no, it's not the Storms. I don't know what it is, but it's not—no wait." His eyes took on that far-off gaze again. "It's the border, the northern border. Adair is on the northern border, and something has happened up there. Something important. Something that changes everything."

"What—" one of Tremane's generals began, but Tremane just shook his head, dumbly.

"I don't know," he repeated. "I just know—it's something completely new."

"What's on the northern border?" someone else asked, and looked at Elspeth for the answer.

She had one for that question, but she had turned as pale as Tremane. "Iftel," she said, and her hand clenched tight on Darkwind's. "Iftel. The one place in this part of the world that *no one* knows anything about."

"So that's the message?" Tremane said, his eyebrows rising. "Just that? Nothing more?"

With his recovery, the meeting among Darkwind, Elspeth, and Tremane that had been interrupted had been moved back to the office in his quarters, but by now they had all forgotten whatever it was they had been talking about, for a message had come by way of signal-towers from the North. Unfortunately, it only confirmed that something had happened, and gave them very little other information.

"That's all there was, sir—Your Majesty—" the aide recovered from his mistake. "Just that the border with Iftel suddenly opened, and a new delegation of something friendly was coming down here to meet with you. I'm afraid," he continued apologetically, "that the signal language is not very specific."

"The signal *did* say they were friendly, though? You're sure you're not misreading that?" If Tremane's voice was sharp with anxiety, Darkwind couldn't blame him.

"No, sir, that much is *quite* clear," the aide said with certainty. "The old man at the signal did say that the term used was one that he hadn't seen very often, but that it was definitely noted as being friendly."

"Thank the gods for small favors," Tremane muttered, and sighed, running a hand over his chin. "Well, now I know what it—ah—*feels* like to have the Iftel Border open up. That's useful information. But how whatever is coming expects to travel in this winter weather, I can't begin to imagine."

"Peregryn and his men did," Darkwind pointed out. "There's no reason to suppose others can't, but it will take time for them to arrive, perhaps weeks on foot, ten days by horse."

"By then, I might even have a throne I can sit on without worrying if it's going to break and drop me on my rump," Tremane sighed, then laughed. "Listen to me complaining about a flimsy throne! As if that was the worst thing we have to face!"

"A delegation from Iftel," Elspeth mused, twisting one of the rings she wore around and around. "They've always allowed a single envoy from Valdemar inside their land, so long as it was a member of the Merchant's Guild—but never anyone from the Mercenary's Guild. And they would never permit Heralds inside." She shook her head. "The envoy never would tell us much, only that they "preferred peace" but weren't particularly interested in any exchanges with us."

"Very insular," Darkwind commented, quite well aware that this was a case of the goose complaining that the swan had a long neck. *One can hardly call the Tayledras anything but insular.*

"They could have good reason for being insular," Tremane pointed out. "When was the first time people of Valdemar encountered them?"

"Quite some time after the Founding," Elspeth admitted. "Their barrier was already in place then, at least according to the Chronicles. It was a merchant who was first allowed inside, and it has mostly been merchants who crossed it since." She smiled deprecatingly. "They may be insular, but like the rest of us, they enjoy buying things." Darkwind hid his own smile, for that last shot had been meant for herself. She had been unable to resist spending some of her own money on a few odd trifles that had turned up in the loot of the Imperial storehouse.

"So they could have encountered someone or something extremely dangerous before they ever saw you," Tremane pointed out, his eyes speculative, as he probably tried to envision what could have been so terrible that it caused an entire country to erect a magical barrier to keep out intruders. That it was a barrier that had survived centuries and baffled the magic powers of Ancar, Falconsbane, and the Empire alike made it all the more intriguing.

"They probably did," Darkwind put in. "In those early days, there were terrible things that far north. There was at least one Tayledras Vale somewhere about there, and *our* Chronicles report that at some time while they lived there, they encountered and defeated a Dark Mage much like Ancar's servant Falconsbane, but with a larger following."

He did not add that this mage probably had actually been Falconsbane in one of his earlier incarnations. Tremane neither knew about Falconsbane, nor likely cared; the only person still concerned with Ma'ar-Falconsbane was An'desha, and only because An'desha still held those critically-important memories. But as for the rest of them. . . .

Falconsbane is dead, with the past, and this time he will stay that way. And about damned time, but we have more important things to worry about. The sober glance that Elspeth cast his way said virtually the same thing. For now, the situation was grave enough that even isolated Iftel was opening her borders and sending representatives to them; there was no leisure to dwell on the past.

"I don't know what, if anything, these representatives of Iftel might offer you," Darkwind cautioned.

"If nothing else," Tremane mused, "perhaps we can get them to part with the secret that makes up their Border. It's shielded them from the worst of the Storms so far; it might be able to shield us as well."

"Provided these people arrive here before the question becomes academic," Gordun, Tremane's chief mage, reminded him dryly. "It's a long way to the northern border and the going is difficult; by the time they get here, the Final Storm could have left us in ruins here."

Tremane nodded ruefully. "A good point, though it was an entertaining thought while it lasted. Well, that brings up the next decision; what shall we tell our newest Baron tomorrow about the Final Storm?"

"Hide, and finish your card games quickly?" one wag suggested. There was a general, strained laugh, and then the discussion moved into the serious channel of what to do in the immediate future. Eventually, late that night, precisely what should be told to the Baron and his entourage had been worked out; enough to make him understand the gravity of the situation, but not so much that he would panic. Panic would be bad for Peregryn and his people as well.

Over the course of the next couple of days, the Baron got his pick of surplused supplies, was given a review of troopers interested in resettling up north, and got his briefing and warnings about the Final Storm. He and his own advisers were philosophical about that last; there was nothing they could do to stop it, and they could only hope that the physical effects were limited to places with no human populations. During the first of the storms, caught both by the initial storm waves and the reflected waves from the Iftel Border, they had suffered more damage than anyone yet reporting in. "We have already had a half-dozen people unfortunate enough to be caught in one of the things we are calling 'change-circles,' and they were changed even as beasts are," Peregryn said, with a shrug of deeply-felt helplessness. "The fortunate died."

"And the unfortunate lived," added one of his advisers grimly. "Though often, that was not long, when they made the mistake of approaching others for help. It wasn't always their bodies that changed, at least not outwardly."

Tremane exchanged a significant look with Darkwind. This

was something he and his people had thought of at about the same time the potential for trouble occurred to the Allies. But while those in Valdemar had been concerned with prediction of where the change-circles would occur, and thus preventing people or large animals from being caught in one, the people in and around Shonar had planned on what to do *when* a human became a monster.

Until this moment, that had been nothing more than a possibility. Now they knew that there *were* transformed humans somewhere out there in the north, and it was time to put some of those plans into action in case the hapless victims trekked south. Tremane wrote something on a small slip of paper and passed it to a page to take to his clerks. The orders, already written out, would go into the troops' daily briefing. In essence, they were simple enough; *Humans have been caught in the Storms and changed. If a boggle shows intelligence and no aggression, be wary—but* leave it alone *long enough for it to show its intentions.*

There had been some debate on the subject, with a minority objecting to the mere idea of giving a boggle the chance to attack first, and a second minority wanting to make attempts to communicate with every boggle that even paused for a moment before attacking. Finally, to end the debating, Tremane had exercised his royal prerogatives and decreed the language of the order, which predictably did not entirely satisfy anyone, not even Tremane himself.

Darkwind had noticed, however, that Tremane had applied enough of the Imperial manner not to care if anyone was satisfied (including himself), so long as his decree did the job for which it was intended.

Neither of them could ever have guessed the immediate effect of that simple order.

Not more than two days after sending Baron Peregryn and his entourage and gift sledges off, during yet another ceremony of seisin—this time for the benefit of a very old Squire who had sent his informal pledge some time earlier, but who had not felt equal to taking the winter journey until now—they learned exactly why the signal-towers had said that some*thing* was coming down from Iftel.

No one there could have expected just what the some*things* were.

Tremane had just added his blood to the soil that old Squire

Mariwell had brought with him, when a great clamor arose up on the walls of the manor. Darkwind started and looked up automatically, although he wouldn't be able to see a thing through the stone walls and ceiling. With great presence of mind, Racky took the casket of earth from Tremane's hands, mixed the contents quickly, divided them and handed the old man his own casket back, while all about him, his elders were behaving skittishly, staring and muttering among themselves, hands on empty scabbards. Before Tremane could send to find out what the cause of all the ruckus was, and right after Racky pressed the casket of soil back into its owner's shaking hands, one of the King's bodyguards came bursting into the Great Hall, his face as white as the snow outside.

"Boggles over the castle!" he cried. "Oh, by the gods! Great, huge, flying boggles! So many they cover the sky! Oh, gods, help us. . . ."

Elspeth held up her hand to shade her eyes, and squinted up at the dark shapes hovering in the brilliant blue sky above the courtyard. It was too soon yet to say just what these "boggles" looked like, other than the fact that they were winged, but there was something about those black V shapes and the way that they swooped and soared that looked tantalizingly familiar.

They remind me of Treyvan and Hydona, but they don't fly exactly the same way. Could they be gryphons? There've been rumors of gryphons in the north for years now. . . .

"Remember your orders, men," Tremane called to the nervous sentries on the walls and towers above. "No shooting without provocation."

Pray they don't take simple swooping as provocation!

"There're exactly twenty-one of them," Darkwind said absently from her right, as he peered upward into a sky blindingly bright. He bit his lip and she sensed that he was thinking hard for a moment, then his eyes narrowed as if he had just made a decision. He extended his gloved hand to Vree, who transferred his perch from the shoulder to the gauntlet with that intensity of gaze that told Elspeth he was getting silent instructions from his bondmate.

A heartbeat later, Darkwind flung Vree upward, and the bondbird pumped his wings skyward, heading straight for those twenty-one mysterious Vs. "I'll know in a moment just—" He began, his eyes half closed.

Then, unexpectedly, he laughed, the sound echoing across the otherwise silent courtyard and making just about everyone in Tremane's escort jump and stare at him as if they suspected he had gone mad. He brushed his snow-white hair back from his forehead, and pointed up at the "boggles," then at Vree, who had reversed his climb and was making a leisurely descent.

"Tell your men to put their weapons away, King Tremane," Darkwind called, holding out his gloved fist for the returning forestgyre. Vree flared his wings, ruffling Darkwind's hair, and landed as lightly as a bit of thistledown, settling his talons gently around the leather-covered wrist. "I suspect that's your delegation from Iftel up there, and if they can see half as well as my old friends Treyvan and Hydona can, they aren't about to land until there's no chance that they'll wind up becoming feathered pincushions."

:They *are* gryphons, then?: Elspeth asked, feeling a strange thrill of excitement. :Could these be more of the "missing Companies" from the days of the Mage Wars?:

:Could be; even with the distortion of looking through Vree's eyes, these gryphons don't look quite like the ones we've seen. Millennia of separation from the parent stock would do that, I suspect.: Darkwind continued to peer upward as the Imperial guards reluctantly put down their weapons at Tremane's shouted orders. :It's either that, or some unbelievably clever Adept managed to duplicate the gryphons we know, and I doubt that's possible.:

Whatever was or was not possible, it was soon obvious that Darkwind was right about the gryphons' eyesight. As soon as the last spear was grounded and the last arrow put back in its quiver, the hovering specks above descended with a speed that put Vree to shame, and made Elspeth recall what her mother's falconer had once said: *"If you want to know what the fastest bird in the world is, ask the falconer who's just had his prize peregrine carried off by a stooping eagle."*

Not only did the gryphons descend with breathtaking speed, they did so with artistry. They dropped in a modified stoop that followed a tightly spiraling path down into the relatively small courtyard, one after the other in a precise formation, like beads on a string. As the first of them backwinged

hard, kicking up a wind that drove debris all over the courtyard and made those who had not been prepared for the
amount of air those huge wings could push shield their faces,
Elspeth wanted to applaud the theatrical entrance. The huge
creature landed on the cobbles of the court as lightly as Vree
on Darkwind's glove, touching down with one outstretched
hind-claw first, then settling neatly an eyeblink later, posed
and poised with wings folded, like a guardian statue in the
middle of the expanse of stone.

The next followed a moment after, and the next, until the
remaining twenty were ranged in a deliberate double half-circle behind their leader, all in the same precise, regal posture.

As Darkwind had indicated, they did not look *quite* like the
gryphons of k'Leshya. These creatures were heavier of beak,
neck, and chest; like eagles, rather than stocky and broad-
winged like hawks, or lean, large-eyed, and long-winged
like falcons. In color they were quite unlike the gryphons of
k'Leshya, who were as varied in color as the creatures they
had been modeled after. These gryphons were a uniform dark
brown from beak to tail, a color with some patterned shading
in a lighter brown, but nothing nearly like the malar-stripes
or masks of the falconiform gryphons, or the variegations of
the hawk-gryphons, with their bright yellow beaks and claws.
The effect was very impressive to someone who had never
seen any two gryphons who looked precisely alike; as if someone had deliberately made up a wing of gryphons that
matched in every way, like a matched set of horses in a parade
group. They looked every bit as intelligent as Treyvan and Hydona, and their yellow eyes watched every move made by the
humans before them with calculation and speculation. The
heavier beaks made their faces look oddly proportioned, at
least at first, but Elspeth found herself swiftly growing used
to the new variation.

Each of them wore a harness and pack very similar to the
ones the Kaled'a'in gryphons often wore, made of highly polished leather of a rich reddish brown, with polished brass fittings. The apparent leader also wore a neck-collar and chest-
piece that looked as if it had been derived from armor some
time in the far distant past. Now it served only to bear a device
of three swords, hilts down, points up, with a single heraldic
sun above the middle. Elspeth glanced at Darkwind, who

shook his head slightly; whatever it signified, he didn't recognize the symbology.

The gryphons waited, motionless except for the rising and falling of their chests, watching for someone among the humans to make the first move. The Imperials and Hardornens, one and all, stared back at them, faces pale and limbs rooted to the spot. Elspeth thought of her first sight of gryphons, and couldn't blame them for not moving. Here were creatures, twenty-one of them, with sickles on their front and hind claws, and meat hooks twice the size of a man's head in the middle of their faces—she wouldn't have been eager to rush up and embrace them in the name of brotherhood either.

"I suppose it's up to us," Darkwind said, a touch of amusement in his voice. He stepped forward, Elspeth a scant pace behind him, Gwena following at Elspeth's side, until he stood in comfortable speaking range of the leader, who regarded him with the unwavering, scarcely-blinking gaze of the raptor.

"Welcome to Shonar, capital of Leader Tremane of Hardorn, in the name of the Alliance," he said in careful Kaled'a'in. "I am Darkwind k'Sheyna, representative of the Clans of the Tayledras of the Pelagirs, the Shin'a'in of the Dhorisha Plains, and the Kaled'a'in of k'Leshya Vale and White Gryphon. This is Elspeth, daughter of Selenay, ruler of Valdemar, and Companion Gwena, representatives of the peoples of Valdemar, Rethwellan, and Karse. Behind me are Leader Tremane, of Hardorn, and his officials and advisers."

Elspeth knew only enough Kaled'a'in to follow what Darkwind was saying; she could not have hoped to make the same speech herself. Kaled'a'in was handicapped by not having a word for "king;" the closest was "leader" or "ruler," and it gave no sense of the size of what was ruled. Darkwind's three peoples freely borrowed whatever local term applied, but she suspected that he was afraid that the gryphons before him would have no idea what the Hardornen titles meant. The chief gryphon listened attentively and with great concentration, and waited for a moment after Darkwind had finished to see if he would add anything. When Darkwind said nothing more, but made a slight bow, the gryphon opened his beak. He replied in a clear enough voice, but his words were in a form of Kaled'a'in so drastically different from anything she knew that she could only recognize the origin and not what the envoy said. Now it was Darkwind's turn to listen, closely, and

with immense concentration, brows knitted into an unconscious frown as he followed the carefully enunciated words.
She did not venture to break his concentration by Mindspeaking to him.

:*I don't suppose you're picking up anything from them, are
you?*: she asked Gwena, as Darkwind made a reply of which
she only understood half the words, none of them in sequence.
She guessed that he was elaborating on who was what, and to
whom the gryphon needed to apply for reception of his delegation.

:*Not a thing, they're shielded, and shielded hard,*: came the
helpful reply. :*It would be useful to have an Empath with us
at the moment, but I don't think there's anything other than
a fairly reasonable level of anxiety in them at this point.*:

In the gryphon's reply, Elspeth caught the word, "Hardorn,"
and Darkwind's face cleared. "It would be a great deal easier
if you *could* speak in the language of Hardorn, sir," he replied
in that tongue. "I fear that time has changed the language you
speak from the one taught to me."

"A grrreat deal of time, young Brrrother-To-Hawksss," the
gryphon rumbled, with evident amusement. "A verrry grrreat
deal of time by anyone's measurrre. I am Tashiketh pral Skyl-
shaen, envoy from the land you know as Iftel to the court of
King Tremane, who we have been told has been chosen for his
office by the land, as it was in the old days." He waved a huge
taloned hand in an expansive gesture at the twenty gryphons
poised behind him. "This is my wing. These are the representatives of the twenty *hrradurr* of Iftel, courageous and worthy
of their offices, who each won the right to fly in my wing in
the *bahathyrrr*."

The *hrradurr* were evidently subdivisions of Iftel—though
what the *bahathyrrr* could be, Elspeth could not even begin to
guess. She made a quick hand-gesture behind her back, hoping
Tremane would take the hint and come up to be presented,
but he was already moving before she gestured. With quick
wits, he had already anticipated what was needed the moment
that the gryphon began to speak in Hardornen.

He walked forward with grace that could only be trained
into someone who began learning the peculiar "dance" of
court movement at a very early age. When he reached Darkwind's side, he bowed his head in a slight acknowledgment to
Tashiketh. The gryphon in his turn made a deep obeisance to

the King, then carefully extracted a packet of folded papers from a pouch at the side of his harness and handed them to Darkwind who in turn gave them to Tremane.

"The land of Iftel sends greetings to Hardorn's new ruler, oh, Tremane, once of the House Imperial," the gryphon said, in his strangely accented Hardornen. "We have been sent by the Assembly of Peoples and He Who Made The Barrier to bear the greetings of our Assembly and our Peoples, and to offer you our personal assistance in current and future difficulties. We are," he added, with a lift of his head, "authorized to assist you in any way."

Elspeth could guess at the thoughts running through Tremane's head at the moment, though he gave no sign of them as he gravely thanked Ambassador for his greetings and his offer.

He can't take this offer seriously. Likeliest is either that Tashiketh is not aware of what he is actually promising, or that this is a polite custom of Iftel, a standard speech, and the offer is not meant to be anything more than an expression of polite esteem.

That, of course, was only logical. As welcome as the aid of a full wing of gryphons would be, how could an ambassadorial delegation be expected to perform *any* services that did not directly benefit their own land? And certainly there was no reason to believe that such a blank card had been given to King Tremane to fill in as he cared to. He could, conceivably, ask them to do something too dangerous for his own men to try. If they were harmed, he would have to face the consequences, but it made no sense to think that Iftel would be willing to put its citizens in danger.

Of course, Darkwind and I and our entourage are perfectly willing to put ourselves in danger—and do—but that's because we aren't really just envoys, we're representatives of the Alliance and we're performing as Hardorn's military allies as well as our other duties. In a sense, we're a very small military unit as well as ambassadors.

The next thing that *must* be running through Tremane's head as he surveyed the half-circle of twenty-one very *large* gryphons, was where on earth was he going to put them?

He *couldn't* put them in the stable nor in one of the barracks, surely he must see that. The stable simply wasn't suitable, even if her Companion and Darkwind's *dyheli* Brytha were willing to put up with it, and the earth-sheltered barracks buildings would probably give creatures of the air great screaming fits of claustrophobia. She considered the gryphons, their size, and their probable needs. They *would* all fit in the Great Hall; could that drafty barn of a room be made habitable as well as elegant? Each of the several towers of the manor would probably hold four or five gryphons in each of the topmost rooms, which were mostly used as armories and weapon storage for the sentries that were posted there; would the gryphons consent to being split up? If they would, there was at least access to the air from the trapdoors in each of the tower roofs. Fortunately, thanks to the spacious barracks now available, and the fact that a large number of staff persons (mages, Healers, and other auxiliaries) now were housed in the city rather than in the manor itself, the overcrowding that had been making life so difficult in the early days here had been overcome. There *was* room in the manor for the gryphons, at least on a temporary basis. But from Tashiketh's speech, this was intended to be a permanent delegation, and they would need permanent housing.

Tremane made a graceful, rambling speech of welcome, probably while he was trying to think of housing options.

There are still some unused buildings in Shonar. Would the gryphons be willing to be housed in an "embassy" in the city?

But if they did, what would they use for servants? Gryphons required a lot of tending; there were any number of things that they couldn't do for themselves. Lighting fires, for instance; talons were not good at manipulating firestrikers, and feathers were dismayingly flammable. The gryphons of k'Leshya had specially trained *trondi'irn* to see to their health and well-being; Treyvan and Hydona had done without such help, officially at least, for several years—but the k'Sheyna *hertasi* had helped them unofficially. What would these gryphons do? Did they even guess that the people of Hardorn and the Empire were unready to host them?

Tremane finally ran out of things to say, and so did Tashiketh. They stood on the cobblestones and looked politely at one another for a moment, and it was Tremane who finally broke the silence.

"Now I must confess that I and my people are simply not prepared for anything other than strictly human ambassadors," he said, in a burst of that un-Imperial frankness that was becoming a welcome characteristic of his. "We were somewhat thrown off-balance when the Alliance sent two nonhumans, the Companion Gwena here, and her colleague the *dyheli* Brytha, who intends to present himself to you later. We were completely unprepared for them, but they were gracious and generous enough to accept the stable as perfectly adequate, though it was scarcely that."

Gwena bowed in graceful acknowledgment of the compliment, and Tashiketh glanced at her curiously, then returned his attention to Tremane.

"To be honest, Ambassador Tashiketh, I do not know what we are going to do for the comfort of you and your entourage," Tremane confessed ruefully. "I can only think of three possibilities, and none of them are ideal. There are four tower rooms that might do, if you'd be willing to split up into groups of four or five?"

At Tashiketh's headshake, he went on doggedly. "Then there is only the Great Hall, or taking a building in the city itself—"

"But that was what we had intended to do, take a building and make of it our permanent Embassy," Tashiketh interrupted gravely. "We have brought with us the hire of the building, of staff. We knew that your resources are stretched, and had no intention of straining them further. If we could just spend a few days here, somewhere, that would be enough, surely. As soon as we have established our own place, we will remove to it."

If Tremane sighed with relief, he was schooled enough not to show it. "We shall be happy to house you in the Great Hall for as long as it takes for you to establish your Embassy," he replied with commendable ease, as out of the corner of her eye, Elspeth saw the young Seneschal breaking away from the rest of the group and pounding at a dead run toward the nearest doorway to put Tremane's intentions into effect. She hid a smile; that was one benefit of having a staff composed entirely of military people. Instead of arguing that something couldn't be done, they ran off and made it happen.

"If you would be so kind, then, I would ask you to send a messenger to some representative of your city, that we might establish ourselves as quickly as possible?" Tashiketh asked, and she thought she caught a sly glint of humor as he added, "And in the meanwhile, perhaps you have someone who would conduct us in a tour? This is the first time I have seen a wholly-human city; the differences are apparent even at a distance."

Elspeth tried not to choke, for this was *so* clearly a diplomatic gesture to ensure that Tremane's people had time to get suitable quarters for the gryphons ready! Tashiketh and his wing must be exhausted and were probably also ravenous; to ask for a tour under those conditions bespoke a consummate diplomat. *:Volunteer to give him the tour yourself; I'll go help advise Tremane's people on the care and feeding of gryphons,:* she quickly told Darkwind, who smoothly volunteered his services as soon as she made the suggestion.

The Iftel delegation and their reception committee quickly broke into three groups; one of humans, one of mixed humans and gryphons, and one of gryphons only. Tashiketh, Darkwind, and an escort of amused Valdemaran Guards and two solemn and militant gryphons went off for a brief tour of the grounds as built and fortified by Tremane's people. The rest of the gryphons stationed themselves in the courtyard like a group of sober and businesslike young Guard-trainees to wait for their leader's return. Gwena returned to the stable by herself, as Elspeth went with Tremane and his people, and volunteered her expertise as soon as they were out of gryphonic earshot.

Within a relatively short period of time, the Great Hall had been stripped of the trappings of power and refurbished as temporary housing for twenty-one gryphons. This turned out to be a great deal easier than she had thought it would. Remembering what Treyvan and Hydona had done, Elspeth and the Supply Sergeant went over the lists of surplus and stores, until they found enough equipment to make the gryphons reasonably comfortable, then she commanded a squad of sturdy fighters in carrying out every bit of furniture. Stage curtains and painted backdrops were sent for, to help keep the chill of the stone walls at bay, and a rainbow of rugs brought in to soften floors. Every featherbed that could be spared was brought in once the rugs were down and the draperies up, until there were twenty-one good "nests" covered with as many thick blankets and throws as a gryphon could want. Twenty of the nests were arranged along the walls, with the twenty-first up on the dais, and hastily-rigged curtains put up that could partition off that part of the room to make an individual chamber. As privacy, it wasn't much, but at least it was a good gesture in that direction, and if Tashiketh preferred to keep the curtains open, he could.

The largest soup kettles available were brought and filled with fresh water for drinking, with large, deep soup bowls arranged on a table beside the kettles in case these gryphons preferred to drink from a small vessel rather than plunge their prodigious beaks into a larger one. That took care of drink, and Elspeth advised the cook what kinds of raw meat, fowl, and fish best suited their new guests. The room looked quite odd by the time they were done, but strangely, not at all shabby. There was a curious sort of harmony in the painted canvas scenery backdrops, separated by velvet stage curtains, covering the walls, and between the bewildering variety of rugs, blankets, and throws covering the floor and the nests, the end effect was something like being inside an extremely luxurious tent.

:We're ready,: she told Darkwind, as the last of the carpenters cleared their ladders and equipment out, and the first of the kitchen staff began arriving with whole sides of beef and baskets of fish.

:That's good, because I'm running out of things to show them, and I doubt they're going to be able to express even polite interest in warehouses and latrines.: Darkwind sounded distinctly amused, and Elspeth had the feeling that Tashiketh was proving to be quite good company.

She cleared out herself, leaving the young Seneschal to do the honors on behalf of Tremane, and decided that she had best report what she had so cavalierly ordered to the King himself.

But someone had already gone to fetch him, for he met her at the door, with his escort and hers in tow.

He surveyed the transformed room with some surprise and a great deal of relief. "Bless you, Herald Elspeth," he said with feeling. "I'd have had my carpenters trying to cobble up gigantic cadges or floor perches, or something of the sort—which wouldn't have been a disaster, but it would have delayed things while Tashiketh explained what they really needed. Will this be warm enough, though?" he added, looking at the hangings with a slight frown of uncertainty. "This place is notoriously drafty."

"It will do," she replied. "Their feathers keep them as warm as our winter cloaks do, and they really only need to stay out of extreme cold and drafts. The hangings will block the drafts well enough, and they *can* wrap themselves in rugs and blankets to sleep. Add charcoal braziers carefully tended, and they should be fine. They'll need one of your Healers—a good, brave person, who will find them a challenge and not something to be afraid of—and about four servants to run errands, watch the braziers, and fetch things at all times."

"A Healer?" Tremane asked with surprise, signaling to one of his aides. "Why a Healer? They look healthy enough to me."

"Gryphons have peculiar strengths and weaknesses; the ones I know always try to have a specially trained helper around them to keep them healthy," she explained. "A Healer is the closest we have to that, and I expect that Tashiketh will be willing to explain their needs." She coughed, hiding her expression behind her hand. "The hardest part will be finding a Healer and a handful of servants brave enough to come tend to 'boggles.' "

But it was Tremane's turn to smile knowingly. "Not as hard as you might think, Elspeth of Valdemar," he said lightly. "We of the Empire are made of sterner stuff than that."

And so it proved; Tremane had not one, but *two* Healers eager to have access to the gryphons, and there was no problem in getting volunteers from the ranks for the light duty of acting as servants to the Ambassador and his entourage. As soon as Tashiketh and his corps had been installed, pronounced themselves "delighted," and dined, they had their Healer and their servants waiting for orders.

Tashiketh had displayed surprise when he saw the quarters, if an onlooker knew what to look for; he had shown more surprise and pleasure at the quality of the hospitality. He dismissed the would-be *trondi'irn* and three of the four servers as soon as he and the others had eaten, with thanks and the information that they all needed to rest after their journey. He asked the fourth server to stay, to watch the braziers, and in case any of them required something after they retired, which the man was not at all loath to do. The other three made themselves comfortable in a niche in the hall close by, and got out the inevitable dice.

"Are they going to sleep, really?" Tremane asked Darkwind, as the King and his small entourage left the gryphons to their privacy.

"Probably so," the Hawkbrother replied. "Even given that they flew here in order to reach us, that was a tremendous distance they covered in a very short time. Judging by the amount they ate, they're going to sleep the sleep of the sated until well past sunrise tomorrow."

Tremane ran his hand over the top of his balding head, looking, at the moment, nothing like a King. "I thought that having earth-sense dropped on me was confusing," he said, slowly, looking honestly bewildered. "They're huge and like nothing I've ever been near before. *Now* what do I do? How do I treat them?"

"You have dinner with Elspeth and me, and you simply accept them as any other foreign ambassadors," Darkwind advised. "This is a great honor, yes. It is also the first time Iftel has sent out representatives who were not human. This can't be any easier for them than it is for you. You may not be used to having gryphons as ambassadors, but *they* aren't used to being ambassadors in the first place."

Tremane looked at him oddly for a moment, then began to laugh. And if there was a faint edge of hysteria to his laughter, Elspeth couldn't blame him.

Tremane's men trampled their way purposefully through the snow, hauling burdens, readying sledges and animals, shouldering packs and weapons. Darkwind guided Tashiketh and his ever-present gryphon-guards through the gates and toward the worst of the congestion, stopping often to allow someone with a more urgent task get past them.

"What is all this excitement concerning?" Tashiketh asked, watching the activity swirling around them with curiosity brimming over in his large golden eyes.

"I was about to explain it to you," Darkwind replied, quickly stepping out of the way of a man burdened with an entire bundle of spear shafts. "We had a very unexpected and unpleasant message last night."

"Ah! Now I regret vacating our palace quarters so soon!" the gryphon said brightly. Tashiketh and his own entourage had established themselves within two days of their arrival in an old inn very near the manor, cheerfully vacated by the owner at the sight of the odd, octagonal gold coins offered for its purchase by the treasurer for the gryphons. They had chosen the inn because of its large rooms on the second floor, each of which had its own balcony, and several of the staff were quite willing to stay on and serve such relatively undemanding masters. Now Tashiketh and his escort of two moved between the inn and the manor every day, taking part in daily Court and Council sessions, showing extreme interest in everything Tremane did. So far, they had neither interfered in the business of Hardorn nor done anything other than tender an opinion when asked for one. It was Darkwind's thought that they were acting in very similar fashion to the way that Treyvan and Hydona had behaved when they first came to k'Leshya Vale—willing to offer advice, but making no move to push in where they might not be wanted.

But the cause of this particular uproar had occurred very near midnight, long after the gryphons had retired for the night. The gryphons Darkwind knew did not find it necessary to be purely daylight creatures, but Tashiketh and his group had not been trained from their youth to be explorers and navigators of the unknown, and their experiences here were probably wearing them down. Between the cold and their strange surroundings, they felt much more comfortable taking to their own, warm quarters after dark, and not stirring out until daylight. So when the messenger pounded in on an exhausted horse last night, reporting that one of Tremane's newly-sworn liegemen was under attack by one of his neighbors, the gryphons were blissfully asleep. In the excitement, no one had bothered to wake them or even send them a message, and by the time anyone thought of doing so, it was already daylight and Darkwind was on his way to the gates to escort Tashiketh inside.

There was nothing in the simple attack of one set of humans upon another that would have alerted Tremane through the earth-sense, so the attack came as a complete surprise. A substantial amount of last night had been devoted to planning a defense, and with dawn the men in the chosen barracks were roused, briefed, and moving by the time Tashiketh appeared at the gates.

Darkwind, who met the gryphons here every morning, explained the situation to him. Tashiketh stopped, just out of the way of traffic, and stared at him in perplexity.

"But it will be very difficult to fight in this season, will it not?" he asked, very slowly. "And with the possibility of the mage-storms resuming soon, that could make it more difficult yet."

Darkwind nodded. "How could it not be?" he replied. "But if King Tremane does not come to the aid of this liegeman, then every other bandit who thinks to make himself King in place of Tremane will think himself free to do what he wills."

"But why did Tremane not call upon us?" Tashiketh asked, with a surprised and even injured expression. "Did we not offer to be of all assistance to him? And would his enemies not find the sight of a gryphon wing descending upon them enough to terrify them into submission? Why, look you how frightened his own people were when they *knew* that we were coming—how much more so must his enemies be?"

Now it was Darkwind's turn to stop in his tracks and stare at Tashiketh with shock and incredulity. "But you are ambassadors!"

"We are *allies*," Tashiketh replied firmly. "Even as you, Brother-to-Hawks. I am not only the Ambassador, I am the leader of this force, which members have drilled and trained together. Is it not preferable to quell disturbance with the application of a small force, rather than to wait and meet war with a greater one?" He clicked his beak and then gryph-grinned, in the way that Darkwind was so familiar with in Treyvan. "Besides, we are bored. It will be good to show our fighting prowess. It is what we are born, bred, and trained for."

"I thought that there was no fighting in Iftel," Darkwind blurted, as activity swirled all around them. "I thought that your Border prevented any such thing!"

Now Tashiketh sobered. "Simply because we do not make war on other nations, nor permit those nations to make war upon us, that does not mean that we do not prepare ourselves for war or for the day when the Barrier might fail us. I cannot tell you how long we have trained. . . ." He shook his head. "All my life, all the life of my father, and his, and his, and so far back I cannot begin to count the years. We have always trained and contested, and will always train and contest. And when the need is there, we fight."

Then he roused up his feathers, and moved so quickly that Darkwind was left behind, completely unprepared. "Come!"

he shouted. "We go to this King, and we tell him in a way that will make him believe!"

As Darkwind knew, even when on the ground, gryphons could move very quickly when they chose. He was left behind as Tashiketh and his escort charged into the manor, bent on offering themselves as potential victims on Tremane's altar. And he was afraid, terribly afraid, that Tremane would accept them.

But when he reached the council chamber, he found that although Tremane *had* accepted their offer, it was with conditions—and reservations.

"Tell the men to stand down," he was ordering as Darkwind entered. "I'll try Tashiketh's way, but—*but*—" he said, turning to the exultant gryphon and raising his voice. "You, sir, will obey the orders of your commander, that is, *me*, and you will make the preparations that I tell you to and adhere to the conditions that I set."

Darkwind could hardly believe the transformation that a few moments had made in the dignified gryphon. Tashiketh and his two escorts were wildly excited, hackles and cartufts up, eyes flashing as their pupils expanded and contracted rapidly, their talons flexing against the wooden floor and leaving gouges that would be the despair of Tremane's housekeepers. These were no longer the strange ambassadors of an even stranger culture, these were warriors, and he wondered how they had kept their nature hidden beneath those serene exteriors.

"We have the time, if you and your wing are determined to fly a warning against these people, to *take* the precaution that is needed to prepare you," Tremane said sternly, every inch the commander. And now Darkwind wondered at the transformation in the King as well. Here and now, there was no uncertainty, no hesitation. *This* was the Imperial Commander, a man who knew both planned warfare and scrimmage fighting, the man who had been entrusted with the conquest of Hardorn. "There is time enough for you to see what maps we have of the area and speak with those of Shonar who have relatives in the contested area. I would have you see my armorer, so that he can make you breast- and side-plates to protect you from arrows, and helmets to defend you from slung shot, if there were time enough." Tashiketh opened his beak to protest, and Tremane swiftly overruled him. "Not a

word, sir! *I* am your commander, *I* have been fighting these
people, as you have not, I know what they can and cannot do,
and *I* will decree the terms under which you will fight. I will
not dictate your tactics, sir, for that is your purview, but I can
and will decree what I need for your safety!"

He looked so black and angry that Darkwind thought for a
moment that Tashiketh would take offense. But one of the
two escorting gryphons muttered something under his breath,
and Tashiketh burst into laughter.

"What did he say?" Tremane asked, his anger fading.

"He said, 'What a surprise, to find after all these centuries,
a commander who is more concerned with saving our blood
than spending it!' And he is right." Tashiketh bent his head in
submission to Tremane's will. "We will follow the wishes of
the commander who does not waste anything. I'll send Shyre-
stral to bring the rest, and we will see your maps and plans
rather than improvising solely upon what we find there."

In so short a time that Darkwind was astonished, the gryphons were lined up in three ranks for a none-too-hasty briefing.
Only one somewhat bewildered man, who had only visited
the place once, could be found to tell the gryphons about the
lay of the land in that area. He found himself overwhelmed by
the gryphons' relentless questioning over details of the region's wind currents.

On the fourth day after the messenger had arrived, the
gryphon wing flew off to confront the enemy, and Darkwind
and everyone else watched them fly off with mingled hope
and dread. The gryphons seemed full of confidence and good
humor; they might have been going off on a pleasure jaunt.

Except that their behavior showed Darkwind very clearly
that their hunting and killing instincts were roused. When
they were not moving, they were intensely alert, heads up,
eyes taking in everything, bodies poised. When they moved,
it was with bewildering swiftness and utter sureness, as
deadly and beautiful as the dance of warrior and sword. They
took no notice of the snow beneath their claws, of the cold
breeze; their eyes were on the blinding blue sky, and they
could not wait to be up and out. When they took to the air,
they leaped up, catching the shivering wind in their talons
and conquering it.

"You're sure they will have a chance?" Tremane asked, as

the wing vanished into the blue distance. "I keep feeling as if I'm sending them to their doom."

"Gryphons were originally created as fighters," Darkwind replied slowly. "Very versatile ones. It's in their blood, and a millennium or two isn't going to change that."

"They may have been created as fighters, but are they trained?" Tremane said, his voice sounding strained. "I know what my men can do—but these creatures? Granted, their opponents aren't as well-equipped or skilled as my men, yet it only takes a single well-aimed arrow to kill someone. And you tell me that Iftel has kept war away from her borders for as long as the Valdemarans have known them. How can they be ready for this? Surely—"

"Forgive me for interrupting you, but has Tashiketh told you how his twenty wingmen were chosen?" Darkwind replied, before Tremane could voice much more in the way of anxiety.

The King shook his head.

"I thought not. Let's go inside where it's warm," Darkwind told him, as the sharp wind cut through the seams of his coat and chilled him. He shivered involuntarily and stamped his numbing feet to warm them. "I believe I'm about to surprise you."

The group retired to Tremane's study; several of his other staff members, who had overheard the exchange, had managed to tag along. The gryphons had excited a great deal of interest among the Imperials and Hardornens alike, and Darkwind didn't at all mind assuaging some of their curiosity. It was a close fit for all of them, but Tremane gave no hint that he wanted any of them to leave.

"I've managed to learn a bit about the way things are done in Iftel, at least as far as the gryphons are concerned," Darkwind told the group, once they were all settled in a circle of chairs, Tremane's only a little larger and more elaborate than the rest. "It's not the peaceful paradise you and I might have imagined."

"Oh?" Elspeth said. "But they won't even let the Mercenary's Guild establish a Guildhall there!"

Darkwind could only shake his head. "I don't know of their origin, but because of what I have learned from Tayledras history and some Kaled'a'in information, I have a few guesses.

Tashiketh either doesn't know the answers, or has been ordered to pretend that he doesn't, so this is speculation."

Tremane uttered a scornful little cough. "Darkwind, at times your insistence on hedging is maddening. *Tell* us! Don't keep saying it's only your opinion."

Darkwind chuckled, not at all offended. "Certainly. I think that the citizens of Iftel are descended from some of the forces that were cut off when the Mage of Silence's stronghold was overrun. There were gryphon-wings with several of the armies, and since female gryphons by and large are a bit larger and heavier than the males, females always fought alongside males, often their mates, so there would have been a breeding population."

"You mean some of these gryphons are female?" one of the generals blurted, looking completely taken aback.

Darkwind laughed. "You didn't even look between their haunches, eh? Yes, some are female. Probably half; males also spend as much time tending the young as females, since they feed their young the way young hawks are fed." He raised an eyebrow at the general's stunned expression. "Oh, come now—you didn't think anything with a beak like that could suckle milk, did you? *I* wouldn't want to see the result if one tried!"

The general winced, and Tremane himself made an expression of sympathetic pain.

"As for the concept of females being poor fighters, I would not venture that opinion around Herald Captain Kerowyn of the Skybolts if I were you," Elspeth added crisply. "She is likely to invite you to have a practice session with a few of her ladies—or worse, with her!"

Darkwind watched the general in question as he took a second and third glance at Elspeth, finally *saw* the calluses and muscles, and realized that Elspeth was not the pampered princess he had thought. "So much for physiology; I am assuming that they *must* have come from Urtho's people, because gryphons are created creatures, and I can't imagine where else they could have originated. We know from Kaled'a'in stories that some of Urtho's people were cut off from their own forces—they knew what was going to happen when the enemy overran the last stronghold," Darkwind continued. "I guess that they threw up hasty Gates—Portals, to you—and just tried to get as far away as possible. They succeeded, and ended up in fairly hostile country, and then the Cataclysm happened and the Storms began. At some point, *something* put up the Barrier; Tashiketh isn't being very forthcoming about that either. The problem with putting a wall around you, though, is that it walls you in as well as other people out. So, in order to keep from killing each other or losing such self-defensive abilities altogether, the Peoples of Iftel organized their aggressions."

Tremane looked troubled. "Organized? How?"

Darkwind sighed, for he was of two minds about what he had learned. He understood *why*, and sympathized, but he wasn't happy about *what* they had chosen to do. "Games, but games that verge on being blood-sport. If Tashiketh is telling the truth, no one *has* to participate, but in the highest and most competitive levels, there is real possibility of serious injury and even death. Serious wargames; Tashiketh says that in his part of Iftel there are several deaths among participants in every round of competition. That was how his wing was formed; every single one of these gryphons is the winner of contests in his district that pitted him against opponents of his own and other races, coming at him singly and in a group, and using weapons that were merely *blunted*, not rendered harmless."

Tremane blinked. "Oh," he said, thoughtfully. "Interesting. They aren't as inexperienced as I assumed."

"That isn't all, of course," Darkwind went on. "Each preliminary winner was required to participate in intellectual contests as well; what those were, I don't know for certain, but they probably included memory tests and logic puzzles. Tashiketh was the overall winner of everything. And the reason that the delegation is made up entirely of gryphons is that only gryphons would have been able to get here before the Storms started again. Now you know the gist of everything that I have learned or guessed."

Tremane and the others seemed somewhat taken aback by the fact that the right to be an ambassador had been determined by a series of often-deathly-violent contests, but Darkwind privately thought that was a more logical means of choosing someone for an important post than some other methods he had heard of from supposedly "civilized" lands. Picking someone to whom you owed a favor, or someone whose family was important, or worst of all, giving the job to whoever paid the most for the honor—all those were recipes for sheer disaster, and whoever used such means probably got the disasters he deserved. Granted, most ambassadors didn't have to compete in highly dangerous war games, but then, most ambassadors weren't also authorized to participate in their allies' real conflicts, either. He just wished that the contests weren't so lethal.

"Are *you* confident in their ability as a fighting unit?" Tremane asked him bluntly. Darkwind nodded.

"I know *my* gryphons, and I know that these are well-trained," he replied. "I also know they aren't stupid. I don't think they would have been nearly so eager to volunteer if they thought your opponents had working magic."

"Ah!" Tremane exclaimed, and chuckled. "I see. They don't expect to come within range of a normal distance-weapon, is that it?"

"Probably not; *they* can stay out of range of arrows and drop large, heavy objects down on the enemy." Another of the generals started to chuckle, as if he found the idea vastly amusing. "Or spears, or firepots—"

"Or any number of things that are inconvenient when crashing through one's roof," Elspeth interrupted, before the good gentleman could wax eloquent. "But telling you that they were going to do *that* would not have sounded nearly as heroic as they wanted to appear."

"So, we will let them believe that we are still cherishing the illusion that they flew off to battle talon-to-sword with our foes," Tremane said firmly. "If they *choose* to tell us what their tactics are, we will then praise their cleverness. Otherwise, we will be effusive in our praises of their bravery. In either case, they will succeed in making it clear to trouble-makers that *we* have a formidable ally that they do not; they will accomplish what they set out to do, which is to win this single scrimmage, and that may be all we need. I would rather have a bloodless victory than any other kind."

"I've taken the liberty of ordering a congratulatory feast of wild game, sir," the Seneschal said diffidently. "I was afraid that if we left it too long, we would never get the meat thawed in time."

Tremane nodded his agreement absently, which relieved the poor lad, who was still afraid to order anything on his own that might have a serious impact later. In this case, ordering a feast *might* lead to a shortage later. Darkwind privately doubted that, having seen the stores of frozen meat himself, but it was a possibility. Perhaps more than a possibility, when he recalled the sheer mass of food that Treyvan and Hydona could put away without hesitation. But now that Tremane had given his approval, the young Seneschal clearly felt much easier in his mind.

I do miss Treyvan and Hydona, and their two little feathered fighters. I miss tumbling and playing with the little ones, and feeling Hydona preen my hair, and watching Vree dive after Treyvan's crest-feathers. And I miss their deep voices, their affection, and advice.

"Now, gentlemen and ladies," Tremane said, his tone turning somber, "Let us consider what we must do if our allies fail."

"It isn't likely, I don't think," Darkwind offered. "A single gryphon, half-asleep, can defeat a squad of fighters with less effort than it takes to preen. This is a group of twenty-and-one, fully awake and eager!" Several of the attendees laughed, looking quite convinced of that by what they had seen of the creatures. "But you're correct, of course. Preparations should be made for less than total victory."

The rest of the day was spent making plans for just that contingency, but as sunset reddened the skies to the west, the victors came winging home, quite intact, and with the foes' leader's personal banner, a letter of surrender, and a pledge that he would come in person to swear his allegiance, all clutched proudly in Tashiketh's talons.

The cheers that rose to greet them as they replicated their previous graceful landing in the courtyard were prompted as much by relief as by joy in the victory, but they didn't need to know that.

Darkwind assured one and all that a tired gryphon was a starving gryphon, and Tashiketh's second in command nodded firmly. At the feast, to which the tired gryphons were immediately ushered, Tashiketh formally presented the surrender and pledge, and then modestly revealed the secret of their victory.

"First we dropped rocks through their roofs," he said, with a faintly cruel chuckle. "Then we dropped *one* firepot on a thatched outbuilding, and circled in three subwings of seven each. After six passes, we threatened to drop more. That got their attention long enough for us to claim that we were a mere fraction of the winged army that King Tremane could command if he chose. And I hinted that we weren't too particular about waiting for provisions to arrive in a case like that, and were inclined to help ourselves. The idea of *hundreds* of us descending out of the sky, smashing big holes in every roof, setting fire to things, and snatching and carrying off who-knew-what to eat, had them in a panic. If that idiot leading them hadn't surrendered on the spot, I think they might killed him, and served him to us on a platter with a good broth on the side!"

Several of the generals laughed heartily at this, and even Tremane smiled. Darkwind thought it best to interject a cautionary note.

"It won't do to make them think you're going to carry off children for snacks," he warned Tashiketh under cover of the laughter. "How could they trust a King who'd let his 'monsters' feed on children?"

"No fear of that," Tashiketh soothed. "I made sure we were eying the sheep when I said that, and added a bit about how tasty fresh, fat mutton was, and allowed as how we could decimate their every flock and herd in a matter of days and just feel stronger for being so well fed. For a people on the edge of starvation, accepting surrender in place of that sounds very appealing. Our rules of combat have always stressed that we're not to intimate that we eat thinking beings. We might not have done this in earnest before, but we've had plenty of training."

"Good." Darkwind relaxed enough to chuckle. "I wish I'd seen their faces when you told them that you were only the vanguard. And of course, *they* would never know when you were bluffing."

"It wasn't all bluff." Tashiketh said smugly, then suddenly took an extreme interest in his food, as if he realized that he had said too much.

Well. Well! Darkwind took an interest in his own meal, as if unaware that Tashiketh had let fall something important. *So Iftel has more interest in Tremane's welfare than I thought. Enough that they would back him with a significant force? It certainly sounds that way.*

If they would send an army to help him, what else would

they be willing to offer? The secret of the Barrier? Other secrets?

And how much of that would be of any use against the coming Storms, especially the Final Storm?

Or would so little be left after that last blow that none of this would matter?

"You could not possibly have conceived of anything more likely to have turned you into the Army's favorites," Elspeth told Tashiketh, as a roar went up from the watching crowd. Five of Tashiketh's subordinates climbed, crawled, flew, leaped, and contorted themselves across a torturous obstacle course under the bright noontime sun. It was cold enough to numb feet encased in boots and several layers of stockings, but that hadn't prevented the now-usual crowd from showing up as soon as the contest began. Typically, the former Imperial soldiers had gathered to watch, cheer—and then bet on the outcome. This was probably the most exciting entertainment in the entire country about now.

There was not a great deal in the way of entertainment in Shonar, in spite of the presence of the King here; every time the one and only Bard in the town composed a new song, the tavern where he played was crowded to capacity for days, and the soldiers did their best to enliven otherwise dull days and nights with mixed results. One of the highest-priced items to be had among the soldiery was a deck of cards. But now there was a new and novel source of spectacle in their midst, one with all the finest attributes of a fair, a race, and a real contest. Since Tashiketh never participated except to practice alone, the outcome of any given competition was always subject to the whims of chance, which made it perfect for wagering. That in turn made it more attractive yet, if that was possible.

"Would it harm me in your esteem if I confessed that this was a deliberate choice, making our contests public affairs?" Tashiketh asked Elspeth, gravely.

"Hardly. I would simply congratulate you on your intelligence," she replied promptly. "The only question I have is why stage these obstacle things at all? There are other ways of keeping you all in fighting trim."

"Because we must. Our hierarchy changes as the results of the contests change, and as our own ranking changes, so will the rankings of our various counties. And *that*, at year's end, will decree where discretionary tax funds are spent." Just as he made that surprising assertion, Tremane joined them, relatively anonymous in a plain brown soldier's cloak with the hood pulled up against the bite of the cold wind. Tashiketh did not turn his head or appear to notice, but a few moments later, he addressed the King directly.

"So, King of Hardorn, I am given to understand that you are exceedingly curious about my people. I finally have leave to answer your questions, for you have proven yourself to be an honorable ally and worthy to hear the full tale of our land." Now Tashiketh moved his head to gaze into Tremane's astonished face with mild eyes. "Ask," he said. "The time for secrets is past."

Whatever Tremane's faults, an inability to think quickly was not one of them. "Darkwind k'Sheyna believes that your people were descended from one part of the armies of the mage his people served, specifically the one called Urtho," he said. "Are you?"

Tashiketh laughed, a deep rumble that came from somewhere down in the bottom of his chest, and he roused his fathers with a shake. "Yes. The shortest version of the tale is this. Our several Peoples were all serving the Third Army. Urtho made it his policy to group all the folk of a particular land into one Army, rather than dividing all of them amongst his Armies. However, the humans of the Third, serving a God who decreed that those who had magic power should be His priests, had no mages of their own. They had no prejudice against working with those of other faiths, and so had a group of mages assigned to them, mages who had nothing whatsoever in common with them, not even nationality. Also attached to the Third were a wing of gryphons with their *trondi'irn*, a pack of *kyree*, a surge of *ratha*, a knot of *tyrill*, and a charge of *dyheli*."

What am I hearing? Tyrill? Ratha? How did they get into this story?

"And these are your Peoples of Iftel?" Tremane asked.

"What is a *ratha?*" Darkwind asked, at the same moment.

Tashiketh wasn't the least perturbed by being bombarded with questions. "These are our Peoples, yes. *Ratha* are from the far north, and are to the mountain cats what *kyree* are to wolves. *Tyrill* I think you know already, Brother-To-Hawks."

"Only by legend," Darkwind replied, feeling a bit dazed. "They were one of Urtho's last creations, a larger race of *hertasi*, and there weren't many of them."

"But, oh, they breed with such enthusiasm!" Tashiketh laughed, tossing his head so that the freshening wind ruffled his feathers. Behind him, another cheer rose (together with some groans) as one of the other gryphons did something clever. "They learned it from us gryphons. There are plenty of them now! Well, to make this as brief as possible, the Third, whose emblem I wear, was cut off from Ka'venusho at the time of retreat. They chose to Gate to the remotest place the mages could think of, hoping they would be beyond the reach of Ma'ar and the destruction that would ensue when Urtho's Tower was destroyed by its master. But there was a problem."

"Not enough power," Tremane guessed shrewdly.

"Nowhere safe to go?" asked Elspeth.

"No Adepts," hazarded Darkwind.

"A little of all three," the Ambassador explained. "Their Priests—the humans—had remained behind in their own land to protect their people. The only Adept with them strong enough to raise a far-away Gate was someone who, at the time, was thought to be a barbarian shaman from the far north. They had to go to the remotest place *he* knew of—his home, not the gryphons' home, nor that of their human charges, not anywhere near it. There wasn't much choice; they took the escape that was offered, ending in the north of what is now Iftel. They thought to wait out the destruction, then be reunited with the others. But no sooner had they all gotten across, then something terrible happened, worse by far than anything they had expected."

"The Cataclysm," Darkwind said aloud. "The Tower *and* Ma'ar's stronghold destroyed, and the interaction of the double release of terrible forces."

"And needless to say, they did not know the cause for many years. They only knew that things were impossible, that there would be no way to find their friends and fellows, that there would be no way for the humans of the Third to find *their* way home. And almost as bad, it soon became obvious that they had not gone far enough; they ran into a fresh Army of

Ma'ar's." Tashiketh shook his head. "It must have seemed as if they had come to the end of the world, that everything evil had won against them, and was about to annihilate them. Battered by the mage-storms that followed, on the verge of attack by superior forces, and unable because of the high number of wounded to travel to someplace where they might escape the worst of the effects, they did the only thing they had left to do. The humans prayed to their god, Vykaendys—"

That name struck Darkwind like a blow to the head. *"Who?"* Darkwind blurted, as Elspeth's eyes widened.

"Vykaendys," the Ambassador repeated. "The Holy Sun, from whom all life—"

Elspeth interrupted. "Ambassador Tashiketh, do the humans of your land use a different language from the gryphons?"

The huge gryphon nodded. "The sacred language is different," he replied. "The shared language is a combination of several tongues, and Old Gryphon is very like that tongue you spoke to me when first we met. Do I take it you wish to hear something of the Sacred Tongue of Vykaendys?"

"Please," said Elspeth and Darkwind together.

Tashiketh rattled off a few sentences, and Darkwind looked to Elspeth, who had a better command of languages than he did.

She listened very closely, as her eyes widened further until the whites showed all around. "I'm not a linguist," she said when he has finished, "But I would say that this is to Karsite what the Iftel gryphon tongue is to Kaled'a'in."

Darkwind whistled. *:No wonder Altra kept insisting that the Border would only recognize himself, Karal, Ulrich, or Solaris! The God of Iftel and the God of Karse are one and the same! Isn't that going to put a Firecat among the pigeons!:*

Gwena chose that moment to add her own observation. *:Oh, this is interesting indeed. Solaris doesn't know this, but Altra does. I wonder why and why he hadn't told her?:*

"They prayed for protection, right?" Elspeth asked the Ambassador. "And the god established the Border to keep their enemies out?"

"Precisely," Tashiketh agreed. "And of course Vykaendys did exactly that, answering their prayers. He is the one who ordained that we send our representatives beyond the Border to help as we could with the current crisis. He sent us to Hard-orn once He knew that Hardorn again had a King who had been bound to the land. Otherwise, given the gravity of the current situation, we would, of course, have been sent into Valdemar. All creatures must work together to survive the last Storms, but Vykaendys is pleased to welcome the land that lies between the two that He governs, as a brother-country rather than an enemy-state."

Elspeth shook her head. "Of course," she replied.

:I can't help wondering what Solaris is going to make of this when she finds out about it,: Elspeth added to Darkwind. :Although, in retrospect, it's fascinating, the ways in which gods answered the prayers of their followers—the Star-Eyed creating the Dhorisha Plains for the Shin'a'in who had renounced magic, and granting the Tayledras the power to protect themselves with their magic while they healed the land a bit at a time. And now the Sun Lord, creating a barrier around Iftel—:

Darkwind wondered if He had done something similar for Karse just to hold through the Cataclysm itself. The Karsites were certainly close enough to the source of the Cataclysm to have needed such protection. But wait; the Sun-priests are mages. Maybe the Sun-priests are their equivalents of the Tayledras, and Vkandis gave them access to great power to protect themselves the way the Tayledras did. The greatest dangers after the Cataclysm lay in the monsters that had been created. Could that be where and why the Sun-priests got the ability to summon and control demons so effectively? Now that was an intriguing thought!

There was no way of knowing without having Karal to ask, and even then it might not be canonical information. But Altra was obviously privy to noncanonical truths, and if he was inclined to share them with nonbelievers—

If he is, we might learn more than we ever wanted to know.

But Elspeth had been thinking further ahead than he. As Tremane asked more detailed questions of Tashiketh, she drew Darkwind and Gwena into a close mind-link.

:What are the odds that we can involve gods in all of this?: she wanted to know. :Vkandis, Kal'enel, either or both? The power of a god might save us.:

:Or it might cause a whole lot more trouble than any mage-

storm, however powerful,: Darkwind warned. *:We can't know.:*

:But I can ask Florian to ask Altra,: Gwena said. *:And perhaps he can ask An'desha as well.:*

Darkwind shook his head doubtfully. *:Don't count on any real help,:* he told them. *:The Star-Eyed is disinclined to interfere, Vkandis may be fundamentally the same. They may be able to help us only after the disaster strikes, and be unable to do anything to prevent it from coming—because we have that power, if only we make the correct choices, and They will not take that right to choose from us.:*

Gwena nodded mentally, but Elspeth's mind-voice seethed with frustration. *:But how can we make the right choices if we don't know what they are?:* she fumed.

:If we knew what to do, then they wouldn't be choices, they would be plans,: Darkwind chided gently.

He didn't blame her, and he didn't have the heart to tell her that the "right" choice, from the point of view of a god, might not be the one that prevented a second Cataclysm. Gods tended to take a much longer view of things than mere mortals, and what they considered to be good in the long run might be pretty horrible for those who had to live through it.

I'm sure that Baron Valdemar's people heartily wished him to the bottom of the Salten Sea during that first winter in the wilderness, he thought soberly. *And certainly it was terrible for the last Herald-Mages of Vanyel's time to be the last of their kind. But in the long run, those were good things for most of the people of Valdemar.*

This was probably not the time to point this out to her, however.

:All we can do is what we've always done,: he told her with utmost sincerity. *:We must do our best. Then, even if things turn out badly, we will know it was not from any lack of trying on our part.:*

She sighed. *:I do wish you weren't right so often,:* she said forlornly. *:I rather enjoyed being able to rail against Fate and the Unfairness Of It All.:* But she pulled herself a bit straighter and nodded.*: Whatever happens, we'll survive it, and we'll build on what's left.:* She glanced around, and her mouth twisted wryly. *:All our peoples do seem to be rather good at that.:*

He squeezed her hand in agreement. :*And we will do it together*, ashke.: He could not help thinking about the group at center of Dhorisha, picking through the remains of the Tower, without experiencing a feeling of chill. Whatever happened— yes, he, Elspeth, and the others here would probably survive it.

But what of his friends in the Tower? Would *they?*

As he turned his attention back to the conversation at hand, his stomach gave a sudden lurch, his eyes unfocused for a moment, and he felt very much as if the ground had dropped out from underneath him. Then the world steadied again, but as he looked from Tremane to Elspeth and back, and saw the same startled look in both their eyes turn to sick recognition, he knew what had just hit him.

The mage-storms had begun again. Hints of their building power were beginning to overcome the Counter-Storm. They were not strong enough yet to cause any problems, but it was only a matter of time.

Darkwind understood.

This was the first sign of the coming Final Storm, and their respite before it struck would be measured in, at best, weeks. Their survival was in doubt, and even if they did survive, whether they would prosper afterward was in deep question. There were hundreds of variables, and just as many major decisions. There were key uses of power and defense, solving of mysteries and understanding of connections. Like each segment in a spiderweb, the failure of any of those elements could collapse it all, and cost every one involved—everything.

Firesong, Need and An'desha

Nine

"What is wrong with your friend Firesong?" Lyam asked Karal in a whisper, as Firesong went off to a remote corner of the Tower to brood—or as he called it, "meditate"—for the second time that day. "The others are all working together over the notes for the cube-maze, but he keeps going off by himself, he says to think. Is that usual for him? Is he ill, do you think? Or have the frustrations begun to weigh upon his soul?"

"I'm not sure," Karal replied, although this behavior of Firesong's wasn't particularly news to him. Living together as closely as they all were, it wasn't possible for any of them to deviate from normal behavior without the others noticing And Firesong was certainly acting oddly—though not with that selfish oddness that made him so dangerous before.

There were several signs that this bout of solitary brooding was far different than the last. For one thing, Aya kept cuddling close to him, tucking his head up under Firesong's chin while Firesong held him and scratched gently under his wings, and it had been Aya's avoidance of his bondmate that had been one sign that his temper and thoughts were tending in dangerous directions. He wasn't tinkering with odd magics either; he was sitting in out-of-the-way corners, staring into space, as if Firesong sought the privacy in his mind that he could not get in the Tower. But those bursts of "meditation" always seemed to end in a sharp and thoughtful glance at Karal, and given some of the past difficulties between them, that didn't make Karal feel entirely easy about his possible thoughts.

"Huh," Lyam said, and scratched the top of his head with a

stubby, ink-stained talon. "Well, he doesn't seem to be getting much done, an he's giving me collywobbles with the way he just sits and stares. If he's gotten into a blue funk, maybe one of you ought to shake him out of it."

Karal made a face. "I'm not sure any of us want to *shake* Firesong out of anything, but I suppose it can't hurt if I talk to him. If there's a problem, maybe Silverfox could help him with it, or something. Or maybe it's a problem he doesn't want to get Silverfox involved with, and maybe I could help him." He made a face. "After all, I'm supposed to be a priest, and that's the sort of thing that priests are supposed to do, right?"

Having said that, he knew he had talked himself into the position where he was going to have to do something about the situation. Lyam nodded encouragingly to him at that last statement, so before he could find a reason to put it off, he got to his feet and trailed off after Firesong.

Altra invited himself along, sauntering casually at Karal's heels. As Karal glanced inquisitively down at him, Altra blinked guileless blue eyes at him. :*I thought I'd come along, too, just in case you needed me,*: the Firecat said idly. Karal did not ask "for what?" since he knew the answer already. There wasn't a great deal that Altra couldn't shield him against, if Firesong turned angry or dangerous, or both.

He found the Adept in the chamber containing one of the mysterious contrivances (one made of wire, odd plates of some sparkling material, and gemstones) that looked far too delicate to warrant the label of "weapon." Aya was with him, cuddling inside his jacket. Aya's long tail trailed comically down from beneath the hem, as if the cascade of feathers belonged to Firesong. The Adept stared at the softly glowing stones with an intense look on his face. He turned to face the entrance when he heard Karal's deliberate footstep, but he did not seem particularly surprised to see the Karsite.

Karal approached him gingerly, but there was nothing in Firesong's slight smile to indicate anything other than welcome. As he edged around the wire-sculpture weapon, Karal tried to think of a lateral approach to the subject, and failed to come up with a good one. So he decided to go straight to the heart of the matter, and make no attempt at being clever.

"You've been wandering off by yourself for the last couple

of days, and we're a little concerned about you," he said bluntly. "It didn't seem right to go behind your back and pester Silverfox to see if you were all right, so I decided to ask you directly. Is there anything wrong?"

"Other than everything?" Firesong asked archly. "We *are* in a very precarious position here, you know."

"Well, yes, but—" Karal fumbled. "I mean—"

"There's nothing wrong, or rather, nothing wrong with *me*, Karal," Firesong interrupted, with a smile for his bondbird, as Aya stuck his head out of the front of the Adept's jacket, saw who it was that Firesong was talking to, and tucked himself back inside. "But I'm glad you came to find out, because I have a few questions that really concern only you. Here, sit." He patted the floor beside him, and Karal lowered himself down warily. "Karal, Karse and Valdemar fought a generations-long war, and I can understand that anyone from Karse might feel very negative about certain figures of Valdemaran history, but you are bright enough to reason things through for yourself and not just take everything you are told in without ever examining it. So, given that, here's a history question; what do you know and what do you think about Herald-Mage Vanyel Ashkevron?"

Karal stared at him, a bit confused by the abrupt change of subject, for the initial question Karal had asked about Firesong had nothing whatsoever to do with a figure of ancient history like Vanyel Ashkevron.

But it was a very interesting question, given all of the changes Karal's own life and thoughts had been going through. It might, on the surface, seem like the question had no relevance in any way to the situation in the Tower, but he knew Firesong better than that, and Firesong *had* to have an ultimate purpose in asking it.

"I'm going to have to think aloud, so bear with me," Karal said, finally. "As you probably guessed, according to *our* history, Vanyel Demonrider was absolutely the epitome of everything that was terrible about Valdemar. Every child in Karse used to be told that if he was bad, Vanyel would come and carry him off. He was a Herald, a rider of a demon-horse, and the implacable enemy of all Karse stood for. He was a mage, which was anathema, of course, and he had the audacity to be a very powerful mage, one who could turn back the demons that the most highly skilled Priest-mages could raise, which made him even worse. And if that wasn't bad enough, it is said by some chroniclers of the time that he could break the compulsions that the Priests put on their demons and send them back against their own summoners, which made him the King of the Demons so far as our people were concerned."

"That's your history," Firesong replied, watching Karal with peculiar intensity. "How do *you* feel about it?"

"I'm getting to that." Karal rubbed the back of his own neck, trying to sort out his thoughts as he loosened tight muscles. "I do think it's supremely ironic that the worst accusations about Vanyel have to do with him riding a demon-horse and being a mage, when our own Priests were mages who summoned demons and controlled them."

Firesong's sardonic smile had a note of approval in it. "No one has ever dared to claim that the causes of warfare and the sources of prejudice are ever rational." He scratched Aya under the chin, and was rewarded by a particularly adorable chirrup. "And religious fervor is often used as an excuse for a great many socially unacceptable behaviors."

"That's religion as an excuse. Sometimes it seems to me that when religious fervor enters the mind, the wits pack up entirely and fly out the ear," Karal replied a bit sourly. "But worst of all is when powerful, ruthless people use the religious fervor of others to further their own greed."

Aya poked his head out of the jacket again, as if he found what Karal was saying very interesting. Altra settled himself at Karal's feet, and there was nothing in the Firecat's demeanor to make Karal think his own religious guide disapproved of anything he had said so far.

"All that is true in my experience," Firesong replied with one of his brilliant, perfect smiles. "Though I'm not *that* much older than you. So, what do *you* think Vanyel was really like?"

Karal shrugged. "Of course, I am sure that he must be a very great hero to the Valdemarans; the fact that my people considered him to be such an evil enemy would make that a simple conclusion to come to. Given that he was fighting what *I* now know to have been very power-hungry and entirely amoral men, most notably one of the worst Sons of the Sun we ever had in all our history, I suppose that he was only doing his duty to protect *his* people against the rapacious land grabbing of mine. I—cannot say that I like that thought. It fills me with shame, in fact." He paused, and a final thought floated to the surface, one that seemed to define the situation. "I can only say that not even his enemies in Karse ever tried to claim that *he* led any armies over the border into *our* land, and the same cannot be said of the Karsite commanders. Now, I can't pretend to tell who was right and who was wrong in those areas where both sides claimed to have been attacked first, or were provoked into attacking, or where magic, sabotage, and assassination were allegedly employed, but I can tell that the Valdermarans never took armies into Karse, but my people certainly waged war up into Valdemar."

"Very even-handed," Firesong replied approvingly. "No side is always in the right. Now, we'll change the subject again. I need a religious opinion from you. What do the Sun-priests have to say about ghosts?"

"As in, what?" he asked. "Unquiet dead? Haunts? Spirits who return to guide?"

"All of those," Firesong said, making a general gesture. "Some religions deny that any such manifestations exist, and some religions are written around them as a form of ancestor worship. What does the Writ of Vkandis say?"

"The Writ says very little." He frowned, trying to think of what it *did* say. "Now that I come to think of it, what it *does* say is rather interesting. According to the Writ, no one who is of the Faith, whether the purest soul or the blackest, could possibly become a ghost. Anyone born or brought into the Faith *will* be taken before Vkandis and judged—'sorted' is the word used in the Writ. *And the good shall be sorted from the evil; no spirit shall escape the sorting. The evil will be cast into darkness and great despair, into fear and pain, to repeat their errors until they have learned to love and serve the Light of Vkandis. And the good shall be gathered up into the rich meadows of Heaven, to sing His praises in the everlasting rays, to drink the sweet waters and bask forevermore in the Glory of the Sun.* That's the actual quote. There's a great deal more about who shall become what rank of angelic spirit, and what each kind does, but I have a suspicion that all of that is a clerkly conceit. I've got an earlier version of the Writ that doesn't have any of those lists in it."

"Some people even have to have their afterlife ranked, arranged, and organized," Firesong chuckled. "I hate to say this, but being gathered up to lie in a meadow sunbathing and singing for all eternity is *not* my idea of a perfect afterlife. I should be screamingly bored within the first afternoon."

Karal laughed. "Maybe not for you, but think about the poor shepherds who were the first Prophets, living in the cold, damp hills of Karse, with rain and fog and damn poor grazing most of the time."

"I suppose for them, rich meadows and sun forever would be paradise, wouldn't it?" Firesong raised his eyebrows. "All right, so Karsites can't become ghosts—but what about other people?"

"Well, that's not in the Writ. But there is a tradition that the unblessed dead become the hungry, vengeful ghosts who roam the night. That's why most Karsites won't venture out after dark without a Priest to secure their safety." But Firesong's question had asked about more than mere Karsite tradition, it had been about what Karal himself thought. "As a Priest, I *can* exorcise ghosts, in theory. I'm supposed to be able to send any unblessed spirit to the sorting even if they aren't of the Faith, if they want to go. The Writ is kind of vague about what happens to heathen who have the misfortune to worship someone besides Vkandis. Most people assume that they'll be sent to eternal punishment, even if they are *good* people, but the Writ really doesn't *say* that, it just says that they will be sorted and sent to 'their places.' It doesn't say what those places are. For all *I* know, those places could be right here on earth."

Tre'valen and Dawnfire are ghosts of a kind, and if what Lo'isha and An'desha have been saying is true, then some of the Kal'enedral are ghosts, too. Or if they aren't ghosts, they certainly aren't physically alive the way Florian and Altra are. So there's no reason why Kal'enel couldn't have "sorted" them Herself, and decreed that their "place" was here.

"Well, what about the Avatars?" Firesong asked, echoing his thoughts. "Do they count as ghosts?"

"If they aren't, I wouldn't know what else to call them," Karal admitted. "And even if they aren't 'blessed' in the Karsite sense, they are anything but evil or hungry. They certainly aren't vengeful either, so there's no reason for me to interfere with whatever they are doing." He thought a bit harder. "The thing about exorcism is that if you want to be exact about it, there are two kinds. One kind just throws the ghost out of whatever it's possessing and bars it from coming back—it can still go possess something else somewhere else. The other kind blesses the ghost, opens a path for it so it can see where it's supposed to be going, and gives it some help to break the last bonds with the world and send it on its way if it's ready. But it has to *be* ready. Most Priests combine both kinds, hoping that once the spirit is cast out, it will see the Light and realize it shouldn't be here, but I've also seen reports about spirits that just seemed confused about the fact that they were dead, and in that case, the Priest only used the second kind of exorcism."

"All very well, but suppose you were to see something that you knew was a ghost—not an Avatar, or anything obviously under the direction of anyone's god. What would you do about that?" Firesong asked. "Would you feel that you *had* to do something about it?"

It was a good question. According to some Priests, he would *have* to try exorcising anything that looked or acted like a ghost, but that would include the Kal'enedral and the Avatars, and he dashed well knew that he wasn't going to even *breathe* the word "exorcism" around them! "Personally, I suppose I would try to exorcise anything that was harmful, send on anything that was ready, and leave everything else alone."

He still didn't see what relevance any of this had to their current situation, but presumably Firesong had some idea where he was going with all of this.

Firesong appeared to make up his mind about something, for his expression became a bit more animated and less contemplative. "Look," he said, "I've been asking you all these questions because I need your help, yours and Altra's, and there are some religious problems involved. I made the—acquaintance—of some real ghosts, and you wouldn't mistake them for anything else. One of them is an ancestor of mine. Physically, they're bound to a place up north, right up at the northern border of Valdemar."

Oh, no . . . he must be afraid that when the Final Storm hits, these ghosts of his are going to be destroyed or hurt in some way. Karal interrupted him. "Firesong, I hope you weren't planning on asking me to exorcise them. I mean, I'm sorry that one of your ancestors is physically bound to the earth, and if I could, I would be glad to help him, but I don't think it's possible. I told you, all I would be able to do without the spirits being ready, is to force them out of the place they were bound to. Even so, I doubt I could do anything for them at such a great distance."

Now it was Firesong's turn to interrupt him. "No, Karal, that was *not* what I had in mind!" he exclaimed, but he seemed more amused at the conclusion that Karal had leaped to than annoyed. "Hear me out. An'desha, Sejanes, and I all agree that we simply need more *mages* here at the Tower, powerful mages, and we're just not going to get them here to us in time. We need Adepts at the least, and every Adept within physical range of the Tower is needed right where he is. We can't build Gates to bring in human or nonhuman Adepts from farther away, and Altra can't bring in anyone mortal—but what about ghosts?"

Ghosts. One of Firesong's ancestors. North of Valdemar. And an Adept. The trend of the questions suddenly formed into a pattern, and Karal stared at him in mingled horror and fascination. "This ghost—this ancestor—it wouldn't be Vanyel Ashkevron, would it?" he asked, his voice trembling in spite of his effort to control it. He felt the hair on the back of his neck rise. Discussing Vanyel Demonrider in abstract was one thing. Seriously discussing bringing him here was another!

He wanted to beg Firesong to tell him that it was *not* Vanyel Ashkevron he was talking about, but one look in Firesong's face told him differently.

:*I think it would be a very good idea, Karal,*: Florian said diffidently. :*Vanyel is an Adept. If it is possible, I think it should be done.*:

"I won't ask how this came about," Karal said flatly. "I won't ask how *you* discovered that Vanyel Demonrider was still . . . in existence." He closed his eyes and shook his head. "I cannot believe I am hearing this."

:*Boy, if you require more votes on this, you have mine,*: said the sword Need. :*I've met the man, though I doubt he'll recall it. He and Stefen would be a tremendous asset to the group here. They* might *even give us that edge we need to beat this thing.:*

Firesong smirked. "The sword is saying that we need an edge. How appropriate. In any case, the Avatars actually suggested it. There are some things in the cube-maze notes that suggest we're going to need—well, more skilled people than the last time. The only way we can think of to get the spirits down here is to send Altra," Firesong said. "We think that Vanyel, his Companion, and his friend can link themselves to something small enough for Altra to transport."

"We?" Karal asked weakly. "How many of you discussed this?"

"All of the mages," Firesong told him. "That included Need and the Avatars. And we all agreed. We think we're about to find our answer on the cube-maze device, which is our first choice, but we need more help to make it work."

Karal looked down at Altra, who gazed back up at him with interest. "And what do you have to say about this?" he asked the Firecat.

:Seriously? I think it might work, but I don't know for certain. I'm not a mage as you think of one, but the others seem convinced. There is only one consideration, and that is why they wanted to talk to you.:

"So you were already a party to this?" Karal sighed. "I might have known. What's the consideration?"

:A very practical one. This borders on interference; if I were to just do as you ask, I would be exceeding my own authority. In order for me to do this, we would need permission from a higher authority, and I cannot be the one to ask for permission.:

"I have the feeling that you are not referring to Solaris when you speak of needing permission from a higher authority." Karal bit his lip.

:You are correct, and you are the only Sun-priest here,: Altra said calmly. *:So you are the one who must make the petition. I cannot, and I cannot do such a thing without that permission. I may advise, guide, and run limited errands up to a point, but this is past that point. I hate to sound like a copper-counting clerk, making a fuss about a technicality, but if these spirits were Karsite and not Valdemaran, there would be less of a problem.:*

"Because of the old enmity?" Karal asked, surprised. "But it was the Sunlord Himself who ordered truce with Valdemar in the first place!"

:No. Because these spirits were bound where they are for a reason, and I don't know that this reason has been fulfilled. They may not even know that. Now, even if their purpose is not yet fulfilled, they could choose to come here anyway, disobeying the One who offered them the task. But without first receiving permission of Vkandis, I cannot choose to help them come without the risk that I would be disobeying as well, and I do not choose to take that risk.:

"I wouldn't ask you to," Karal replied. "I suppose that means I don't have much choice in the matter."

:Judging by the way your friends are staring at you, I would say not.:

Karal looked up, already feeling pressured and guilty, to meet three sets of eyes—

Well, Need didn't *have* eyes as such, but he sensed her looking through Firesong's, and Florian stood in the doorway, gazing at him with a completely heartrending expression in his huge blue eyes.

The combined weight was too much to bear. "I'll have to go outside," he gulped, and managed not to stagger as he passed Florian.

He remembered somehow to find his coat, heavy boots, and gloves and pull them all on, but the trip up the tunnel was a complete blank in his mind. He knew very well what he had to do; he'd witnessed many petitions offered up by Solaris and her most trusted Priests, and had studied the form as part of his own education in the priesthood. Like many of the core portions of the Sunlord's Faith, a petition to Vkandis was deceptively simple.

The only requirement was that a petition must be made in the full light of day. In the Great Temple, this was accomplished, of course, by virtue of the many windows cut in the upper dome. Here, of course, Karal had only to walk outside. As befitting a religion founded by poor shepherds, who had little but what they could carry on their backs, or perhaps the back of a single donkey, there were no special vestments or vessels, no trappings of any kind. The only vessel needed was the Priest, and the only "vestment" a pure and single-hearted belief that the prayer would be heard. It might not receive a "yes," but it *would* be heard.

Karal, more than many, had every reason to hold that faith in his heart. He knew that Vkandis would hear him; did he not have Altra with him to prove that? His only question was if *he* was ready, was worthy, to be answered in any way, even with a "no."

He walked a little distance off into the snow, putting a tall drift between himself and the Shin'a'in camp, until there was no sign of activity but his own footprints trailing behind him. Beside him was the Tower, looming over everything, as it loomed over their lives. All around him was the dazzling whiteness of the snow, no less than knee-deep in some places, and deeper than that in most. This was a thicker snowpack than he had ever seen before.

It was also thicker than the Shin'a'in had ever seen it before, or so he'd been told. This was a terrible winter, and it could so easily get worse—assuming that the Plains themselves survived the Final Storm and what might happen to those ancient weapons still in the Tower.

Even if I'm not worthy, the cause is, he finally decided, and turned his face up to the sun, spreading his arms wide.

Some took great care with each word when they made prayers for a particular purpose, but Karal and his mentor Ulrich had never seen the sense in that. "They are like courtiers, trying to find the most unctuous phrase in hopes that their prince will throw them a bauble," Ulrich had said in disgust. "There is nothing in the Writ about making fine speeches for Vkandis' ear. Vkandis understands us far better than we could ever find words for."

So Karal simply stood with every bit of him open to the light of the sun, the light that stood for the greater Light, and let that Light become all that he was. He kept his petition to the bare facts.

This is how we stand. This is what we have been doing. This is what we need to do. We know that this will not guarantee our success, but we think it is necessary. Will You grant your permission for Your servants to do this?

This was the first time he had ever made such a prayer alone, and he trembled all over at his own audacity. He made of himself nothing but the question, and waited, like an empty bowl, for the answer.

The sun burned on in the endless blue of heaven, as he struggled to lose himself in the Light. And in the moment that he actually did so, Vkandis showed His face.

The sun blazed up, doubling, tripling in size; he felt the light burning his face even as he held his gaze steady and un- flinching.

You can bear the Light. But can you bear the place where there are no sheltering shadows?

The sun split into two, three, a dozen suns, surrounding him in a circle of suns, creating a place where there could be no hint of darkness and nowhere to hide. The suns settled upon the earth around him, dancing upon the face of the snow, but neither melting nor consuming it. Still he waited, all fear burned out of him, empty of everything but faith and the wait- ing, and he breathed steadily and deeply once for every dozen heartbeats.

You can bear being without shadow. But can you bear being only in Light?

The dozen suns blazed up again, and began circling around him, faster and faster, until they blurred into a solid ring of white light. Then the ring flared and he had to cover his eyes for a moment; and when he looked again, he stood, not in the snow of the Plains, but in the heart of the sun, with light above and below, and all about him, in the heart of the Light, and the Light became part of him.

But this, he realized, was not a completely new experience. Although he had not had the memory until this moment, *this* was what had happened when he acted as a Channel for the release of the great energies of the first weapon they had trig- gered. The Light had taken away his fears then, and it did so again, then illuminated every corner of his heart. Yes, there were faulty places, poorly-mended places, even spots of faint shadow—Karal saw and acknowledged those, as he renewed a pledge to see them made good. *But,* he said silently to that great Light, *what I am does not matter. This thing that I ask is not for me, nor even for these few who are here with me. This is for all our peoples; and for peoples we do not even know.*

The Light answered him with a question of its own. *Is this also for those of the Empire?*

He replied immediately, and simply.

Yes.

Had he not alrcady pointed out that most of the people living in the Empire had nothing to do with the terrible things their leaders had done? Why should they not be protected?

Even your enemies? came the second question.

He answered it as he had the other. *Yes.*

If protecting his enemies was the cost of protecting the innocent, then so be it. Fanatics said, "Kill them all, and let God sort them out." He would rather say, "Save them all, and let God sort them out, for we have not the right to judge."

There was a timeless moment of waiting, and the Light flooded him with approval.

Then that is My answer, came the reply. *Yes.*

The Light vanished.

He found himself standing in the snow, his feet numb, his eyes watering, with his entire being filled with the answer. He was a scintillating bowl full of *Yes,* and he carried that answer back to the Tower as carefully as an acolyte carried a bowl of holy water.

"You don't remember anything?" Lyam asked, alive with curiosity, as he helped Karal carry a new set of notes up to the storage chamber. Karal shook his head regretfully, and watched where he was putting his feet. The last few steps out of the workroom were worn enough to be tricky.

"All I remember is going out into the snow. After that— nothing, until I woke up again with the answer." He made an apologetic face. "Sorry, I know you'd love to note all of this down, and it's not a priestly secret or anything, but I just can't remember what happened."

The *hertasi* lashed his tail, perhaps with impatience. "You could have just gone out, come back, and pretended to have the answer," Lyam began. "Not that *you* would have, but—"

"That wouldn't be as easy as you think. I might have fooled anyone but Florian and Altra, but *never* either of them," Karal replied firmly. "And I'm not sure it would have fooled Need; I think she was a priestess before she was a sword, and if she was, she'll have ways of knowing when people make up answers they say are from their gods."

"If you say so," Lyam said, though his tone was dubious.

"And it wouldn't ever have fooled the Avatars," he continued forcefully. "How could it? How could you *ever* fool them about something like that?"

Lyam conceded defeat at that; although he might not be completely convinced of the supernatural nature of Florian, Altra, or Need, he was *entirely* convinced that the Avatars were something altogether out of his experience. He regarded them with a mixture of his usual intense curiosity mingled with awe and a little uncertainty. Karal found that mildly amusing. He had the distinct feeling that right up until the moment the *hertasi* first met the Avatars, little Lyam had been something of an agnostic—willing to admit in the reality of something beyond himself, but not at all willing to concede that it had anything to do with him and his everyday world. Like many another historian before him, Lyam was only convinced by verifiable facts. That was what would make him a good historian, rather than someone who was content to repeat all the same old erroneous gossip. The *hertasi* and his mentor Tarrn believed passionately in the truth, would do anything to find out the truth, and would probably do anything to defend the truth. They might find exonerating reasons for a friend who robbed another of property, but if that friend falsified historical documents or concealed relevant facts, they would show him no leniency.

Karal and Lyam arranged the notes in order with the last batch and sealed up the now-full box and put it with those holding Tarrn's precious chronicles. "If you've got a moment, could you give me a hand?" he asked Lyam. "You're better at handling hot rocks than I am."

"That's because you humans are poorly designed," the *hertasi* replied with a toothy grin. "You should have nice thick skin on your hands, preferably with a toughened outer hide or scales, so you can pick up things without hurting yourselves."

"Remind me to ask for that option, the next time I order a new body," Karal countered, as Lyam followed him into the bedchamber. "Then again, isn't that why you were created?"

"To make up for your human shortcomings?" Lyam laughed. "Why, *yes*. Someone besides divine beings needed to.

And just try getting some ghost or Avatar to cook a good meal or mend clothing! We're indispensable!"

Karal laughed with Lyam, and had decided, given the sad condition that Altra had been in when he'd come back from delivering the teleson to Haven, that he would be prepared for a similar situation. When Altra returned from the Forest of Sorrows, he would find food, good water, and a warm bed waiting for him, already prepared and standing ready. The guess was that Altra could return at any time after two days had passed, so in the afternoon of the second day Karal had arranged for all those things. The moment Altra returned he could eat and sleep without even having to ask for food or a warm bed. Karal kept heated stones tucked into the bed he'd made up, and as the warm, meat-laden broth he prepared got a little thick and past its prime flavor, he was usually able to find someone willing to eat the old while he prepared a new batch.

Lyam had been the latest beneficiary of Karal's cooking, and so he wasn't at all averse to helping Karal place more heated stones into the bedding. "So, what do *you* think of all this?" the *hertasi* asked. "Doesn't it seem kind of strange to be bringing in *ghosts*? I've never even met anyone who'd ever seen a ghost before this, had you?"

"It's no stranger than the Avatars, and they're ghosts, I suppose," Karal replied honestly. "I've never seen a ghost either before I got here, but it really doesn't bother me."

Lyam rolled his eyes with disbelief. "How can you be so calm about this? Firesong is planning on bringing a *spirit* here, and an ancient hero at that! Why, that would be like—like calling up Skandranon, or—or Baron Valdemar, or—or the first Son of the Sun! Aren't you excited? Or scared?"

Logically, Karal knew he should be both those things, and yet he couldn't manage to dredge up any real feelings about the situation. It just didn't seem real enough to him, or, perhaps it was only as real as he'd gotten used to. It was not that he was precisely numb about these sorts of events, it was just that long ago he had crossed over his threshold of amazement and now things were only a matter of degree. "Vanyel Ashkevron lived a *long* time ago, Lyam," he said after a long moment of thought. "I know that you're quite passionate about history and to you things that happened hundreds of years ago are as vital as things that happened last year, but honestly, I can't get very emotional about this. Especially not after having met living people who were considered to be very serious enemies of Karse before the Alliance, and discovering that they were really quite like people I knew at home. You know, I'll believe these spirits are going to be here when they arrive, and until then, I don't see any reason to get excited."

"What do you mean, you discovered enemies of Karse were like people you knew?" Lyam wanted to know, as he tried unsuccessfully to juggle three recently-smoking stones. They thudded one by one onto the ground and he scuttled after one that was rolling away, then tucked the last of the hot rocks into Altra's bedding. He flicked his tail as his only comment.

"I actually *know* people who lost family members to Captain Kerowyn's mercenaries, and then, she turned into one of my teachers when I got to Haven," Karal told him. "I found out that she didn't actually eat babies, and she wasn't any more of a monster than any good military commander. And another one of my teachers was a gentleman called Alberich, who actually deserted Karse and his position as a Captain in the Army. He was Chosen, by a Companion who smuggled himself right into Karse! They called him 'The Great Traitor' before the Alliance, and yet I found out later than he was instrumental in bringing the Alliance about. If you believed everything you heard, he was half demon and half witch and was perfectly capable of any atrocity you could name. He turned out to be a great deal like Kerowyn, except maybe his sense of humor is darker than hers."

"Interesting," Lyam said, his eyes lighting up. "I don't suppose you'd be willing to tell me about all that?"

He reached into the pouch that never left his side and took out a silverpoint and paper as he asked that, and Karal didn't have the heart to refuse him. He told the story of his own journey into Valdemar, which seemed to have occurred a hundred years ago, and to some other person entirely. He answered Lyam's questions as best he could, and as honestly as he could, even when the answers made him look rather stupid. Since Lyam was very interested in the details of his thoughts as his opinion of Valdemar and its inhabitants changed, he was as open as possible.

In many ways, he was a bit surprised at the change in himself as he tried to explain himself to Lyam. The talking and questioning helped to fill the time and allay his anxieties, too, and for that reason alone he would have been glad of Lyam's company.

There was always the possibility that all of this would be for nothing; Altra could go and request help, even present Firesong's personal petition to his ancestor Vanyel, but that didn't mean that the spirits were going to cooperate. For one thing, they might not be who they claimed they were. For another, they might not be very interested in helping old enemies. After all, Altra was a representative of Vanyel's old nemesis— and for Vanyel, what was ancient history to Karal was very much a part of his personal memory. This could all be a plot. They could be constructing a trap to hold the spirits here, far from Valdemar and the border they were supposed to be guarding.

The spirits might also be unwilling or unable to leave what had been their home. They hadn't in all this time, so why would they now? They might simply not be able to *help*, and why make the long and dangerous journey to the Tower just to sit and do nothing?

They might not be willing to take the chance that this might start out to be a need for their services, but turn into a situation where Karal could eliminate them entirely. After all, once they were *here* and in his power, Karal might change his mind about them and take it into his head to try an exorcism.

Then shortly after dawn on the third day, Altra returned, and all the doubts were resolved.

Karal was in his bed, and Lyam shook him out of a dark, deep, and dreamless slumber. It took him a moment to understand what the *hertasi* was trying to tell him.

He scrambled out of his bedroll and pulled on his clothing from the night before as soon as it penetrated into his sleep-fuddled mind that Altra was back. He filled a bowl with the hot, rich meat broth he had waiting on a little charcoal brazier, and followed Lyam out into the main room.

Not only was every member of their own party gathered around the Firecat, but a goodly number of the Kal'enedral as well. And if Altra had looked worn out when he brought Sejanes and Master Levy in, he looked positively flattened now. He lay on the floor, panting and disheveled, surrounded by people who all seemed to be talking at once. Without paying any attention to anything else, Karal pushed in among the others and placed the bowl of hot broth under Altra's nose. The Firecat cast him a look of undying gratitude and plunged his face into it, taking great gulps of the liquid rather than lapping it up daintily as he usually did.

:They need a physical link to the real world,: he said as if he was continuing an earlier statement. Karal reflected that being able to Mindspeak was a great advantage in mealtime conversation; you could go right on talking and no one would ever accuse you of bad table manners. It was also fascinating to him that Tarrn, Altra, and Florian could all make their thoughts heard even by those, like Sejanes and Master Levy, who did not have the Gift of Mindspeech themselves. *:So there it is; and I do wish there had been an easier way to transport that bit of wood here than by having me fetch it. It will take them a bit of time to use it to bring themselves here, so be patient. If I'd had to bring them as well, I would have run the risk of losing them in the Void. Besides, Vanyel doesn't particularly care for Gates, and Jumping is a lot like Gating, especially now.:*

"Why wouldn't an Adept care for Gates?" Sejanes wondered aloud when the Firecat's Mindspeech had been related to him.

"Let's just say that I had some unpleasant experiences involving Gates in the past," replied a new voice, a pleasant and musical tenor that had the peculiar quality of sounding as if it came from the bottom of a well, a quality that it shared with some of the Kal'enedrals' voices.

Karal looked where everyone else was looking, but saw no new person there, only an old, decrepit, weather-beaten wreck of a musical instrument. It might at one time have been a lute or a gittern or some such thing; there was no trace at all of its original finish, nor its strings or tuning pegs, and it had probably not been playable for centuries. If this was the physical link that Altra had brought with him, it was certainly a peculiar choice.

"On the whole, I would just rather not have to deal with Gates at all if I have any choice in the matter," the voice continued, and the air above the old instrument began to shiver. *"You'll have to give us a few moments here, as my*

new friend Altra said. None of us are used to drawing our energy from ley-lines and nodes anymore, and we're rather out of practice."

"We're in no hurry, Ancestor, and we have had some interesting experiences involving you and Gates ourselves," Firesong replied calmly, as the hair on the back of Karal's neck began to crawl of its own accord. It had been all very well to tell Lyam that he was neither excited nor afraid when the arrival of these spirits had been an abstract concept, but now. . . .

Now there was an atavistic chill running down his spine, a cold lump in his stomach, and the knowledge that he would really rather be anywhere but here, as the shimmering air developed three glowing forms, which took on substance even as he watched. First, there were only two vaguely human shapes and another, larger one that might have resembled a horse. Then the shapes became more defined and detailed, although they never actually attained the solidity of the Kal'enedral or the fiery substance of the Avatars.

Maybe that was why he was suddenly afraid; the *leshy'a Kal'enedral* looked just like any of the others, and the Avatars were so exotic as to fit in the same categories as Firecats and other manifestations of the gods. But there was nothing solid about these, nor so alien that he could bear them because they were so new to him.

The first to become really clear was a strikingly handsome man, and if this was Firesong's ancestor Vanyel, it was obvious where he got his beauty. There was no color to any of these spirits, so Karal could not have told if the clothing this spirit had chosen to "wear" happened to be antique Herald's Whites or not, but the cut was like nothing he had seen in his lifetime. The spirit had long hair, though not as long as Firesong's or Silverfox's, and "wore" no jewelry of any kind. He searched the group gathered around him, and his gaze lit on Karal and remained there. In spite of the ghost's smile, Karal was *not* reassured.

"So this is our young Sun-priest," the spirit said, as Karal froze. *"If I ever have the opportunity, remind me to tell you of another young servant of Vkandis that I met, who proved to me that not all of the folk who used Vkandis' Name to justify their actions should be lumped together into a single category."* The spirit's smile widened—quite as winsome a

smile as anything Firesong had ever produced—and some of Karal's chill melted away. But not, by any means, all of it. For some reason—perhaps simply that these beings looked, acted and *sounded* exactly like what they were supposed to be— Karal found Vanyel entirely unnerving.

As the second spirit manifested, Karal didn't find him any easier on the nerves, perhaps because he couldn't seem to make up his mind whether to look like a muscular, square-jawed fellow who was a bit taller than Vanyel, or a slight, tri-angular-faced, large-eyed lad who was shorter and more slen-der than the Herald-Mage. Just looking at him made Karal feel dizzy, and when the third shape came into focus, it didn't help any, for it wavered between the form of a Companion and that of a determined woman with a firm chin and the look of a hunter about her.

:If you all don't mind, I'd like to see that bed Karal has been keeping warm for me,: Altra said firmly, and when Karal looked down, he saw that the Firecat had polished off every drop of the broth, and was on his feet, swaying a little.

"You go ahead, my friend," Vanyel said genially. *"We three need to have our first consultation with the mages, and hav-ing too many people trying to explain things at once is not going to get us anywhere. We will try to keep the noise down so you may rest better."*

Since Altra did not look at all steady, Karal picked him up bodily and carried him to that waiting bed, with Florian pac-ing alongside him, offering a shoulder for support. Lyam cleared the way ahead of them, quite authoritative for such a short fellow. Altra was quite limp with exhaustion, and Karal wondered if he should say anything forbidding Altra to make any more Jumping expeditions. Did he have the right to de-mand such things?

:That's the last. That is absolutely the last,: Altra said weakly as Karal laid the Firecat in his warmed bed. *:I know you aren't seeing any physical manifestations of the Storms right now, but believe me, where I have to go, they're there. It was like trying to swim a river in flood, and cats are not particularly suited to swimming, let me tell you. I do not have the strength to try that a second time.:*

"Good, because I was going to ask you not to," Karal re-plied. "I don't think I could stand losing you."

:Well, you won't. That's that advantage of having a Cat instead of a Horse as a partner; we don't go running off to sacrifice ourselves at the sound of the first trumpet call,: Altra said, feebly winking at Karal on the side opposite of Florian. *:We're sensible. And right now, my sensible side demands some cosseting. I want sleep:*

:Oh, do go right ahead and sleep,: Florian said with mock-indignation. *:Don't mind us, we just want to gather worshipfully around your slumbering form and tell stories about your bravery and virtue.:*

:Fine, you do that, and about time,: the Firecat replied in the same spirit. *:Just don't wake me up.:*

And with that, he closed his eyes, his even breathing seeming to indicate that he *had* fallen straight asleep.

"Well, what do *you* think?" Karal asked the Companion, certain he was about to get a litany of praise thinly disguised as a lesson in Valdemaran history.

:I think that I'm hoping our latest visitors remain unmanifest most of the time,: Florian replied promptly, his uneasiness quite apparent in his mind-voice. *:Yfandes gives me the—what's Lyam's term for it?—the collywobbles, that's it. They're all three dreadfully intimidating.:*

"Really?" Karal arched an eyebrow at him. "I didn't think you could be intimidated by anything!"

:I can, and she's it.: Florian was quite serious, and it was Karal's turn to put a steadying hand on his shoulder. *:Not even a Grove-Born gives me the urge to kneel and knock my head on the ground the way she does!:*

"Well, don't do that," Karal advised. "For one thing, you'll hurt your head. For another, I'm sure you have nothing to feel inferior about."

He knew how Florian felt, though, and he sympathized. Hopefully these newcomers would stay invisible; if he couldn't see them, maybe he wouldn't keep having the urge to do some bowing and scraping of his own.

"Ghosts and spirit-swords, Avatars and *leshy'a Kal'enedral*—we have more not-mortal things around here than we have mortal ones!" he complained. "And when you add in bondbirds and *hertasi* and *kyree* and Companions, the weird creatures outnumber ordinary humans to the point where we're a minority!"

:*It could be worse,*: Florian pointed out pensively. :*This could be a Vale. Or k'Leshya Vale! Then you'd have* dyheli *and* tervardi *and gryphons, and I don't know what all else. Only the gods know what weird pets the K'Leshya brought up out of the South with them.*:

Karal just sighed and sat beside Altra with his chin on his hand. "The worst part of it is that a mind-talking horse is the *most* normal of all the folk around here!"

Florian only whickered, and mind-laughed weakly.

Fortunately for Karal's peace of mind and Florian's sense of profound inferiority, the three newcomers mostly remained "unmanifest" to save energy, and simply tendered advice to Firesong by means of Mindspeech. Karal had the feeling that Vanyel was a little hurt that the Karsite was so nervous in Vanyel's presence, but there was no help for it. Karal himself wasn't entirely sure why Vanyel made him so edgy. It might simply have been that the Herald-Mage was everything that Karal was not, but without the somewhat inflated self-esteem of his descendant Firesong. It might have been unconscious residue from all the "Demon Vanyel" stories he'd been told as a child. And it might only have been that Vanyel was so obviously everything that a Karsite feared about the night, and although Karal had been working with stranger beings, Vanyel's presence was simply the one bit of strangeness that was too much.

He had his own problems that were similar to Florian's— the fact that of all of them, *he* was really the most ordinary, and aside from his ability as a Channel, apparently the least necessary. He was not brilliant like Master Levy, nor a mage like Sejanes or Firesong; he could not translate the ancient texts as Tarrn and Lyam could, nor had he the knack of amusing everyone and helping them see solutions to their problems as Silverfox did.

It was Silverfox, however, who made him realize that the things about him that were the most commonplace were the ones that made him the most valuable in this group of those who were out of the ordinary.

"I'm glad we have you here, Karal," Silverfox said to him the next day, as he shared stew that Altra had not been awake to eat with the *kestra'chern.*

"Me?" he said with surprise. "Why?"

"Because your strength is that you are forced to handle wildly extraordinary events and people—and you just *do* it, without complaint. You set the rest of us an example. After all, if you can handle all this, *we* should certainly be able to."

Karal made a face. "I think I'm being damned with faint praise," he replied ironically.

"It isn't meant to be faint praise," Silverfox said earnestly. "What I mean is that you are finding great strength and grace inside yourself, and you prove to the rest of us that we should be able to do the same." He gazed into Karal's eyes with intense concentration. "You keep us centered, reminding us that there is a world out there beyond these walls. You give us perspective in this rather rarefied company, and help keep us all sane." His smile was just as charming as anything Firesong could conjure. "In your own way, my dear young friend, you are a constant reminder of everything normal and good about the world that we are trying to protect."

Karal blushed; that was all he could do, in the face of words like that.

:He's right, you know,: Altra seconded. :It isn't the great mystics and saints who do the real day-to-day work of keeping people's faith firm, it's the ordinary priest—the good man who goes on being good, no matter what he has to face. Ordinary people know in their hearts that they could never withstand the trials that a saint undergoes, but if they see a person who is just like they are, and watch him bearing up under those trials, they know that they can do it, too. And as for the great ones, when they see an ordinary man bearing extraordinary burdens, they are inspired to take on far more than they might otherwise do.:

Now he was blushing so hotly his skin felt sunburned.

"Meanwhile, we *are* having to face a crisis," Silverfox continued, his smile fading as he sobered. "And it is coming on us swiftly. Firesong wanted me to tell you that they're going to use the cube-maze, after all."

That cooled his blushes in a hurry, and he nodded. Silverfox reached for his chin and tilted it up, looking deeply into his eyes, then nodded as if satisfied by what he saw there. "You know that this is the best choice of all of them," he stated. "Firesong says that of all the weapons, this offers the most gain." He said nothing about risk, but he didn't have to, for Karal already knew that the risk of using any of those weapons was great, and they really could not know how great until they triggered one.

Karal nodded. "And I knew that it was quite likely I would have to work as a Channel again. It's all right; I'm not afraid this time."

Strangely enough, he wasn't. "He wanted *me* to tell you, so that you would know he doesn't intend you to have to bear any more than any of the rest of them." Silverfox's ironic expression filled in the rest—things best left unsaid. Karal knew, though, that Firesong would not be able to lie successfully to the *kestra'chern*, and Silverfox would not allow him to put Karal in for more than an equal share of peril. In a sense, Silverfox was vouching for the Adept.

Karal shrugged awkwardly. "The cube-maze was their first choice the last time, they just couldn't come up with enough information to make it work. I'd *rather* be channeling for something that is their first choice, rather than their third or fourth."

He didn't pretend to understand half of what the mages were talking about, but the device they called a "cube-maze," which resembled a pile of hollow cast-metal cubes stacked rather randomly atop one another, was supposed to have had a nonliving core to do the channeling. Either Urtho could never get the thing to work correctly in the first place, or else the core was no longer functioning. In either case, there was no one here that was capable of making a device to act as the channel. That meant Karal was the only hope of making this thing work. It *might* work better with a living channel; that might have been one of the reasons it had failed in the first place. A living channel could make decisions; a nonliving channel couldn't.

Like the other devices here, the cube-maze didn't look anything like a weapon. It was rather pretty, in fact; there was an odd sheen or patina to the blue metal surface that refracted rainbows, like oil on water. One of the truly strange things about all of these weapons was that none of them looked alike. It was difficult to imagine how the same mind could have come up with so many dissimilar devices.

"Karal!" Master Levy hailed him from the main room. "The teleson is free, and Natoli is on it."

Silverfox cut short Karal's attempt at excusing himself politely. "Go, off with you!" the *kestra'chern* said. "You can talk to me anytime, and I'm not half so pretty as Natoli is."

That last comment made him blush all over again, but this time he didn't care. His long-distance romancing of Natoli appeared to charm everyone. They all stayed discreetly out of the way when he spoke to her, and they all seemed to go out of their way to give him occasions to talk to her on the teleson.

Altra followed on his heels, to act as the facilitator for the conversation. It was amazing that Altra didn't ever tease him about anything that passed between himself and Natoli, but even Altra apparently regarded the growing relationship as a private matter between the two of them, and not for any outsider, not even a Firecat, to intrude upon. No matter what either of the two said to each other, Altra never commented on it, either during the conversation or afterward. In fact, Karal was able to completely forget about Altra's presence most of the time.

But Natoli had disturbing news for him that had nothing whatsoever to do with their personal matters. "Elspeth and Darkwind reported that they are already getting Storms in Hardorn," she said gravely. "They aren't dangerous yet, but it's only a matter of time before things degenerate. We have already started preparations here to handle whatever comes up."

"That's probably why the mages and all finally made up their minds which device to use," he told her. "I suppose Master Levy must have agreed on their choice, since he is the one doing the mathematical modeling for the solution." He hesitated, and looked down at his hands a moment, then looked back up and told her the truth. "I'm going to have to be a Channel again."

She didn't say anything, but her face grew pale and she bit her lip. "Well," she finally managed, "that's what you're there for. You have to do your job, just as I have to do mine." She rallied a bit. "Speaking of my job, I'm in charge of some of the emergency plans. We're going to have to evacuate the Palace at the very least, and maybe even parts of Haven, just in case that node under the Palace goes unstable. All the highborn have gone home, and as of today they've dismissed the Collegia and sent the trainees home as well. Even the Healers have dispersed. The trainees that don't have homes to go to are supposed to go off with their Masters if they're Bards, off to one of the Houses of Healing as Healer-trainees, or riding circuit with full Heralds if they're still in Grays. It's a little crazy around here, since things still have to get done, and it's getting to be that whoever has a pair of hands free just does whatever it takes. They say that the gryphons will stay until the last moment and set spells to keep out looters, then they'll fly away. It'll be a relief when everyone is actually gone."

He didn't have to ask why she was still there; she could not sit back while others were in danger any more than he could. She would probably remain there until the very end because that was what her father would do. Herald Rubrik was in Karse, so perhaps she felt it was up to her to take on the familial duties. "Well," he replied. "You do what you have to, right? If your job is to be there, then you need to do it." Clumsy words, but he hoped they told her what he wanted to say— that he still would never ask her to stop doing what she considered to be her job just to be "safe." If there even *was* any place "safe" anymore. "I want you to know that I really don't think any of us here are in any more or less danger than you are," he continued, trying to give her reassurance. "The one thing I *am* concerned about is that after the last time, the others here are all so fiercely determined to protect me that I'm more afraid for them than I am for myself."

She smiled tremulously. "You would be anyway. Just promise me that you'll let them take care of you. Not at the expense of getting the job done, but let them protect you from what they can."

"If you'll do the same," he demanded. "Before you go flinging yourself into exploding boilers, wait and see if someone more suited to that particular job is already doing it! You know, it just *might* be that, capable as you are, someone else would manage that particular rescue a little better than you!"

"You drive a hard bargain," she retorted, and shook her head, a little of her old humor returning to her eyes. "All right, I promise."

"And so do I," he pledged softly, and basked in her smile.

*   *   *

The wind of a full-scale blizzard howled and whined outside the windows of his suite, and icy drafts forced their way past windows and thick curtains, but Baron Melles didn't care. Enveloped in one of the heavy woolen tunics that had become fashion out of necessity, with a second layer of knitted winter silk beneath that, he brooded pleasantly over the reports of his network of spies within the households of the members of the Court. Virtually every one of those pieces of paper reported a new attitude toward him on the part of anyone of any importance.

Fear. He was delighted at their reaction. They might hate him, they might envy him, they might (rarely) even admire him for his ruthlessness—but they all feared him now, and feared to have even the appearance of opposing him.

He shifted his weight in his chair, and repositioned his feet on the warming pan beneath his desk. His last object lesson was more effective than he had thought it would be, and had spread far beyond the immediate household and friends of his target. Clearly it was *much* wiser and more expedient to show that the children of his would-be enemies were vulnerable than it was to threaten the enemies themselves. And as for those who had no children, well, there wasn't a single one of them who didn't have *some* other person for whom they cherished tender feelings. Anyone who would threaten a child obviously would have no difficulty with targeting an aged and infirm parent, or a sibling, or a lover. Even Tremane had dependents he would have been very upset at losing—that old mage, Sejanes, for one.

It was ironic in many ways, for it would have been very easy for any of them to make him or herself invulnerable. There had not been another person besides himself here at Court who had read and understood the lesson old Charliss had given to them in the course of his own life: *Trust no one, care for no one, depend on no one.* They had all persisted, even in the face of obvious disadvantages, to fall in love, make friendships rather than alliances, and allow themselves the cracks in their armor that *relationships* made.

Tremane never knew that he made me what I am today, even as he made me his enemy when we were cadets. He betrayed me to the Colonel, and ruined my career in the Army. And for what? Because I was doing what everyone else

*wanted to do, but didn't have the intelligence or the audacity
to try. I trusted him because he said he was my friend, and
he betrayed me. Without that, if I had remained in the cadet
corps as he did, I would not have seen Charliss' example for
what it was.*

He had stopped being a sheep that day and had become one
of the wolves—as any of them could have. Well, that was all
their own fault, and their stupidity, and that was why he was
the Emperor's Heir and not one of them.

Not even the memory of that long-ago humiliation of being
cast out of the corps could spoil this triumph. He had finally
achieved the goal he had set for himself that day—to make
anyone of any importance look at him and fear. It was in this
mood of unusual good humor that General Thayer found him,
and destroyed his mood with a single sentence.

His valet Bors showed the General in; Thayer wore a regula-
tion Army cloak over his uniform tunic, and fingerless gloves
to keep his hands warm. Melles greeted him with pleasure,
although he did not rise.

But Thayer had not come to make a social call. "Melles,
we're in trouble," he rumbled. And as usual, the General came
straight to the point without even waiting to take the chair
that Melles offered him.

Where had that come from? "How can we be in trouble?"
Melles asked, with more than a bit of surprise. "We've got
order in the smaller cities, and the larger ones are coming
around. Food is getting in, and you're even making a small
profit. Rioting has stopped in most places, and the subversives
are beginning to be regarded as lunatics. We might have lost
the lands Charliss brought under the Imperial banner and
some of the provinces, but—"

"But the Army doesn't want you in charge," Thayer replied,
bluntly. "That last little trick you played was one too many.
The word from the field is that they don't intend to establish
order just to put a baby killer on the Iron Throne. Word of your
power play has been traveling farther and faster than either of
us thought it would. I don't know how, but in spite of everything, virtually everyone I've contacted already knows all
about it, and knows that you were the one who put the body
in the crib." He scowled. "That was a stupid ploy, Melles.

Your average soldier may be a hard man, but the one thing he won't put up with is threatening a baby."

Melles frowned. "But there was nothing to link me with that incident," he objected.

Thayer snorted with utter contempt, as the wind rattled the windowpanes and a draft made the candle flames flicker. "Please. Not everyone is an inbred idiot, especially not in the Army. You're an assassin, however much you pretend not to be; everyone knows it, and everyone knows you're the only one who not only could have done what you did, but who is cold-blooded enough to follow up on the threat if you had to. And I repeat to you; the Army won't support a baby killer, and there's an end to it.

A cold anger burned in the back of Melles' throat, as cold as the howling winds outside. "That's fine sentiment from people who kill for a living," he said with equal contempt. "I'm sure they ask the age of every peasant with a boar-spear who opposes them in the field, and make certain to leave insurgent villages untouched in case they *might* kill a few children."

Thayer's face flushed with anger, but somehow he kept his temper even in the face of Melles' provocative words. "I could point out that the Army operates under certain laws, and that when a soldier kills someone, he does it openly, under conditions where his opponent has an equal chance of killing *him*. But that would be specious and we both know it—and it's not the point."

"Oh?" Melles asked sardonically. "And just what is the point?"

"The point is that the average soldier *believes* all those things," Thayer said, pounding the desk for emphasis. "Whether or not they are true. Truth has no bearing on this, and you damned well know it. The average soldier thinks he is going to defend the honor of the Empire against *adult* enemies, and that makes him feel superior to any assassin, and vastly superior to someone who not only threatens the safety of a child, but threatens a child of his own people."

"Never mind that this same noble soldier would skewer the children of a rebellious village without a second thought or a moment of hesitation," Melles grumbled, although he saw the logic in Thayer's argument. Thayer was right. The truth didn't matter here, and he, who was a practiced hand in manipulating perception, should have known that. "Very well. What's to be done?"

Thayer sighed, and finally sank into the chair Melles had offered. "I don't know," he admitted. "It's not only the Commanders that are talking rebellion, it's the Generals, and the rank and file, and they aren't amenable to the kinds of coercion you can use on the nobles of the Court. Unless we can do something about this, we're going to lose them, and the moment Charliss becomes a Little God, they're going to put someone of their choice on the Iron Throne and you and me in the ground."

Melles ground his teeth in frustration, for Thayer was right. Although, unlike Tremane, he had never gotten out of the cadets to serve in the military forces of the Empire, he knew the structure and makeup. The Generals were mostly men who had made a career of the military, as had their fathers before them. Their wives were the daughters of similar men, their families all related to other military families. They employed former military men as guards and servants, employed the wives of such men as maids and housekeepers. Their positions were embedded in multiple layers of protection, and they could not be dismissed or demoted out of hand. The High Commanders could be eliminated, for they were mostly nobles like Grand Duke Tremane, but there was no getting rid of the Generals. They were like a wolf pack; you couldn't separate a victim, for none of them stood alone, and if you made a move against one, the whole pack would consolidate long enough to tear your throat out before going back to their own internal jockeying for power.

"You can't touch them, Melles," Thayer warned in an echo of his own thoughts. "If you try, they'll destroy you. They won't put up with that kind of threat, and they'll close ranks against you. Press it too far, and they'll call a coup against you. Not even your personal guard can protect you against an entire Company coming to kill you."

"It's gone right down to the rank and file, you say?" he asked, his thoughts swirling as wildly as the snow outside.

Thayer nodded, and Melles cursed them all in his mind. He couldn't even order every General within reach of the capital to come to a meeting, seal the room, and kill them all at once. If he tried, the entire Army itself would rise up in revolt. It was only when the Generals were corrupt and hated by their men that you could get away with a tactic like that.

"We're only in trouble, we aren't defeated yet," he said at last, as a few ideas began to form out of the chaos. "They might have good communications, but I have better ones. I have a few more throws of the dice coming, and *I* can pick the dice." He began to smile as he saw how he could completely subvert the entire problem.

Thayer regarded him curiously, and with a certain grudging admiration. "Have you got something up your sleeve that you haven't told me about?"

He nodded. "I'm not even going to try to deny their rumor, instead I'm going to give them something else entirely to think about. I always have more up my sleeve that I haven't told anyone about," he replied smugly. "And you should never underestimate the power of the clerical pen."

"What you can't find, you can manufacture, hmm?" Thayer hazarded. "Just what, exactly, do you have in mind? Are you going to give them a different enemy to concentrate on?"

Melles just laughed. "I won't have to manufacture anything. With enough records to search, I can find just about anything I need, and you know yourself that this Empire creates enough paperwork to fill entire warehouses. Give me a few days and I can find all the right evidence to convince the Army that I'm the one they should be supporting, show them that having a so-called 'baby killer' on the throne is the *least* of the things they should be worrying about, and in the meantime, I can woo them."

"Woo them? Like reluctant girls?" Thayer made a rude and suggestive noise, but Melles wasn't offended, now that he had the bit in his teeth.

"Wait and see," he responded, plans already growing in the back of his mind that would probably astonish the older man. "Just wait and see."

Thayer was not convinced, but was certain enough of Melles' competence to be willing to buy him some time to work on the schemes that he promised. Thayer stood up, saying so in as many words.

"Just remember that I can't give you too much more time," he warned. "And it's going to take a great deal to overcome the way they feel about the baby incident. I'm still not certain you're taking that seriously enough."

"Just remember what I told you about the common man and what he needs and wants," Melles replied. "Then remember that the Army is composed of those same common men— just with a little more training and a bit of discipline."

"Hmm." Thayer looked thoughtful at that, and took his leave. As soon as he was gone, Melles called in all five of his private secretaries.

They were all men, like his valet, of varied talents and some interesting training. All five of them were so nondescript that no one would ever notice them in a crowd. And all of them were adept at getting into even the most carefully guarded records, simply by knowing how to impersonate virtually any type of clerk in the Empire and how to forge anything but the Imperial Seal. When a clerk arrived with appropriate documentation and a request to see something, or even to carry it away, it took a hardier and more independent soul than existed in the Imperial Civil Service to challenge him.

"You—" he said, pointing to the first in line. "I want you to go over the military pay records, find out all the units with pay in arrears, and who is in charge of their pay." He pointed to the next two. "You and you—go through the records of the units sent to take Hardorn. I want you to match up the requests for supplies and reinforcements with the orders issued to fill those requests. I also want the record of every request that was denied, and on whose authority." He pointed to the last two. "You two get access to Emperor Charliss' private papers, or at least the ones that are in the Archives. I want all the correspondence between Tremane and Charliss from the time he left for Hardorn to his last known message. Go!"

The five clerks departed, scattering like quail before the hunter. He didn't need to give them any further orders about *how* to get access to those papers; one of the reason that these men were no longer *in* the civil service was that they had initiative. Neither initiative nor creativity were rewarded in the Imperial Civil Service, and those with both often grew frustrated and looked for employment elsewhere.

Melles next called in his private treasurer.

"You get down to the Imperial Exchequer. I want to know how much out of the military budget can be spared in hard

coin and how much in goods. Tell the Exchequer that I suspect the Army's pay has been bollixed up, and we may have
to make good in a hurry if we don't want trouble on our
hands." He thought for a moment, and dredged up the relevant fact from his memory. "If he balks at telling you, just say
something about the road budget; it doesn't matter what, just
work it quickly into the conversation."

The man nodded, grinning; every Imperial Exchequer
skimmed a certain amount off the top, it was expected, so
long as they were clever enough not to get caught at it. But
if they *were* caught, the penalties were severe. Melles knew
precisely where the current Exchequer was skimming and
even had a rough idea of how much; he had made it his business to know, planning to use the information at the right
moment. There could be no better moment than now. A good
card was no better than a bad one if you never played it.

The treasurer left, and Melles called in his final choice in
this campaign of seduction, one of his odder employees. This
rather elegant specimen was ostensibly Melles' personal poet
and playwright, but although the man was mediocre cre-
atively, he was an absolute genius at propaganda. Melles
didn't use him often, but he was, like the valet, the appropriate scalpel for certain types of surgery. Melles was doubly
fortunate in that the man enjoyed the writing of manipulative
propaganda almost as much as poetry. He had told his patron
once that when he wrote the former, he considered that he
was writing a different kind of drama, one in which the words
manipulated the actors, instead of the other way around. He
enjoyed seeing how his works played out on the larger stage
of the real world.

And as a peculiar kind of reward, Melles regularly financed
the production of poetry readings in opulent surroundings,
seeing to it that the right critics were flattered, fed, and given
enough strong and exotic drink to make even the worst drivel
seem inspired.

"I hope you aren't in the throes of creation," Melles said
cautiously, for this was one individual who could not be coerced, only persuaded. But his loyalty to Melles was based on
firm self-interest and was utterly trustworthy. When bought,
he stayed bought—and no one aside from Melles himself
knew that he was anything other than a peculiar affectation.

It was expected that someone of Melles' status patronize the arts in some way, and a poet was the cheapest and least intrusive sort of artist to have on one's staff. "I have a rather extensive job for you," he continued. "I hope you aren't preoccupied."

The man smiled urbanely and crossed his legs with conscious elegance. He was something of a dandy and rather fancied himself as a popular man with the ladies. His salary from Melles enabled him to cut quite a figure of sartorial splendor among not only his peers but also his superiors. "What do you need my skills for? As a repairer of reputation? I've been planning what to do for you since the moment the rumors began to fly." He shook his head, and then waggled his finger in mock-admonition. "My dear patron, you have been very injudicious. This could ruin you yet, if it isn't carefully handled."

Melles did not make the retort he felt hovering on his tongue. The man was worth his weight in gold, and was arrogant enough to be quite aware of it. Instead, he got right to the point. "It isn't the Court I'm worried about; they're ineffectual enough, and like sheep, they'll follow anyone with the right bell around his neck. No, it's the Army that's giving me trouble." He leaned forward over his desk, to emphasize how serious he felt the situation was. "They've decided they don't care for the idea of someone with my ethics on the Iron Throne."

The poet pursed his lips. "That could be troublesome. I don't know quite how to handle the Army—unless you already know what you want to say?"

"I do. Believe it or not, I want you to report the exact truth." Melles smiled thinly at the poet's surprise. "We're going to concentrate on the plight of my old rival, Tremane," he continued lightly. "I want you to spread the story of how he and his command were abandoned out beyond the farthest reach of the Empire. Be creative; go on about the horror of being sent off to die in utterly unknown lands. Find the right words to convince people that *I* had nothing to do with the abandonment of Tremane and his men in Hardorn. Then convince them that I had no idea that I would be Charliss' next choice for his successor. Say that I feel that the times are so radically changed that I have changed with them. Say I personally am so busy trying to keep the Empire together that I have no interest in pursuing my old vendetta against Tremane himself."

That last could get him in a certain amount of difficulty with the Emperor if Charliss got wind of it, but he was willing to take that particular chance.

The poet pursed his lips in thought. "It's a novel approach," he admitted. "And it just might distract soldiers from the stories of dead bodies in baby cribs. After all, you didn't actually kill the *baby*, you only dumped the body of an assassin there. Whereas Tremane and his men were abandoned in Hardorn; that's without a doubt and with no particular reason to leave them out there."

"That's exactly what I'm looking for," Melles encouraged. "And soldiers have more in common with other soldiers than with brats in cribs. They will have empathy for Tremane's forces. Why weren't they called back while it was still possible to construct Portals that worked between the Storms? Don't place any blame yet, but raise as many questions in peoples' minds as you can, particularly in the Army."

"I can do that," the poet said decisively, losing a great deal of his languid pose as his own imagination set to work. "I'm very good at questions. What about answers?"

"I'll give you more to work on when I have facts," Melles promised. "For right now, this will be enough. Get people talking, get their minds on something else besides my little jokes." He signaled that the man could go.

"Gossip and rumor, opiates of the dull, can for the clever be the stuff that dream are made of," the poet said sardonically, as he smiled, standing up as gracefully as he had sat down.

"My dreams, at any rate," Melles chuckled, watching the man's elegant way of walking—elegant, but not at all effeminate. It was rather like a wolf at the stalk, and he made up his mind to copy it.

The first of his seekers came back within hours with an accurate account of the Army pay records. As he had suspected, since every district governor was individually responsible for seeing to it that the units within his jurisdiction actually *were* paid (even though the pay actually came out of the military budget), there were several instances where pay was in arrears, sometimes significantly. As he went over the figures with his own accountant, the secretary he had sent to interview the Imperial Exchequer also returned.

That gave him his first move in the new game.

He waited until the next day, then descended on the major figures of the Imperial Civil Service, trailing a string of clerks all bearing stacks of paper. With great fanfare and a fine speech written by his pet poet, he "revealed" the terrible injustice that had been done to the loyal soldiers of the Empire.

"But it is not your fault," he continued, before anyone could get angry at having yet *more* work heaped on him. "You are doing the best you can in terrible circumstances!" He went on at some length, praising the overworked clerks for sticking at their jobs even when they had to wade through blizzards to get to their desks, shiver in the drafts when they arrived, and fight worse weather to go to a cold home with short rations once they returned at the end of a long day's work. "I have brought you the help of my *own* clerks to see you through this crisis," he said, as his men took over empty desks or any other flat space with a chair. "I am sure you do not want our brave soldiers to suffer, but I do not want you to suffer either!"

With that, he set off a frenzy of paper pushing to get every soldier's records and pay up to date. Some of the pay had to be made in goods rather than coin, but he made certain that the clerks arranged it so the goods in question were more valuable on the gray market than the actual pay they were substituting for.

It was all taken care of in a single morning; not too difficult, when he doubled the existing workforce and had all of them concentrate on the one task, putting all other work temporarily aside. He then formally went to the Commanders and promised to personally make up for the other deficiencies that had cropped up, usually in the way of resupply. He made a great show of embarrassment, as if he had only now discovered these problems. He didn't know if anyone believed him, but he made a point of assigning his own people to make certain that existing problems were corrected and further ones reported to him so that he could see that they were dealt with.

As he had hoped, although there was some suspicion that he was trying to buy the Army's favor, he began to get some grudging acceptance. This was especially true once the stories began to circulate of how he had uncovered all these problems personally.

Then his poet went to work, sending out his insidious little stories and questions, making the ordinary Imperial soldier wonder just what "supposed mistake" could have left Tremane's people out in the cold, so to speak. An added bonus came when he got word back that the rank-and-file had a few other, unanticipated questions. Such as—a question of whether the late pay was really just bureaucratic bungling, or if Certain Parties had ordered the pay held back as a form of punishment. After all, if Grand Duke Tremane and all his men could be abandoned, what was a little delay in paying out wages?

But the crowning touch to the entire plan finally went into effect when Melles' clerks found that correspondence between Charliss and Tremane. And he could not have manufactured a better final letter than the one that arrived for the Emperor's personal perusal just before the Portals went down and stayed down.

It was bad enough that Tremane had begged, over and over again, for critical supplies that were never sent, for more men, and especially for more mages. But it was the final letter that made Melles positively gleeful both from the standpoint of seeing his old enemy brought low, and for the strength of the "ammunition" it gave him.

For in that letter, which was accompanied by strategic maps, Tremane begged the Emperor to allow his men to retreat, vowing that he himself would remain behind and attempt to hold what had been taken with a corps of volunteers. He pleaded with the Emperor not to visit punishment upon men who had done nothing to deserve it, and to permit them to escape while it was still possible to hold Portals to the Empire open long enough for them to pass through.

And although Melles himself was no strategist, it was painfully obvious from the maps that Tremane's position was utterly untenable. No one, not even a military genius, could have saved the situation.

In a handwritten directive, the Emperor ordered his secretaries to make no response to this desperate plea, on the grounds that Tremane would have to solve the situation in order to prove his worth, thus condemning Tremane's forces with him. At that point, the best outcome for them was exile—and the worst was massacre.

He took that letter with the note in the margin to General Thayer, who in turn leaked the information to his own Commanders, who sent it on down the line. He managed to conceal his triumph in a show of distress so perfect he even fooled Thayer.

By this time the Army was outraged. The Emperor had betrayed them, betrayed the sacred bond that was supposed to bind the Emperor and the men who served him. The rumors of Melles the "baby killer" were forgotten in this new, and far more personal outrage, and even the lowest private began to recall how it was *Melles* who saw that the pay was put right, and *Melles* who made sure the supply wagons got through.

Melles, and not the Emperor. And in that moment, he had them.

That was the point where he got an odd invitation from General Thayer; an invitation to dinner, but not in the Palace. This was to be a private dinner, in an upper room of a very well-known and luxurious inn usually frequented by wealthy bachelors who didn't care to keep staff or cooks.

There were just a few things "wrong" with this invitation— the most obvious being that Melles was not and had never been part of the social circle that made use of this particular facility. The inn itself was suffering some of the privations of every other eatery; the fare now was far from the former standards, and in fact was inferior to anything he could get in Crag Castle. And it was halfway across the city; the mage-storms struck twice a day now, with the result that the weather was utterly unpredictable, and there were often "things" prowling the streets, animals and even humans changed by the Storms into misshapen creatures that bore little resemblance to what they had been. The once-rats were bad enough, but the other creatures required that one travel with an escort of heavily-armed men after dark.

He turned the invitation over and over in his hands, considering it. It could be a trap, of course, designed to get him where he would be vulnerable and eliminate him. But somehow, he didn't think so. To meet in a public tavern in so remote a place suggested a need for secrecy. The private salons of these large inns had separate, outside entrances, so that people could come and go without being seen. This had the earmarks of a conspiracy.

I had better go. If anyone is going to make an attempt on the Emperor—assuming that is why they want me—I had better be in a position to advise them.

It wasn't the best plan, but it was better than allowing them to make an attempt that would fail, and would alarm Charliss. The Emperor was already unstable, and it wouldn't take a great deal to set him off on a campaign to purge the Court.

And if necessary, I can always turn them in myself, proving my loyalty to Charliss. That would be the court of last resort, however, if he could not persuade them to hold off until he was ready. Betraying them to Charliss would cost him so much difficulty once *he* was Emperor that such a move was not advisable unless there was no other possible course of action.

There was the possibility that this invitation was the setup for an assassination attempt on him, but he didn't think that they would be that stupid. An assassin himself, as they well knew, he would be a very difficult man to take down. Granted, a large number of men could overpower him, but as he had already proved, he was, despite all appearances, still perfectly capable of defending himself and killing or maiming several of them before they managed to kill him. Such an affair would be noisy and leave many witnesses who would have to be silenced or eliminated. He would have his own men with him, who would also have to be silenced or eliminated, and those men would have the superiors they reported to and families of their own who would miss them. It would turn into a nightmare of murder, and be impossible to cover up. They had to be aware of all of that.

With great reluctance, he called his valet and ordered clothing for the cold, arranged an armed Imperial escort to take care of the hobgoblins, alerted his personal bodyguard, and ordered a carriage-on-runners; nothing else could handle the icy streets now. People had to step up from their doorsteps to the street instead of down, for there was rock-hard, packed snow to the depth of the knee on most of the streets, snow that would not be gone until spring.

He was just glad that he had invested every bit of his magecraft in shielding; mages who had not done so were in a state of near-collapse every time a Storm passed through. He barely noticed; he got a headache just before each Storm, a bit of disorientation during it, and a touch of nausea afterward. Nothing was bad enough to even interrupt his reading. But another Storm was due about the time he expected to be on the street, and anyone who was likely to be severely affected by the Storms could find himself in deadly danger in a situation of that nature. A person walking alone could collapse and freeze to death, he could be set upon and robbed, and a person riding in a conveyance could *still* freeze to death without his escort noticing.

He wondered how many marginally-Talented mages had been caught and hurt or killed that way. *If so, that simply cuts down on the number of idiots with mage-power,* he reflected, as he pulled on a second set of gloves over his first set, and worked his feet into heavy sheepskin-lined boots. It was difficult to be both dressed for warmth and for elegance, and he opted, at least in his outermost garments, for the first.

The journey to the inn was something of an unpleasant ordeal, and he wondered at the number of people who still continued to make their daily trips from home to place of employment, went out shopping, or indeed, did *anything* that took them out of doors. The weather was hideous, as it was more often than not now. There was the usual blizzard blowing, driving snow deep into the fabric of one's clothing, making it impossible to see the linkmen bearing lanterns who lit the way for the driver, if they got more than a few paces ahead of the carriage. And yet there *were* other people out on the street, including some women, which amazed him. His escort changed places regularly, so that some rode while others walked.

When they were about a third of the way to his destination, a pack of hobgoblins attacked—hairy things that scrabbled through the snow on all fours, drooling and howling with hunger, their ribs clearly prominent even through their heavy brindled coats of fur. This time, it appeared that they were Changedogs, rather than Changechildren, which made it a bit easier on the escort; the men had a difficult time killing things that cried like babies and had human eyes or faces. It wasn't too difficult to beat the pack back, leaving a few bleeding, fur-covered bodies in the snow. So far, Changed creatures were routinely less intelligent than the creatures they had been changed *from*, and Changedogs were probably the most stupid of them all; they kept charging straight ahead even when that tactic clearly did not work. The exception was Changerats, which were more cunning and vicious, and swarmed in packs of several hundred. There were laws about Changed animals and people now; if your pet or relative was Changed, the only way to keep it (or him) was to take it to an Imperial examiner who would verify that it was no danger to humans or livestock. There were few Changechildren being kept and sheltered by relatives. Most were actually killed by their own families the moment they Changed, for the horror stories circulating about the bloodbaths some of the Changed had wrought in their own households did not encourage compassion. A few who found themselves Changed had killed themselves. Most of the Changechildren who roamed the streets as hobgoblins had come *from* the streets—were beggars, thieves, and other street people who had no relatives to eliminate them and no interest in anything other than survival.

The rest of the journey was spent nervously watching for another pack of attackers. When they finally did arrive at the inn, it was fully dark, and in the interest of keeping his employees satisfied enough to keep their mouths shut, he distributed a generous purse among them so that they could entertain themselves in fine style in the common room while he met with Thayer and Thayer's guests in the private room above.

His men entered the common room at the side entrance; he entered the main entrance, stepping out of the screaming wind and snow into a sheltering foyer, softly lit and blessedly warm and attended by a discreet footman. Music played faintly somewhere; a full consort of wind and string instruments. The footman directed him up a staircase to the right to another foyer, this time attended by one of Thayer's personal servants, who took his snow-caked outer clothing and directed him inside the door behind him.

He was not at all surprised to see that besides Thayer, virtually every other important military leader in the area of the capital was there already, waiting, with an excellent supper (as yet untouched) set up on a sideboard. All eyes were on him as he entered, and the murmur of talk that had been going on stopped for a moment, then resumed.

He took his place beside Thayer, was introduced to those he did not know personally, and Thayer's servants proceeded to serve all of the guests. He watched them carefully, and noted that they only served him food from dishes that everyone shared, and only after stirring up the contents within his sight, so that there could be no "special" little spot that had been prepared for him with poison. He kept his approving smile to himself, and pretended not to notice. Dinner conversation was not precisely light, since a great deal of it had to do with the roving packs of hobgoblins and suggested means of eradicating them, but it had nothing whatsoever to do with politics. There was another peculiarity of Thayer's servants; they never handled knives themselves, deferring to Thayer for carving of meat, and they were unarmed. As for Thayer's guests, they were *conspicuously* unarmed. Everything that could have been done to reassure a professional killer that he was safe among them had been done.

So, it wasn't to be an assassination attempt after all. That meant it was a conspiracy.

And the moment that the meal was over, the dishes cleared away, the wine poured and more left in decanters on the table, and the servants sent off, the conspiracy was revealed.

They wanted to be rid of Charliss before he did any more damage, and they were perfectly willing to send him on to Godhood a little sooner.

He listened to them with great patience, making no comments, only nodding occasionally when they seemed to require it. They were understandably angry at many of the things that had been going on, and his revelations concerning Tremane had essentially been the trigger for all their pent-up frustrations. They were quite prepared to eliminate the Emperor themselves, and had a good, solid plan for doing so. He told them as much, and commended them for having a plan that took care of almost every aspect of the situation.

"*Almost,*" he repeated with emphasis. "But I would be remiss if I did not point out the major flaw in your plan. And I do not blame you gentlemen for not considering the aspect I have in mind."

"Which is what, exactly?" asked General Thayer, who was acting as the primary spokesman.

"Magic." He held up a hand to forestall any objections. "I know that, given how your own mages are acting with the increasing severity and frequency of the mage-storms, that mages seem an insignificant aspect to you. Please believe me; they are not. You have determined that the spells binding the Imperial Guard to Charliss are broken and have not been replaced; that is good news, but those are not the only magics you need to worry about. Charliss himself is a powerful mage, and his power is augmented by an entire corps of lesser mages whose minds have been his for many years. They spend themselves to ensure *his* continued prosperity, and that is what you are not seeing in dealing with your own mages, who would do no such thing. Surely you gentlemen recall seeing Charliss' mages before—that group of rather blank-eyed individuals who trail about after him like so many adoring, mindless maidens trailing about after a handsome warrior?"

He looked around the table, and saw to his satisfaction that although there was disappointment in their faces, there was reluctant agreement there as well, and nods all around.

"At the moment, Charliss is only moderately inconvenienced by the Storms, as opposed to the vast majority of mages, who are prostrated by them." He steepled his fingers together thoughtfully, and considered his next words. "As a mage myself, let me explain to you, if I may, the true effect the Storms are having on mages—and that is primarily in our *choice* of actions. The choice for a mage at the moment is simple: Preserve all of your own power for shields, or work other magics and have each Storm that passes send you to your bed for hours, recovering." He saw more nods, as the Generals recognized the effects he had just described. "Because Charliss is using the power from his corps of mages, he can shield *and* work other magics, and not suffer. That is what makes him dangerous, still. You might well get past his guards, even past his personal bodyguards; you might get past the protections put in by his personal mages, but by then he will be alerted and you will never get an assassin past his own defenses."

There were still a few of the generals who were not convinced; Melles saw it in their closed expressions.

"There is one more factor to be considered here, and that is what would happen afterward," he continued. "The old man still retains the loyalty of too many people—including most of the truly powerful mages of the Empire—who consider me to be an upstart. As it happens, most of them favored Tremane, who was a personal favorite of the mages who taught him, many of whom are now quite influential. I do not know if the truth of what happened to poor Tremane would turn their opinion against the Emperor, but if you remove him now, you will not give that truth a chance to work in their minds."

Now he had all of them; the last of the skeptical looks was gone, replaced with resignation.

"Please wait," he said, at his most persuasive. "The Emperor has made no attempt to say or do anything about the truths that are spreading about his treatment of Tremane. I suspect this is because he is living in a very narrow world of reasoning at the moment. He wants revenge on Tremane for 'betraying' the Empire, and he may believe that people assume he cut Tremane off after that 'betrayal' rather than before. The Hundred Little Gods know that by now he may even believe that himself!"

A couple of the oldest of the Generals pursed their lips and looked just a touch regretful; some of the youngest only looked smug. Both expressions were probably prompted by the same thought—*how far the Emperor has fallen!* The old were thinking that Charliss' mental deterioration could easily be something they would experience if they were unlucky; the young were thinking only that it was terrible for someone that old, in that state, to still be in power.

Melles continued, seeing that he was bringing them to the line of thought *he* wanted them to follow. "Charliss looks physically worse with every day that passes. He may die soon on his own; his life is sustained by magic, and that is eroding no matter how desperately he shores it up. Let things take their natural course." He allowed himself a small, modest smile. "After all, I *am* the one who is really holding the reins now; Charliss is too busy concentrating on survival. Waiting will harm nothing in the long run. With time, I may be able to persuade those same mages that Charliss is using them with no regard for the cost to them, and no regard for the *real* enemy we face—the Storms."

Thayer looked around the table, and seemed to take some kind of unspoken consensus from his colleagues. "Very well," he said. "We will hold our hands. We agree that the real danger to the Empire is the mage-storms and the continuing refusal of the Emperor to adequately deal with them. *You* must see what you can do to convince the mages that Charliss is no longer capable of dealing with the true priorities of this situation."

He sat back in his chair and nodded. This was exactly how he wanted *everything* to fall out, and he relished the moment even as he relished a single sip of wine. If he were to prosper as Emperor, the Empire itself must survive and prosper; in order for that to happen, he *must* redirect the energies and attention of the Empire on the Storms and their effects. Just now, the energies and attentions of the Empire were seriously divided between one selfish old man who had outlived his usefulness, and the struggles to survive through worsening conditions. Either Charliss must go, or the Empire, for only one would survive through the Storms.

"I will deal with the mages, and believe me, we *must* have them," he said. "Remember, Tremane is our key. Even as the Army realized that Charliss had betrayed and abandoned one of their own, I believe that with time, I can persuade the mages of the same."

"Good." Thayer held out his hand. "Strange times make for strange allies, but sometimes those are the best. The Army is with you."

"And I," Melles pledged, with no sense of irony, "am with you as well. It is a pity that poor Tremane did not have as many firm allies."

Elspeth had just finished describing the latest results from the group in the Tower, as relayed from Rolan to Gwena, when Tremane's face suddenly went white. "Gods," Tremane said through gritted teeth. "Here comes another one."

He meant another mage-storm; he felt them first, as they traveled over the face of Hardorn. They made him tremble all over, churned his stomach, and muddled his head. But that gave Elspeth, Darkwind, and Tashiketh time to brace themselves before the onset of the Storm hit them as well. At the moment, the effects were still not *too* bad, although every mage endured some unpleasant physical symptoms in direct proportion to how powerful he or she was. But the circles of changed soil had already begun to appear again, and it could not be too much longer before the weather shifted back to the terrible blizzards that had ravaged the countryside, and before more "boggles" appeared as living creatures were changed by wild magic. They were just glad they had the formula to predict *where* those circles would appear.

Elspeth grasped the arms of her chair and clenched her own jaw; it didn't help, it never did, but at least it gave her something to do while the Storm rolled over her. Meanwhile, Father Janas watched them all with worried, wondering eyes, for he was no mage, and felt nothing when the Storms came.

This was a short, intense Storm. When it was over, she let out the breath she had been holding, let go of the arms of the chair, and put her head down on her folded arms on the table.

"Oh, I do not *like* that," Tashiketh sighed. "I do not know how you bear it."

"You bear what you must," Darkwind replied philosophically. "And there are worse things to contemplate than having one's lunch jump about in one's stomach."

"And that brings us back to the topic we were discussing," Tremane said, his clenched hands slowly loosening as color returned to his face. "I do not wish to cast aspersions upon the ability of your friends, Lady Elspeth, but I feel we *must* assume that the party in the Tower will not find a solution to the Final Storm. My concern is and must be for this land and these people; how am I to protect them? Is there any way that I can take in the damage myself, instead of having it come upon the land? Can I use earth-magic and the earth-binding to instruct the land to heal itself and to prevent the creatures here from being twisted out of all recognition? Have you any ideas at all?"

Father Janas shook his head. "You could take the ills of the land upon yourself, my son, but not for long before it killed you. You cannot bear what the land could and live."

"I don't have any ideas yet, but we have several kinds of magic that we can incorporate," Elspeth mused aloud. "Tremane, I don't think the damage to the land is going to be that terrible, but what I am afraid of is that the nodes are going to—go to a critical point where they cannot be controlled. That they are going to become rogue. I'm very much afraid that the Final Storm is going to turn them into something like the rogue Heartstone that Darkwind and I dealt with."

"That is my concern also," Tashiketh agreed. "I fear that is precisely what may occur, and such a thing would be very like having a continual Storm in one place. As power fed into it, it would continue to grow. This would be a very bad thing."

"Shelters, shields," Darkwind muttered, frowning and glaring at nothing. "The trouble with such things is that they are *going* to fail; I don't know how we could possibly make them strong enough to survive what is coming."

Elspeth got up and paced restlessly beside the windows. The weather in Hardorn had deteriorated again, but it was not yet as foul as it had been before the last protection went into place. They were currently between snowstorms, and the sun shone down with empty benevolence on the dazzling fresh snow. Elspeth was not looking forward to the resumption of blizzards, but at least the increase in the number of snowstorms was keeping the number of curiosity seekers down. Virtually everyone who *could* come in himself to pledge to Tremane had, and a few days ago, their old friend Father Janas appeared with another casket of earth, collected from all of those who wished to pledge themselves and their land to their new King and could not come in person. Now Tremane "felt" virtually every part of his realm, which was both an advantage and a disadvantage. He knew where every trouble spot was, and when a Storm began its march across the face of Hardorn, Elspeth was personally quite glad that it was Tremane who experienced the sickness of his land, and not her.

But now the system of signal-towers was fully functional again, and at least warning could be sent out when something did go wrong out in the hinterlands. The precise locations of where the circles of altered land would fall were sent out well in advance of the Storms by means of the towers. If things were not precisely under control, at least they were in a better state than they had been. There was *one* authority in Hardorn again, and resources were not being wasted on warfare. A few skirmishes with Tashiketh's gryphons had put an end to further fighting.

There was still the pressing problem of how to protect the nodes and the Tayledras Heartstones. She was all too conscious of the Heartstone right under the Palace at Haven; if *that* went rogue, it could very well destroy the Palace, all the Collegia, and perhaps a good section of Haven as well. The loss of life would be horrendous. The Palace complex had been partially evacuated, but with mixed results and quite a bit of ongoing confusion. She had seen enough magical destruction in the capital of Hardorn; she had no trouble envisioning the same level of destruction visited on her own home.

She started to shake, just thinking about it, and turned her gaze to look out the window for a moment so that no one in the room would see her face and the expression she wore. As so often happened these days, her timing was just right. She was the first to see and recognize the latest arrival to Tremane's court.

The procession was just entering the courtyard as she glanced down at the gates, and the glitter of the sun on shining metal and blinding gold and white trappings caught her eye first. Then she saw the standard, and who rode beneath it, and she gasped, catching the attention of everyone else.

"Oh, gods—" she said, feeling as if she had just been struck a numbing blow to the head and had not yet felt the pain. She wondered wildly for a moment if she was hallucinating; there was no way that she should be seeing what she saw out the window. "Oh, ye gods, this cannot be happening! This is too strange even for me."

"Elspeth?" Darkwind said, catching the timbre of her voice without knowing what caused it. "*Ashke,* what's wrong?"

The chair legs grated on the wooden floor as he hastily shoved his seat back. He got up and hurried to her side; unable to speak, she simply pointed out the window.

His eyes widened, and he choked, completely unable to get even a word of exclamation out.

"King Tremane," Elspeth managed to say as Darkwind was struck dumb, "You have a very important visitor, and I think you had better get down to the courtyard *now.*"

"Why?" he asked, a little resentfully, for he had gotten rather tired of meeting so many delegations in the cold over the past several weeks.

"You should just—do what she says," Darkwind managed to croak.

Tremane looked skeptical. His tone took on an edge of sarcasm. "Who's here? The Emperor?"

"No," Elspeth replied. "Solaris, High Priest of Vkandis and Son of the Sun and her entourage." She glanced down again. "And the Firecat Hansa," she added.

Behind her, there was a muffled curse, and the sound of a chair clattering against the floor as it fell over, and by the time she had turned to see what Tremane was doing, he was already gone.

"We'd better go down there, too," Darkwind finally managed to get out. "We should be there to welcome her." She nodded, and gestured to the fascinated gryphon to accompany them.

By the time they reached the courtyard, however, Tremane had already given Solaris as respectful a welcome as anyone could have wished, even the Son of the Sun and the Mouth of Vkandis, given that she had arrived with no warning. And she in her turn had remained polite, which was all that Elspeth could have hoped for, given the circumstances.

"I have been traveling for many days at the express orders of Sunlord Vkandis," Solaris was saying, as Elspeth got within earshot. "It was, I believe, at precisely the moment when *you* were bound to the land of Hardorn that—"

Then she caught sight of Tashiketh—who had reared up on his hind legs and was holding his foreclaws extended in a peculiar manner that was obviously a ritual salute. And Solaris stared at the gryphon with a look of shock and complete disbelief on her face, her hands automatically moving to form a similar salute.

That's odd; she's seen gryphons before. So why is she looking at Tashiketh as if he were some new kind of creature?

As she stared at him in complete disbelief, Tashiketh intoned something in that odd gabble that Elspeth thought sounded like Karsite. Evidently, so did Solaris, who blinked and stammered something back. It was the very first time that Elspeth had ever seen the Son of the Sun taken aback by anything.

:Evidently Vkandis has a streak of the practical joker in

Him after all,: Darkwind commented with a touch of amusement. *:Otherwise, He would have warned her.:*

:Perhaps this is meant to be an object lesson. That just because she is the Mouth of Vkandis, she doesn't necessarily know everything about the Sunlord,: Elspeth answered.

Tashiketh replied, and Solaris responded. Evidently they were going through a set series of greetings and responses. Finally the little ritual came to a close; Tashiketh dropped back down to all fours again, and made a very courtly bow.

She looked from Tremane to Tashiketh and back again. "How long, sir, have you had this gentleman at your Court?" she asked very carefully.

"Since a few days after I was bound to the earth," Tremane replied. "Tashiketh informed us that he and his entourage were sent because of that particular event."

"As was I," Solaris murmured, still staring at Tashiketh. "And now I know *why* I was sent here, rather than being told to send representatives as I did to Valdemar."

:I have the feeling that it wasn't just to consult with Tremane,: Darkwind said wryly. *:Now she knows that her God has been sharing his attentions. This could be rather amusing.:*

The Firecat Hansa, who was sitting very patiently on the front of Solaris' saddle, reached out and patted her on the shoulder with his paw. *:We are about to have a blizzard descend, Sunborn,:* he said politely. *:If you would all be so kind, good people, it would be best if we could move inside.:*

As with his compatriot Altra, Hansa could apparently make himself "heard" in Mindspeech even to those who did not share that Gift. Elspeth saw startled looks all over the courtyard, as even Tremane's guards experienced someone talking inside their minds for the first time in their lives.

"I beg your pardon, Sir Hansa, of course we can," Tremane said instantly, and with commendable aplomb. "Allow me to conduct you to appropriate quarters myself." At that moment, to confirm Hansa's prediction, the warning horns blew from the walls, signaling that a physical storm was moving in quickly from the west.

And Tremane did escort them, probably thanking his Hundred Little Gods that he had set up one of the towers as guest quarters for important folk and their followers. The last set of guests had just vacated the premises; the tower was clean and waiting for the next set. It was a matter of moments to take them there, turning over the entire tower to Solaris and her relatively small entourage. Although Darkwind excused himself, Elspeth went along as the official representative of Selenay, and because she was anxious to talk to Solaris if she could. Solaris' escort consisted of a few *very* professional and tough-looking guards, and several Sun-priests. Just as the last of their baggage came up from below, the blizzard Hansa had warned was coming did indeed descend, and Tremane took his leave of them to see that the usual precautions were in place.

The moment he left, Solaris dropped some of her detached and "official" manner. Looking at Elspeth and Tashiketh, she raised an eyebrow in an inquiring manner. "Would you care to remain while my people get us settled in? I should be glad of the company; it has been a stressful trip."

"I think we would both be pleased to remain, Holiness," Elspeth said carefully, and Solaris laughed, tossing her cloak aside and removing the heavy gold collar she was wearing. A robed attendant took both and carried them away.

"Just 'Solaris,' little sister," the High Priest replied. "There are few enough who can call me by that name, and you are certainly one who has that right." She removed a few more pieces of regalia and set them aside, then sank down in the chair nearest the fire while the wind shook the walls. Hansa immediately leaped into her lap and settled there. "Do take a seat, Elspeth," Solaris continued. "Sunborn Tashiketh, I am not certain *what* to offer you."

"The floor will do, Most Holy," the gryphon said with careful courtesy, and settled himself there as Elspeth chose another chair. "I hope you will forgive me, but how is it that you did not know that Vykaendys was—"

"Was watching over both our lands? I suspect it is partly because that knowledge was lost while corrupt Priests held the Sun Throne. As to why Vkandis did not choose to reveal this fact to me until now—" She spread her hands wide. "The God moves in His own way, and in His own time. Presumably He had a reason for sending me here to be hit over the head with this revelation."

"I suspect that He sent you here for more than that reason, Most Holy," Tashiketh replied respectfully.

"If you are here, *who* is holding the Sun Throne?" Elspeth blurted, unable to restrain her curiosity. "I thought you couldn't leave for any length of time, that there were still those you did not entirely trust."

"Oh, *that* is a tale in itself, and some day I will tell you all of it, but in short, I am here because Vkandis Himself sits on the Sun Throne at this very moment," Solaris said. As Elspeth started with surprise, Solaris nodded. "I mean that quite literally. It is the second great Miracle of my reign; the great statue of Vkandis came to life again during a Holy Service over which I was presiding, then ordered us all to follow and walked out of the Temple, shrinking as He moved, until He reached the throne room, where He took the throne."

Solaris spoke so matter-of-factly that she might have been discussing the terrible blizzard outside, rather than something that was, quite clearly, a miracle in every sense of the word. Elspeth was as fascinated by her attitude as by what had happened. She saw no reason to doubt anything that Solaris told her, for Solaris would not have left Karse without a compelling reason and an unshakable guarantee that her Throne would be waiting for her when she returned.

"When He had seated Himself, He let it be known that I was traveling into Hardorn on a life-or-death mission at His behest, and that in token of the fact that I was His true-born Son, He would be holding the Sun Throne until I returned," she continued. "He swore His protection to Karse against the Storms. At that point, the statue became a statue again— except, of course, it was literally rooted to the Sun Throne. It wasn't an illusion, either; the great statue is quite *gone* from the pedestal, and the smaller version in place on the Throne. And in addition, there is a peculiar barrier around Karse itself. People can come and go through it, but it *is* quite visible, and it seems to resemble the barrier around Iftel that Karal described to me." She smiled a bit wryly. "Now it seems clear *why* it resembles that barrier. The Sunlord has had practice."

Solaris might *seem* to be matter-of-fact, but as Elspeth listened and watched, she realized that Solaris was profoundly moved and awed. Elspeth found this a great deal easier to understand; how could anyone *not* feel awe at such an occurrence?

"I doubt that anyone will have the temerity to claim your

place, given that particular demonstration," Tashiketh said dryly. "And so Vykaendys directed you here?"

"Precisely, and it was not the easiest journey I have ever undertaken, though not the worst either. Our robes earned us respect and safe passage, though no one really recognized us as Sun-priests." One corner of her mouth twitched. "I will admit it came as something of a shock to learn that Tremane had been Bound to Hardorn. That puts him on an equal basis with me, in some ways, and it was not what I would have expected to see happen. Still, it is probably good for Hardorn." She laughed softly. "I also have a confession that I might as well make to you both. I am taking a certain amount of sadistic pleasure in this. He is going to suffer physical discomfort, even terrible pain from time to time, he agreed to this, he even volunteered for it, and I think that between this and his *geas* of Truth-speaking, he just might be able to atone for his actions in the past."

"He spoke to me in private of what he had done, sending the assassin," Tashiketh admitted. "I believe he regrets his actions more with every passing day."

"Well, he should," Solaris said firmly. "I cannot even begin to describe the anguish he caused, not only to myself and Karal, but to those who knew and cared for all of his victims. But although I am not prepared to forgive him yet, I am willing and ready to work with him. I *am* an Adept of a peculiar bent, as I suspect you have guessed. I think we may be able yet to find ways to protect ourselves through this crisis."

"I hope so," Elspeth said fervently. "I *hope* so."

"With Vykaendys' help," Tashiketh replied with absolute certainty, "we shall."

Tre'valen and Dawnfire

Ten

Firecats had a real cat's ability to make a person feel as if she was a particularly stupid student and the cat was a teacher fast losing patience. *:Vkandis' protection is temporary,:* Hansa said firmly, looking for all the world precisely like the Cat-statue at the feet of Henricht, the first Son of the Sun. Poor Henricht, even as a statue, looked singularly unprepossessing; the Cat, however, looked as if *he* should have been sitting on the Sun Throne. *:It cannot last through the Final Storm. The nodes in Karse are as vulnerable as any. The protection is only meant to prevent people and beasts from Changing, and to prevent the greater part of the priesthood from falling ill twice and thrice a day.:* He bent his head then, and washed a paw with great daintiness. *:You and your priests will have to do your share like everyone else. If nodes go rogue, you will be dealing with the unfortunate results.:*

Solaris sighed, but not with disappointment. Elspeth thought that her sigh sounded more like someone who had just heard unpleasant news she had nevertheless expected.

"Shields," Darkwind muttered, pacing, as Vree followed his movements with interest from his perch in the corner. "That has to be the key. But *how* do we create a shield that will hold through even the Storms we have now?"

Elspeth pummeled her mind for something she remembered out of—a Chronicle? No, it was a story that Kerowyn had told about one of the mages her grandmother had trained. "Why only *one* shield?" she asked. "Why not layered shields, shields within shields? Kerowyn told me about something like that; the mage layered lots of weaker shields instead of one strong one, and kept replacing them from the inside as they were taken down from the outside. If you could do that, keep replacing the innermost shield every time the outermost was destroyed—"

"Interesting, and yes, it has been done before, and quite successfully," Darkwind said, knitting his brows in thought. "Multiple shields *are* more effective than one strong shield. But we can't put a mage beside every node, and if we don't, how could we keep replacing shields as they came down? You can't shield from the *outside* once the initial shield is up, and how would we do it from the inside? That is the problem of course, and a spell—or series of spells—would have to be crafted for that."

"If we could. How would we continue to supply the energy to create the shields in the first place?" Tremane objected. Solaris gave him a withering look. "You would be sealing the perfect energy source *within* the shield," she replied, with an unspoken "fool" hanging off the end of the sentence. "That would be the least of our problems. And if the energy were to be exhausted and all the shields fail, well, an exhausted node would be no more dangerous than no node. If there's no power to act upon, there will be nothing to go rogue."

"Apologies, but things work somewhat differently where I am from, and we did not handle magic wells that way," Tremane offered. Tremane did not take offense at her manner, perhaps because she was at least participating in these experimental sessions and demonstrating that she was not going to take out her animosity toward him on Hardorn and its people in general. He grimaced as if he was getting a headache. "Then if we could simply find a way to keep a node spawning its own shields until the energy ran out—"

"This is all very nice in theory," Elspeth pointed out impatiently. "But even if we could do that, we haven't the time or the resources to run about the countryside slapping a shield-spell over every node!"

"Well, actually, we wouldn't have to do that, at least not here—" began Tremane.

"There are Priests enough in Karse to shield every node there," said Solaris at the same time.

"And that works for Hardorn and Karse." Elspeth frowned.

"But what about Valdemar? And the Pelagirs? And elsewhere?"

"Hmm," Tashiketh rumbled, moving his gaze from Solaris to Tremane and back again. "There is an answer to that question already in our hands."

Hansa and Father Janas switched their gazes between the two rulers also, as Solaris and Tremane exchanged a very peculiar look.

There was something rather odd going on there, and Elspeth hadn't a clue to what it was all about, but the tension between those two suddenly increased a hundredfold.

"I do not *like* you," Solaris burst out, as she abruptly got to her feet and stood, glaring at Tremane. "I do not like you at all! Ever since you and your heathen army came here, you have stood for everything I find detestable—expediency above honor, craft above wisdom, guile above truth, self-reliance above faith! I do *not* like you!"

And with that, she gathered her robes about her and swirled out, Hansa padding in her wake. The heavy silence that followed her outburst made even their breathing seem loud.

"What in hell was that all about?" Elspeth asked, bewildered. She had never seen Solaris lose control like that before.

Tremane looked at the door that Solaris had closed—not slammed—behind herself. "I'm not sure," he replied, "but it might have to do with a solution that involves a personal compromise on the part of the Son of the Sun." He appeared to make up his mind about something and stood up. "If you four can work on the problem of a self-renewing shield-spell that can take power from a node-source without the intervention of an Adept, I will go and speak with Solaris, and see if my guess mirrors actuality rather than just an outburst of frustration."

He nodded at all of them, and left as well.

Darkwind snorted. "A self-renewing shield-spell that takes power from a node without an Adept. At least he was only asking the impossible!"

But Elspeth wasn't so certain. "Don't Tayledras Heartstones do self-renewing spells, like the Veil? And they don't need an Adept around to make *them* work."

Darkwind started to object, then got a thoughtful look on his face. Tashiketh rested his beak on his foreclaws, looking expectant. "They do," Darkwind replied slowly. "And I was about to say that nodes aren't Heartstones, but Heartstones *are* a kind of node. Let me think about this one for a moment."

Father Janas simply shrugged. "I haven't the least idea of what you're all talking about," he said cheerfully. "Tremane asked me to sit through this because I know how the earth-binding and earth-magic works. Other than that, my friends, I'm fairly useless. But it does seem to me that for your controlling factor, you could *use* earth-energy, the very slow and subtle energies that underlie everything, the ones even hedge-wizards and earth-witches use. Those are fundamentally unaffected by the Storms."

Tashiketh raised his head and nodded eagerly; Darkwind looked at Father Janas as if he had unwittingly uttered something profound.

Elspeth had come late to magic and thus undergone a forced-growth process like a hothouse plant. She had never actually worked with such primitive energies as Janas described. But the theory seemed reasonable to her, and both Tashiketh and Father Janas obviously were familiar in detail with how those magics operated. "Well, why don't we just pursue that particular hare until we either catch it or it goes to cover?" she asked decisively.

"It is these energies with which Vykaendys created the Shield-Wall," Tashiketh said thoughtfully. "This is why there is less magical energy to spare within Iftel itself than there is in other lands. It is constantly going to renew the Shield-Wall. If this works, there will be little energy to spare in any of the lands when the Final Storm has passed."

"And the alternative?" Elspeth replied. "I don't think any of us want to contemplate *that*. Most of us have been doing without a great deal of magic ever since the Storms started, and I doubt that it is going to be too much of a hardship."

"Except for the Vales," Darkwind sighed. "But as you said, the alternative is a great deal less pleasant." He regarded the three of them with an expression so mournful that it almost made Elspeth want to laugh. "I will need your help in asking me very stupid questions, for we will somehow have to unravel the processes by which Tayledras make Heartstones and link them into spells like the Veil. I am so *used* to being able to do such things that I cannot tell you *how* I do them. This," he concluded with resignation, "is going to be a very great deal of difficult work, all of it mental."

He was right; it was. They were still only in the earliest stages when Solaris and Tremane returned, and Darkwind remarked via Mindspeech to Elspeth that since there were neither knife wounds nor signs of violence on either of them, the talk must have gone well. Neither of them said anything, and both of them acted as if they did not particularly wish to discuss what had occurred.

The group was not able to get beyond the most basic of understandings that day, nor for several more days, although they all worked feverishly to put together their solution. Only Tremane did not spend every waking hour of the day deep in research and testing; Solaris remarked cryptically that he didn't need to, since his presence was only necessary when they had a solution ready to try. Whatever had passed between them had cleared the air considerably, for Solaris had stopped making her acidic comments and was even distantly friendly to him at times.

Perhaps, not so ironically, it was the discipline and methodology they had learned from Master Levy and the other Master Artificers that enabled them to dissect magic logically, apply the laws they had learned, and find the fundamentals that allowed the magic to work in the first place. Finally, they had all the pieces of a solution; thanks to Darkwind, they all knew how to make a node behave like a very weak Heartstone and how to tie one into a self-sustaining spell. Unlike a Tayledras Heartstone, nodes could only support *one* such spell, but one was all they would need. They knew how to use earth-energy to power the second spell that would control the first, triggering the spawning of a new shield when the outermost collapsed. Now came the question to which they had no answer, unless Solaris and Tremane already knew it—how to reach every node at the same time.

Then, at last, Tremane rejoined the group.

"Earth-binding," he said succinctly. "Every Tayledras Vale will be able to control the nodes in the territory of that Vale; Solaris will be able to reach the nodes in Karse, the King in Rethwellan the nodes in his land, and so forth. Those leaders will have to undergo the ritual, but the gods know it's simple enough, and once they do, they can *immediately* protect their nodes."

Elspeth looked askance at him, but Father Janas nodded. "I thought so," he said with satisfaction. "This is one of those few times when the King can affect the land, rather than vice versa."

"I am not looking forward to this," Tremane added bitterly. "When we take this to the next level and involve the entire country, it is going to be extremely unpleasant. But it isn't going to kill me, and I would rather spend a week recovering from the aftereffects of this than have my people face a single node gone rogue. So, let us test our theory on the nearest node to Shonar, and if it works, we will then make all of Hardorn into our second test."

Something about his tone made Elspeth think that the effects of the full-country test were going to be something worse than merely "extremely unpleasant;" she had the feeling that this was going to require every bit of courage Tremane possessed. But there was nothing she could do about it, and she knew very well that her mother would have willingly sacrificed herself in the same cause, as would Solaris, or any other good ruler.

The test on the single node was far less difficult than Elspeth had envisioned; first the controlling-spell was set in place, then the node itself was altered to allow for the linkage of a shield-spell directly to it. This was the part that only an Adept could do, so it was up to Darkwind as the most practiced of all of them in this particular kind of magic, while Solaris "watched" with single-minded intensity.

Then, when everything was in readiness, Darkwind triggered the spell, just before the next Storm came through.

If Elspeth had not been "watching" at the time, she would never have believed that it was possible, for between one moment and the next, the node disappeared, and in its place was a shielded spot into which ley-lines fed but nothing came out. Then the Storm swept in, and they all waited out the effects.

When they had recovered and were able to "look" again, the node was exactly as it had been before the Storm, shielded and safe.

Tremane looked very much like a man who has received

both incredibly good news and incredibly bad news at the same time. "Well," he said, "we know it works."

"How soon do you want to try protecting all of Hardorn?" Father Janas asked him gently.

"Now," he said decisively. "We have until late tonight before the next Storm comes in, and I don't want to be able to sit and brood on this."

Solaris sat straight up and looked him in the eyes. "Tremane Gyfarr Pendleson of Lynnai, don't you *dare* sit there and pretend to be a martyr! What you are about to endure, *I* will also have to, and Prince Daren of Valdemar, and Faramentha of Rethwellan, and whoever it is in Iftel—"

"Vykaendys-First Bryron Hess," Tashiketh said helpfully.

"The Son of the Sun in Iftel, and a half-dozen Hawkbrothers and at *least* one Shin'a'in," Solaris concluded.

:Not to mention as many other leaders we can reach as we think will have lands in jeopardy,: Hansa added helpfully. *:There will be a great many leaders with dreadful headaches before this is all over.:*

"Exactly! You will not be alone in this, and although you *may* feel fear because of the justifiable guilt you bear for your other actions in the past, I can assure you that the land will *not* let you die!" She rose to her feet, full of anger and some other emotion that Elspeth could not put a name to. "If you are afraid, then be a man and admit it, and let us help you through it! *You* should know that if you are too afraid, the land will resist what we are about to do. We may not be able to overcome that resistance, for the land takes its cues from you."

:That's Solaris talking, but it's also something else,: Darkwind said, in Mindspeech tightly focused and tense. *:I wonder if Tremane realizes it?:*

:Vkandis?: Elspeth asked, but even as she said it, she knew that it was the wrong answer.

:Since when does a male use all of someone's names to scold him?: Darkwind asked, a little of the tension ebbing. *:No, Solaris is acting as a Mouth for a different power, and I suspect that if you asked Father Janas, he'd be very familiar with it. Probably her annoyance with Tremane and her familiarity with being a Mouth opened her up to acting as an inadvertent channel for it.:*

Elspeth sent silent agreement, after casting a quick glance
at the priest, who was watching the little scene with a faint
smile on his lips. Darkwind was right. Only a woman—a
mother—would scold someone using every one of his names.
And wasn't the earth often referred to as Mother? Looked at
in that light, there were some subtle physical changes in Solaris that gave more clues. For one thing, she looked more—
feminine—than Elspeth had ever seen her.

The scolding did what it was supposed to do, which was
annoy him enough to make him willing to admit to a weakness; and in a way Elspeth could feel very sorry for poor Tremane, who hadn't asked for any of this, and had borne up very
well under it all. He stiffened his back, looked up into Solaris'
eyes, and said, with quiet dignity, "You are right, Solaris. I am
terrified. I am accustomed to using power, not having it use
me, and the prospect of giving up control over myself to *anything* gives me the horrors. Doing it with the lives of thousands of innocents in the balance is terrible beyond my ability
to articulate."

Whatever had Solaris let her go, and the anger faded as she
sat down. "It isn't so bad, being used by this kind of power,"
she said softly. "You will be exhausted when it is over; perhaps a little ill, though I don't think it will be very bad. I think
the power will use you gently, if you don't resist it. Sometimes giving up control in a greater cause is the noblest thing
one can do in one's life." She hesitated a moment longer, then
it looked as if some wall inside her gave way. Her expression
changed completely. "Perhaps you are rightfully afraid that
some of us, who have grievances with you, may not protect
you with a whole heart. You would have been correct in fearing that not very long ago; I might not have moved to help
you if I saw that you were in danger." She took a deep breath
and plunged on. "That is no longer true; I forgive you, Tremane of Hardorn, and if it is any more comfort to you, young
Karal, who has greater cause to hate you than I, forgave you
before I did. The man who loosed the assassin that murdered
our friend was an Imperial Commander, subject to the orders
and whims of an Emperor with no morals and no scruples, and
you are no longer that man." Now she looked shamefaced for
a moment. "The Sunlord himself told me that I must forgive

you if we were to succeed, but until this moment, I could not."

Tremane looked at her with astonishment, and offered her his hand; she took it in a firm handclasp that said far more than words could have. "Thank you for that; I know what it cost you," was all he said.

Then he released her hand and looked at the others. "Well? Shall we begin?"

As far as Elspeth was concerned, there was very little for her to see or do, other than to feed mage-power to Darkwind, who in his turn did things with it that she could neither see nor follow, although she knew in theory what he was doing. She was what they all called the "anchor" and she brought in the power, directed, and refined it. Tremane searched for the node, and "held" them all there when he found one. Darkwind built the node into a matrix that would permit a single spell to be linked into it. Father Janas constructed the controlling spell that triggered the main spell, using the loss of a shield as the guide for activation. Solaris built the main spell, which created the nine nested shields using power from the node, and Darkwind linked it in. Then, once that node "disappeared" because it was now shielded, Tremane moved their viewpoint on to the next node. In the end, by the time they were done, Tremane was so completely exhausted that he could not even move, but as Solaris had promised, he was neither ill nor in pain. They had worked through him to reach every node in Hardorn and replicate the same shields and spells they had tried on the first node. This was the only way they *could* have reached all of the nodes without going to them physically; in a sense, since Tremane was bound to all of Hardorn in a very *physical* fashion because of the blood and soil he had ingested, they actually were working there physically.

They completed their work just as the next Storm came through, and had the satisfaction of seeing their work hold. And Tremane got a small reward out of it after all; since the nodes were no longer being battered by the energies of the Storm, *he* was suffering only about half of the physical effects he had been enduring with every Storm-wave. This made him feel half again better.

"That in and of itself made this all worth while," he said weakly, but with a smile, and then they sent him off to bed.

"He feels as though he will sleep for a week, but it won't be more than a day or so," Father Janas said with weary satisfaction. "He'll be back on his feet and hard at work shortly. Now do you need anything to alert the peoples in your homes?"

"I will send two of my fastest flyers—mages both—back with the exact instructions in the morning," Tashiketh rumbled, his eyes alight with pleasure at their success. "And if you will permit me, Most Holy, more will convey you and Hansa back to your own land to save you as much time as possible; as many of your escort as care to remain here can, I suppose, and the rest can follow you at their own pace."

Solaris gave him a puzzled look. "I would appreciate it no end, but how do you intend to do this?" she asked. "I assume you mean me to fly with them, but I can't imagine how that could work properly."

"A basket, suspended between them. It is perfectly safe," Tashiketh assured her. "There are some minor spells on the basket to make it and the contents light; you can renew these easily enough, and the only thing you will need to take care with is that you go to ground during Storms.

"Our gryphons use the same means," Darkwind seconded. "It's safer than you'd think. You'll be able to cross into Karse within a few days, even with having to land twice or three times a day as a Storm passes."

"Then I thank you, for I will have to seal off the Temple as well as our nodes, and whether or not Tremane will believe that, it will be a harder task than this." Her words were still a little sardonic, but she smiled, and Elspeth sensed that Solaris would no longer be able to say in truth that she hated Tremane of Hardorn.

"And you?" Father Janas asked Elspeth and Darkwind. Darkwind answered for both of them.

"It is already accomplished," Darkwind said, his voice heavy with tired content. "Gwena has sent the word to Rolan; Rolan has sent it on to Skif's Cymry, who will detail it to the Kaled'a'in of k'Leshya Vale. *They* will see to it that Tayledras and Shin'a'in alike have the information, and our nodes and Heartstones will be protected within days. Messages will go from Valdemar to every White Winds mage in every land, and from there—wherever the word needs to go."

"Your Companions are useful friends," Father Janas said with envy. "Perhaps there will be room for them in Hardorn in the future." He looked shyly at Solaris. "And there should be room for Temples to the Sunlord as well, I should think. When it all comes down to it, what is done for the cause of Good is done in the name of every Power of the Light."

She smiled; the first open, unshadowed smile that Elspeth had seen on her face since she arrived here. "And on that very optimistic note, I shall thank you and beg leave to go to bed myself," she said, getting to her feet. "Hansa and I have a long journey in the morning."

"Room for everyone," Darkwind echoed, as he and Elspeth walked slowly to their own quarters. "That is not so bad a way to conduct one's land."

"I know," she replied saucily. "We've been doing it that way in Valdemar for some time now."

And now, at least, we have some assurance we will continue to be able to, she thought. *And now we can spare some prayers and energy for Karal and the rest where they are. May all our gods help them, for we cannot.*

Emperor Charliss sat in, not on, the wooden Throne in his private quarters, and plotted revenge, for revenge was all he had left to hold him to life. His mind was clear, despite the hellish mix of drugs his apothecary had concocted on his orders, to dull his pain and sustain his failing body. That was because the mix included drugs to keep his mind from becoming clouded. Outside his quarters, a physical blizzard raged, as it had raged for the past three weeks. The mage-storms, too, passed through Crag Castle several times every day, leaving most mages shuddering with the aftereffects. He wasn't suffering from that difficulty, though; or if he was, it was insignificant in the light of the degeneration of his body.

Although he did not appear to take any notice of what was going on outside this suite, such was not the case. He knew very well what Melles was up to; discrediting the Emperor even with the Imperial Army, spreading truths, half-truths, and lies to make it appear that only Baron Melles had the welfare of the Empire in his heart. He was also quite well aware

that Melles was doing a fine job of holding the Empire together, even if it was with devious and dubious means. He
knew that Melles was using the Emperor's treatment of Tremane as a weapon to bring the feuding political factions of the
Empire together under Melles' control. It was a ploy that
would not have occurred to Charliss, but in retrospect, given
that Melles was detested by at least a quarter of the Great
Players in the game of Empire, and feared by another quarter,
the only way he could have united them was to find a common enemy they could hate worse than him.

None of that mattered, for he no longer cared what Melles
or any other living man did. His priorities were different, and
much more personal.

The spells that kept his worn-out body going, that rein-
forced failing organs, were themselves failing. Each time a
Storm came through, he lost more of them and was unable to
replace all the spells that were lost.

He saw no way of being able to save himself; he was dying,
and he knew it. He could no longer move under his own power
anymore; his servants carried him from bed to Throne and
back again, all within the confines of his private quarters. The
long, slow decline he had anticipated had accelerated out of
all recognition.

He was not afraid, but he *was* angry, with the kind of calcu-
lating, all-consuming anger only a man who had lived two
centuries could muster. He had been cheated of the last, precious years of his life, and he knew precisely where to lay the
blame for it.

Valdemar.

He had sent his scholars on a search for that benighted land
and its origin, and had learned things that gave him all the
more reason to assume that it was *Valdemar* that had unleashed these Storms across the face of the land. Valdemar
had been founded centuries ago by rebellious subjects of the
Empire who had escaped into the wilderness too deeply to follow. But time and distance were no barriers to revenge, as he
himself very well knew. The rulers of Valdemar had probably
been plotting this attack against the Empire ever since their
land was founded. A plot such as this one would have taken
centuries to mature, centuries to gather the power for. These
Storms could not have been generated by anything less than

the most powerful of Adepts working together in concert; such a weapon was fiendishly clever, diabolically complicated.

In the end it might have been his own actions in reaching for the land of Hardorn that triggered the long plots of Valdemar and gave them the opportunity to destroy those who had driven them out of their homes so long ago. He should have read the return of his envoy from Hardorn, dead, with the blade belonging to Princess Elspeth between his shoulders, for the serious warning it really was. *You're too close, and we'll finish you;* that had been the real message. Like a nest of bees, he had ventured too near, and now the insects would swarm him and destroy him.

It didn't really matter what the cause for their actions was, nor did it matter whether he could have done anything to prevent this. The Storms had been unleashed, *he* was dying, it was all the fault of Valdemar, and he was going to see to it that Valdemar didn't outlive him—at least, not in any form that the Valdemarans themselves would recognize. Like a wild bear making a final charge, in his death throes he would destroy those who were destroying him.

He had everything he needed; all of the magic of the local nodes, plus all that of his coterie of mages, plus a great deal he had hoarded in carefully-shielded artifacts. Every Emperor created magical artifacts, or caused them to be created; he could drain every one of them. Every mage he had ever worked with, whether he was one of Charliss' private group or not, had a magical "hook" in him, one that tied him back to Charliss. The moment Charliss cared to, he could pull every bit of that mage's personal power and use it as if the mage was one of his personal troupe. The smartest of the mages had, of course, discovered and removed that hook—but most of them hadn't, and Charliss could use them up any time he cared to.

But his own time was rapidly running out. The shields protecting those hoarded objects weren't going to last through too many more Storms, nor were the resources of his mage-troupe, nor of the mages he had hooks in. If he was going to use this power, it would have to be soon.

He sat supported by the tall back and heavy arms of his mock Throne, and contemplated the methods of vengeance. What could he do to finish them, these upstart Valdemarans?

What form should his attack take? He wanted it to be appropriate, suitable—and he wanted it to do the most damage possible.

What would the best allocation of his resources be? *It's obvious. Release all the power at once,* he decided. *Release it as the wave-front of the Storm passes, and use it to augment what the Storm does. Make it the worst Storm that the face of this old world has ever seen.*

The results of that should be highly entertaining, and since he would release it as the Storm passed from east to west, most of the Empire would be safe.

But Valdemar—ah, Valdemar would have no idea that the blow was coming. The results of such an enormous release of power would be devastating—and amusing, if he lived to watch it, and to collect his information.

Everything from Hardorn to far beyond Valdemar, and from the mountains in the North to the South of Karse, would erupt with Nature driven mad. The weather was already hideous; this would make it unbelievably worse. Earthquake—there would be earthquakes in regions that had never known so much as a trembler, as the stresses in the earth built to beyond the breaking point. Fire—volcanoes would erupt out of nowhere, pouring down rivers of molten rock on unsuspecting cities. Physical storms would spawn lightning that in turn would ignite huge forest fires and grass fires. Blizzards would bury some areas in snow past the rooftops, while floods would wash away the country elsewhere, and mudslides make a ruin of once-fertile hills. Mountains would fling themselves skyward, and the earth would gape as huge fissures opened underfoot. Processes that normally took millennia would occur in a single day or less. There would be no place that was safe, no place to hide. And when the wrath of Nature was over, the Changed creatures would descend on the demoralized and disorganized survivors.

It would be everything he could have wished for. He just wished he was going to live long enough to properly gloat over it; once the energy was released, Charliss would have no more magic to sustain him, and he would die. But so would most of his enemies. Anyone and anything that lived through it all would probably wish for death before too very long.

Tremane would be caught in all of this, of course, which

would give him revenge on the faithless traitor—revenge that Melles had been too cowardly or too lazy to take. Lazy, probably; Melles never had been one to pursue targets that were out of his immediate reach; he could always manufacture excuses to obviate any need to do so.

Well, he would take matters into his own hands, then.

It was possible that the extra energy released wouldn't just wipe Valdemar off the world—it might rip through the Empire and its allies as well. The chaos he was about to unleash could have far-reaching effects.

He didn't care. He was long since over caring about things that meant no immediate improvement in *his* well-being.

Why should my Empire outlive me? he asked himself, seething with resentment over the fact that the Empire as a whole was not willing to make the sacrifices to sustain him. *I gave them my life and my attention—my entire life. Was I appreciated? Beloved for being stern with them? No. Not at all. They took and took. Now they pay for their greed. They should have thought ahead and appeased me.*

And there was no reason to make life any easier for Melles either. Let him patch something together from what was left, if, indeed, there was anything left. Let Melles see if he could actually do something with the crumbs and shards. It would serve that effete bastard right.

He smiled slowly, thinking of how Melles would react. The Baron had been progressing *so* well in imposing order on the chaos left in the wake of the Storms. He must feel so proud of himself, and be so certain that he had everything under control now. It would be delicious to see how he crumbled as everything he had worked so hard for vanished before his eyes.

Revenge; on Valdemar, on Tremane, even on Melles for daring to succeed—that was all Charliss had left, and he would take it. By the time he was finished, the known world would be driven down to the level of cave-dwelling, nomad-hunter survival. If Melles reclaimed anything at all as an Empire, it would be an Empire no bigger than this city.

I will destroy it all. His hands clutched the arms of his chair, and he felt his dry lips cracking as his smile widened. When he set off the final cataclysm, when he ignited nations to form his funeral pyre, he would prove he had been the greatest and most powerful Emperor to ever live.

No one would ever surpass him as he burned the world to light the way to his grave, and the darkness that followed would be a fitting shroud.

Karal felt peculiarly useless at this moment in time, although in a little while he would be just as important as anyone else in the Tower. He watched the others making last-minute preparations, and wished wistfully that he could use the teleson to talk to Natoli; it might have relieved his nerves. He sat quietly where he'd been told to sit, immersed in a peculiar mixture of terror, resignation, and anticipation. He knew he could do what they were going to ask of him, but he couldn't think past that. Even when he tried, he was unable to imagine a single moment *after* their task was done. Was that only because he was frightened, or because once it was over it would *be* over for them, forever?

He was still acting as the Channel for this "weapon," but this time he would not be in the physical center of the group. This time the main participants—himself, Firesong, An'desha, and Sejanes—would stand in square formation around it, and it didn't seem to matter what direction each stood in, so long as they were spaced equally around it.

There was another difference this time. Each of the "mortal" participants would be shielded by those who were not. Karal had Florian and Altra; An'desha would be protected by the Avatars, Firesong by Need and Yfandes, and Sejanes by Vanyel and Stefen. Yfandes had attached herself to Firesong without comment, perhaps so that each of the participants would have two protectors. Aya was to be kept strictly out of the way, in the care of Silverfox, with the rest of those who were not participating. *They* would all be in the workroom below, with the hatch closed. Firesong and Sejanes had determined that the shields on the workroom were as much purely physical as magical. There were properties in the stone that insulated from magical energy. The workroom had been cleared of anything remotely magical in nature, and stocked with tools, food, and water, so that if the worst happened and the survivors were sealed inside, they had a chance to dig themselves out.

The cube-maze was the exact opposite of whatever device was used to unleash the Cataclysm in the first place, and the

Adepts had surmised that it had been created as a fail-safe. As they now understood it, all of Urtho's magic had been released at once when he dissipated the bonds of all of the spells on everything that was not inside the specially shielded areas of the Tower. At the same time, a similar device had done the same to all of Ma'ar's magic in his stronghold, thus creating the Cataclysm as the two reacted together in violent and sometimes unexpected ways. They had partly replicated that when they set up the Counter-Storm.

This time, if their research and planning paid off, they were going to reverse that; they were going to open up something that would swallow all of the magic energies converging on this spot and send it all out into the Void. At least, they hoped that was what would happen. They didn't know what was going to happen at the other original release point, but Ma'ar had not been the tinkerer that Urtho had been, and had not been known for having workshops to experiment in. There were probably not any of the dangerous devices there that there were here—and in any case, the site was at the bottom of Lake Evendim. Whatever happened there would take place under furlongs of water, and far from any populations of human or other beings.

No one knew what would follow when they closed the device as the last of the energies were swallowed up. They all had some theories. Master Levy insisted that since no energy could be destroyed, it would all go elsewhere; his suggestion was that it would become a kind of energy-pool in the Void that mages could all tap into. He also warned that resistance to energy flow usually manifested as heat, and there was a very real possibility that despite their best efforts all here would be charred to death partway through. This earned the mathematician a few sour looks, which were returned with an apologetic smile. Both Lo'isha and Firesong were of the opinion that all the energy would come right back into the "real" world, as if a flood was swallowed up and came back out of the sky as rain, like the water in a fountain, endlessly cycling from pond to air and back again.

Whatever happened, the only certainty was that all the old rules of magic would go flying right out the window. No one even knew if all of this energy was ever going to be accessible anymore. They might end up with a world that was fundamentally without magic, though that was fairly unlikely.

As Urtho had said in the placards that he had left, this would have been a suicidal device to use as a weapon; once it was opened, it would have proceeded to swallow all the magic in its vicinity—in fact, it was quite likely to drain all the rest of the weaponry in here dry—and it might even have swallowed up the mages who opened it. But with the tremendous energies of this Storm breaking over it, the device would probably have all the energy it could possibly handle.

The plan was to take down the Tower shields and open it as the Final Storm hit, feed it all the energy of the Storm until it couldn't take any more or melted down, and close it again under control if it was still active.

Storms were coming in all the time now, and although the Tower shields were still holding, they had been forced to evacuate the remains of the Shin'a'in camp some days ago as a blizzard like none of their hosts had ever seen before raged across the Plains. Similar weather ravaged Valdemar, Karse, Hardorn, the Vales—

Probably everywhere else, too, Karal thought, listening carefully. *And it's supposed to be spring out there.* If he paid very close attention, he could ignore all the sounds coming from inside the Tower, and was able to pick out, very faintly, the howling of the winds outside. You couldn't even stand out there, the wind would knock you to the ground in a heartbeat. It was a good thing that they had evacuated the Plains weeks ago; tents wouldn't take this kind of pounding, and no horse, sheep, or mule would survive exposed to a storm like this.

As for the Vales—Firesong said that the Tayledras were incorporating the magic that shielded nodes with the one that formed the Veil that protected each of their Vales. Hopefully, these would hold; if not, they would have to live as the scouts did from now on, exposed to the elements, without their little lands of artificial summer.

Karal wished he knew what was going on in Karse; Altra would only say that Solaris had the situation well under control, and that most of the people were being well cared for. He hoped that his family was all right, though since they *were* living in a fairly prosperous village, they should be. The ones in real danger would be the remote farmers and shepherds who, isolated and alone out in the hills and mountains, might not have gotten warning in time to get to adequate shelter.

He hadn't thought about his family in a long time; the Karal that had helped his father in the inn's stables was another person entirely, and he knew that if his mother or father were to pass him in the street, they would not recognize him. And he would have nothing whatsoever in common with them. He had always expected to change as he grew up—but not this radically.

He tucked up his legs and rested his chin on his knees, thinking wistfully about all he had left behind—all he would leave behind if this effort failed. When it came right down to it, there were only a handful of people who would actually miss him if he didn't come out of this, and most if not all of them would recover quickly enough. Natoli probably wouldn't exactly *recover*, but she would manage, and go on to make something good out of her life. And meanwhile, he would have done something important with *his* life, and there weren't too many people who could actually say that. The thought, though bleak, was curiously liberating.

He had made his good-byes to everyone except those who were still in the Tower itself, down in the workroom; he still had time, and this might be the moment to take care of that little detail.

He got to his feet and slipped down the stairs, hoping to find Tarrn and Lyam alone. He was lucky; Lo'isha, Master Levy and Silverfox were still up above, with the handful of Shin'a'in who were still here, wedging doors to other weapon rooms open and helping to drag the cube-maze out of its little room into the main one. No matter what else happened here, they were at least going to accomplish one thing Urtho could not; they were going to render every other weapon in the Tower inactive.

Their industry left the workroom mostly untenanted. Only Aya sat nervously on a perch in the corner, while Lyam and Tarrn puttered about, storing things away more efficiently.

He stood uncertainly on the stairs, and it was Tarrn who noticed him first. :*Well, young one, it is nearly time,*: the *kyree* said, looking unusually solemn.

"I know," he replied, sitting down on the bottom steps. "I

came to tell you both that I'm very glad I knew you, and I learned a lot from both of you."

They left what they had been working on to join him. "I am very pleased to have been your friend, Karal," Lyam said earnestly, taking Karal's hand in his own dry and leather-skinned claw-hand. "I hope we will be able to continue that friendship after Tarrn and I have gone back to k'Leshya."

:And you figure prominently in my Chronicles, young scholar,: Tarrn said gravely, with a slight bow of his graying head, giving Karal what the young Karsite knew were the two most important accolades in the *kyree's* vocabulary—being called a scholar and being told he had a prominent place in the history Tarrn was writing. *:In days to come, cubs will be astonished that I actually had the privilege of your friendship.:*

An awkward silence might have started then, but at that very moment, Silverfox came trotting down the stairs, followed by all the rest. "It's time, Karal," the *kestra'chern* said, and gave Karal a completely unself-conscious hug. "They're waiting for you."

"Good luck, boy," Master Levy called, and cracked an unexpected smile. "Don't disappoint Natoli; she's expecting you to take careful notes and tell her all your observations."

Lo'isha only clasped his hand warmly and looked deeply and gravely into his eyes, and the rest of the Shin'a'in paused long enough to give him the nod of respect they normally only accorded to Lo'isha.

Each of them in his own way was saying farewell—giving him what encouragement they could—without doing anything that might unnerve him or shake his confidence. He knew that, and knew that they knew it as well. And he knew that he *should* be afraid, but somehow all his fear had passed away as he made those farewells, as if each of them was taking a little bit of it with them, so that he could be freed to do his task.

He walked quickly up the stairs; Firesong and An'desha waited up there to lower the hatch down into place, once again sealing it behind shields both magical and physical. The cube-maze was the first thing he saw as his head came up out of the hatchway; placed in the center of the room, it was curiously dwarfed by the sheer size of the place.

It looked very pretty, a piece of abstract art, gleaming with blue and purple reflections in the light from overhead. Sejanes was already in his place, flanked by the two wisps that were Vanyel and Stefen. Dawnfire and Tre'valen, looking far more solid, waited on either side of An'desha's position, and another white wraith stood beside the place where Firesong would stand. Firesong already had Need in a sheath on his back, and as he took his stand, he drew the mage-sword and held her.

An'desha moved to his place between the two Avatars, a closed-in expression on his face, as if already concentrating on what he was going to do. Sejanes had his eyes closed and his hands cupped in front of him. As Karal took his own place, flanked by Florian and Altra, Firesong made a little movement that caught his attention, and as he glanced at the Hawk-brother, Firesong gave him a wry grin and a one-handed sign for encouragement. Somehow, that made him feel better than he had all day, and he set his feet with more confidence.

As the terrible energies broke over them, Firesong was to open the device, and hold it open; next to being the Channel, his was the most dangerous task. An'desha and Sejanes were to act as funnels and control the energies as they converged on Karal, keeping a steady flow. Surges would be particularly dangerous; if a surge of power overwhelmed Karal, he might block the flow. If that happened, it would feed back on all of them. It was also the job of Sejanes and An'desha to "homogenize" the incoming energies by mixing them, for a flood of only one kind might do the same thing. Karal would actually transmute them before feeding them into the device.

"Are we ready?" Firesong asked, looking around the circle at all of them. Each of them nodded, and Karal saw for a moment, in each of their faces, the same resignation that he himself felt.

They all think in their hearts that they are going to die. They're putting on a brave face for the rest of us.

And he did the same. Despite all their care and planning, this could go horribly wrong, and if it did, it wouldn't just be *one* of them that would take the brunt of the punishment, it would be all of them.

:Here it comes,: warned Altra, and then there was no time to think of anything else.

Charliss waited, tense with anticipation as he had not been in decades. This would be perhaps the most powerful spell that had ever been cast in the history of the world since the Cataclysm; it would certainly be the most powerful spell ever cast in the history of the Empire. And for all that, it was such a deceptively simple thing—just a spell that released all of the energy of every magical object and person within Crag Castle that Charliss had any control over. This would probably kill all of his mages. If it didn't, it would certainly leave them disabled for many weeks, and might well destroy their minds. That had a certain piquant pleasure to it, for this spell would definitely kill its caster, and Charliss was not at all averse to taking an escort with him when he died.

The only emotion within his breast now was rage; it left no room for anything else. It really left no room for any thought but revenge.

He might well be the last Emperor, and that thought had the sweetness of revenge. More so since no one would ever know that *he* was the one who had done this—those few who knew he was spell-casting thought it was of the usual sort, that he was trying to extend his life a little longer.

They would probably blame Melles for this, since the mages who would die would all be mages closely allied with Charliss. That was even sweeter. Melles would have all the blame as the man who had destroyed the Empire, and Charliss would acquire the virtues that Melles did not have in contrast. Melles would be the terrible villain, and Charliss the saint that he destroyed.

What a subtle revenge!

The only thing that would make it better would be to know for certain that he was taking Tremane down with him. But never mind. One couldn't have everything—and if Tremane didn't actually *die* in the catastrophe that Charliss unleashed, he might well be among those who wished he had.

Charliss gathered the threads of his power in his hands, and waited for the Storm to break.

It was a strange little gathering, here in the Great Hall of Tremane's manor. Tashiketh and the four gryphons that were left with him, part of Solaris' escort of Sun-priests that had remained behind to help, Elspeth and Gwena, Darkwind and Vree, Brytha the *dyheli*, all of Tremane's mages, the two old weather-wizards from Shonar itself, and Father Janas, all arranged in concentric circles around Tremane. Anyone with even the tiniest bit of Mage-Gift was here, and they would all be working on a single task; to create and hold a shield. If they could hold it over Shonar, they would—if that proved impossible, they would try to hold it over the castle, and if that failed, just over themselves.

The scene looked and felt unreal and dreamlike, but Elspeth was doing her best to control a fear that was as deep and all-pervasive as the fear in a nightmare. For once, the menace looming over Elspeth was invisible, implacable, and faceless. There was no villain, no Ancar, no Falconsbane; only a terrible thing that had been loosed millennia ago and was now coming home, too ancient, impersonal, and powerful to grasp, yet too real not to terrify.

Nevertheless, the danger was real enough, and it would be worse if the group in the Tower failed. There had been a blizzard howling across the face of Hardorn for the past three days, the strangest such storm that Elspeth had ever seen. Greenish lightning somewhere up above the solid curtains of snow illuminated the entire sky in flashes, yet revealed nothing but white. There were reports of whirlwinds, and of spirits riding the wind, strange creatures blowing before it. None of these reports had been verified, but Elspeth would not discount any of them.

Every time that Storms came through, the effect was worse—although every one of the node-shields held with no apparent problems. But this Storm was going to be worse, much worse, than any of the previous lot. This was the return of the initial blast that had caused all of the storms, so long ago.

As for what would happen if the group at the Tower failed—no one could predict that, except that it would be terrible. Nature already raged out of control; could they deal with *years* of this?

Never mind. It was out of her hands, and that was what felt the most unreal of all. She had never been in a position where she was utterly helpless to do something about her own peril before, never been in a case where she had *no* control over what was going to happen. She felt demoralized and impotent, and she didn't like it one bit.

Darkwind squeezed her hand, and Gwena rubbed her soft nose against Elspeth's shoulder. Well, at least she wasn't facing this alone; no one else in this room had any more control over the situation than she did.

"It's time," Tremane said hoarsely. "It's coming."

And now it was too late to think about anything but joining mind, heart, and power with the others, disparate as they were, and shield and hold with grim determination. . . .

"Now," Firesong said between his clenched teeth, as the Storm broke over them. Around them, the stone of the Tower rumbled and groaned, like a carriage-spring being twisted beyond its ability to return to normal. This time was unlike all the previous experiences with the energy of the Storm, in that it had a distinct sound—a hollow, screaming roar accompanied by a steady increase in air pressure. Firesong held Need up between himself and the cube-maze, spoke some apparently private words to the sword, and did something to the taut fabric of magic that Karal half-saw, half-felt—

Then the cube-maze scattered motes of light along its surfaces, toward the apex of the topmost cube, and a ring spread outward to the farthest edges of the device—and all inside that ring vanished, and in its place was what could only be described as a great Darkness. The Void. The Pit.

Karal sensed it pulling on him and let it; Florian and Altra held him anchored as he let some inner part of himself meld with that awful darkness in the center of their circle. Then there was nothing but Light and Dark; the Pit in the center, and a coruscating, scintillating, rainbow-hued play of light and power all about it. Karal felt part of himself opening to it, sensed that he had become the conduit to send that power down into the Pit, which swallowed it hungrily but did not yet demand more than he could feed it.

All of his attention was on the Pit before him; he sensed explosions of energy behind and to all sides, and the energies around him oscillated furiously.

He tried to contain them and shove them into the dark maw, but the Pit had reached the limit at which it could accept them.

He heard shouting; it sounded like An'desha's voice, but he couldn't make out what the Shin'a'in was trying to tell him. Off to his right, a shining shape emerged from the chaos of swirling, flashing light, growing brighter with every moment.

It was Firesong, with Need glowing white-hot in his hands. He trembled in agony but refused to give in to the obvious pain of his blistering flesh.

Melles paused outside the Emperor's doorway—for once unguarded, thanks to the complicity of the Emperor's personal guard. With the *geas* binding them in loyalty to the Emperor now quite gone, they were all of them able to think for themselves, including Commander Ethen, who had replaced the now nerve-shattered Commander Peleun. In the past several weeks, they, too, had seen and heard enough—not *quite* enough to take things into their own hands, but enough to make them willing to leave their posts for a carefully-staged "emergency."

There was no sound in the white-marble corridor except for the ever-present screaming of the wind. Even sheltered inside their glass chimneys, the candle flames that had taken the place of mage-lights flickered in icy drafts strong enough to have earned the name of "breeze." But these gusts were no zephyrs, and the blizzard out there wasn't half as powerful as the Storm now breaking over them was likely to *make* it.

The Emperor was going to be utterly engrossed in his spell-casting; over the past several days, Melles had made a point of going in and out of the Emperor's chambers and the Throne Room on one pretext or another during a Storm, and he knew that Charliss was completely oblivious to everything around him when he was spell-casting.

If the Emperor had put half the effort on holding his crumbling Empire together that he was spending on maintaining his crumbling body, Melles would not have felt so impelled to remove him now.

If he had done so, Melles would not have half the allies he now had either.

He walked boldly into the Emperor's quarters, as he had any number of times over the past few days, as if in search of an official paper or something of the sort. He ignored the unconscious mages sprawled over the furniture in the outer

room, taken down either by the Storm itself or the Emperor's
ruthless plundering of their energies.

The Emperor would not be here or in his bedroom; Melles
already knew that Charliss had ordered his servants to carry
him into the empty, cavernous Throne Room and placed him
in the Iron Throne itself. He made a tiny hand-sign to the
two bodyguards standing on either side of the door, a pair of
bodyguards from his own retinue, inserted into the Emperor's
personnel with the collusion of the Guard Commander. They
acknowledged his presence with a slight nod and stood aside.
He opened the door to the Throne Room carefully, a fraction
at a time, as he sensed the Storm building to an unheard-of
fury, and a new and oddly-flavored spell building inside the
room in concert with it.

He wasn't certain *why* the Emperor had taken to casting his
magics while in the embrace of the Iron Throne, wearing the
Wolf Crown, but it made his own task easier. There would be
no witnesses and a dozen entrances through which a murderer
could have made his escape, assuming that there were even
any murmurs of foul play. He frankly doubted that would be
the case. People were far more likely to point to all of the loyal
bodyguards on duty, each within eye- and ear-shot of the next
pair, and believe the report of suicide.

Despite the roaring fires and a half-dozen charcoal braziers
around Charliss' feet, the room was icy, but not still. Charliss
could already have been a wizened corpse, hunched over in
the cold embrace of the Throne, eyes closed, white, withered
hands clenched on the arms. Only the yellow gem-eyes of the
wolves in the Crown watched him, and he fancied that there
was a look of life in those eyes, as they waited to see what he
would do. But wolves protected only cubs and territory, and
they had no interest in protecting individuals once those individuals were detrimental to the welfare of the pack. They
would not hinder Melles in what he intended to do.

There was a tightly-woven, furiously rotating spell building
up around the Emperor, a spell somehow akin to the Storm
outside. Did Charliss think to tap the power of the Storm now
to bolster his failing magics? If so, he *was* mad.

The spell neared its peak. After years of watching Charliss
spell-cast, Melles knew the Emperor's rhythms and patterns.
If he was going to strike, he had better do so now. He slipped

a sharp dagger, pommel ornamented with the Imperial Seal, out of the hem of his heavy, fur-trimmed tunic. He had purloined this very dagger out of the Emperor's personal quarters two days ago; it was well known to be one of Charliss' favorite trophy-pieces and virtually every member of the Court would readily identify it as his and no one else's.

Now. Before Charliss woke from his self-imposed trance, realized his danger, and turned all that terrible energy on *him*.

As only a trained assassin could, Melles flipped the dagger in his hand until he held only the point between his thumb and forefinger, aimed, and threw.

The dagger flew straight and true, with all the power of Melles' arm and anger behind it. With a wet *thud*, it buried itself to the hilt in Charliss' left eye. The Emperor was killed instantly, left with a slack-jawed version of his self-absorbed expression.

But the spell he had been about to unleash did not die with him.

For one instant, Melles felt the chill hand of horrified fear clutch his throat, as it had not in decades, and he waited to be pounded to the earth as the rogue spell lashed out at him.

The gathered energies, with no direction, and no controls, whirled in a vortex of light around the Emperor's body for a moment, obscuring him. Rays of light shot upward, punching holes through the darkness, leaving scorched spots in the ceiling. Other sparks jumped and careened, arcing back to the sword points arrayed in ominous fans behind and around the Iron Throne. The crackling sparks disappeared with a flash and a soft sizzle. Then suddenly, the vortex stilled, and a moment later, the gathered energy invested itself in the Iron Throne, leaving it glowing for a moment before returning— apparently—to its original state.

Melles let out his breath in a hiss, walked tentatively over to Charliss, and reached for the Wolf Crown. He touched it for just a moment, and he could have sworn that the pack-leader on the front of the crown grinned at him.

Then he removed the dagger from the dead man's eye; a thin trickle of blood followed the removal of the blade, but it took less force to pull it out of the skull than Melles had feared. The corpse of the former Emperor was already falling to pieces. He examined the wound; it could be made to look less serious. He made a few more facial wounds with quick stabs, as if Charliss had cut himself about the face in a mad frenzy. Then he placed the dagger in Charliss's hands, clenched both the flaccid hands around the hilt, pressed the point to the Emperor's breast, and shoved, piercing the heart.

He checked to make certain that he had not gotten any blood on himself, more as a reflex than anything else; he had been a professional for too long to have made so foolish a mistake.

Then he strolled casually out the door, nodding to the guards as he passed. In a few more moments, they would go in, find Charliss, and report that the Emperor, distraught and deranged by his failing magic and crumbling health, had committed suicide.

And long live the new Emperor, may he reign a hundred years.

Karal was on his knees. Altra was beside him, a glowing cat-image under his groping hand. Florian stood braced between him and the Pit, a horse-shape of Fire against the darkness. To his right, looming out of the swirling, fluctuating energies, Firesong still stood like a blinding statue of a warrior with upraised sword—a high keening sound that somehow penetrated the roar in Karal's ears came from Need, as if the sword had somehow acquired a voice. To his left, there was no sign of An'desha, but two bird-human shapes with feathers of flame wove a restless web all about a shadowed core. He couldn't see Sejanes at all across the Pit.

He sensed the energies around them were winning. They couldn't feed the Pit fast enough, and their protectors were burning out.

And yet, he was no longer afraid. Even if they didn't survive, they *had* fed enough of the terrible power into the Pit to prevent a second Cataclysm. As he gazed on the burning image of Florian, great peace descended on his heart, and he faced the terrible, glorious, mystical fire without flinching. Once again, he stood in the heart of the Sun and knew he was welcome there. He opened himself up to it fully, and lost himself there, past fear, past pain, past everything but the Light.

And then his awareness of self evaporated, and there was nothing more.

The light was gone; the Light was gone. There was nothing but darkness, yet Florian's image still continued to burn against that dark.

He was lying on his back. His groping hands encountered rough blankets over him, then warm fur.

"I think he's awake," said Lo'isha in a low voice.

He coughed, cleared his throat, and replied, "I am awake. How is everyone? Did the light fail?"

His question was answered with the kind of heavy silence that only occurs when someone has unwittingly asked a question that has an answer that will make him very unhappy.

"Firesong has been . . . hurt," Silverfox said gently. "An'desha and Sejanes are quite all right, only tired."

He tried to sit up, and felt hands on his chest holding him down. "How badly hurt is Firesong?" he asked urgently. "Can I see him? Where's Florian? Haven't you got any lights going yet?"

Again, that awkward silence, and then the answer came to him, to his last question at least, as Lo'isha asked, very softly, "What can you see?"

"Nothing," he whispered, stunned. "Only—Florian—"

"It seems that those whose guardians were entirely spirit fared the best," said Lyam in that dry way of his.

The fur draped over his legs moved. :Florian is gone, Karal,: Altra said, in the gentlest tones that Karal had ever heard him use. :I am the only one of the protectors to survive the experience. I am sorry.:

Karal moved his head, and still saw nothing but darkness and the fiery image of Florian in reverse silhouette against it. He swallowed, as the full impact of realization hit him, and felt hot tears burning their way down his face. Florian—gone? Protecting him? He blinked, but nothing changed in what he saw—or rather, what he didn't see.

"You see nothing, Karal?" Lo'isha persisted. He shook his head dumbly.

"What about Firesong?" he asked, around a cold lump in his gut and a second lump in his throat. "Is he—like me?"

"No, but—the sword, Need—she exploded in a mist of mol-

ten metal in his hands. His face and hands are badly burned."
That was Lyam. "I just sent Silverfox back to him."

Although tears of mourning continued to trickle down Karal's face, he nodded. "Good," he managed. "I don't really need a Healer. . . ." He let his voice trail off, making a kind of question out of it.

"No, Karal," Lo'isha said, with a comforting hand on his shoulder. "I'm afraid a Healer won't do you any good right now."

"Then, just leave me with Altra for a bit, would you?" he asked, and after a while, he heard them get up and move away. He felt Altra settle on his chest and legs, and began gently scratching the Firecat's ears. Tears slid down his cheeks, and Altra continued to rasp them away.

:Karal?: Altra asked, after a long silence. He answered the Firecat with a fierce hug.

"Just stay with me," he whispered.

:I'll never leave you, Karal,: Altra promised. *:Never. Not for as long as you live.:*

Firesong remembered the exact moment when Need lost her battle to shield him, which was right after Yfandes had evaporated into motes of energy. She had screamed—a warning, he thought—and he had let her go and flung one arm over his eyes to protect them. All he remembered after that was pain.

He hadn't ever lost consciousness, and right now, loss of all awareness would have been a blessing. Silverfox had given him something that turned the terrible agony into bearable agony, but he still *hurt*. Almost as bad was the knowledge of what had happened to him. *He* knew what he looked like—and worse, he knew what he was *going* to look like. No Healer would be able to keep scar tissue from forming, and his face—

He struggled to keep back tears, tears of pain, tears of loss. *Yes* he had been vain, and why not? His face had won him all the lovers he had ever wanted, and now no one would ever give him a second glance.

A touch on his arm made him start and open his tightly-closed eyes. "*Ashke*, I am here," said Silverfox, his face full of concern. "Are you in pain?"

"Better to ask, what *doesn't* hurt," he replied, trying to

make a feeble joke of it. "I am trying not to scream; it is very impolite, and would frighten An'desha."

"We have sent the Kal'enedral out for stronger pain-drugs," Silverfox told him tenderly, resting one hand on the part of his arm that was not burned. "They should be back soon. The blizzard stopped, and the snow is melting, and in a little we will have gryphons or horses here to take you to k'Leshya. Kaled'a'in Healers are very good." He hesitated, then added, "It is a pity they are not good enough to help Karal."

That snapped him out of the slough of self-pity he was wallowing in. "What about Karal?" he asked sharply.

"I think—he has lost his sight." Silverfox looked away for a moment.

Lost his sight! For one bitter moment, Firesong actually envied him. Better to lose his sight than to go through life, scorned and pitied, to have people look away from you because they could not bear the sight of you—

But even as he thought that, he rejected the thought with anger at himself. *You fool,* he told himself scornfully. *You vain, self-important fool! You are* alive *with all your senses; you are neither crippled nor incapacitated, and you still have Aya.*

As if to underscore that last, the firebird trilled a little from his perch beside Firesong's pallet.

Poor Karal, came the thought at last. "Poor lad," he sighed, "Florian, and this—" then involuntarily whimpered as the movement sent pain lacing through the burns on his face. He felt tears start up, and soak into his bandages.

Silverfox cupped his hands at Firesong's temples, and started into his eyes with fierce concentration. As Firesong looked into his eyes, some of the pain began to recede, and he almost wept again, this time with relief. "I will be glad—" he gasped, "—when those pain-drugs arrive."

"They cannot arrive soon enough for me," Silverfox muttered, then managed something of a wan smile. "You are being much braver than I would. I cannot bear pain."

"It is not too bad, except when I am alone," Firesong said, still gazing into those warmly compassionate eyes.

And somehow, those eyes softened further. "In that case, *ashke*, I will never leave you," the handsome *kestra'chern* said softly. "If you think you can bear to have me here."

And for a moment, Firesong forgot any pain at all.

An'desha lay curled up with his face to the wall, and Karal could tell by his shaking shoulders that he was weeping silently. The view through Altra's eyes was rather disconcerting, given that Altra's head was about at knee-height, and he had to look up to see peoples' faces when they stood. But at least now, with Altra glued to his leg and lending him the view, he wasn't bumping into things, nor tripping over them.

Karal knelt down beside An'desha's pallet, and put a hand on his shoulder. "If you keep this up much longer," he said, trying not to dissolve into tears himself and make things worse, "you're going to be sick."

An'desha only shook his head violently, and Karal tried to remember exactly what it was that Lo'isha had told him.

"An'desha blames himself for the loss of the others, especially the Avatars," the Kaled'a'in had said. *"You* must *persuade him to walk the Moonpaths, or—or it will be bad for his soul, his heart. I have not been able to persuade him."*

The older man had left it at that, but there was no doubt in Karal's mind that he knew how An'desha had managed to help him through his own crisis of conscience. Altra had seconded the Shin'a'in's request as soon as Lo'isha was off tending to some other urgent problem. After that, how could Karal have possibly refused?

"There wasn't anything you did or didn't do that would have made a difference for the better," Karal persisted. "How could there have been? We tried to do more than Urtho could, and it *still* came out better than we had any reason to expect!"

"I should have known about those other weapons," An'desha said, his voice muffled by his sleeve. "I should have known what they'd do when they started to fail."

"How?" Karal asked acerbically. "Those were *Urtho's* weapons, not Ma'ar's! How could you have known what they were going to do? ForeSight? When not even the ForeSeers were able to give us decent advice?"

One red eye emerged from the shelter of An'desha's sleeve. "But—" he began.

"But, nothing," Karal said with great firmness. "You aren't a ForeSeer, and you don't have Urtho's memories, you have

Ma'ar's. And if you'd go walk the Moonpaths, you'd find out from the *leshy'a* that I'm right."

An'desha winced, blanching, which looked quite interesting though Altra's eyes. "I can't—" he began.

Karal fixed him with what he hoped was a stern gaze, even though he couldn't feel his eyes responding the way they should. "That sounds exactly like what someone who's been thrown says," he replied. "What do you do when a horse throws you?"

"You get back on," An'desha said faintly, "but—"

"You've already used 'but' too many times." Karal patted his elbow. "Try saying, 'all right,' instead."

"All right," An'desha replied obediently, then realized he'd been tricked. Karal wasn't about to let him off.

"Go," he said, and got unsteadily to his feet again. Instead of looking down, he sensed that his head was in a position of looking out, echoing Altra's head-posture. "Go walk the Moonpaths. I want you to, Lo'isha wants you to. That ought to be reason enough, right there."

Having finished what he had to say, and having partly tricked An'desha into agreement, he left and returned to his own pallet, far from the others, where he sank down onto it, exhausted by holding back his own emotions, and cried himself to sleep.

"Karal."

He looked around, startled. He wasn't in his bed in the Tower anymore; he was standing in the middle of—of nowhere he recognized. There was opalescent mist all around him, and a path of softly glowing silver sand beneath his feet. Not only that, but it was his own eyes that he was looking out of, not Altra's.

Where was he? This wasn't like any dream he had ever had before. In fact, it was rather like the descriptions that An'desha had given him of the Moonpaths. But that was a place that only Shin'a'in could reach, wasn't it?

Wasn't it?

"Of course not," said that voice again, teasingly familiar. *"Anyone can come here, they just see it differently. But Altra thought that after all you've been through, you probably wouldn't want to visit SunHeart for a little."*

This time, when he turned around, there *was* someone there—or rather, four someones, two male and two female. Two of them, the ones standing hand-in-hand, with vague bird-forms swirling about them, he recognized immediately.

"Tre'valen!" he exclaimed "Dawnfire! But—"

"*Oh, heavens, you didn't think we'd burned up or some such nonsense, did you?*" Dawnfire laughed. "*It takes more than a storm of mage-energy to destroy a spirit! We just lost the parts of ourselves that held us in your world, that's all.*"

"You did?" said someone else, incredulously, "That's all?" Karal found, without any surprise at all, that An'desha had somehow come to stand beside him. "But, why didn't you come back when I called you then?"

"*Because—well—we can't.*" Tre'valen actually looked shamefaced. "*I'm afraid that we overstepped the bounds of what we were actually permitted to do to help you. The Star-Eyed wasn't precisely put out, but. . . .*"

Dawnfire interrupted him. "*You'll have to come here to meet us from now on,*" she said ruefully. "*But if you're going to be a shaman, you ought to get all the practice you can in walking the Moonpaths anyway.*"

"All I can think of is how glad I am that I didn't—" An'desha began, but it was the strange young man that interrupted him this time. He looked very familiar, but Karal could not imagine why. Thin and not particularly muscular, but with a build that suggested agility, he had sandy brown hair that kept flopping into his blue eyes, and a friendly, cheerful manner.

"*Nothing you did or didn't do made any difference in what happened to us, An'desha,*" the young man said. "*Part of it was purest chance, and the rest was that we took on more than we had any right to think we could handle, and we managed to carry it off anyway. We dared. Right, Karal?*"

At this point, Karal had an idea that he knew who the young man was, and he gave voice to it. "Right—Florian," he replied, and was rewarded by a wink, a flash of a grin, and a nod. "But if this is where all of you came—after—where are Vanyel, Stefen, and Yfandes?"

"*Free of the forest for one thing, and high time, too, if you ask me,*" Florian replied. "*And probably if you ask them. I suppose it seemed like a good idea at the time, but I suspect they were stuck there a lot longer than they thought they would be.*"

Karal hadn't the faintest idea what Florian was talking about, and some of his bewilderment must have shown on his face. Florian chuckled.

"*Never mind,*" he said. "*Basically, they've made decisions about their destinations, and they didn't have a lot of time to make sure they got properly placed, so they've already gone on. I can't tell you what they decided, but it's going to be fine. As for me,*" he continued with a wink, "*I've made mine, too, but I wasn't so picky. It should be obvious if you think about it, but don't tell any Heralds, all right?*"

Karal nodded solemnly; Florian's decision *was* obvious, though he doubted that his friend was going to look anything like he did at the moment when he returned to the world.

Then again, maybe he would. Karal branded that face into his memory. If in fifteen or twenty years' time, Karal—or rather, Altra—saw a Herald who looked like this, they would both know who it was.

I'd better remember that he won't remember, though, and not go rushing up to him and greet him as my long-lost friend.

Even though that would be precisely what he was.

"Florian—" he faltered, and continued. "I've never had a friend like you."

"*Well, you'll have one again in time,*" the irrepressible Florian interrupted. Evidently he was in no mood for sorrowful good-byes or recriminations. He cut short any other attempts at speech by embracing his friends. "*Now, you go back to Valdemar and get into as much mischief as possible with Natoli, and I'll go take care of my business, and eventually we'll meet again. It's not 'good-bye,' Karal, it's 'see you later.' All right?*"

What else could he do but agree, and return the hearty embrace? With a cheery wave, Florian faded into the mist, and was gone, leaving Karal behind with tears in his eyes and a smile on his lips.

Now he was alone with An'desha and the old woman.

This must be Need, he realized, listening to her give An'desha some tart and intelligent pieces of advice. "*And as for you, young man,*" she said at last, turning her clever gaze on him, "*I heartily agree with that young scamp, Florian. You're too*

*sober by half, and just because you can't see things for your-
self, that's no reason to go back to that gloomy country of
yours and sit in a corner and mope. Go get into mischief with
that young lady of yours; I had plenty of apprentices like her
in my time, and I suspect she'll keep you hopping and she
won't let you feel sorry for yourself."*

"Probably not, my lady," he replied politely, thinking that
her assessment of Natoli was remarkably accurate for someone who didn't actually know her.

*"Now, since you asked earlier, as for me, I'm taking a long-
delayed rest. Maybe you'll see me and maybe you won't, but
I'll be damned if I ever go sticking myself into a piece of steel
again!"* She gave both of them a brief hug. *"Now, you both
stop ruining good pillows with salt water, and go and get
some living done."*

And with that, she turned and stalked off into the mist,
leaving him and An'desha alone. Tre'valen and Dawnfire had
already vanished while their attention was on Need.

"Now what?" he asked.

He looked at his friend, who shrugged, but with some of his
old spirit back. "I suppose we'd better do as she says," An'desha said. "You know her. If we don't, she's likely to turn
around and kick us out." He toed the soft silver sand for a
moment, then added, "I'm glad you made me come here."

"I'm glad you let me," Karal replied, and smiled, feeling
more peace in his heart than he had ever expected to have
again. "Now, let's go home."

Karal looked back through Altra's eyes, over the tail of his
Shin'a'in riding horse, a lovely and graceful palfrey. It felt very
strange not to be riding Florian, but he supposed that he would
get used to it after a while. Firesong rode behind him, supported by a saddle that the Shin'a'in used for riders who were
ill or disabled, watching everything around him with his eyes
shining behind the eye-holes of the mask covering his half-
healed face. Firesong's mask was a wonder, not only because
it was as extravagant and beautiful as one of his elaborate
robes, but because he and Lyam had made it of materials they
had scavenged from things in the Tower during the fortnight
they had waited. With a base of leather and adorned with bits
of crystal, wire, and feathers that Aya himself had carefully

pulled from his tail and brought to Firesong while he still lay half-healed in his bed, it probably would have fetched a small fortune from a collector of such things. But Firesong was dissatisfied with it, and was already designing new ones.

All around them, the Plains were blooming in a way that the Shin'a'in said they had not seen since the Star-Eyed herself walked there. One could hardly see the grass for the flowers, which painted the landscape in wide swathes of color. The land had gone from deepest winter to the heart of spring, all in the space of a fortnight. Through Altra's eyes, Karal took in the incredible beauty with a sense of awe and wonder. According to the messages that Altra had brought from Solaris in Karse, all their friends in Haven, and Elspeth in Hardorn, the phenomenon was not confined to the Plains. All the world was in blossom, as if to make up for the ravages of the Storms.

Sejanes and An'desha had been working to discover just how magic operated, and as soon as he was able, Firesong had joined them. It had not been long before they discovered that there were no ley-lines anymore, no nodes, no huge reserves of mage-power. Magical energy had been dispersed fairly evenly across the landscape; and there wouldn't be any large magics for a very long time. That meant no Gates, of course, but it was no hardship to ride through a countryside where the sun shone down with kindly benevolence, where birds serenaded every step of the way, and there was such an all-pervasive perfume of flowers, both night-and day-blooming, that it even permeated their dreams at night. And once the clever Kaled'-a'in found the means to make the carry-baskets light using the small magics that still worked, they would make the rest of their journey by air.

Karal had been given the choice of going home to Karse—a shorter journey by far—or back to Valdemar. But when all was said and done, it had not been a difficult choice. One of the first messages from Solaris had been strictly for him, commending his actions, and asking him if he would, as a personal favor to her, resume his work in Valdemar both as the Karsite envoy and as the head of the Temple outside Karse. "With the visible evidence of your sacrifice," she had written, "no one in Valdemar will question your authority. Additionally, you will be dealing with the representatives of Iftel—creatures I confess I find somewhat unnerving. The Sunlord has decreed some odd things in Iftel, and I frankly do not think that outside of you there is a single Priest in the entire Temple who could treat these peoples as anything other than heretics. I do not want to offend these new brothers and sisters in any way, but I fear that if I assigned anyone else to Valdemar and Iftel, there would be blood spilled before long. However, if you want to come home, I will understand, and find a way to cope."

The message had come on the day when they were all deciding whether to go to their homes or back to Haven.

Tarrn and Lyam had elected to return to k'Leshya, which was no surprise at all. Silverfox and Firesong, however, were going with them. Karal had half expected Firesong, at least, to want to return to his own people, but the Adept had smiled behind his mask and simply shaken his head, the crystals and bits of metal dangling from the mask tinkling softly.

"No one remembers what I looked like before in k'Leshya," he said quietly. "And—besides, Silverfox wants to be there, and it *is* a familiar Vale." It was plain in his voice, burned lips or not, that being with Silverfox was the primary reason.

An'desha rode with them, but he would not be leaving the Plains. He had elected to remain and study with Lo'isha, taking the vows of the shaman. Karal had been surprised at that as well, especially as he had been earnestly practicing magic alongside Sejanes and Firesong during the time that they waited for their hosts to put a caravan together for them.

"There is no prohibition on magic among the Shin'a'in now," An'desha explained with a chuckle. "There is no reason for one. I suspect that Lo'isha has it in mind for me to be the teacher to the new mages among us, in time. I should like that," he finished softly, with a tone of contentment in his voice that Karal had never heard before. "Ma'ar in all of his incarnations gave nothing of himself. I shall perhaps be able to balance that, eventually."

So Lo'isha and An'desha would leave them at the edge of the Plains, and Silverfox, Firesong, Tarrn, and Lyam at k'Leshya Vale. Master Levy and Sejanes were going on, of course, and they would be joined by the Heralds who had carried the messages from Haven telling the mages and rulers of other lands how to keep their nodes from going rogue.

And Karal would be going with them. After all the advice

from the spirits on the Moonpaths, he was hardly surprised when Natoli sent him a message of her own, asking him to come back to Valdemar. "I can be your eyes, too," she had written. "And you can be my good sense, which I seem to have a distinct lack of. I think I need you." Confused grammar, but not confused thoughts. He had been afraid for a little that despite the surety of others, she might not want to see him as less than he had been; he knew now that he should have given her more credit than that.

So he *would* be going on with Master Levy and Sejanes; back to duty, back to love. But most of all, back to a place he was already thinking of as home.

Altra would stay with him to provide him with "eyes," but he had the love of friends, awareness of himself, and hope for the future to give him vision, vision without sight, perhaps, but as true and clear as anyone could imagine.